RYDEVILLE ELITE BOOK 1

CRUEL
Intentions

USA TODAY BESTSELLING AUTHOR
SIOBHAN DAVIS

Printed by Amazon
Paperback edition © June 2019

ISBN-13: 9781072089865

Editor: Kelly Hartigan (XterraWeb) editing.xterraweb.com
Cover design by Robin Harper https://wickedbydesigncovers.wixsite.com
Photographer: Sara Eirew
Cover Models: Anthony Desforges and Hélène Bujold
Formatting by Polgarus Studios

AUTHOR'S NOTE

Although this book is set in a high school environment, it is a dark bully romance, and it is not suitable for young teens due to mature content, graphic sexual scenes, and cursing. The recommended reading age is eighteen+. Some scenes may be triggering.

PROLOGUE

Waves crash against the empty shore, summoning me with invisible arms, and my feet move toward the icy water as if I'm pulled by a string. I'm numb inside. Hollowed out. And I just want to put an end to this... charade that is my so-called life.

I never remember a time in my seventeen years on this earth where I had free will. Where every aspect of my life wasn't controlled and mapped out.

And I'm done.

Done with the mask I've no choice but to wear.

Done with the elite crap I'm forced to participate in.

Done with that monster who calls himself my father.

I want out, and the turbulent sea offers me salvation. I scarcely feel the deathly cold water as it swirls around my ankles like the tempting caress of a destructive lover. My silk robe offers little protection against the bitter wind whipping my long dark hair around my face, and goose bumps prickle my skin in everyplace it's exposed.

I walk farther into the water, my body shivering and shaking as the wild waves lap at my calves. An eerie voice echoes in my mind, urging me to stop.

Imploring me to go back.

Pleading with me not to give up.

Suggesting my world is about to change.

I ignore that taunting voice, tilting my head up, surveying the crescent moon in the dark nighttime sky, casting strangely shaped shadows on the land below. My ears prick at the sound of splashing behind me, and my heart beats faster as adrenaline courses through my veins, but I don't turn around.

"Hey. Are you okay?" a deep masculine voice asks from close by.

I'm standing knee-deep in icy-cold water in the middle of the night in minuscule clothing. Does it fucking look like I'm okay? My snarky alter ego mentally responds to his question, but I remain mute. I can't summon the energy to speak or to care what the stranger thinks of me.

I just want him to go away. To leave me alone. To at least give me this.

But no such luck.

He wades through the water, his darkened form brushing against my arm as he moves around me, positioning himself directly in my line of sight so I've no choice but to look at him.

A flicker of warmth enters my chest as I stare into sultry brown eyes that are so deep they're almost black. The glow from the moon casts a shadow around his form, highlighting his masculine beauty in all its glory. He's wearing low-hanging cotton shorts and nothing else. His bare chest is an impressive work of art that speaks to incredible dedication in the gym. His cut abs are so sharp they look painted on. But it's the tattoos on his chest and lower arms that grab my attention. None of the guys at Rydeville High would dare ink their skin. It wouldn't fit the reputations they've so carefully cultivated or suit their obnoxious parents' plans for their futures. The elite wouldn't dream of lowering themselves to something so provincial.

This guy is an enigma, and the first sparks of curiosity ignite inside me.

My eyes trail up his delectable torso, refocusing on his face. He's watching me carefully. Absorbing my gaze like he wants to bury deep inside me and figure me out. My fingers itch to run along the fine layer of scruff adorning his chin and jawline. To mess up his hair which is styled long on top and shorn close to his skull on both sides. A craving to explore his chiseled cheekbones, and to taste his full lips, hits me out of nowhere, reminding me I'm still very much alive.

I can't ever recall having such a strong, physical reaction to a guy upon sight. None of the guys back home have affected me so potently, except for Trent—he makes my skin crawl with the barest of looks—but this is the complete opposite.

One glance from this stranger heats my blood and stirs desire low in my belly. I cock my head to the side, intrigued and aroused, my previous self-destructive mission all but forgotten.

We don't speak. We just stare at one another and an electrical current charges the small space between us. My body emerges from its semi-comatose state, and I'm equally hot and cold. A shiver works its way through me, and I wrap my arms around my slim frame, desperately trying to ward off the biting cold air clawing at my pale skin.

"You need to get warm." The stranger extends his hand. "Come with me."

I wrap my hand around his without hesitation, and we tread through the water back toward the shore. His callused palm is firm against my skin, sending a flurry of fiery tingles coasting up and down my arm. We don't speak as we emerge from the sea, walking across the clammy sand toward a small wooden cabin in the near distance. I hadn't noticed it when I first arrived because I had singular focus.

A thin stream of smoke creeps out of a narrow chimney, and I watch the cloudy spirals with fascination as we walk hand in hand toward the neat wooden structure. In the distance, a sprawling mansion occupies prime real estate, the property submerged in darkness at this late hour.

He pushes open the door, stepping aside to allow me to enter first. A blast of heat slaps me in the face from the roaring open fire, and my body relaxes for the first time in days. The cabin is small but cozy and welcoming. The main room contains a compact kitchen with a stove, sink, and a long counter with three stools. On the right is a three-seater couch positioned in front of a coffee table and a wall-mounted TV over the fireplace. A side room suggests a bedroom with en suite bathroom, and that's the extent of the space.

My bedroom is bigger than this entire cabin, but it isn't half as inviting.

A bright rug resting atop the varnished hardwood floor, the soft colorful throw on the couch, and an abundance of vibrant cushions injects a comfortable, lived-in feel. The old bookcase tucked into the corner between the wall and the door is crammed full of books, DVDs, and mementos, creating a homey atmosphere. The only light is from the flickering flames of the fire and an old-fashioned lamp on top of the coffee table.

He shuts the door and steers me in front of the fire. On autopilot, I raise my palms, relishing the heat as it wraps around my chilly skin. He moves around behind me, but I don't turn to look. I stand in front of the fire, allowing it to thaw my frozen limbs and fracture the layer of ice surrounding my heart.

"Sit down," he commands in that rugged voice of his, draping a blanket around my upper body.

I sink to the ground without a word, tucking my knees into my chest as I peer at him. He drops down in front of me, gently uncurling my legs, drawing one into his lap as he dries my damp skin with a soft blue towel. We stare at one another as he dries both my feet and legs, and that same pull from before pulses between us, rendering some invisible connection.

"I feel like I know you from somewhere, yet I've never seen you before," I admit, eventually finding my voice.

He stalls with his hands on my feet, piercing my gaze with his intense chocolate-colored one. "I know," he says after a few beats.

When he tosses the towel aside, I move closer to him, sitting up on my knees with my body resting on my ankles. I keep my eyes locked on his as I reach up and touch the shorn side of his head, my fingers trailing over the velvety soft hair, tracing the edge of his skull tattoo. It was too dark outside to notice it, but now, I'm even more intrigued by this elusive, hot stranger who appeared out of nowhere to rescue me.

The tattoo is in the shape of a cross, and I wonder if the symbolism means something personal to him. All I know is it's sexy as hell, and my body naturally responds to him, arching in closer.

He pulls my hand away from his head, pressing a feather-light kiss to the sensitive skin on my wrist, and I feel his tender touch all the way to the tips of my toes. His gentle touch is in direct contrast to his edgy look. With his defined abs, bulging biceps, and ink-covered tan skin, he looks like the quintessential bad boy every girl gets warned about. "Why were you out there?" he asks, keeping his gaze locked on mine.

I could lie, but I'm tired of all the lies.

I'm tired of saying what's expected and pretending to be someone I'm not.

"I didn't want to feel anymore."

There's a pregnant pause as he stares at me, no doubt wondering if I meant that sincerely. "What would you have done if I hadn't spotted you?" he inquires, still trying to puzzle me out.

I shrug. "Kept walking most likely." Allowed the sea to claim me as I'd originally intended when I'd given Oscar, my bodyguard, the slip, and driven here.

"Who are you? What's your name?"

I cup his face, deciding on the truth again. "I'm nobody. I'm invisible. I don't exist except to obey their commands."

A slight frown creases his brow. "If you're in trouble. If—"

"Don't." I cut across him. "I don't want to talk about it."

Silence engulfs us for a few beats. "What do you want?" he asks, his voice dropping a notch, sounding wholly seductive, although I'm unsure if that's on purpose or not.

"I want to feel something real," I reply without uncertainty. "I want to let go of these chains that bind my body. To feel like I'm in control even if it's only an illusion." My eyes stay locked on his, and electricity crackles in the air again.

He rakes his gaze up and down the length of my body, his heated stare lingering on my chest as my nipples harden. His eyes flit to my mouth before he licks his lips and drags his gaze upward. His eyes bore into mine, and butterflies scatter in my chest, my heart beating faster and faster as my body heats in a whole new way. "I can help with that."

This time, there's no doubting his intent, and my core aches with need. My gaze drills into his eyes, projecting my acceptance and permission.

Nodding slowly, he pulls me onto his lap, circling his arms around my waist. "Are you sure?"

I bob my head. "Please make me feel alive. Make me feel like me. Remind me why I should live."

It's crazy.

I don't know him.

He doesn't know me.

But I feel more hopeful in this moment than I have in years.

Slowly, he brings his face to mine, brushing his lips against my mouth. I close my eyes as my body sags in relief. Snaking my arms around his neck, I angle my head as he caresses my mouth with his luscious lips. His kiss is unhurried and worshipful. His mouth moves leisurely and seductively against mine, and this kiss is unlike any I've ever experienced before.

Trent kisses with years of pent-up anger and aggression behind his punishing lips, and it makes me feel dead on the inside. This stranger's tender kisses unravel the knots that usually twist in my gut, breaking through the walls that cage my heart, allowing warmth and pleasure to invade every single part of me.

I meld my lips and my body to his, straddling his hips and gasping as his hard length nudges against the softest part of me. He rocks his hips gently in expert, measured movements, and a burst of desire shoots through me, overtaking logic and warning and common sense.

I shouldn't be doing this here with some guy I don't know.

It would enrage my father, my twin brother, Drew, and my fiancé, Trent, if they saw me, but that thought only spurs me on, strengthening my resolve.

He stands, holding me to him, and I tighten my legs around his waist as he walks toward the bedroom. Our mouths never separate as he lowers me to the bed, and we gradually shed our outer layers.

I've never been naked in front of any guy before. Trent repeatedly tries to strip me bare, but I enjoy denying him. Now, I spread my legs for this beautiful, rugged stranger, with no hint of nerves or vulnerability, admiring his gorgeous body as he pulls a condom out of his bedside table and rolls it over his impressive length.

We don't talk, but words are redundant. He settles between my thighs, bringing his hot mouth to my pussy, and I almost lift off the bed as he devours me with his tongue and his fingers, quickly bringing me over the edge.

No man has ever done that to me before, and the pleasurable sensations coursing through my body are wholly new. When I come down from the best orgasm of my life, he climbs over me, kissing me passionately as his hands caress my small breasts. His roughened fingers tweak my nipples like he's plucking strings on a guitar, rolling them skillfully until they're taut peaks, and it's not long before I'm writhing in need again.

He positions himself at my entrance, stalling to look at me. "Are you sure this is what you want?" he asks, and another little chip melts off the block around my heart.

No one has ever cared to ask me what I need or what I want, and tears prick my eyes at the obvious concern in his eyes.

"Yes. I want to do this with you."

His eyes are glued to mine as he slowly inches inside me. He stops halfway in, sweeping his fingers across my cheek. "You're so beautiful." He nudges in a little more. "And so tight." He flexes his jaw, and I can tell he's exercising caution. When he pushes in a little more, a sharp sting of pain jolts through me, and I wince.

His eyes pop wide as he holds himself still. Shock splays across his face. "You're a virgin?" he splutters.

A sly smirk slips across my mouth. "I was."

"Fuck." He leans down, kissing me so sweetly I feel like crying. "You should've said."

And have you change your mind? Not likely.

Thoughts of losing my virginity to that psycho Trent were part of the reason drawing me to the sea tonight. I've been holding him off for years, but with the wedding approaching, I know I can't hold out much longer.

Denying him that victory only adds to the joy of this moment.

But it's way more than wanting to one-up Trent.

I want to give my body to this gorgeous stranger.

To enjoy this one night where I can take something for myself before returning to the gilded cage I live in.

"It doesn't matter," I say, bucking my hips up in encouragement. "I want this with you. Right here. Right now. Nothing has made so much sense in a long time."

He inspects me for so long I fear he will pull out and change his mind, but then he pushes the rest of the way inside me, and I swallow my cry of pain. He peppers little kisses along my neck and my collarbone, gently kneading my tits as he slowly rocks back and forth inside me. "I'll go slow until it doesn't hurt anymore," he whispers across my now overheated skin. "And if you want me to stop, I will."

"I don't want you to stop," I say, threading my fingers through the longish dark strands of hair now falling over his strong brow. "Keep going."

He makes love to me then, only picking up his pace when I confirm it no longer hurts, but he's never rough, completely attentive to my needs, and he brings me to a second orgasm as his own climax hits.

I'm sprawled across his warm body, a few hours later, listening to the comforting beat of his heart, watching his chest inflate and deflate in slumber, wishing I could stay here in this little beach cabin with this beautiful stranger for eternity.

But I know that's only wishful thinking. A fantasy I can't entertain. Bringing anyone into my life risks theirs, and that'd be a poor way of rewarding this man who has given me a night I will cherish for the rest of my life.

Although I hate to leave him like this, it's for the best.

He can't know who I am or understand the implications of what we've just done.

Reluctantly, I ease out of his warm bed and his life, feeling a pang of overwhelming sadness as I get dressed, preparing myself to leave him behind. He looks peaceful in slumber, like a tattooed guardian angel, arriving at the perfect moment to help put things in perspective.

If I'd followed through tonight, they would have won, and I know my dead mother wouldn't want that for me.

I'm stronger than that.

I might be a pawn in a game I don't want to play, but that doesn't mean I can't win.

I need to strategize.

To plan my victory so I can escape the tortured future lying in wait for me.

Determination surges through my veins, and I smile adoringly at the beautiful man who has given me so much more than his body. "Thank you," I whisper, blowing him a kiss. I wish I could taste his lips one final time, but I don't want to wake him. It's better that I leave like this.

My hand is curled around the door handle when I spy a pencil and sketchpad on the coffee table. Without stopping to second-guess myself, I tear a strip off the end of a blank page and pen a brief note.

You can't possibly know this, but you saved my life in more ways than one tonight. You have reminded me why it's important to survive. Given me the strength to fight for what I want. And you have given me a precious memory I will hold close until my dying breath. Thank you. A.

As I close the door and head back toward my car, back to a life I despise, I know I'll be reliving this special night every day for the rest of my life.

But I had no idea that sleeping with this stranger would set certain things in motion. Things that couldn't be undone. And I certainly had no idea that I'd come to hate him and desperately resent giving him my virginity.

CHAPTER ONE

"Get your hands off me!" I shove at Trent's broad shoulders, pushing him back a couple steps. He immediately reclaims the space, thrusting his face into mine. "This fucking frigid act is getting old, *darling*," he sneers, enunciating the last word so I'm left in no doubt of his derision.

Aesthetically, Trent is a gorgeous guy—golden-blond hair, striking blue-gray eyes, strong masculine jaw, high cheekbones, and an impressive body that is ripped in all the right places—but the person behind the exterior is repulsive and totally beyond redemption.

Believe me, I've tried. Once I realized I was stuck with the douche, I did my utmost to bring out the best in him.

But you can't extract something that doesn't exist.

Trent isn't a nice guy.

Trent isn't a decent guy.

Trent embodies everything wrong with the society we live in and everything I want to run screaming from.

But I have no control over my life, and I'm on this speeding train regardless of how badly I want to jump off.

His hands dig into my hips, and he thrusts his obvious arousal into my stomach. I work hard to swallow my disgust. Although it's tempting to push his buttons more, he's been drinking, and I remember what happened the last time we got into it when he was hammered. A shiver tiptoes up my spine at the memory of him shoving his cock into my mouth while he had me pinned on the bed, his ass pressing down on my chest, as he fucked my mouth with no mercy.

How can a guy look so angelic and be so evil? Trent grinds against me, pawing at my chest and slobbering all over my neck.

At first glance, his mouth is utterly kissable until he opens it, shattering the illusion with the venom that regularly spews from his mouth.

Trent is the stereotypical rich kid. Spoiled, arrogant, and smarmy. He has sailed through life, handed everything on a silver platter, and he thinks his shit doesn't stink. Most everyone trips over themselves to give him everything he needs, especially the posse of women who fight for a temporary place in his bed, and his ego is floating somewhere in orbit.

Which is why he can't fathom my lack of interest and my disdain. Especially since we're engaged and scheduled to walk up the aisle next year.

"Stop!" I push his chest, forcing his vile mouth away from me. "My father's home, and all it'll take is one scream," I threaten.

He narrows his eyes, and his mouth twists into a malevolent grin. "Have you forgotten Daddy Dearest is the one who brokered our marriage deal? Or the reason he'll do anything to ensure it goes ahead?" He takes a step forward, reclaiming the space between us again.

I prod one finger in his firm chest. "Have *you* forgotten *your* father was the one who insisted I remain a virgin until our wedding night?" I take his evil grin and throw him back a smug one. "Or has he changed a generations-old rule because you can't keep your grabby hands to yourself?" I tilt my chin up. "Call one of your fuck buddies.

I'm sure they'll be more than happy to suck your dick."

Trent smirks as he extracts his cell, holding it to his ear. I fold my arms across my chest, waiting for the charade to play out.

The funny thing is, he genuinely thinks I care.

News flash—I couldn't care less.

"I need your ass," he barks into the phone, not even attempting to disguise it's anything but a booty call. "No, Rochelle. I literally mean I need your ass. I'm filling all holes tonight, baby. Be ready."

Asshole. He knows how I feel about that bitch.

Grinding my teeth, I work hard to keep my annoyance at bay.

I know Trent fucks around. *A lot.* And, I honestly couldn't give two shits. I shudder to think what'd happen if he didn't have his fuck buddies. Although Christian Montgomery made it a condition of the marital agreement negotiated with my father when I was ten—yes, *ten*—that I remain a virgin until my wedding night, Trent has been badgering me for sex for the past two years. I'd rather skin myself alive than willingly give myself to him, so I've spent two years fighting him off.

Occasionally, I'll feel generous and blow him.

Usually, he'll just take what he wants.

But he's a selfish bastard with no regard for my needs, so it normally means he fucks my mouth, forcing me to swallow, while he tugs at my breasts, sometimes making them bleed.

It's much worse when he's been drinking, so I have some idea of what lies in wait for Rochelle when he arrives at her place.

But I can't find it within myself to feel sympathy. Rochelle is the closest I have to an arch-nemesis at Rydeville High, and Trent knows how much we despise one another, which is why he deliberately called her in my presence.

Keeping up appearances is nonnegotiable if you're a descendant of one of the founding families. It's something ingrained in Trent,

Drew, Charlie, and me from the time we were little. And my father is the perfect example of how to act like a raging manwhore behind closed doors while presenting as the perfect law-abiding citizen.

Everyone knows Trent fucks around on me, but provided he's discreet, it's permitted.

Drew is engaged too, but he treats his fiancée with respect, while Charlie doesn't lower himself to bedding high school girls. However, if they wanted to whore themselves out whenever they felt like it, they'd get pats on the back.

Jane and I can barely piss without someone breathing down our necks.

Jane Ford is my best friend—*my only friend*—and she's also Drew's intended.

My twin and I are both destined for arranged marriages once we graduate a few weeks after our eighteenth birthday, thanks to the "business" deals our father made with the other elite patriarchs.

Trent rubbing my nose in it is not considered gentlemanly.

Mostly, I don't care.

But Rochelle grates on my nerves. Making sly digs in contravention of the code. Shooting me filthy looks when the guys aren't watching. Playing juvenile pranks, like stuffing stupid shit in my locker. Thinking she's someone important because Trent screws her sometimes. But she comes in handy, occasionally.

Like now.

If Trent thinks I'll change my mind because he intends to fuck my enemy, he's another think coming. "Knock yourself out, stud," I say, smiling pleasantly at him. "And make sure you wrap it before you tap it. Wouldn't want you to catch an STD."

Trent throws back his head, laughing. "Jealous much?"

No. Definitely not.

He grabs hold of my arm, yanking me into his hard body. "I'll ditch the bitch. Just spread those pretty legs nice and wide, and let me fill you up." He nips at my lower lip, dragging it between his teeth, drawing blood.

"I will never voluntarily have sex with you." I attempt to wrestle out of his arms, but it's futile because he's way too strong. He could overpower me easily, and it's happened too regularly to count. "You repulse me." I glare at him, watching his nostrils flaring as he grips my upper arms tight. "You'll have to force yourself on me if you want any because I will never make it easy for you."

His fingers dig into my flesh, hurting me, but I refuse to cry out. To show any signs of weakness. "You say that like it turns me off." He jabs my stomach with his hard-on while one hand slides down to cup my ass. "Like it would stop me." His finger prods the crack of my ass through my clothes, and I flinch. "Hate sex is the best." His mouth crashes down on mine, and I press my lips together, denying him access, refusing to kiss him back. His kiss turns vicious, his mouth punishing, as he bites my lips, drawing more blood, but I don't back down.

I'm used to his game.

When he pulls back, his eyes almost black with fury, he grabs my crotch, squeezing hard, and pain slices through my core. "This is mine. And I'll have you. I'll rip you apart, tear you to pieces until your resistance is futile." He shoves me away with such force I lose my balance and tumble to the ground.

He may well deliver on that threat when he finds out I'm not untouched, but I'll cross that bridge when I come to it.

"What the fuck, man?" Drew barges into my bedroom, shoving Trent in the chest, his handsome face red with rage. "How many fucking times do I have to tell you?!" he hollers, extending his arm and helping me to my feet. My twin tucks me beside him in a protective stance, scowling at the blood coating my lips. "Quit this shit, or we're done, Trent. I fucking mean it this time."

Trent slants an amused grin in Drew's direction. "You say that like you've any choice in the matter. We're in this for life. You're stuck with me, whether you and your bitch of a sister like it."

"You can't speak to Abby like that. And I won't let you treat her like this."

Trent squares up to Drew. "She's mine to do with as I please. Butt the fuck out. I don't tell you what to do with Jane."

"Because I treat Jane with respect," Drew retorts, dragging a hand through his dark brown hair.

Trent snorts. "You're so fucking pussy-whipped. Why you want to tie yourself to the same pussy for life is beyond me." Trent slaps him on the back, shaking his head. "You should pound as many chicks as you can before you settle down."

"Ugh." I step in front of the warring boys. "You're gross. They love each other, that's why." I know it's a foreign concept to him, but I hate how superior he acts around my brother. Like he deserves some life medal for being a player. "Go, Trent." I push him toward the door. "Go to that skank and fuck her up the ass. See if I care."

"You're going to Rochelle's?" Drew queries, raising a brow.

"Your sister won't spread her legs, as usual, and I'm all fired up." He winks at me. "Lucky for Rochelle."

"We had an agreement," Drew protests, and it's the first I've heard of it. "And you're already breaking it."

"You decided I should cut Rochelle loose. I didn't voice an opinion either way." He saunters toward the door, and a layer of tension lifts from my shoulders. "Convince your precious sister to put out, and I'll consider it," he tosses over his shoulder, before leaving, the noise of his shoes echoing in the wide hallway as he walks away.

Drew slowly turns around, inspecting me quickly. "Did he hurt you anyplace else?" he asks, pulling a handkerchief out of his dress pants and gently dabbing at my lip.

The guys were at some function in the gentleman's club downtown with their respective fathers. Hence why Drew is dressed like he's attending a funeral. And why Trent is wasted. I hate the way women are treated within the elite social circles, but there are times I'm glad we're excluded from things.

I harrumph. "You have to ask?" I push the short sleeves of my dress up to my shoulders, skimming a finger over the bruising already blossoming on my upper arms.

Trent never leaves a mark in a visible place.

Appearances and all.

That's something else he has in common with my father. That and the obvious shared psycho gene. Thankfully, Drew seems to have escaped that trait, although he's as arrogant and power-obsessed as Daddy Dearest, so he definitely inherited some of his DNA.

I like to believe there's more of Mom in me.

Drew rubs a tense-looking spot between his brows. "He's on edge because of this upcoming trip."

The guys are leaving next weekend for Parkhurst, some bullshit elite training camp they attend a few times a year. Although the guys will go on to college after graduating high school next May, they will each assume some official responsibility within their family business, fulfilling more public obligations, and this month-long camp trip is part of their preparation.

"Don't make excuses for him," I say, turning around and holding my hair up.

Drew unzips my dress, casting his warm brown eyes to the floor as I slip it off and pull on my silk nightdress. "I'm not. You don't understand the pressure that's on our shoulders."

I whirl around on him, my eyes blazing. "Don't talk to me about pressure! At least you get to have a career and a life! What choices do I have?" I flap my hands about.

"You've got college to look forward to, and Christian Montgomery has agreed you can wait until you get your degree before producing an heir."

"Am I supposed to be grateful?" I shout even though I'm venting at the wrong person.

"You'll want for nothing, Abby." He tenderly cups my face. "And you and Trent will make beautiful babies together."

I push him away, disgusted at the turn in our conversation. "Go away, Drew. I can't hear this tonight."

His features pull into a tight grimace. "Stop being such a whiny bitch," he snaps. "You know how important the alliance with the Montgomerys is. We've both got parts to play."

I pull back the silk covers on my large four-poster bed, crawling inside, needing this day to be over. "I know, Drew. I've heard this my entire life. I don't need you to constantly reinforce it."

"Sure, I do," he says, perching on the side of my bed, losing his fleeting anger. "Because you've got too much of Mom in you, and I see how badly you want to rebel." He tucks me in under the covers, like he used to do after Mom died when I'd have regular nightmares. Except back then, he'd usually crawl into bed alongside me. "But you can't, Abby. Stop fighting Trent. Give him what he wants, and he'll change. He just wants you to love him."

"He just wants to fuck me," I retort.

"Is that such a bad thing?"

"His dick is rotten to the core, and his touch makes my skin crawl, so that'd be a yes." Drew sighs. "Maybe if he wasn't so aggressive with me all the time. Maybe if he respected me as you do with Jane, things would be different, but he doesn't, and they aren't."

While the Ford family isn't one of the founding families, they are respected within the upper echelons of elite society, known as the inner circle, and our father was keen to secure a formal alliance.

Marriage between both families will ensure that.

Jane's father insisted on a virginity clause too, but Drew and Jane are hot for one another, and they couldn't wait. Unlike me, Jane adores her father, and she doesn't want to disappoint him, so, even though she's already sleeping with my brother, her father doesn't know.

Any time Jane sleeps over, her parents assume she's staying with me, but she usually sleeps in Drew's bed. My father actively encourages it, because he loves getting one over on Mr. Ford and he's a sexual deviant. The private sex room in our basement attests to that.

When I see my brother and Jane together, all loved up and mooning at one another as if no one else exists on the planet but them, I feel the odd stab of envy. If Trent and I were in love, I'd be happy to let him into my bed. But I fucking loathe Trent with the heat of a thousand suns, and I'd never willingly sleep with him.

"Just don't do anything stupid, sis." Drew presses a kiss to my forehead. "We already lost Mom, and I couldn't bear to lose you too."

"I won't," I lie, sitting up and hugging him. "But I won't be Trent's punching bag either."

"Let him in, Abby," Drew beseeches. "It'll make for an easier life."

And as my brother pulls the door closed behind him, I wonder if there's some wisdom in his words and if I should make some alterations to my plan.

CHAPTER TWO

"I can't believe you're leaving on Friday for a whole month." Jane pouts, clinging to Drew as we walk from the parking lot toward the entrance doors on our first day back at Rydeville High.

It's senior year.

Our last year here before we graduate and move to the private college campus across the other side of town. "I'll miss you."

Drew tightens his arm around her shoulders. "I'll miss you too, babe." He presses a loving kiss to the top of her head, and she melts into his side.

"Will you miss me?" Trent asks in a husky voice, keeping a firm hold of my waist as we walk.

The early morning sun glints off the massive diamond on my ring finger like a giant fuck you from the universe. "Like I miss snow on a glorious summer's day," I retort, earning a dark scowl in response. Drew shoots me a warning look over his shoulder, and I remember the promise I made to myself last night. Forcing back bile, I slide my arm around Trent's waist, smiling sweetly at him. "That was mean of me. I apologize. Of course, I'll miss you."

Trent's eyes narrow suspiciously while Charlie, also known as,

Charles Barron the Third, chuckles. "Your acting skills could use a little brush up," Charlie teases, smoothing a hand over his slicked-back jet-black hair.

"I'll get straight on that," I joke, as Trent digs his fingers into my waist.

The crowd parts when we approach the main entrance, stepping aside to allow the elite to enter. A reverential hush descends as we take the steps toward the doors. The guys nod at a few of their inner circle as we pass by. When we reach the top step, Rochelle almost magically appears like an unwelcome apparition, licking her lips and opening another button on her white uniform shirt, exposing even more of her ample cleavage. She grins at Trent. "Hey, baby."

Drew shucks out of Jane's embrace, urging her to the side as he glares at Trent. Trent keeps a tight hold of me as he brings us face to face with the girl he was fucking last night. "What did you call me?" he asks in a low tone, a muscle clenching in his jaw. Her smile falters. "And what makes you think you can speak to me?" She noticeably gulps, looking sideways at Drew and Charlie with a pleading look on her face. "Don't look at them. They won't help you." Trent grips her chin, keeping his other arm locked around my waist. "Now, do you have anything to say?"

"I'm sorry, b—Trent. I just thought, after last night—"

Trent lets go of me, grabbing her around the neck and shoving her inside the building. Drew, Jane, and Charlie follow us in, the crowd trailing behind them. "Let me make one thing clear," Trent growls, slamming her up against the wall. "You mean nothing. You're a hole to fuck when I'm bored or drunk, and you're not even a good fuck at that."

Her eyes widen, her skin turning a bluish-gray as Trent tightens his hold on her neck. "If you disrespect me, disrespect my fiancée, in public, like that ever again, I'll bury your skank ass in the woods and let animals pick the flesh from your rotting bones." Trent increases the pressure around her neck before letting her go. Tears well in her eyes, and her hands automatically move to soothe her sore neck. "You are nothing. You are the dirt under my feet. Less than insignificant. Do you understand?" he demands, pinning her with hard eyes.

Her lower lip wobbles as she nods, fear transparent in her gaze.

This is why there are rules and places in our society. Why girls in the lower echelons— those from new money—are rarely given the time of day by the elite. For three hundred years, our families have controlled Rydeville, each generation ruling supreme in Rydeville High during their teenage years.

It's more than tradition.

It's law around these parts.

Parents enroll their kids here, fully understanding the hierarchy.

They know our families' histories. How it was Manning, Montgomery, Anderson, and Barron who founded Rydeville on the north shore of Massachusetts back in the eighteenth century. How the town prospered as the businesses started by the four families developed exponentially, growing into the multi-billion corporations that our fathers' control today. Those same businesses Charlie, Drew, and Trent will inherit soon.

Rochelle thought she'd broken through the social barrier, and a whole host of eager girls were lining up to get on their knees for the three hottest guys in school.

Today, that fantasy shatters.

Trent puts her in her place in front of an audience for a reason.

To teach the others their rightful place in the order of things.

She knows better than to approach one of the elite without being summoned. Stupid girl. I shouldn't feel sorry for her, but I do. I've been the focus of Trent's dark glare and hurtful words before, and I don't call him a psycho for nothing.

Trent is unhinged.

Hands down, the most damaged and the most fucked up of the elite.

I might dislike this girl and her pitiful attempts to bully and belittle me, but she's done me a favor. While Trent's been fucking her, he's left me alone, and I figure I owe her for that. But I can't show compassion toward her in public, so I paint a snarl on my lips and level a derogatory glance over her body. "Cover yourself up," I hiss. "Your bruises are showing." I guess Trent is less circumspect about marking his fuck buddies in obvious places.

The screeching of tires from outside draws our attention away from Rochelle. Trent, Drew, and Charlie share a knowing look. "What?" I ask, wondering what intel they've kept from me this time. Out of the corner of my eye, I spot Rochelle scurrying away, tears streaming down her face.

"I thought your father put a stop to this," Drew says, eyeballing Charlie.

"Put a stop to what?" My question falls on deaf ears again, and blood boils in my veins. I step up to my brother. "Andrew." I plant my hands on my hips. "What don't I know?"

"We thought we dealt with the problem," he cryptically says.

"Never trust a fucking Barron to get the job done." Trent pins a sneer on Charlie, but he's too busy stabbing buttons on his cell to notice.

Rumblings from the crowd outside remind us there's a situation to handle. Drew shoots daggers at the people blocking the entrance, and they immediately move aside, clearing a path for us. Trent grabs my hand, pulling me back out through the double doors.

A bright red Ferrari parked at the curb has captured the crowd's attention.

Or rather the two hot guys accompanying it has.

A guy with messy dirty-blond hair is sitting up on the hood, knees bent, blatantly smoking a blunt while shooting fuck-me eyes at a couple of girls gawking at him with their mouths hanging open. His red and black tie is loose around his neck, his white shirt crumpled as if he slept in it, and he's not wearing the obligatory black blazer with the red trim and Rydeville High crest.

The second guy is casually leaning back against the side of the car, his long legs encased in the standard-issue gray uniform pants, crossed at the ankles, emitting a vibe of someone who doesn't care. But his sharp eyes scan the crowd with intent, suggesting he's the leader of this little twosome.

He's the epitome of tall, dark, and handsome with his dark brown hair teased off his face in a classical style highlighting a face models would kill for. He's all angular lines and high cheekbones with full lips and thick brows. A slight smirk lifts the corners of his mouth as he watches his friend flirt with the gaggle of girls now swarming his side.

Fuck. There'll be hell to pay for this later.

Drew and Charlie hang back for a second, waiting for Trent and me, and we approach the car as a team.

This isn't our first rodeo, and we know what to do.

Trent puffs out his chest, eyeballing the dark-haired guy. "You don't belong here, Hunt. So, take Lauder and Marshall, wherever the fuck he's hiding, and hightail it back to New York like good little minions."

The smirk grows on Hunt's face as he pushes off the car, standing tall. Lauder's flirtatious expression transforms as he jumps down off the hood, landing right in front of Trent. Hunt moves to stand beside him, and they share some unspoken communication.

Lauder drags on his blunt, inhaling smoke deep into his lungs, his cheeks hollowing out as he eyeballs Trent. Trent clasps my hand harder, and tension is palpable in the air. The crowd has grown quiet and you could hear a pin drop.

Lauder blows smoke out of his mouth, directly into Trent's face, and I don't need to look at him to know he's enraged. The familiar musky scent swirls around me, tickling my nostrils.

Hunt's smirk turns full blown, and I glare at him. His astute hazel eyes focus on me, and, holy fucking hotness, this guy is the definition of sex on legs. Not as sexy as the hot stranger I gave my V-card to but a close second. He rakes his gaze over me, and his slow perusal of my body is like a sensual caress. Trent squeezes my hand so hard it's a wonder I have any feeling left in my fingers.

"Unless you want to wear a body bag, I suggest you take your fucking eyes off my fiancée," Trent growls, aggression seeping into the air. He's like this with every guy who risks looking my way, and it's the main reason I have no male friends at this school, outside the elite. Even the guys in the inner circle are terrified to speak to me.

Lauder's head whips sideways, and he whistles low on his breath. His piercing blue eyes almost appear laughing as he checks me out. He winks, grinning widely, showcasing a set of matching dimples and a dazzling set of pearly whites. With his tousled hair, stunning eyes, and flirtatious manner, he's every bit as attractive as his buddy.

No wonder the girls at the curb were creaming their panties.

The only reason I'm not drooling are the three guys flanking my side.

I made the mistake of using a guy junior year to try to prove a point to Trent. I didn't even kiss Fenton. I just flirted with him a little, and he was foolish enough to flirt back. Later that night, Trent beat him so bad he ended up in the hospital with several broken ribs, a smashed jawline, and severe concussion. He never returned to school, and I stopped trying to teach my unwanted fiancé a lesson.

Now, I avoid any reckless flirting with guys to protect them.

But Lauder isn't in the know.

"Fuck. Me." He steps into me, cupping my cheek in a super-quick move. "You're beautiful."

"And you're out of line." I remove his hand from my face, deliberately ignoring the little spark from his touch. "Do you always touch women without their permission?"

"I've never been refused," he says, pulling on the blunt again.

"You have now," Trent answers before I get the chance.

"He always speak for you?" Hunt inquires, arching a brow.

"I'm well able to speak for myself. And you heard my fiancé. You're not welcome here." I bore a hole in the side of his skull. "Leave."

"Damn. I love an authoritative woman. Really fucking turns me on," Lauder adds, rubbing a hand over his crotch.

"If we have to physically remove you, we will," Drew says, stepping forward and snatching the blunt out of Lauder's fingers. He tosses it behind him for one of his minions to dispose of. "And stop eye-fucking my sister."

"Andrew Hearst-Manning," Hunt says, jerking his chin up as he levels a stare at my brother. "Son of Michael Hearst, CEO and majority shareholder of Manning Motors, the largest global car manufacturer, and Olivia Manning, daughter of the legendary Davis Manning, both now deceased. Twin to Abigail Hearst-Manning," he continues, casting another glance my way, "who will become Abigail Hearst-Manning Montgomery after she weds Trent Montgomery the Second upon graduation next summer. How am I doing so far?"

"Less than average," Charlie cuts in, ending whatever cell phone conversation he was having. "If you expect to impress us with a basic Google search, you're sorely mistaken."

Charlie is correct—all that information can be gleaned online. And all the locals know our second name should be Hearst but because the Manning name carries so much weight, our birth certs contain a double-barrel name.

Technically, I'm Abigail Hearst-Manning but everyone calls me

Abigail Manning. It's the same for Drew, and it's something Father approves of. I've often wondered why *he* didn't legally change his name.

"Spoken like a true Barron," Lauder says. "And you look like a stereotypical rich prick with a point to prove." He clicks his fingers, looking behind us. "You." He points at someone. "Catch." He throws his car keys, and they soar over our heads. "Park my baby. If anything happens to her, I'm holding you responsible." He levels two fingers at the sorry bastard before grabbing my hand and bringing it to his mouth. He winks as he presses a kiss to the back of my hand, deliberately ignoring the steam billowing out of Trent's ears. "Until we meet again, oh beautiful one." Hunt snorts, shaking his head.

"Later, assholes," Lauder says, bumping Trent's shoulder as he forces his way through the elite, taking the steps two at a time.

"It's been entertaining," Hunt deadpans, straightening his tie as he follows his buddy into the school.

"What the fuck is going on?" Trent fumes, sending poisonous vibes in Charlie's direction.

That's a question I wouldn't mind the answer to either.

CHAPTER THREE

"L et's walk and talk," Charlie says. "We can't be late for class on the first day." I roll my eyes when no one's looking. Perfection must be draining, but Charlie never shows it. He's the most compassionate and considerate of the three male elite, but he takes his role so seriously.

Every word that leaves his mouth, every action and reaction, is carefully measured.

Charlie has never engaged in any conduct that would bring shame on the elite or the Barron name. I've rarely seen him lose his temper, and he never hooks up with anyone from school, preferring older college chicks.

He's the only one not being forced into an arranged marriage because he has something the rest of us don't—parents who dote on him and one another. His parents believe in love, so they're allowing Charlie the freedom to choose who he wants to marry and when.

It's a continuous bone of contention with Daddy Dearest and Christian Montgomery, not least because it shows a disregard for tradition. But Charles Barron, Charlie's father, likes to push the boundaries and challenge the old rules, and he doesn't seem to care if it causes conflict in the ranks. It's not like he's answerable to my father and Trent's; however, if I were in his shoes, I wouldn't pit myself against those two rottweilers. Their loyalty to one another only extends so far, and if Charlie's dad continues to push things, he could find himself on the outs.

Charlie is a lot like his dad in many ways. While I can always rely on him to have my back, and he's intervened in arguments with both Drew and Trent on copious occasions, he keeps his cards close to his chest, and he comes across as quietly manipulative behind that charismatic, affable front he wears.

At least with Trent and Drew, what you see is what you get, but Charlie is like those mute swans we studied in biology last year—all beautiful and pure until their territory is encroached, and then they attack. I've yet to see Charlie attack, but I know he's capable of it, and I sense he's the most vicious one of all.

Drew has ushered the crowd into the building, and we climb the steps behind them.

"Your father said he'd deal with this, so why the fuck are they here?" Trent barks, running dangerously low on patience reserves, as usual.

"Who are they?" I interject, ignoring the blistering look Trent slings my way.

"Sawyer Hunt and Jackson Lauder," Charlie confirms, shoving his hands in his pockets as we step into the hallway.

The names ring a bell, and I trawl through my mind for the details, my eyes widening as I fit the puzzle pieces together. "Sawyer's father owns Techxet, and Jackson's dad is that crazy idiot who owns the world's most successful Formula One team, right?"

"Yes, although Lauder runs a bunch of different teams. Not just at Formula One level. With Camden Marshall rounding out their merry band of thieves, they consider themselves the new money elite," Drew scoffs, pursing his lips.

It's no secret there's little love lost between Rydeville's old money elite and the new money elite who have moved into the area in more recent times.

The hypocrisy is astounding, but I gave up trying to apply logic to our society years ago.

That my brother has referred to them as thieves isn't a throwaway comment either. All the traditionalists believe the new money elite are out to steal their crown and their status, and they will stop at nothing to drive them away. To deplete them of their wealth and reputation. To leave them with nothing.

And it's not confined to Rydeville alone. I know at least some of the weekend conferences the guys have attended this past year were organized for strengthening ties with other old money elite in different states.

It's a sick world I inhabit, and it's the driving force behind my escape plans.

I don't want to exist in a world where women are expected to look pretty and churn out babies while turning a blind eye to their husbands' philandering ways.

Where progress, hard work, and determination are frowned upon unless you are part of the old money elite.

Where power and control are the primary aspirations and it doesn't matter who you trample upon on your way to the top.

Where nefarious deals, criminal deeds, and acting with no moral compass is encouraged and applauded.

"Where is that fuckwit Marshall, anyway?" Trent inquires, his jaw still rigid with tension.

"I don't know," Charlie replies, "but he's definitely enrolled."

"And why is that?" Trent demands, slamming to a halt outside our lockers. "I thought Marshall liked to stay hidden like his recluse of a father."

Jane and I deposit some surplus books in our lockers while the guys talk.

Charlie shrugs. "Maybe he's coming out of his shell, or he keeps a low profile on purpose."

"They can't be here," Drew supplies. "And Father will be furious when he finds out your father didn't end this like he promised."

"He had to use it as leverage to release us for the month for the training camp," Charlie coolly replies. I don't know why the guys must attend during school term. Every other year, they've gone during school breaks.

"Bullshit," Trent snaps. "We control this school. The founding fathers built it, and our massive donations keep the coffers overflowing."

"That wasn't the only reason," Charlie continues, unruffled. "Lauder bribed Principal Sayers with a place on a Formula Three team for his son."

"That dipshit still thinks he can race professionally?" Drew asks, arching a brow.

"Apparently," Charlie says. "But the pièce de résistance is Hunt. Sawyer's one of the most sought after QBs and after Bradley North's accident, we're down a QB." Trent rubs at his temples. "Fuck this shit."

"We'll get rid of them when we come back from the trip," Charlie says. "There's no point bitching and moaning about it now."

"We can't leave Abby to deal with this alone," Trent says, as I shut my locker and rejoin him. His fingers automatically thread through mine.

"I'll handle it, and I'll have the inner circle as backup."

"I don't like it," Drew says, slinging his arm around Jane as we walk toward our homeroom.

"I hate it," Trent agrees. "And if that fucker Lauder lays another finger on my woman, I'll flatten his ass to the ground."

I firmly believe that's all I am to him.

A possession.

A status symbol.

A pretty bird to keep locked in a cage.

A toy to be played with when the mood takes him.

"I can deflect any unwelcome advances. And Oscar and Louis barely leave my side." Except when I blackmail them into turning a blind eye, but the elite don't need to know about that.

"Your bodyguards aren't permitted within the school grounds, babe," Trent says, stopping in front of the door. "That's where you're most exposed."

"Thanks for the vote of confidence," I snap.

"Babe." He cups my face, worry flitting across his face in a rare display of concern.

There are brief moments where I see a different side to Trent.

Flashes of the little boy he used to be.

Moments where I believe he might be capable of feeling something.

But they're so fleeting I usually forget they exist.

Looking at him now, at the transparent fear on his handsome face, it would be easy to fall for him.

But I never forget the monster who lives inside.

I can't afford to.

Not when my life is at stake.

"I know you can handle yourself. But these guys didn't come here without an agenda. They're up to something, and I don't like leaving you vulnerable."

Without warning, he kisses me. Usually, I shove him off when he attempts any display of intimacy, but I'm changing things up in a new game, so I kiss him back, feeling his pleasant surprise as I don't resist.

Of course, Trent being Trent, he *has* to push it, forcing his tongue into my mouth and devouring me as he grabs hold of my ass, pulling me flush against his body, his dick hardening the longer we kiss. He gives zero fucks to our audience, and if he wasn't such a jerk, I'd probably like that about him.

A throat clearing breaks us apart a few minutes later. Drew swats the back of Trent's head. "That was fucking gross, and now I can't unsee it."

Trent smirks, grabbing my boob through my shirt to further piss him off. This time, I don't hesitate, slapping his hand away. "You're such a pig."

"But I'm *your* pig," he retorts, nipping at my earlobe.

"Lucky me." Instead of using my usual sarcastic drawl, I beam at him as if butter wouldn't melt.

"Getting more convincing." Charlie chuckles in my ear, and I slap him away too, hauling my bestie out of my brother's embrace, linking our arms.

"Get lost, losers. We're out of here." I don't wait for their response, opening the door and dragging Jane inside with me.

Two things are the hot topic of gossip all morning—Rochelle's public takedown and the new guys' arrival. The place is buzzing with excitement, and I've never seen the cafeteria so full. Chad and Wentworth are on door duty, following the elite's orders.

They refuse entry to the poor sap who was forced to park Jackson's Ferrari and the girls who were flirting with him this morning. They stand there arguing, crying, and stomping their feet while the sap dutifully walks away, understanding he broke the code even if it isn't his fault.

The guys step aside to allow Jane and I to enter, nodding respectfully at us. We go to our usual table, and Trent hops up, pulling out a chair for me. "Hey, darling." He smiles before pecking my lips in an uncharacteristic sweet gesture. "You can sit. I already got your lunch." I blink excessively as I stand rooted to the spot, thinking it can't be this easy. Perhaps he's grown a conscience, and he feels bad about the Rochelle thing. Either way, I'll take a pleasant Trent over a grumpy, foul-mouthed Trent, any day.

Jane sits beside Drew, like always, and they share a long kiss, *as usual*. Charlie sits on my other side, without a female companion, *as usual*. The rest of our table is occupied by senior members of the inner circle. Trent slides his arm around the back of my chair, scooting in closer. I level a suspicious glance at him. "Why are you being so nice?"

"I didn't realize it was a crime to be nice to my fiancée?"

"And what about Rochelle?"

His lips curve up. "I knew you were jealous."

I roll my eyes, stabbing a piece of chicken with my fork, popping it into my mouth so I don't say something I shouldn't.

"I'm done with her. You have my word." He leans his face closer to mine. "You know you're the only one I love. The only one I respect."

I arch a brow in disbelief. "You love me?"

He frowns. "Why would you even question that?"

"Because you seem to hate me more than you love me."

"I could say the same to you." He could, and it'd be the truth in my case.

He winds his hand through my hair, clasping my neck and pulling me to him. His lips brush against mine in a soft kiss, one I never believed him capable of. "I don't want to fight with you anymore," he whispers over my mouth. "And I want you to know I'm one hundred percent committed to you now. There will be no other girls. I promise."

The last thing I need is this backfiring on me, so I carefully construct the next words out of my mouth. "I'm glad to hear that, Trent. And I'll give you my word to stop fighting you too on one condition."

"Name it."

"That you respect my wish to remain a virgin until our wedding night."

I need to buy time.

It's as simple as that.

His Adam's apple jumps in his throat. "I want to respect that. I do. I know you're trying to abide by the deal, but I've got needs, babe."

Swallowing my distaste, I plant my hand on his thigh, pressing my mouth close to his ear. "I can attend to your needs if you promise penetration is off the table."

He cups my face in his large palms, probing my eyes for the truth. I've mastered the art of lying to men's faces, so this isn't a biggie for me. "Agreed." He kisses me hard, and I let my hand glide higher, brushing the tip of his cock. He sucks in a sharp gasp, kissing me harder.

"Trent." Drew's clipped tone censures us, and we draw apart. "Not the time or place," he adds as sounds of a commotion at the door reach our ears. We turn around as one, not surprised to find Jackson and Sawyer debating with Chad and Wentworth. Drew stands. "I'll deal with the fuckers."

"No." I stand. "Let me." All three guys eyeball me. "I'll be the one remaining elite while you're gone. I'll be in charge, so it's best to start now. Unless you don't trust me?"

Drew reclaims his seat. "Have at it, little sis." I flip him off. So what if he was born fifteen minutes before me?

Charlie nods, smiling, and I smooth a hand down the front of my gray skirt.

"You've got this, darling." Trent swats my ass as I walk away, and I want to swing for him, but I draw deep breaths instead.

My heels tap noisily off the hardwood floor as I stride briskly toward the door. "Is there a problem?" I ask, my gaze bouncing between Chad and Wentworth.

"They refuse to go away," Chad explains.

"You can let them in." I offer Jackson and Sawyer my most disarming smile. I've already decided that the best way to control these wannabes is by appearing gracious. Denying them will just lead to battle, and despite my bravado, I'm not sure it's a battle I'd win alone.

"But Trent said—"

"Are you questioning my authority?" I cut Wentworth off with a harsh stare.

"No, but—"

I shove him up against the wall, pinning my arm underneath his chin. "There are no buts. The only response is yes, Abigail. Do you understand?"

Little beads of sweat form on his brow. "Yes, Abigail."

I let go of him, straightening his tie and slapping his cheek. "There's a good boy."

A loud chuckle emits behind me, and I turn to face Jackson and Sawyer. "I'm sorry about that." I usher them inside with a wave of my hand. "It won't happen again."

Sawyer stares at me, trying to bury his way into my head, but I just offer him another blinding smile. Jackson slides up to my side, pressing his mouth to my ear. "So fucking hot," he whispers. "We should go out sometime."

"I have a fiancé."

"Your fiancé is a slutbag douche. You're far too good for him."

I don't disagree.

"A friendly word in your ears, gentlemen." I curl my finger at Sawyer, motioning him forward. He steps up, never losing eye contact. "Things will go south quick if you don't abide by the rules. You seem reliably informed, so I'm sure you're aware. Trust me, this will be easier for everyone if you adhere to the code." I eyeball Jackson. "That means no disrespecting any of the elite and no hitting on me."

"I don't play by the rules, baby," Jackson says, curling his finger around a lock of my hair. "I was born to break 'em," He waggles his brows, and it's easy to see why so many girls fall for his charms.

According to the gossip mill, the guys were kicked out of their private New York academy for engaging in a drug-fueled orgy with several of the younger female teachers.

"And I'd break all the rules for you," he adds, his warm breath fanning over my face.

"I'm not interested." I take a step back to clear the fog in my brain. I reckon I have about ten seconds before the guys appear and take control. I can't lose face in front of the newcomers. "And don't say I didn't warn you." I spin on my heel and stride back to our table with my chin up.

"What the fuck, babe?" Trent predictably hisses when I reclaim my seat.

"Do not start with me, Trent. I'm either in control or I'm not." We face off, and a quiet hush descends upon the table.

"You're in control," Drew reaffirms. "But I hope you know what you're doing."

"I think it's a smart move," Charlie interjects. "Keep your enemies close and all that."

"But not too close," Trent snipes.

"Aw, baby. Jealous much?" I love turning his words back on him.

"Of that fuckwad?" He glares at Jackson over his shoulder. "Not fucking likely."

CHAPTER FOUR

I take a trip to the bathroom before afternoon classes resume, stumbling upon an upset Rochelle. She's huddled in a circle with her cronies, and they are doing their best to console her. All four heads jerk in my direction when I walk in, but I ignore them, attending to business and keeping my mask in place as I step toward the sink to wash my hands.

They haven't spoken in the minutes since I arrived, but I know they've plenty to say. I can almost feel the daggers embedding in my back as I dry my hands. I turn around, homing in on Rochelle, disgusted at the bruises creeping up her neck and lining her throat.

And those are just the ones I can see.

Trent is a fucking animal, and a surge of remorse slaps me in the face. It relieved me sending him off to her last night, and I feel partly responsible. "Are you okay?" I ask.

"As if you care!" she snaps.

"I know this isn't the first time, so why do you keep going back for more?"

"Because I love him!" She shoves me in the chest, but I'm strong from ballet and weekly sessions with my self-defense instructor, and I barely even flinch.

"He will never love you back."

"Because you think he loves you?" she sneers, looking me up and down the same way I did her earlier.

"Because the only person Trent loves is himself."

"Whatever, bitch. You're pathetic. You can't keep him satisfied long enough to keep him out of my bed."

I can't let this go on any longer. If this convo was just between the two of us, I could risk it, but not with an audience. Grabbing her hand, I yank her wrist back, pushing my face right up in hers as she winces. "Let's make one thing clear. He was in your bed because I permitted it. And I can remove that permission as easily as I've given it."

She doesn't need to know Trent has already made that decision himself.

"You seem to be under a misconception, and it's time I set you straight. I'm an elite." I twist her wrist harder, and she cries out in pain. None of her so-called friends even attempt to help, and I'm glad at least some girls are smart enough to obey the code. "And the rules refer to me too. I've been lenient on you, but that ends right here, right now."

I've enough on my plate handling the new guys, and I need to ensure Rochelle gets the message. Twisting her wrist farther, I hear the snap as the bone breaks. Tears leak out of her eyes while shocked gasps emit behind me. "Cross me again, and you'll end up with more than a broken wrist."

I don't wait for her reply, flinging my hair over my shoulder and exiting the bathroom.

The rest of the week passes uneventfully. Jackson and Sawyer keep their noses clean and stay out of our way. I'm not naïve enough to think my little pep talk worked.

No.

They're biding their time.

Waiting for Marshall to show up and the guys to leave before they make a move. I'm sure of it.

They take the same seat in the cafeteria at lunch, always sitting by themselves, but none of us miss the surreptitious looks sent their way by most of the female population.

Friday is the guys' last day here for a month. We held a meeting at our place last night to go over the plans in their absence. So, we're waiting for Sawyer and Jackson, at their table in the cafeteria, by prior arrangement.

"A welcoming committee?" Jackson slaps a hand over his chest. "For little ole me? You shouldn't have."

"Are you always this dramatic?" I ask, folding my arms across my chest.

"Always. Interested now, baby?"

"Not if you were the last guy on Earth and humanity's survival rested on us," I lie, because, honestly, if I was free to fuck whoever I wanted, I'd happily fuck him.

"Ouch," Sawyer deadpans, oozing lethal charm. "I see rumors of your claws are not unfounded."

"Enough," Trent growls. "We want a meeting. After school. West parking lot. Don't be late."

"You're late," Drew says as the two wannabes stroll up to us, ten minutes after the parking lot has emptied.

"What you gonna do?" Jackson taunts. "Write me up?"

"Maybe Abigail will break a bone," Sawyer adds, letting me know he's heard about Rochelle.

"Don't tempt me, jackass."

"That also seriously fucking turns me on," Jackson adds, thrusting his hips forward.

"Is there anything that doesn't turn you on?" I retort.

"Other dudes and the Kardashians," he blurts, fake shivering. "But apart from that, not a lot."

"We didn't ask you here for comedy hour," Charlie cuts in. "Where is Camden Marshall?"

"Why do you want to know, and why the fuck should we tell you?" Sawyer answers.

"If you've forgotten, we run this school, and we don't need to give an explanation," Drew supplies. "What's the deal with him, and no bullshit."

Jackson shrugs, leaning back against the hood of Trent's car, lighting up a blunt. "He had family shit to attend to, but he'll be here Monday. Anything else, Your Highness?"

I smother a snort of laughter. Sawyer watches me circumspectly out of the corner of his eye, not missing anything, and that helps eliminate my sudden burst of hilarity.

"We're heading out of state for a while," Trent says.

"We got the memo," Sawyer says, crossing his arms. "Parkhurst, right?"

"What the fuck do you know about Parkhurst," Trent demands, narrowing his eyes.

"We know enough." Sawyer straightens up, letting his arms fall to his side as tension bleeds into the air.

I've heard mention of Parkhurst over the years, the training camp for male members of the elite, but I haven't been able to find out a single thing about what kind of camp it is or what goes on there. No amount of bribery works on any of the guys. Apparently, they've sworn an oath not to discuss it with outsiders, and that includes female elite. It's been a major source of tension between us over the years, so I've no clue how Jackson and Sawyer know about it.

Charlie, Drew, and Trent exchange looks, but I can't read into it. Jackson looks amused while Sawyer is on high alert, knowing he's pressed a button, waiting to see how they react.

Drew clears his throat. "Abigail is in control in our absence." He steps right up to Sawyer. "If any of you give her trouble, you'll be answerable to us when we return."

"We're quaking in our boots," Jackson tosses out, leaning fully back on the hood, blowing smoke circles into the air.

"Get the fuck off my car," Trent barks.

Jackson slides off the car, sauntering toward Trent with the blunt extended toward him. "You need to chill out, man."

"Fuck. You." Trent brushes his hand aside.

"Told you dudes aren't my scene. I'm a pussy lover, through and through." He sends a devilish glint my direction, and I can't decide if he's brave, stupid, or just doesn't give a shit. "You need to ride his cock more often, beautiful. Maybe he'll chill the fuck out then."

"Lauder." Sawyer pins Jackson with a cautionary expression, and he holds up one palm in a conciliatory gesture.

"My bad. Abigail's in charge. No hitting on her. Got it." Jackson grins, and I wonder if anything fazes that dude.

"We done here?" Sawyer inquires.

"Pass the message onto your buddy Marshall," Charlie adds as Trent takes my hand, steering me toward his car.

"Enjoy your *vacation*," Sawyer says, enunciating the word, raising hackles on the back of my neck. Then they walk off as if they don't have a care in the world.

"I'll miss you, baby," Trent purrs, buttoning up his pants.

I won't. I didn't realize attending to Trent's needs meant sinking to my knees daily, but I do what I have to, and there's no denying he's more pliable now I'm showering him with affection.

"Me, too. This week's been good," I lie, wrapping my arms around his neck and pressing my body against his, fighting the bile swimming up my throat.

"Remember what I said," he says, sliding his hand underneath my skirt, cupping my bare ass cheeks. "I want photos and videos. Daily. I need plenty of ammo for the spank bank."

Gross. "I haven't forgotten." But if he thinks I'm sending him explicit pictures of myself, he's delusional. As if I'd give him that kind of ammunition to use against me at some future point. Not a chance in hell.

"Lean on the guys, if you need to," he reminds me. "Especially Chad. He'll do what needs to be done."

"Stop worrying. I've got this," I say with more confidence than I feel.

"Be good." He kisses me hard, yanking me against him, before releasing me and stalking out the room.

I flop down on my bed, sighing in relief.

One month of freedom from blowjobs, punishing kisses, and faking it.

I silently fist pump the air.

Jane's gentle sobs yank me out of my euphoric mood, and I push up on my elbows as my brother enters my bedroom, cradling his crying fiancée under his arm.

Poor Jane. Not seeing Drew for a month is akin to chopping off a vital limb. Those two are tied at the hip, so this will be hard for her. I hop up, giving my brother a one-armed hug because Jane refuses to relinquish her hold on him. "I'll look after her," I promise as I kiss Drew's cheek.

"I know you will," he says, kissing the top of my head. "And look after yourself too. I want daily updates."

I nod, prying my friend out of his arms. Drew kisses her one final time, whispering in her ear, and then he leaves, dragging a hand through his hair, his frustration, and concern, palpable.

"Shush, babe," I say, hugging my friend. "He's not going forever. He'll be back before you know it."

"You can say it. I know," she whimpers, swiping at the hot tears coursing down her face.

I frown. "Say what?"

"That I'm pathetic." She laughs a little, perching on the edge of my bed, her long blonde hair falling in straight lines around her face.

I drop beside her. "Don't do that. Don't put yourself down. You love him, and you'll miss him. There's no shame in that."

"Do you think there are girls at the camp?" Her pale blue eyes glisten with more unshed tears.

I shake my head. "It's a male-only training camp." Although, I'm sure there is female staff at the facility, and they probably bring in hookers and strippers for those who want to fuck, *like Trent*, but I won't share my theories with Jane because it'd upset her. "Why do you ask?"

She looks at me like I've grown ten heads. "Drew's used to sex on the regular, and we've never been apart this long before. What if he's tempted?"

"Firstly, eww. Secondly, my brother worships the ground you walk on and he's never cheated on you, so why would he start now?"

Doesn't she understand she holds all the power?

Drew's in love with her, and I honestly don't think he'd jeopardize what they have. And, for reasons I haven't worked out yet, Daddy Dearest needs this alliance with the Fords. He does nothing without an agenda, and he wouldn't marry Drew off unless he's getting something valuable from it. Drew craves our father's approval in a way I've never understood, so he won't do anything to mess up his relationship. I'm certain.

"I know he wouldn't purposely cheat on me." She worries her lip between her teeth. "I'm probably being stupid. It just bugs me we don't know what goes on there. What if it's a more elaborate version of your dad's sex dungeon and that's why they claim they can't tell us anything?"

I'd love to laugh in her face, but it's not inconceivable. I've never thought that's what goes on there, but who's saying she's wrong?

"Maybe it is," I say, shrugging. "But we'll never know, so the best thing you can do is put that thought out of your mind and focus on the fact my brother loves you deeply. He wouldn't do anything to hurt you."

"You're right," she says, perking up. "And there are plenty of ways to keep our sex life alive even if we aren't sharing the same airspace."

I nudge her in the ribs, and she falls off the side of the bed, grumbling. "You deserve it," I murmur. "Unless you want me to puke my guts up, please stop mentioning my brother's sex life."

She giggles, crawling back up onto the bed, and we watch some TV before she leaves, arranging to meet for lunch in town tomorrow.

I take a shower, dress in my pajamas, and pop my head into the corridor, telling Louis I'm beat and I'm going to watch some TV and crash.

His eyes linger on my braless chest for a moment too long, and I see some things haven't changed.

You think he'd have learned by now.

His penchant for fucking younger girls is the reason I get to sneak off when it suits me while he's on shift.

I noticed he was a perv and set the whole thing up. Invited a couple of girls from the inner circle over for a sleepover one night, arranging it so both girls made their interest clear. Louis isn't that old. Mid-to late twenties, I guess, and he's handsome if you're into guys with cropped hair, a six-pack, and little between the ears. I picked two girls who dig older dudes, knowing they'd be into it and up for the challenge.

Honestly, it was like feeding candy to an innocent kid.

Even easier than I predicted.

Louis was so busy screwing them he didn't notice me taking photos from my hiding place in the closet. Now, I dangle those shots over his head whenever I need to. Both girls were under the age of consent, so not only would he lose his job, but he'd also go to jail. He hates my guts now, but I couldn't care less once he turns a blind eye when I need him to.

Louis is a sleazebucket, and I don't feel bad for setting him up because he deserves it, but I hated blackmailing Oscar.

Oscar is the nicer of my two assigned bodyguards. He's in his forties, married with two kids, and he's a devout family man. This job means everything to him because of the health and educational benefits, and he won't jeopardize that.

So, I know he'll never divulge details of the night of my aunt's funeral when I snuck out, only returning in the early hours of the morning.

He doesn't know where I went.

That I was on the verge of throwing my life away until a hot stranger rescued me. Or that I gave him my precious virginity.

But he knows losing track of me for six hours is a sackable offense, which is why I have him by the balls now.

I don't feel good about it, but I do what I have to.

After locking my bedroom door from the inside, and turning the TV up loud, I shed my pajamas in favor of black skinny jeans, a black tank, and a light black hoodie. I lace my sneakers, smooth my hair back into a ponytail, and pull the hood up over my head before disappearing into the secret tunnel behind my wall.

I discovered the tunnel by pure accident fourteen months ago. I'd lashed out at the wall in a fit of rage after a vicious argument with Daddy, pressing a hidden lever in the process and watching, with tears drying on my cheeks, as the wood paneling retracted, revealing a set of steep stairs.

I pad down the stairs now, the pathway ahead of me automatically lighting up when my foot hits the bottom step. The panel slides shut behind me, and I walk with purpose upon the granite floor.

I was intrigued when I first made the discovery because I was expecting a dusty, damp, decrepit old tunnel with cobwebs, mold, and crumbling walls—because our house dates back to the eighteenth century—but it was immediately obvious this tunnel was a more modern addition with the clean stone walls, granite floor, automatic lighting, and electronic locking mechanisms.

Our lavish mansion has been in the Manning family for generations, passed down to Mom after her father died when we were kids. Mom's only other surviving relative was her sister, Genevieve, but she'd shunned the family business once she graduated from college, taking her trust fund and moving to Alabama where she ran her own chain of florist shops until she passed five months ago.

Responsibility for upholding the Manning family tradition thus fell to Mom.

Like me, I know she had little choice.

Her marriage to my father was unusual because his family wasn't of the same standing. Mom died when I was seven, so I never got the full story from her, and I've spent years wondering why my grandfather chose Michael Hearst for her husband. I know their marriage wasn't a happy one, and I still remember hearing my mother's screams as that bastard beat her, but there are so many questions left unanswered.

Like who built this tunnel and why?

Aunt Genevieve confided some stuff in me from her deathbed. Relaying her belief that my father orchestrated the car accident that claimed my mother's life.

She urged me to leave.

To get out.

Terrified the same fate lies in store for me.

Her theories, and her death, sent me running into the sea that night, and I'm ashamed to admit that even to myself, because she didn't confide in me to end my life.

She did it to save me.

And if I'd killed myself that night, I would've made a mockery of her trust.

I bend down in front of the door, prying the loose stone free of the wall, and retrieve the box I stashed there. I punch in the code on the digital pad, and the lid springs free. Removing the burner cell, I tap out a text to Xavier confirming I'll be at the rendezvous point in twenty minutes. Zipping the cell in the pocket of my hoodie, I grab some cash and my gun, checking the safety's on, tuck it in the band of my pants, and head out into the dark night.

CHAPTER FIVE

After a pleasant lunch with Jane the following day, I return to the house, cussing under my breath when I spot the familiar silver and black cars parked out front.

Trent's father drives the Majestic S70—Manning Motor's most popular car with obnoxious, wealthy pricks who have more money than sense—while Charlie's father insists on driving a silver Bentley, much to my father's disgust. I get a secret thrill out of his disobedience, and I love that he challenges the traditions in several ways. Don't get me wrong, Charles reveres the old traditions, but he's always seeking ways of modernizing the legacy, and if it was up to him, most of the ancient archaic rules would be abandoned.

I sigh as I approach the house, hoping their plans haven't changed. I presumed the fathers would've left for Parkhurst by now, and I was looking forward to not seeing Daddy Dearest for a few days. Having the house to myself is only an illusion of freedom, but I take the wins where I can get them.

I step foot in the marble lobby, quietly closing the heavy mahogany door behind me. I set out toward Father's study with my stiletto heels tap-tapping off the floor as I walk, deep in thought.

I have the means to escape now, thanks to the large chunk of change Aunt Genevieve left me on the sly. I have cash stashed in a few different places, but most of the millions she left me is safely hidden in an offshore account she opened in my name.

And, thanks to Xavier's connections, I have a fake ID and other necessary paperwork securely stowed in my box in the tunnel.

But I'm not naïve enough to think I could vanish without a trace. I believe my father arranged my mother's death because she was attempting to flee and she planned on taking Drew and me with her. I have vague recollections of her telling me we were moving to a new house shortly before she died.

I know if I vanished, my father would pull out all the stops to find me. I refuse to look over my shoulder for the rest of my life, so I need ammunition. I need something to hold over my father to force him to let me go, so I avail of every opportunity to snoop.

The fact the fathers are still here means something has happened, and I want to know what.

I stop in front of the large gold-encrusted mirror to reapply my lip gloss and run a comb through my hair. Then I run my hands down over my form-fitting red dress, checking my reflection carefully, ensuring I look ladylike and refined.

Father won't let me step foot around town unless I'm dressed the part, and I long since gave up rebelling against it.

I have bigger battles to pick.

Pleased with my appearance, I rap firmly on his study door, not waiting for an invitation before stepping foot inside.

All three men tip their heads up as I walk into the room. Charles Barron, Senior smiles warmly at me. Daddy scowls, and Christian Montgomery, my future father-in-law, undresses me with his eyes in a way that never ceases to send chills all over my body. Fucking sleazeball.

"What have I told you about barging in here?" Father barks,

swirling the amber-colored liquid in the glass in his hand.

"I knocked." I flutter my eyelashes, wearing my most innocent expression.

"What do you want, Abigail?" He sighs.

"I wanted to remind you of my ballet recital next Friday. Will you be home in time?"

My father leans forward in his chair, glaring at me. "I'll be there. Have I ever missed one?"

No. But it's not like you're there because you want to cheer me on or you're proud of me. You're there because it's what's expected. "Okay. Have a good trip, Father." I nod at Charlie's and Trent's fathers. "Mr. Barron. Mr. Montgomery."

As I exit the room, I leave the door slightly ajar, not enough you'd notice but enough for me to eavesdrop.

"She grows more like Olivia with every passing day," Barron says.

"Don't remind me," my father growls.

"My son is a lucky man," Montgomery adds.

"We need to conclude this business and be on our way," my father says.

"We can use this to our advantage," Barron says. "They've come to us. They're on *our* turf. We can control how this plays out."

"The timing couldn't be worse," my father says.

"It's deliberate," Montgomery agrees. "Can she handle this?"

"She's tougher than she looks."

"All females are weak, especially the pretty ones," the jackass Montgomery replies.

"It will be a good test," Barron suggests.

"Perhaps," my father supplies. "But either way, there's no choice. If things turn ugly, our sons will clean up the mess when they return."

"So, it's agreed," Barron says. "We won't intervene."

"For now," Montgomery adds.

The scraping of chairs alerts me to the impending danger, and I slip off my heels and race down the corridor in my bare feet, heading toward the bedrooms.

I'm contorting my arms awkwardly, struggling to pull the zipper on my dress down my back when my door bursts open unexpectedly.

Panic presses down on my chest like a heavy weight as I come face to face with my future father-in-law. Oscar stands in the doorframe behind him, doing little to hide his anger. "Do you mind?" Christian Montgomery says, pushing my bodyguard back and slamming the door in his face.

"Why are you here?" I stand up straight, planting my hands on my hips, refusing to be intimidated.

"I wanted to remind you you belong to my son." He walks behind me, brushing my hair to one side, his fingers clutching onto my zipper without invitation. Goose bumps prickle my skin, and a chill creeps up my spine. His warm breath blows across the nape of my neck, and bile floods my mouth. It takes enormous effort not to physically tremble. Or puke.

"I haven't forgotten." I wish I could, but it's shoved in my face too often to ever forget.

"Stay away from Marshall, Lauder, and Hunt," he adds, sliding the zipper down in slow motion.

"I don't know what you're implying, but I've never given Trent any reason to doubt my loyalty, and I don't intend to start now."

I jerk when his fingers brush along the bare skin of my back, frantically trying to get a leash on my panic.

Trent's father has always looked at me in inappropriate ways.

Said things that could be misconstrued.

But he's never touched me—until now.

I step forward, needing to get away from him, but his arm slides around my stomach, clasping my elbow firmly, trapping both my arms as he hauls me back against his chest. Nausea travels up my throat when I feel the evidence of his arousal pressing into me from behind. "Those three will try to get to us through you," he says, way too close to my ear. His free hand travels up my body, cupping my boob.

"Take your hands off me!" I attempt to wriggle out of his hold, but he tightens his grip on my elbow, digging his fingers into my skin in a way I know will leave marks.

"This belongs to my son." He fondles my boob, and my stomach churns sourly.

And me.

I hear the unspoken words, elevating my panic to all new coronary-inducing territory. His hand leaves my breast, moving southward, and I squeeze my eyes shut as he cups my pussy through my dress. "As does this virgin cunt. See it remains that way."

Rubbing his nose against my neck, he inhales. "You smell every bit as delicious as your mother." He licks a line up my neck, and a lone tear trickles out of the corner of one eye as new horrors rise to the surface. "I wonder if you taste and feel like she did," he whispers in my ear, rubbing his hand back and forth across my crotch.

"Get your hands off me. Your son won't be happy when I tell him about this." I hate how my voice quakes, but terror has taken control of my body.

"You won't breathe a word to Trent," my father says, strolling into the room like there's nothing unusual in finding his teenage daughter being manhandled by his best friend. Oscar's head is down, his shoulders slumped, at his position in the hallway, and I know he wants to intervene. "You won't do anything to risk your wedding or this family, because you won't like the consequences." Looking bored, he ignores me, eyeballing his friend. "We're leaving."

I almost collapse in relief when Christian releases me, stumbling away from him and swiping at my errant tears so he doesn't notice. "Remember what I said," he warns, blatantly adjusting the hard-on in his pants. "Stay away from those assholes. That's an order."

"And do nothing to bring the elite into disrepute," my father adds. "Prove yourself capable, and we can discuss giving you more responsibility."

I lift my chin and plant a confident expression on my face. "I will handle it, Father."

Without further words, they both leave the room, and I wait thirty seconds before slumping to the ground, silent tears rolling down my face.

Oscar is beside me in a heartbeat, mopping my tears with a tissue. "I'm sorry," he whispers.

"Don't be," I whisper back. "You can't interfere. They'll kill you or take it out on your family." I've eavesdropped on enough conversations to know my father and his associates are not above kidnapping, torture, murder, and rape.

"Drew needs to do more to protect you," he whispers.

"How?" I shrug. "His hands are just as tied."

Oscar shakes his head. "Drew is the future leader of Manning Motors, and your father has groomed him his whole life to assume his rightful place in the elite. He could make demands, and your father would agree to them."

I very much doubt that, but I'm not in the mood to argue. I just want to erase the last few minutes from my mind and forget it ever happened. "I can't tell Drew what just happened because he'll tell Trent, and he'll go ballistic."

Or maybe I'm more afraid that he won't.

That he fully expects to share me with his father once we're married and living in the Montgomery house. Trent's mother isn't an alcoholic basket case recluse for no reason.

His childhood hasn't been any easier than ours, and I know a lot of that is because his mother fell apart when she lost her two best friends in quick succession. Mrs. Anderson took her own life, and then my mother died in a car accident a few months later, leaving Sylvia without her closest friends. Elizabeth Barron, Charlie's mom, was an out-of-towner, and she never shared the same bond as the other three women who had grown up together.

My brain hurts, and I can't think about this any longer. I need to clear my head, and there are only two things that work for me—dancing and running. I choose the latter, pushing up to my feet. "I need to run," I tell Oscar, sliding the heavy diamond off my ring finger and stashing it in the drawer of my bedside table where it'll remain until I'm forced to put it back on.

Already, I feel lighter.

"I'll get the car while you change."

"Thank you."

He presses a soft kiss to the top of my head, and tears prick my eyes. He's shown me more love and compassion than my own father, and I wonder what it'd be like to grow up in a loving environment. To have a father who protects you instead of continuously throwing you to the wolves.

I run the length of the secluded beach, pushing my limbs faster and faster, as I expunge my fear and cling to my anger.

Fuck Christian Montgomery.

Fuck his son.

And fuck my father.

They won't get the better of me.

They won't control me for life.

I will get out of here.

And they won't stop me.

I'm sweating profusely as I finally flop to the ground, lying down on the grassy dunes as I attempt to recalibrate my breathing. After a couple minutes, I sit up, retrieve my water bottle from my backpack, and greedily drink from it even if the water is warm at this stage. I rip my running top off, using it to mop my brow and the line of sweat coasting between my breasts, before pouring the last of the water over my head, enjoying the trickles of liquid trailing down my face, over my sports bra, and onto my overheated torso.

I lie back down again, closing my eyes, my face warm from the dying embers of the evening sun.

The sea has always beckoned me. Maybe it's because being at the beach is one of the few remaining memories I have of my mother.

I can still see her in my mind's eye, her long wavy brunette locks bouncing everywhere as she raced me toward the sea. Her gleeful laughter as Drew and I buried her in the sand. Her warm hands on my skin as she applied sunscreen. The safety of her arms as she toweled me dry.

Mom loved the beach, and we spent large portions of the summer here. I think that's why it's my favorite place to run. Why I gravitate here whenever I feel sad. Because it reminds me of her. Because I feel closer to her here.

"Penny for them, beautiful," a deep voice says, and my eyes jerk open at the sound of approaching footsteps.

I sit up, eyes narrowing as Jackson Lauder jogs toward me. He's topless, wearing black running shorts that hug his toned hips, and his tight abs flex as he runs.

"You look like you have the worries of the world on your shoulders," he says, dropping beside me.

"I was just thinking about my mom," I truthfully admit.

His eyes probe mine. For what, I'm not sure. "I'm sorry."

He knows. Of course. Hunt clearly did more than basic research. "She died a long time ago." I shrug, like that makes it any easier to live with. It's true it gets easier with time, but I never stop missing her. There isn't a day goes by where I don't think of her. Where I don't wonder what our lives would be like if she was still here. If she'd succeeded in escaping with us.

But dreaming is destructive.

"No measure of time ever completely dulls the pain," he quietly says.

It doesn't. I glance at him, trying not to ogle his gorgeous body or succumb to the lure of his twinkling blue eyes. "Who did you lose?"

A muscle clenches in his jaw. "My sister. She was murdered four years ago."

We have that in common too. "That's terrible. I'm sorry."

He removes a lighter and roll up from the pocket of his pants, instantly lighting it up. He takes a long drag before offering it to me. Given his propensity for blunts, I'm guessing it's a joint. I've never smoked one or taken any drug. It's not permitted, and the elite are my perpetual shadows at any parties we attend, ensuring I don't indulge.

But no one's here now. Oscar is waiting in the car, and even if he wasn't, he couldn't stop me. I don't overthink it, taking the joint from Jackson, ignoring the tingles shooting up my arm when our fingers brush. I inhale deeply, smoke filling my lungs, before spluttering and coughing with tears pooling in my eyes.

Jackson chuckles, taking the joint back. "Of course, it's your first time." He takes a deep pull before passing it back to me. "Living in a golden cage must get boring."

I take another drag, spluttering, but not as bad as last time. "You've no idea," I mutter, handing it back to him. Yanking my hair tie out, I run my hands through my hair. I know it's not smart to open up to any of them, but I'm feeling rebellious today after what happened. Trent's dad told me to stay away from the new guys, and this is my way of sticking it to him.

Jackson looks funny at me but says nothing, and we pass the joint back and forth in comfortable silence. It doesn't take long for a pleasant, hazy fog to cloud my mind, dulling my senses and loosening my limbs. I flop back down on the ground, grinning at nothing in particular. I move my arms and legs, in and out, like a starfish, giggling to myself.

"I think someone's stoned," Jackson teases, leaning over me and smiling.

"I feel great!" I continue moving my legs, in and out, like I used to as a little kid when Drew and I played this game for hours on the sand, sighing contentedly. "I should smoke weed more often." Jackson snorts, pulling another drag as he keeps his eyes locked on me. "Who does that anyway?" I ask. "Goes for a run and then smokes a joint?" I jump up, swaying my body to an imaginary beat, humming under my breath as I practice some of my ballet moves.

"I do whatever it takes to numb reality," he supplies. "Running, smoking, fucking, racing." He smirks as I lose my footing in the sand, taking a tumble.

I brush my tangled hair back off my face, giggling as I wriggle in the sand, wondering why weed is still considered an illegal substance for those under twenty-one in this state. Anything that makes you feel this good should be freely available.

"You should laugh more," Jackson says, looming dangerously close as he sweeps my knotty hair behind my ears. "You look even more beautiful when you smile." He runs his thumb along my lower lip, and my breath hitches in my throat. My giggling stops, and a more intense emotion takes over as we stare at one another, electricity humming in the air. My chest heaves, and a swarm of butterflies invades my tummy as I feel his touch in every part of me. His eyes lower to my mouth as he pushes his thumb between my lips.

I'm blaming the weed for what I do next.

My tongue darts out, tasting his thumb, flicking against his skin in soft strokes. He groans, low at the base of his throat, before his lips crash down on mine, and, in the blink of an eye, we're kissing as if we've never kissed anyone else before.

His lips are challenging, demanding, and hungry as he feasts on my mouth, and I'm giving as good as I'm getting. He pulls me into his hot body, grabbing hold of my ass and yanking my hips against his, pressing his hard length into me, making me moan against his mouth. My hands move of their own volition, exploring the toned planes of his naked chest and his back as our mouths feverishly devour one another. Stars explode behind my closed eyelids when his tongue plunders my mouth, licking and sucking while grinding his hips against me in a way that has my core throbbing with need.

"Ms. Abigail."

I scream, ripping my mouth from Jackson's as Oscar's harsh tone brings me crashing back down to Earth with a bang. I scramble away from Jackson and his cheeky, knowing expression, flirtatious eyes, and swollen lips, as the reality of what I've just done slaps me in the face.

"Shit." I climb to my feet while Oscar retrieves my backpack and discarded running top, glaring at Jackson with thinly veiled disgust.

"See you at school on Monday, beautiful," Jackson says, winking as he rises. "I'll be looking forward to it."

CHAPTER SIX

"**O**kay what has you freaking out so bad?" Jane asks when I materialize in her bedroom the next day. I didn't say much on the phone because I know for a fact my regular cell is bugged, but my bestie can read my moods perfectly, so she already knows something's up.

"I've done something supremely stupid." I pace the length of her room, wearing a line in the plush carpet.

"What?" Jane lands in front of me, taking my hands and leading me over to the couch. *Riverdale* is paused on the screen, and I roll my eyes, not unsurprised. She's addicted to that show, but all her attempts to coerce me into watching have failed.

"I made out with Jackson Lauder," I blurt. She blinks excessively, staring at me in shock, her eyes wide, mouth gaping open like a fish out of water. "Say something," I plead.

The corners of her mouth lift. "Was he a good kisser?"

I groan. "The best." My fingers trek across my lips, and my body tingles all over as I remember the feel of his lips and his hands on me. "But focus!" I nudge her in the shoulder. "What am I going to do? They have warned me to stay away from them. My job is to keep them in line not kiss them!"

"Maybe kissing them will help keep them in line."

My jaw drops to the floor. "Who are you, and what have you done with my bestie?" She giggles. "I can't keep kissing Jackson," I protest. "It was a huge fuckup, and Trent will lose his shit if he finds out. But how do I get Jackson to keep quiet without owing him something?" I bury my head in my hands. "I am never smoking weed again."

"You smoked a joint?" Jane shrieks.

I nod. "It was an epic clusterfuck of a day." I tell her everything that went down with Trent's dad and how I ended up bumping into Jackson on the beach.

"Oh my God, Abby. You should've come here straightaway! I can't believe Trent's dad did that and your father let him!"

"This is the kind of shit they pull." I level her with a serious look. "This is the world you're marrying into." I tossed and turned all night long, unable to sleep, because I'll be leaving her behind to face this shit alone, and she'll need her wits about her if she's to survive marriage to an elite.

"You need to tell Drew. He'll know what to do."

I shake my head. "No. You can't tell Drew, and I need you to promise me."

Her nose scrunches up. "You know I don't enjoy keeping secrets from your brother, Abby, but you're my bestie, so if you really don't want him to know, I won't tell him."

"Thanks." I take her hands in mine. "I know you love my brother and you want to marry him, but this world is corrupt and evil, and you need to prepare yourself for it."

"Now you're scaring me."

"Good." I squeeze her hands. "They're not good people, Jay. What Christian Montgomery did in my room doesn't even register because that's child play compared to their usual shit. They aren't some of the wealthiest, most powerful, most influential men in the country by chance. They have bribed, manipulated, abused, and bullied their way to the top, and they have no moral compass. No conscience. Except for Charlie's dad. I don't think he's all bad, but he's not good either. He does nothing to stop it."

"I'm not completely clueless, Abby. I know they're not angels."

"They're the devil incarnate, Jane. Never forget that."

I pull up at Jane's house bright and early Monday morning, and she clambers into the chauffeur-driven car, plonking down beside me. "You ready for this?"

"No. But I've decided I'm going to pretend like it never happened. Deny is my new favorite word. If Jackson mentions anything, I'll deny, deny, deny till I'm blue in the face."

Oscar is the only other witness, and he won't betray my confidence, so denial seems like my only choice, because I will not ask Jackson to keep quiet and end up beholden to him. That's probably what he wants and what he's expecting. And in case this doesn't work, I already have Xavier on the case, searching into their backgrounds to see what skeletons he uncovers.

In our world, exploiting weakness is a key survival tool. It's why I'm already paying Xavier a small fortune to find something I can use against my father and the elite. Why I'm paying him another chunk of cash to find dirt on the new guys. I've paid for a rush job because I need intel now. I need something in my armory to help me survive this next month.

"With any luck, he'll be too busy welcoming the latecomer to focus on you."

"Hopefully, Camden Marshall acts as a suitable distraction, but I wouldn't hold my breath."

"I wonder what he's like?" she muses, staring idly out the window.

"I spent most of last night Googling him, but it's so weird, there isn't a single photo of him or his family online."

"Drew said they are notoriously reclusive."

"Apparently so, according to the gossip sites. Camden's father has Techxet—Sawyer's father's company—on retainer, and a team of technical specialists is dedicated twenty-four-seven to finding and removing all photographic content and any unsavory online content. I could barely find out anything about him other than his father is Wesley Marshall, owner of a pharmaceutical company called Femerst, and a much-respected philanthropist, and he met Sawyer and Hunt when they all enrolled at a private New York school a couple of years ago."

"I bet he's hot," Jane speculates as our driver pulls into the entrance to Rydeville High.

"Of course, he's hot. I don't need a picture to confirm that. Hot, rich assholes always stick together. We should know."

I spot Oscar fighting a smile through the front mirror.

"Just don't go kissing this one," Jane whispers, her expression half serious, half mischievous.

"Don't worry. I'll be going nowhere near Camden Marshall. Trust me on that score."

"He's definitely hot," Jane says as we enter the cafeteria at lunchtime. Wentworth is on door duty with Henry this time and they nod at us as we pass through. "Mr. Fleming had to reprimand Rochelle and her divas several times during English lit because they kept swooning over him. Apparently, Shelton is in his world history class, and she said he's sex on a stick."

"Figures."

Chad summons me to our usual table with a wave. "I got lunch for you ladies," he says, pulling out a chair for me and then one for Jane.

"Thank you, Chad. That's sweet and thoughtful."

"Suck up," someone recklessly mumbles from farther down the table.

"I think you enjoy being waited on hand and foot," an all-too-familiar voice says close to my ear, and I suck in a sharp breath as Jackson's hands land on the table, one on each side of me, caging me in from behind. He presses his warm body against my back, heating me upon contact.

This shit can't happen, so I ram my elbow back into his gut with force, hitting him a sharp jab to the edge of his rib cage, knowing it will wind him. He loses his balance, stumbling backward, as a loud oomph emits from his mouth. I stand, turning around in time to see Hunt grab Jackson's elbow, steadying him before he hits the ground.

"Not very ladylike, beautiful," Jackson rasps, his breathing a little erratic.

"You deserved it." I drill him with a look. One that says, "act smart and shut your mouth."

"You've got serious anger management issues," Hunt says, pinning me with that intense gaze of his.

"Don't pretend you know me when you don't."

"I think I—"

I step toward Jackson, cautioning him with my eyes, and he stops mid-speech. "Shut your mouth," I hiss in his face.

"About what?" a deep, rich voice asks from behind me. His seductive tone reaches deep inside me, pulling the memories to the forefront of my mind. My skin prickles, and my belly does a weird flip-flop motion.

No fucking way.

I'm afraid to turn around.

Afraid to confront the truth.

Because I'd know that voice anywhere.

Even though we didn't talk much, every aspect of that night is imprinted on my brain.

This can't be happening.

My heart rate spikes, my breathing becomes labored, and butterflies scatter in my chest.

I turn around in slow motion, trying to prepare myself for the inevitable, but nothing could shield me from the vision in front of me.

His sultry brown eyes flash darkly as he stares at me, and his cold, impassive face is a million miles away from the softer, compassionate look I'm familiar with. The sleeves of his white shirt are rolled up to the elbows, showcasing the ink on his arms like a calling card. He's wearing his hair the same way. Shorn tight on both sides with the longest part on top, flipped over to the left. The skull tattoo I repeatedly ran my fingers over taunts me as I almost crumble under his hateful glare. Danger and power exude from him in waves, and the entire room has turned mute as they watch our exchange with bated breath.

"You're Camden Marshall," I whisper, struggling to breathe above the panic running riot inside me.

"Yes, *Abigail*." He spits my name out like it pains him to speak it. "And we need to talk."

CHAPTER SEVEN

"**F**ollow me," I say, proud my voice doesn't crack. Doesn't betray the anxiety coursing through my body. Someone up there sure loves to fuck with me.

"I'll come with," Chad offers, materializing at my side.

"That won't be necessary." There is no way in hell I want him, or any of the inner circle, anywhere near this conversation.

"But Trent said—"

"Trent isn't here," I snap. "Take care of Jane. I'll be back shortly."

I spin on my heel and stride out of the cafeteria, not bothering to check if they're following me. I walk toward the main auditorium. No one ventures in there at lunchtime, and it's the most private place to talk.

"Wow, slow down, beautiful," Jackson says, tugging on my elbow.

I shove him off. "Stop touching me."

"That's not what you—" He stops talking when I fix him with my most venomous look, and I'm pissed when his mouth turns up in amusement. "Do you practice scary evil faces in the mirror before you come to school? Because, I gotta say, your fright face needs work."

I flip him the bird. "That clearer for you?"

He throws back his head, laughing.

"Jackson," Camden cautions as we arrive at the entrance to the auditorium.

I push my way through the double doors, keeping my back ramrod straight and my head lifted, as I descend the stairs, willing my errant pulse to calm down because I need a cool head to deal with this situation. Stopping when I reach the podium, I turn around, clasp my hands in front of me, and school my lips into a neutral line as they saunter toward me.

Jackson is wearing his trademark shit-eating grin, his uniform disheveled like he never irons it, his tie missing, and the top few buttons of his shirt undone, offering a glimpse of the tan skin my hands are, unfortunately, familiar with.

Sawyer is giving nothing away, holding himself assertively as he walks with purpose. Unlike his friend, his uniform is freshly pressed, his shirt fully buttoned, and his tie straight. There isn't a hair out of place on his head, and he exudes calm confidence in spades.

My eyes flit to the guy I've struggled to evict from my head since that fateful night at the beach. Camden is a ball of hateful energy as he stalks toward me, not even attempting to shield his loathing. His eyes are darkly vicious as he glares at me, his mouth pulled into a sneer, but it doesn't detract from his hotness.

It only adds to it.

My memory hasn't done him justice at all, and I hate that my body purrs with need, my mouth craving another taste.

I gulp over the messy ball of emotion wedged in my throat. Conflicting emotions race through me.

Discovering I gave my virginity to the enemy both terrifies and excites me. It's even more of an F you to Trent, but that also means I'll be in worse trouble if he finds out. I plan on being far away from Rydeville High before my scheduled wedding day, but Camden showing up here means I'm no longer the sole holder of this secret, and that's a big fucking problem.

Along with the fact he's glowering at me like I'm the second coming of the AntiChrist.

He wasn't shocked to see me which means he already knew who I was, but he didn't know the night we met because I doubt it would've happened otherwise.

Unless he planned it?

My stomach dips as that thought lands in my mind, but I shake it aside. It couldn't have been premeditated. I hadn't planned on going to that beach that night.

It had to have been a coincidence.

A fucked-up one, but a coincidence none the less.

But that doesn't mean he didn't realize who I was and take my virginity as some sick form of control or revenge.

Nausea swims up my throat as my brain grapples to make sense of this.

And while I figure his disgust is because of the rivalry between his kind and mine, I can't help the feelings of rejection that flood my body or the nasty inner voice that says he regrets it. That it didn't mean as much to him as it meant to me.

"Why do you hate me?" I ask, when they come to a standstill in front of me, looking Camden squarely in the eye.

"If you have to ask, you're even more stupid than you look." His voice is devoid of emotion, unlike his hate-filled gaze.

His words dig deep, raising old wounds, and I'm instantly on the defensive. "Fuck. You." My mouth curves at the corners. "Oh, my bad. I already did, and it wasn't in any way memorable," I lie.

Jackson's eyes pop wide, and his mouth falls open, while Sawyer's razor-sharp gaze lands instantly on Camden. "What is she talking about?" Sawyer asks.

I silently kick myself up the ass for my mistake. I presumed his buddies knew, and I wanted to dismiss what we shared before he beat me to it. But, judging from their reactions, Jackson and Sawyer didn't know.

So maybe it wasn't part of some plan because if it was wouldn't his friends have been in on it?

Ugh. I shut my wayward thoughts down. I can analyze it later. Right now, I need to bring my A-game, and I've possibly just made things worse. I need to focus because now the three of them know my secret, and I must find a way of keeping them quiet.

Camden's jaw is rigid with tension, and he doesn't remove his eyes from my face as he answers his friend. "She's the girl from the beach."

Now, it's Sawyer's turn to look surprised.

"You got a thing for hooking up on beaches, beautiful?" Jackson, unhelpfully, supplies, winking at me.

"I was stoned," I say through gritted teeth.

Camden stops eyeballing me long enough to stare at Jackson. Tension bleeds into the air. "Care to elaborate?"

Jackson smirks, and my hands ball into fists at my side. "She was all over me Saturday night. Would've been all over my dick too if her bodyguard hadn't interrupted."

"You kissed me first!" I protest.

"You kissed me back!"

My fists itch with a craving to wipe that smug grin off his face. "I didn't know what I was doing!"

"Is that why I found you up to your knees in the sea, in the middle of the night, your nipples poking through your silk robe?" Camden snarls, putting his face right into mine. "Were you stoned then too? Or was it some pitiful attempt at ending your miserable life?"

"My life isn't miserable," I lie, taking a step back, my calves hitting the edge of the podium.

"The note you left me says otherwise." He removes the crumpled sheet from his pocket, opening it up and shoving it in my face. Before I can make a grab for it, Sawyer has snatched it from Camden's hand. Jackson leans over his shoulder, and they both read it while Camden and I face off.

"Aw, you gave her a precious memory, Cam," Jackson teases, slapping his buddy on the back. "And how was it for you?"

"Below insignificant," Cam coolly replies, digging a hole out of my heart. "I don't fuck virgins for a reason. They have no clue what they're doing." My cheeks flare up as Jackson and Sawyer chuckle. "I should've just left you in the sea and done the world a favor."

Pain slices across my chest making breathing difficult.

What kind of asshole says that to someone who was suicidal?

"It was a mistake. We can both agree to that. There's no need to reference it again." I push past him, desperate to get out of here before I say something I regret.

"Who the fuck said you could leave?" Cam barks, grabbing hold of my arm and stopping me. Warmth seeps from his skin to mine, delicious tremors zip up and down my arms, and I hate how my body responds to his touch so enthusiastically.

I attempt to wriggle out of his hold, but his grip is firm, and he tightens his grasp on my elbow the more I struggle. "Ow." I wince as his palm presses down on my tender flesh.

He shoves the sleeve of my jacket and shirt up, running his finger along the existing marks on my pale skin. "You do this?" he asks Jackson, his face and voice nonchalant.

"Nope," he replies, popping the P. "My money's on the douchebag fiancé."

"Who did this to you?" Cam asks.

"Why the fuck do you care?" I spit.

"I don't. This is about gleaning intel."

I bark out a laugh, still trying to wrest my arm away from him. "And why the hell would I help you with that?"

A cocky grin graces his mouth. "You'll help. Trust me. You'll do exactly what we say."

"You're delusional."

"And you're a stupid, naïve girl who thinks she can play in the big league."

"You don't get to rock up here and tell me what to do. I'm part of the elite. I tell *you* what to do." They all roar with laughter, and heat creeps up my neck and onto my cheeks. Although I abhor violence, because I know that's how the elite rule, I won't stand here and let them belittle me any longer.

I'm done playing nice.

Using my free hand, I reach back around to the gap between our bodies, grab hold of his junk, and squeeze it with all my strength, ensuring I dig my long, manicured fingernails into his flesh. His hold on my elbow releases instantly, and he emits a guttural roar, cussing as he stumbles back, clutching his crotch. I use the distraction to rush past Jackson and Sawyer, scaling the steps as fast as I can.

"Stop her!" Cam pants, his voice laced with pain, and I smile to myself as I pick up my pace.

My palm lands on the door just as I'm wrenched back. I scream, but a hand slams over my mouth as I'm simultaneously lifted against a warm chest. Jackson is climbing the stairs, coming toward us as I thrash about in Sawyer's arms.

"Stop fucking moving," Sawyer grits out, moving down the stairs, and I bite down hard on his hand. "Motherfucker!" he shouts, yanking his hand away, almost losing his hold on me, but he recovers fast. "The bitch bit me!" The arm around my waist tightens as he growls in my ear.

Jackson chuckles. "Told you she was feisty."

"Grab her legs," Sawyer instructs.

"No!" I lift my legs up, shoving them into Jackson's gut before he can get hold of me.

Thank God for ballet and its core-strengthening ability.

Jackson's expression is comical as he wobbles, his arms flailing as he struggles to maintain balance.

Sawyer has a choice to make.

Drop me or let his friend risk injury.

I'm dropped like a sack of potatoes, my shoes flying in different directions, as Sawyer reaches for Jackson, fisting his shirt in the nick of time, halting his backward trajectory.

Ignoring the pain ricocheting along my spine, I crawl away, scrambling to my feet and racing toward the door for a second time. Adrenaline pumps through my veins at the sound of running footsteps behind me. I'm panting as I push through the double doors out into the empty corridor, thinking I'm home free, when I'm suddenly yanked back by my hair.

A scream rips from my throat as stinging pain dances along my scalp. I'm dragged back into the auditorium by my hair, and tears stream out of my eyes as I'm slammed up against the wall. Cam's face is a mask of scary aggression as his hand closes around my throat, and I'm lifted clear off the ground.

I claw at his hand, panicking as I struggle to draw enough air into my lungs. The wall rattles as he shakes me, tightening his grip on my neck while pressing his body flush against mine. "Let's get one thing straight here, *Abigail*. We own you. You are ours to do with as we please." He rocks his pelvis into mine, ensuring I feel his hardening length, and it should sicken me that this turns him on.

But I'm aroused too.

Guess I'm even more fucked up than I thought.

"Pull that crap again, and I'll snap your neck." He digs his fingers into my neck to drill his point home, and black spots flash across my eyes.

"Cam, she's turning blue." Sawyer stares impassively at me as he speaks, but I detect a hint of concern in his tone. Although, it's probably directed at his friend more so than me.

"Dude." Jackson tugs on his arm. "Enough." For once, the smirking, flirtatious look is absent from his face. "We need to stick to the plan."

Cam glares at me one final time before letting go. "There's a new plan," he says, rubbing his hands down the front of his gray pants like they're diseased.

I crumple to the ground, barely feeling any pain as my butt smacks off the floor, too busy sucking in much-needed air to properly register it.

He bends down in front of me, wiping his thumbs under my eyes, his skin streaked with smudged mascara. "You're a mess. Clean yourself up." He stands, looming over me like he thinks he's some god. I flip him the bird because my throat's too sore to hurl insults at him.

"It's cute you think you have any control here." He yanks me up by my hair again, and I cry out. "Congratulations, baby, you're our new toy."

Jackson props against the wall, his eyes lighting up in understanding.

"I'm no one's toy," I croak, cringing at how raspy my voice sounds.

"Oh, but you are," Cam responds with an evil smile. "You will do what we want, when we want it, because if you don't, I'll tell your father and your fiancé you've already given your virginity away."

"You can't!" I struggle to my feet. "They'll kill me!" My father will throttle me with his bare hands if I ruin the deal he's made with Trent's father.

Cam winds his hand into my hair, fisting it and forcing my head back at an awkward angle. I bite back a whimper. He pushes his face into mine, his lips curling in disgust as his gaze rakes over me. "Do I look like I care?"

My heart jackhammers in my chest, and I hate that his spiteful words and harsh glares hurt so much.

Hate he's tarnished the one good memory I had.

Hate it's like everything else in my life—one giant lie.

CHAPTER EIGHT

The guys are waiting at my locker after the last class of the day, and my hands automatically ball into fists at my side. "What do they want?" Jane whispers, her eyes out on stalks.

"I don't know, and I don't care," I lie, lifting my chin and staring defiantly in their direction.

"Hey, beautiful," Jackson says, winking as I come to a halt in front of my locker.

"Screw off, Jackson." I hate how hoarse I sound, and I've been deflecting questions all afternoon about it. I elbow him in the ribs, shoving him aside as I open my locker and grab the books I need. Sawyer stands on the other side of Jane, eyeballing her warily, and I can almost taste her fear from here. "Quit looking at her," I snap.

Cam slams my locker shut before I'm ready, clipping the side of my index finger.

"Motherfucker!" I yell, dropping my books as pain slices across my hand.

Jackson drops to the ground, picking them up, while I pin Cam with a poisonous look. I'm conscious we've drawn a crowd, and the students hovering in the corridor are eager to discover what's going down. "It seems you didn't get the message earlier," Cam continues, his eyes lowering momentarily to my lips. "You don't tell us what to do. *We. Own. You.*"

Jane splutters behind me, and I'm lining up a slew of expletives when a warm hand creeps up my skirt, tracing along my thigh, and I screech. I jump back, caught off guard, bumping into Jane. "Get your hands off me!" I bark at Jackson.

He climbs to his feet, a mock innocent expression on his face as he hands me my books. "Oh, come on now, we both know how much you love the feel of my hands on you." He says this way too loud, on purpose, and the eager bystanders are all ears. Some are recording on their cells.

Calmly, I hand my books to Jane. Then I smile sweetly at Jackson before I punch him in the face. His head whips back, and blood sprays from his nose, little spots landing on Cam and me.

Jackson makes a grab for the lockers, struggling to stay upright, shock splaying across his gorgeous face. Cam looks shell-shocked for a split second before recovering. If looks could kill, I'd be ten feet under with the look he gives me now. A surge of pride overtakes me. I'm glad I was smart enough to take weekly self-defense lessons and that I know how to throw a decent punch.

But I also know when to take my cue.

And it's time to leave.

"Come on." I take my books from Jane, grab her elbow, and steer her away before Cam decides to punch me back. Jackson's shocked laughter follows us as I all but drag Jane out of the building and down to the waiting car. I shove her inside and climb in behind, slamming the door shut superfast. "Let's get out of here."

The driver puts the car in gear, and we glide forward. Oscar turns around in the passenger seat, frowning as he looks me over. "Why do you have blood spatters on your shirt?"

"Because I just punched an annoying boy."

He lifts one brow in amusement. "It wouldn't be the same annoying boy from the beach, now would it?" The amusement quickly fades from his face, confirming he knows exactly who Jackson is.

"Yes. He has some boundary issues, but I think he got the message now."

"If he's bothering you—"

"He's not, and I can handle him."

He eyeballs me for ages, and I meet his challenging stare head-on. Finally, he sighs, shaking his head and muttering, "women," under his breath.

Jane's knee is jerking nervously, and we need to have a private conversation. "We'll be dropping Ms. Ford home first, Jeremy," I tell my regular driver. "And we'd like some privacy, please."

"As you wish, Ms. Abigail."

Jane holds her tongue until the privacy screen is in place and then she detonates. "Oh my God, Abby!" she squeals. "I can't believe you punched him!"

"He was feeling me up. He deserved it."

"He's a pervert," she loyally agrees, "albeit a really hot one."

I lean my head back against the headrest. "These guys will be problematic," I admit. "I need to figure out a way to manipulate them." And there's little time to waste.

Both our phones ping, and Jane whips hers out, gasping as she swipes her finger across the screen of her iPhone. "Someone's just uploaded a video from the hallway online," she confirms my suspicions, "and it's already got two hundred views."

"Let me see that." I snatch the cell from her hand, inspecting the profile, but it's obviously a pseudonym. If the guys were here, no one would dare upload that. I hate that it's only day one and people are already breaking the rules. At least the guys will see I'm taking control of the situation. Even if it's only a façade. Jackson, Cam, and Sawyer have me in a bind, and they know it.

The car turns into Jane's driveway. She faces me, chewing on the edge of one fingernail in a clear tell. "You'd tell me if there was something else going on, wouldn't you?" she hesitantly asks.

"Of course." I hate that I'm lying to her, but I can't tell anyone what they're holding over me.

"What will I tell Drew when he calls?"

"If he asks, tell him the truth."

The car draws to a halt, and the driver gets out, holding Jane's door open. She hugs me. "Enjoy rehearsal and call me later."

Jeremy drives downtown, depositing me in front of the theater we're rehearsing at this week. Oscar comes with me, standing outside the changing room while I shuck out of my uniform and change into my leotard, tights, and ballet shoes. I brush my hair, smoothing it back into a neat bun, loosening my head from side to side in an effort to rid myself of the stress that has invaded every muscle, ligament, and tissue since the lunchtime showdown.

Mom was an amazing dancer, and she enrolled me in ballet classes from the time I was three. I took to it immediately, and I've attended weekly classes ever since. Dance has been my savior in difficult times and an outlet to vent when the pressures and frustrations of my life get too much.

I need this so badly right now.

I enter the auditorium, kissing Madam on both cheeks, and then I limber up as she explains which scenes we are rehearsing today. Our recital of *Swan Lake* is taking place here on Friday night, and we're running through scenes this week for the final time.

The music starts up as she calls us into position. I'm in the lead role this time, playing the tragic Odette, and I glide to the center of the stage, lifting my arms up and tilting my head, holding myself steady until my cue.

The theater fades out as I dance, spinning and turning, my body moving naturally with practiced ease. The music is haunting, and it reaches deep inside me, connecting to my soul. I let go. Allowing the emotion of the scene to sweep me up, projecting me into a different place and time and I'm no longer here, no longer plagued with worries as my body floats across the stage, my limbs exuding passion and longing, as I live and breathe Odette.

When the music ends, I slowly return to the moment, my chest heaving and my brow dotted with sweat, conscious of someone joining Madam in applause.

"Belle. Merveilleux." Madam kisses both my cheeks as I stare at the rows of seating, bile flooding my mouth when my eyes land on the other person clapping.

Jackson is standing, loudly smacking his hands together, as he winks at me. Sawyer and Camden are still in their seats, staring at the stage with neutral expressions.

How the hell did they know I'd be here?

And how dare they invade my private space. My eyes anxiously scan the theater for Oscar as Jackson's applause dies. He's standing by the side of the stage, frowning with his eyes focused on the boys.

"You know them?" Liam inquires, whispering in my ear.

"They're new to my school," I tell my dance partner. Liam is a junior at Rydeville University, and he's a nice guy. We've danced together for years, and he's the closest I have to a male friend, besides Xavier.

"Why are they here?"

"Because they enjoy tormenting me."

Liam's brows climb to his hairline. He's grown up here, so he gets it. "Or they have a death wish."

"That too," I agree. "Not that they seem to care."

Forcing myself to ignore them, I finish rehearsal, but I'm on edge, and Madam can tell.

I get changed in record time, fleeing the dressing room in skinny jeans, a pale pink silk blouse, and black ballet pumps. Dad would skin me alive if he saw me dressed like this outside of the house, but he's not here to complain. Oscar places his arm around my shoulder, escorting me through the theater as he keeps his eyes peeled for signs of the guys.

We step outside, into the fading daylight, and there they are. Propped against the wall, waiting for me.

Jackson is smoking pot, shock horror, and the other two hold poses the wax models in Madame Tussaud's would be envious of.

They watch my every step with calculating intensity, and panic bubbles up my throat. Oscar narrows his eyes at them as we pass, but I keep my gaze focused dead ahead. It doesn't matter though, because I feel their eyes burning a hole in my back the entire walk to the car, and every nerve ending on my body stands on high alert.

I release the breath I was holding the instant I'm securely stowed in the car, for the first time grateful I have a bodyguard and a chauffeur.

I'm still rattled two hours later, sprawled across my bed doing homework, my attention shot to pieces. I check my burner cell for the hundredth time, but there's still no response from Xavier.

A loud knock claims my attention, and I close my book, sliding the cell under my comforter before padding toward my door.

"Ms. Abigail," Mrs. Banks, our housekeeper, says, when I unlock it. "Your friends are downstairs. I've put them in the burgundy living room. Shall I make coffee?"

Jane is the only friend who drops by, and I don't need to be a genius to figure out who's here. "No coffee!" I hiss, racing past her in my bare feet. "They won't be here long enough to drink it."

I'm panting by the time I reach the formal living room. I burst through the varnished mahogany doors with steam billowing out of my ears.

Jackson is standing on the marble fireplace, stretching up as he prods the stuffed moose head with his finger. Camden is slouched on the brown leather couch with one leg crossed over his knee as if he owns the place.

"What the hell are you doing, and how did you get in here?" This would never have happened on Oscar's watch, but Louis is a lazy shit who's begging for an ass kicking. I bet he's in the kitchen stuffing his face with homemade pecan cookies or he's banging one of the younger housemaids in the laundry room.

"I can't believe you live here. This place is creepy as fuck," Jackson proclaims, still poking the moose, as his eyes skim the room.

I don't disagree. Not that I'm telling him that.

Most of the furniture in our house are heirlooms, and, because Father is so focused on maintaining traditions, he's loath to change a damn thing.

All the wooden furniture in this room is walnut, matching the dark wood paneling covering the walls and ceiling. The mezzanine level, with its oppressive railing, casts shadows on the floor below, making the room appear gloomier.

The ornate chandelier in the center of the room doesn't provide adequate light, and the glow from the lamps sitting atop a multitude of tables isn't enough to lift the space. Heavy drapes the color of seaweed hang in straight lines from the only window in the room, blocking most of the natural light.

The only feature I like in the room is the burgundy-and-gold-patterned rug that adorns most of the floor space.

Pulling myself back into the moment, I jab my finger in the air, glaring at them. "Get the fuck out."

"Your language is appalling for someone *apparently* well bred," Camden says, inspecting his fingernails with a bored look.

"And I give zero fucks what you think," I say, striding to the phone on the wall and punching the button for the kitchen. It's answered immediately by an unfamiliar female voice. "Where the hell is Louis?" I snap, watching Jackson move around the room, drinking it all in. Camden stands, eyes narrowing as he makes a beeline toward me. "Well, find him!" I roar down the line. "And I want a word with the security desk. Ask the guard on duty at the gate to come up to the house."

Camden pries the phone out of my grip, slamming it back in its holder before dragging me over to the couch.

At least it's not by the hair this time.

He summons Jackson with a subtle jerk of his head, and he gives up his nosy perusal of the room, sauntering toward us with a lopsided grin. Camden pushes me down onto the couch before sitting beside me, his large hand clamping down on my thigh to hold me in place.

Before I can shuck him off, Jackson is sitting on my other side, his hand moving to my other thigh. Both their legs are pressed against mine, their torsos exuding heat and masculine pheromones as they cage me in with their bodies.

I hate the flurry of butterflies invading my chest and the heat that pools between my thighs, rapidly spreading upward. I could escape their clutches if I wanted to.

But I don't.

And I'm curious to see where they're taking this, so I sit still, letting them believe they have me trapped.

Camden trails his nose up and down my neck, inhaling deeply as Jackson's hand creeps higher up my thigh. "How is it that someone so ugly on the inside looks and smells so beautiful on the outside," Cam whispers, his tongue darting out to lick a line from my ear to my collarbone. I can't control the shudder that snakes through my body, and Jackson chuckles, his fingers inching closer to the apex of my thighs.

"I could ask you the same thing," I reply.

"Ugly isn't strong enough of a word to explain what I'm like underneath this exterior," Cam says, yanking the hair tie from my hair and pulling my head back with the motion.

"Try fucked up. Evil. Twisted," Jackson adds, "and you still wouldn't be close." He slides his hand up my body, brushing the underside of my breast. "We're your worst nightmare, baby."

Cam traces circles with his thumb on the inside of my thigh, and my breath hitches in my throat. "What do you want?" I rasp, struggling to maintain control. My head understands these guys are my mortal enemies, but my body refuses to get with the program.

"Your complete submission," Cam says, nipping at my earlobe.

"Yeah, so not happening," I sneer.

"Your body says otherwise," Jackson says, cupping one breast and kneading it over the flimsy silk material. I move my arm to swat him away, but he clamps down on it as Cam pushes my other arm back with his body, negating my ability to move. I'm now well and truly caged, and I doubt I could extricate myself if I wanted to.

"The elite's rule over Rydeville High ends now," Cam says, watching Jackson fondle my body, a muscle ticking in his jaw. "And you'll help us do it."

"Why?"

"We have our reasons."

"If you want my cooperation, you'll need to share those reasons."

The corners of Cam's mouth lift as his eyes follow Jackson's hand as it moves to my other breast. It's becoming hard to concentrate with the expert way his fingers are teasing my nipples.

"You *are* fucking dumb," Cam taunts. "Because you still don't get it. You don't have any say." He pulls his cell out, swiping across it and holding it out.

All the blood drains from my face as I read over the scanned copy of the arrangement between my father and Trent's. "How did you get this?" Because I haven't even seen the actual paperwork.

"That doesn't concern you."

"What the hell are you doing?" Sawyer asks, striding into the room, a flash of annoyance crossing his perfect face.

"Playing with our shiny, new toy," Jackson replies, grabbing both my breasts in his hands and squeezing.

I swat his hands away now one of my arms is free, glaring at him. "In your dreams, asshole."

"Oh, don't worry, you already have a starring role in my dreams. And now I've added the image of you up on that stage into the spank bank." He presses his mouth to my ear. "That leotard got my dick so fucking hard."

"You're disgusting." I try to lean away from him, but that only presses me up closer to Camden, which is no improvement.

"Let her go," Sawyer says, his lips pursing as he eyeballs his two friends.

"Hey, where the hell were you?" I ask, jumping up as Cam and Jackson stand.

"Little boys' room," Sawyer deadpans, shoving his hands in the pockets of his jeans.

I narrow my eyes to slits. "Bullshit."

"Such a potty mouth," Cam says, shaking his head.

"I'll find out what you were up to." They don't know my father has cameras hidden all over the hallways, some of the living areas, and the exterior of the property.

"Knock yourself out, sweetheart," Sawyer says with a smug grin.

"Tomorrow, you'll invite us to your table at lunch," Cam says, as the three guys move swiftly, trapping me in a circle. Hairs prickle on the back of my neck as I'm caged in, and I hate feeling dwarfed by their smothering presence. Heat rolls off them in waves, and they exude a "don't mess with us" vibe that is equally scary and exciting. "Don't cross us. Don't throw shade. Or you'll be sorry." Cam waves his cell in my face, and I get the message loud and clear.

I'm royally screwed.

CHAPTER NINE

After chewing Louis out and advising Mrs. Banks and the security guard at the gate to put the three guys on the denied list, I dismiss them all and head to the security room, at the rear of the house, where the cameras are stored.

Picking the lock, I slip inside, ensuring no one sees me, and sit down at the desk, quickly hacking into the system like Xavier trained me to do. I pull up all the camera feeds from the last hour, tracking the guys' movements from the moment they stepped foot inside the house.

I watch as Sawyer attempts to open my father's study, smirking at the displeasure etched across his face when he realizes it's padlocked. I fast forward the recording as he runs upstairs, stalking past closed doors, making a beeline for my bedroom.

I press pause, leaning back in the chair, distractedly running my fingers over my bottom lip as I try to figure out how the fuck he knows the layout of our mansion.

Who the hell are these guys, and why have they come to Rydeville?

Placing my elbows on the desk, I press play, watching Sawyer sneak into my bedroom with mounting apprehension. There aren't any cameras in the bedrooms, so I don't have a clue what he was doing. Before I go to investigate, I listen to the feed from the burgundy living room, but Camden and Jackson don't speak, as if they knew there were cameras capturing their every word.

If that's the case, why wasn't Sawyer bothered about getting caught? Do they want me to know?

None of this adds up. I'm lost in thought as I wipe the feed, removing all trace of Sawyer's snooping, lock the door, and walk toward my bedroom.

I tear it apart. Examining every square inch. Pulling up furniture. Checking under the bed. Ransacking my walk-in closet. Inspecting the content of my en suite bathroom. And the only evidence I can find is an open underwear drawer and some missing panties.

Did Sawyer seriously break into my room to steal my panties? And if so, why?

Tuesday dawns, and I'm no closer to finding answers. Xavier is ignoring me, and I'm on edge, still puzzled over what the guys were doing at my house. Morning classes fly by way too fast, and it's lunchtime—crunch time—before I know it.

I spent a restless night tossing and turning over what to do. I've two options.

Comply, and invite them to sit at our table, proving I'm their bitch.

Or call their bluff and buy myself time while I try to dig up dirt I can use against them.

They have something legit to hold over me, but they won't use it yet, because they'll lose their leverage, so I figure I have some leeway to try to find out what their game is. It's risky, and it could backfire, but I've got to try. I can't capitulate at the first threat.

So, I ignore their heated stares when they enter the cafeteria, pretending like I don't see them.

"They're staring at you, and everyone's noticed," Jane whispers in my ear, and I tune Chad out on my other side. He's boring me to tears with some stupid story about a freshman.

Keeping a neutral expression on my face, I lift my chin and stare across at their table. Cam's searing gaze burns straight through me, and his eyes narrow in silent command. I glare back at him, tilting my head up defiantly, letting him know I'm not backing down. We eyeball each other, throwing silent insults at one another as an expectant hush settles over the room. My cell pings, but I ignore it, continuing to face off with my enemy. Jane grabs it, reading the message. "It's from Sawyer," she whispers. "He says last chance, whatever that means."

My heart pounds in my chest, and my palms grow sweaty as terror creeps up on me. They've got something planned. I feel it in my bones. But I can't back down now. I've got to see this through. "Hand me that." Jane places my cell in my palm, and I tap out a quick reply.

Go to hell.

I return my attention to their table, watching as Jackson chuckles and Sawyer and Cam have a brief, heated exchange. Sawyer locks eyes with me, almost pleading, which is confusing, but that's what they probably want. To mess with my head and my emotions.

This is all part of their strategy, and I'm not falling for it.

Cam reaches across the table, grabbing Sawyer's cell, smirking at me as he punches a button.

A chorus of alerts chime around the room and everyone reaches for their cells. Blood rushes to my head, and heat swamps my body, making me uncomfortable, but I maintain a defiant expression. Shocked gasps surround me, but I refuse to look at my phone. I don't want to know what method they've used to humiliate me, because I'm sure that's what they've done.

"Oh my God. Abby." Jane clutches my arm, a look of abject

horror washing over her face. Every head at our table snaps to mine.

"What the fuck?" Chad turns to me with a perplexed expression. "What the hell is this, Abigail? Trent will go apeshit."

Drawing a deep breath, I open my cell and check the message they've sent to the entire school. Color leaches from my face as I stare at my image on the screen. It's from last night. I'm topless. Standing in front of my bed in only my red lace thong as I brush my teeth while watching TV.

Son of a bitch.

They installed a freaking camera somewhere in my room!

My stomach dips at the thought everyone has seen me seminaked, and an anxious fluttery feeling descends on my chest. My heart pounds rapidly, and my hands turn clammy as I fight the nauseous sensation churning sourly in my gut. Rage combines with embarrassment as I struggle to hold onto my composure. But I won't let anyone see how upset I am. And I'm not giving them any tears. I'm a master at disguising my true feelings, so I bottle my emotions up to deal with at a later stage.

Fuck the new elite.

They will not break me.

Working hard to maintain an unruffled expression, I rise, pushing my shoulders back and walking in slow motion toward their table. Jackson locks his hands behind his head, slouching in his chair with a smirk on his face as he watches me approach. Sawyer is masking his reaction, and Camden is glowering at me, as normal. When I reach them, I place my palms down on the table, blanketing the rage building inside me. "You know this means war."

"We accept your defeat," Cam coolly replies.

I'll never surrender to them, but maybe it's best to let them think I have. "I loathe you," I say, piercing him with a hateful look. "And when I'm done, you'll wish you'd never been born."

"Your threats are pitiful, and we both know you're weak. That you'll wait until your asshole of a brother and your asshole of a fiancé return to avenge your honor." He runs the tip of one finger casually around the edge of his coffee cup, while arching a brow, daring me to disagree.

My hands are in a proverbial tie, and I've no choice anymore. As much as I hate my father, he's a master manipulator, and he adheres to that old adage: keep your friends close but your enemies closer.

I need to take a leaf out of his book.

I straighten up, planting a wide smile on my face as I prepare to eat crow. "You're invited to sit at our table."

Cam stands, rubbing his thumb across my mouth, smearing my lip gloss across my face. "Now that wasn't hard, was it?"

I swat his hand away, grinding my teeth as I spin around and stalk back to our table. The only three vacant seats are the ones belonging to Trent, Drew, and Charlie, and the inner circle gawks as Sawyer, Jackson, and Camden drop into their chairs with smug grins on their faces.

"What's going on?" Chad asks, his face turning puce with indignation.

"We're welcoming the newbies, and if you've any issue with that, don't let the door hit you on the way out."

"What are they blackmailing you with?" he asks in a low voice, and I clamp my hand down on his thigh to shut him up.

"I'm being hospitable. That's all." I drill him with a knowing look, and he visibly backs down with a terse nod. Perhaps Chad can be of some use until the guys come home.

"You're dead when the elite gets back," Wentworth says to the three guys who are grinning like their shit doesn't smell.

"For what?" Sawyer replies. "Accepting an invitation from one of their own to sit here? I hardly think so."

"We all know you sent that video," Chad says, folding his arms and daring them to challenge him.

"And I'd like to know how you got it." Wentworth's suspicious gaze bounces between me and them, his implication crystal clear and he's getting on my last nerve.

"What exactly are you insinuating?" I ask, counting to ten in my head.

"Trent's only gone a couple days, and you're already screwing around on him."

I slap him across the face. "Pack your things and leave. You're out."

"You can't do that."

"I think you'll find I can, and I am. Go before I slap you again. Only this time, I won't go easy."

"Fucking whore." His chair crashes to the ground as he stalks off with an imprint of my palm on his cheek.

I glance at the remaining crew at our table. "If anyone else has anything to say, speak up now."

Everyone looks away, finding the floor oddly fascinating.

"I know you've done nothing wrong," Chad says, nodding sincerely. "And I know they're behind this." He sends daggers at them, his fingers painfully gripping the edge of his chair.

Jackson laughs, swiping at his cell. "This is priceless. I can't believe you're pointing the finger at us when you're clearly the culprit."

A frown creases Chad's brow. "What?" he splutters, looking and sounding perplexed.

"See for yourself. You weren't even smart enough to cover your tracks." Jackson thrusts the cell in Chad's face.

Chad's Adam's apple bobs in his throat, and his face pales as he stares at the screen. "Let me guess?" I say, drumming my nails off the table. "It shows it came from your private email addy?"

"I swear I didn't send it."

"I know you didn't, so relax. I'll ensure the elite are informed."

"Can't you do anything for yourself?" a whiny, annoying voice I'm all too familiar with says, as Rochelle slides up to the table, draping one arm around Camden from behind. Her other arm is strapped up, supporting her wrist, which is now in a cast.

"Hey, baby," he says, pulling her down onto his lap.

Bile floods my mouth, but I maintain my composure, disguising my distaste.

Rochelle's eyes glint maliciously as her gaze lowers to my chest. "You'd think with all your money you could at least get your tits done. No wonder Trent went looking elsewhere. No guy wants a girl with small boobs." She thrusts her ample cleavage forward. "They want something they can grab hold of."

Cam chuckles as anger batters me from all sides. His hand glides up her body to cup her left breast. "I couldn't agree more, sweetheart, and you have the best tits in town."

I smile sweetly at them as I gather up the remnants of my lunch. "I think you'll find most of the guys in school agree with you." I stand with my tray on the table in front of me, as I focus on the girl I can't seem to get rid of. "For someone who's such an advocate of cosmetic surgery, I'm surprised you haven't availed of a vaginoplasty yet."

I shoot her a fake sympathetic look. "From what I hear, you're in desperate need of it." I narrow my eyes as I mentally add Rochelle to my permanent shit list. "Especially if you plan on holding onto your Queen Slut crown. No guy wants to fuck a girl with a saggy cunt."

I send the contact to her cell, and it pings in her pocket. "I hear Doctor Gunning is excellent." Or so my father insists every time he tries to force me to schedule breast augmentation surgery. A genuine smile spreads across my mouth as her cheeks stain red and she splutters. "You're welcome." I patronizingly pat her on the head, and anger practically oozes out of her pores.

Without waiting for her to reply, I grab my tray and stalk off with Jackson's loud laughter ringing in my ears.

CHAPTER TEN

I'm still fuming by the time I return to the house later that evening. I messaged Robert on my way, asking him to meet me for a session in an hour. I'm full of pent-up rage I need to expel. But first things first: I need to find and remove the camera Sawyer installed.

I enter my bedroom, retrieve the burner cell from under my mattress—because they've already seen it—and sequester myself in my bathroom with the shower running, praying Sawyer didn't plant a camera in here too. When Xavier doesn't pick up on the first ring, I keep calling until he answers. "About damn time," I snap. "I've been texting and calling you since yesterday. We need to meet."

"I'm not at your personal beck and call," he answers, yawning. "And some of us have outside lives."

"With the retainer I've paid you, I beg to disagree."

"What is it?" His resigned sigh echoes down the line.

"If someone installed a secret camera in my bedroom, how would I discover it?"

Silence greets me for a few beats. "Fuck." Now I've got his attention. "Okay. A detection sensor is the quickest, but I'm guessing you don't have one of those."

"No shit, Sherlock." I'm sure if I asked Oscar or the head of the security team they'd have one, but I don't want this on my father's radar, so I've no choice but to do this alone. "Give me something I can use."

"The best places to hide a camera are in wall sockets, electrical outlets, or behind the TV. Check there first, and if you find nothing, you can darken your room and search for any red or green flashing lights." The phone pings, and I open up Xavier's message. "Install that hidden camera detector app on your iPhone, and scan your room if all else fails. It will display a red glow when you find it."

"You really freak me out sometimes," I admit even if I'm grateful for his criminal mastermind brain.

"You hired me for my freak," he teases, and I roll my eyes even though he can't see me.

"Thanks, Xavier."

"Keep the camera. I can trace the source." I already know the source, but proving it could come in useful.

It's illegal in Massachusetts to record someone without their permission, and this just might give me the leverage I need.

"Okay. And meet me at ten tonight. I expect an update, and don't be late." I hang up before he can argue, slipping the cell into my jacket pocket as I turn off the shower and head back into my bedroom.

I don't bother checking the room or closing the curtains and turning off the lights, downloading the app on my normal iPhone instead, figuring it could come in handy.

I scan the room with my cell, mentally fist pumping the air when a red glow emits from the wall socket just inside the door.

I head to the garage, finding a small screwdriver in the toolbox Drew keeps there and return to my room, unscrewing the front of the socket. "Gotcha." I poke my tongue out, hoping the new elite are seeing this before I pry the small circular silver chip off, placing it in a sealed envelope and storing it in the drawer of my bedside table.

I scan my bedroom and bathroom thoroughly, in case there are any more cameras, but it appears to be the only one.

I'm feeling pretty good as I get changed for my self-defense lesson until Trent calls, and my buoyant mood instantly sours. Typically, he doesn't call when he's at Parkhurst, so there's only one reason he's calling now.

I bet that asshole Wentworth squealed.

Although, it's conceivable the guys got the message too, or they checked the school online boards.

Ignoring him won't work as he'll just call relentlessly, so I reluctantly pick up.

I'm greeted with shouting and a barrage of insults, and every time I attempt to intervene, he shuts me down, so I hang up after two minutes, tossing my cell on my bed as I pull on my yoga pants and a bra top. I'm in the bathroom removing my makeup and fixing my hair into a ponytail while my cell continues to chime and beep on my bed. I glance at it briefly as I'm on my way out the door, stopping when I see my brother's handsome face staring back at me. I pick up Drew's call, walking out of my bedroom and locking it.

It's not like me to lock my room from the outside, but I'm taking zero chances anymore.

"What's going on there, Abby?" Drew asks as I walk with my cell pressed to my ear.

"The new elite is up to something, but I'm dealing with it."

"That's not what it looks like," he says, while Trent continues to rage and shout in the background. "Trent is itching for blood."

When isn't he? "Which is probably one reason they did it."

"How did they get that footage?"

I sigh, knowing he's going to rip me a new one for not telling him about them showing up here unannounced yesterday. I quickly fill him in, keeping it as brief as possible.

"And you're sure there was only one camera?" he asks when I've finished updating him.

"I'm positive." I skip down the main stairs, waving at Robert as he walks through the front door.

"I don't like you hanging out with them even if it partly makes sense. Knowing your enemy is crucial to staying ahead of the game, but I'm worried about the perception. If the rest of the school sees you acting all chummy with them, it'll alter the power dynamics."

"It's only temporary, and I think we need to see how this plays out. It'll be a good test of loyalty."

"One I hear Wentworth already failed."

"That rat bastard." I purse my lips, stopping at the door to the library, motioning Robert ahead with a flick of my hand. "Give me five," I mouth at him before slipping into the dark room.

I don't bother flipping on the lights, walking quietly around the large room, my fingers skimming over the spines of the thousands of books lining the floor-to-ceiling shelves that rim the room on both sides. The only illumination is from the skylight overhead, but it's so high up only trickles of light reach the room below.

"Give me that!" I hear Trent bellow, and then his disgusted voice barks down the line at me. "I can't fucking believe this!" he hollers.

"Keep your panties on," I drawl. "And stop shouting, or I'll hang up again."

"The whole school has seen you practically naked!" he roars. "How the hell did you think I'd react."

"Well, you asked for some nude pics." I shouldn't deliberately taunt him, especially since he's been texting dick pics daily asking me to reciprocate.

"Don't fucking push me, Abigail."

He's so damn predictable. "It's my body, and if I can deal, then so can you."

"Your body is for my eyes only," he growls.

For once, I agree. I wish I'd never let Camden Marshall anywhere near me.

"It's not like I asked for this. Save your wrath for when you return and pinpoint it in the right direction."

"Oh, don't worry, baby. Those assholes will pay."

"And that's why I must be seen playing their game." Drew put me on speaker while I was explaining what's going down, so I know all three of them are listening in.

"Be careful," Trent says, no longer shouting. "We still don't know their agenda, and it's clear they intend on getting to us through you, so watch your back."

"Always. Now I've got to go. Robert's waiting for me."

"Okay. Stay safe. Love you, babe."

I almost drop my cell in complete shock. Trent only professes love when we're in public and it's part of the charade. He's said it now twice in less than a week, but it's complete horseshit. He hates me as much as I hate him. So, this is his possessiveness coming to the fore, he's genuinely worried I'll stray, or he's also playing some game.

"Bye," I blurt, unwilling to return his fake sentiment, ending the call and walking to our indoor gymnasium as my mind works overtime trying to figure out his latest angle.

I creep out of the tunnel, looking left and right, as I always do, to ensure no one is around, but the woods are spookily quiet, the only sound the gentle rustling of leaves and the faint swoosh of the light nighttime breeze.

I glance back at the house in the far distance, looming over the land like some ghastly giant. The red brick façade is barely visible from the rear of the property, hidden behind sprawling vines of ivy.

Darkness cloaks the back windows, the only brightness originating from the exterior lights illuminating the path that runs around the main house, guiding the guards who patrol the grounds at night.

I get a perverse pleasure from the fact I regularly sneak out and no one is the wiser.

I walk with purpose toward the old abandoned shed, retrieving my Kawasaki Ninja 300 and my helmet and pushing my bike silently the last mile through the woods.

Whoever built the tunnel before me—and I like to imagine it was my mother—planned it to perfection. There's no reason for anyone to come to this side of our vast property anymore, and someone blocked the old rear entrance up many moons ago. Dirt and debris are strewn across what's left of the gray stone driveway, and the old, rusted iron gates have long since been boarded up. But someone has upgraded the lock on the wooden side door in recent times, and I reach into the small wall-mounted box, retrieving the key and unlocking the door.

I carefully wheel my motorcycle out, propping it against the wall while I close the door, ensuring it's properly secure. Then I pull my helmet on, straddle the pillion, and kick start the engine, my veins bursting with adrenaline as I shoot out onto the empty road that runs around the far side of our estate.

I always look forward to this ride, enjoying the opportunity to forget reality and absorb the illusion of freedom, reveling in the wind whipping around my body as I coast past expansive fields and open roads. I stick to the less-traveled back roads and adhere to the speed limits, careful to avoid doing anything that would draw attention to me. Father would blow a gasket if he saw me in my black leathers on this bike, and that thought never fails to bring a smile to my face.

I power the engine off and walk the last two hundred meters to the abandoned warehouse Xavier uses as his offsite base. I stand at the paint-chipped corrugated-iron double doors, sticking my tongue out at the overhead camera, chuckling as the doors open and I steer my bike inside.

After depositing my bike and helmet, I walk toward the back of the structure, where I know Xavier is waiting.

"Welcome, partner in crime," he jokes, as he always does when I step into the sealed room. The door automatically locks behind me with a subtle click. You'd never guess this place exists from the dilapidated exterior, but Xavier has spared no expense fitting out his high-tech lair. "Take a pew," he says without looking at me as his fingers fly across the keypad.

"I like the hair," I say, surveying the spiked blue peaks sprouting from the top of his head. Xavier is a chameleon, and he likes to experiment with his style.

He lifts his head, grinning and showcasing a new piercing in his left brow. "I like the tatas," he quips, and I scowl as my eyes dart to the frozen image on the screen—the one of me standing topless in my bedroom.

"Please get rid of that."

"Your wish is my command." He stabs a couple of buttons on his keypad, and the screen dies. "I've removed every trace," he voluntarily adds. "And if anyone tries to upload it again, I'll receive notification, and the workflow I've just embedded will delete the source file and infect the originator's system with the latest Trojan virus." He leans back, wiggling his brows. "You're welcome."

"Thank you. And how did you even know?" I was planning on asking him to do just this, but he beat me to it. Not that I'm hugely surprised. He's not one of this country's best hackers for no reason.

"You mentioned a hidden camera, and it didn't take much to put it together."

"Did you trace the source?"

He shakes his head. "Whoever did this knew what they were doing. They used some sap's email account to cover their tracks, and they triangulated it on a continual loop from there. I could follow the trail, but it'll lead nowhere."

"It was Sawyer Hunt or someone from his father's company." I don't need proof to know that.

He nods slowly, swiveling in his chair. "Why do these dudes have you in their sights?"

"I was hoping you could tell me that."

He pushes the sleeves of his black hoodie up to his elbows, showing off the impressive ink covering both arms. "I haven't found anything you can use yet. You need to give me more time."

"I don't have time. The bastards are blackmailing me."

"With what?" His tongue flicks against his lip ring as he arches a brow.

"I can't say." No one in my circle knows what happened with Camden Marshall, and I want to keep it that way. In recent days, I've thought of confiding in Xavier, but I don't fully trust him even if he appears to be on my side. But a niggling doubt suggests if I can buy his loyalty with cash then so can anyone else.

My statement displeases him.

His eyes harden, and his lips thin. "I would if I could," I add, deliberately softening my tone and gripping his arm.

"It's a fucked-up world when you trust no one," he quietly says, pulling up a file on the screen.

"It is," I agree, leaning forward. "What's that?"

"Some shit I dug up on the Marshalls, but you were right. They have a tight control on this stuff, and it wasn't easy compiling the little I discovered."

"Let's hear it." I remove my jacket, hanging it on the back of my chair, glaring at Xavier when I find his gaze fixed on my chest. "Seriously? You're not even into boobs."

"I could be into yours. They're perfect handfuls, and they looked nice."

"Eh, thanks?" I say before shaking my head. "This is weird. Forget about my tits, and tell me what you found."

"So, we know Camden's father is Wesley Marshall, CEO of Femerst and a notorious recluse who barely ventures out of his office or his estate in Alabama. He married his childhood sweetheart, and they had one child, Camden Everett Marshall. Camden was homeschooled until two years ago when his parents enrolled him in West Lorian Academy in New York where he met Sawyer Hunt and Jackson Lauder. The media had a field day as Camden hadn't been seen in public since he was a little kid. The trio quickly made a name for themselves as the playboys of the academy and frequently hung out with other wealthy brats in New York. Gossip sites and private blogs are awash with recounts of their escapades, but there is no physical evidence. No photos. No eyewitness accounts."

He taps another button on his keypad and the screen changes. "The cops arrested Lauder for illegal street racing this one time, and the media jumped all over it." I press my nose up closer to the screen, spotting the flirty, smug grin on Jackson's face as he's led into the police station with his hands cuffed behind his back.

"I found that in an old archived file on one of the media corporations servers," he continues, "but within twenty-four hours of the story initially breaking, all reports had disappeared, all charges were dropped, and restraining orders were issued to all media outlets to restrict them from reporting anything connected to the incident."

"They have a lot of power," I muse, instinctively knowing them showing up here is some play for ultimate control. My father is planning complete world domination, and if the new elite is preparing to challenge him for control, it could explain why the kids of some of the most powerful men in America today have suddenly materialized in Rydeville. The more I think about the conversation I overheard in my father's study, the more I'm convinced they were talking about Jackson, Sawyer, and Camden.

"Not as much as your father and his associates," Xavier supplies. "But they're snapping at their heels."

"Anything else?" I ask, checking my watch. It's late, and I have to drive back.

"I found one tidbit that's interesting." He prints off an old black-and-white photo and hands it to me. "I found this on a local historical society site by pure coincidence. Recognize anyone?"

I squint at the blurry photo, my eyes popping wide. "That's my father with Trent's and Charlie's fathers," I confirm, pointing at the three boys at the end, attired in Rydeville High uniforms. They were young when it was taken, only fifteen or thereabouts if I had to guess. "Oh my God." I clamp my hand over my mouth, and a boulder-sized lump wedges in my throat. "That's my mom," I whisper.

Xavier squeezes my shoulder. "Yes, and that's Wesley Marshall standing beside her," he says, pointing to a lanky guy with glasses. "That is Atticus Anderson," he continues, prodding the photo with the tip of his finger. The guy who used to be one of my father's closest friends has his hand resting on Mom's shoulder, as he shares a grin with a girl in front.

"And that's Emma Anderson," I cut in, recognizing her instantly. She was my mother's best friend, and a permanent fixture in our house growing up. Until they fell out when Drew and I were four or five. Emma died about six months before my mother did, and I'll never forget her anguished cries as she sobbed herself to sleep night after night, pining for her lost friend.

"No." Xavier's eyes light up. "That's Emma *Marshall*."

My brows knit together. "What?"

"Emma Anderson was Emma Marshall before she married Atticus. Wesley Marshall was her brother. So that means—"

"Emma Anderson was Camden Marshall's aunt." Xavier bobs his head. "You think that has something to do with them showing up?"

Xavier shrugs. "You're the detective. I'm just the paid lackey who digs up the dirt, but I'd follow every lead, and something tells me this is a juicy one."

CHAPTER ELEVEN

I'm exhausted the next day at school, and I can't stop yawning. "All your booty calls catching up to you?" Rochelle sneers from across the table as I'm forced to sit through another unbearable lunch with her planted on Camden's lap.

"Someone has to keep your clients entertained now word's gotten out about your loose vajayjay," I retort, and Jane almost chokes on her soda.

"I think you two should slug it out in the ring," Jackson quips, leaning into my side. "Or do naked mud wrestling. That'd be so hot." His eyes glaze over. "Man, my dick's already hard at the thought."

I roll my eyes as he grabs my hand, pulling it to his crotch, pressing my palm flat against the bulge in his pants. I yank my hand back, hissing at him. "You're vile." And permanently horny, it would seem.

"Aw, is the little virgin scared of cock?" Camden sneers, eliciting a few snickers from the gathered audience.

"Maybe your whore can teach me a few tricks," I bite back.

Rochelle is off Cam's lap so fast it's almost a superpower. Plates crash to the ground as she climbs across the table, yanks me up by my shirt, and head butts me. My chair falls backward, bringing me along for the ride, slamming noisily to the ground, as pain splinters up my spine, and the world tilts. Black spots flitter across my eyes as a heavy weight presses down on my upper torso. My head whips sideways as her cast collides with my cheek, sending shards of pain dancing across my skin and rattling my teeth.

Anger builds, like a tsunami, inside me, and even though my skull throbs and my vision is unclear, I will not lie here and be a punching bag. Acting on instinct, I swing my balled fist around, satisfied when it connects with her jaw. She screeches, and I swing again, wanting to pound her face to a bloody pulp, when the pressure on my chest lifts, and she's pulled off me. "Babe, there's no victory in winning if your opponent is virtually comatose," Cam says, and I force my eyes open at the sound of his voice.

"I'm not comatose," I snap, willing my blurry vision to correct itself.

He hands Rochelle off to Jackson while pinning dark eyes on me, his gaze traveling lower. "Nice panties, but the lacy red thong is my favorite."

I flip him the bird, struggling to sit up unaided. Chad and Jane are being restrained by Sawyer and that asshole Wentworth, who has appeared from whatever hole I told him to climb in to and switched allegiances. I push my skirt down, cradling my throbbing head in my hands, as I struggle to my feet. No one is permitted through to help me, and I'm forced to grab onto Cam's leg to pull myself upright. A teacher hovers on the outskirts of the crowd gathered around our table. "I'll escort you to the nurse's office," he says, glancing warily at Camden.

"That won't be necessary," Cam says. "I'll escort Ms. Manning."

"No," I grit out, trying to ignore the pain scuttling around my skull. "I don't want to go with him."

"You're dismissed," he says, eyeballing the teach, and I watch in horror as he walks away after a brief inner debate.

What the hell is going on around here? Why are people listening to them and blatantly flouting the rules?

Cam takes hold of my elbow, yanking me unceremoniously out of the room. People automatically move out of our way in the hallway, whispering and pointing as Cam drags me to the nurse's office.

"Oh, my," the soft-spoken gray-haired nurse says as we enter her room. "Whatever happened?" she asks, putting her book down.

"Bitch fight," Cam explains, daring me to disagree. Considering I'm the only one in need of medical help, I'd call it more of an assault, but I'm not getting into it with him because he enjoys pushing my buttons.

She sends a disapproving look my way but says nothing, patting the bed and gesturing for me to climb up. "Tell him to leave," I say, refusing to look at him.

"I'm going nowhere, sweetheart."

The nurse looks between us, her features knotting in confusion. "You must leave," she says, but her voice lacks conviction. "It's against HIPPA rules."

Cam smirks. "Does the school board know what you get up to in your spare time, *Marilyn*?" He arches a brow, and the nurse pales. "Didn't think so." He waves his hands about. "Continue."

"Get. The. Fuck. Out," I hiss, wincing as a fresh wave of pain attacks my skull. I don't care what shit he has on the nurse. I just want him out of this room.

"She hit her head hard," Cam says, ignoring me.

"Let me look, sweetie." The nurse gently prods my skull and my forehead and takes my temp and blood pressure before announcing I could have a mild concussion and I should head home to rest up for the remainder of the day.

"Do you have any pain pills?" I ask, struggling to open my eyes under the harsh glare of the overhead lighting.

She hands me some Tylenol, and I swallow them with water before swinging my legs around and sliding off the cot. She's already writing up a report as I exit the room, blatantly ignoring Cam when he follows me out.

"You're going the wrong way," he says.

"I think I know my way around the school."

"The exit's back there."

I harrumph. "I'm well aware." I pierce him with a scalding look. "I'm not leaving."

"You could have a concussion."

"I just have a bad headache, and why the fuck do you care?"

"I don't, but I need you fully functional. At least for the time being."

I slam to a halt, turning around to face him. "Why?"

"That's for me to know and you to find out." He crosses his arms around his chest, and I fight the urge to ogle the way his biceps bulge with the motion. It's not like I'm remembering how it felt to run my hands over every inch of his taut, ripped body.

His smirk says he knows where my mind has gone, and I narrow my eyes, glaring at him. "Oh, I'll find out. Trust me. I have ways and means."

A muscle ticks in his jaw, and my heart speeds up as he dips his head, moving his face closer to mine. "How did you detect the camera so quickly? What other secrets are you hiding, *Abby*?"

"Haven't you heard of Google?" I stare into his dark brown eyes, noticing tiny gold flecks for the first time and hating how much I want to drown in their hypnotic depths.

"You didn't turn the shower on to disguise your internet searching." His warm breath fans across my face, chasing tingles all over my skin. He presses his delectable mouth to my ear, and a shiver works its way through me. "We know you had help, and we'll find out who."

I step back, gloating as I flip him the bird. "Knock yourself out, douche. See if I care."

Somehow, I survive the rest of the day, and I fall into the car after school ends, curling into a ball and craving my bed. Jane deflects Oscar's ten million questions, coming back to my house and helping me to bed. She procures more pain pills from Mrs. Banks, gently rubs arnica cream into the swollen lump on my forehead and the smorgasbord of bruises spreading up my back, and informs Drew of what happened with Rochelle when he calls for his usual daily update.

I'm woken early the next morning by her soft snores, and I chuckle quietly to myself as I tiptoe out of the bed and into the bathroom. While my back throbs and the lump on my forehead is sore to the touch, my head is clear, and I'm grateful I don't have a concussion.

Jane is awake, yawning and rubbing her eyes, when I emerge from the bathroom after my shower. "Thank you for looking after me last night."

"You're practically my sister," she says, hopping up. "Where else would I be?"

I pull her into a hug. "I hope you know how much I love you," I whisper. "How grateful I am to have you in my life. No matter what happens, never forget that."

"Ditto, chica," she says, hugging me back before holding me at arm's length. "How are you feeling today?"

"Head's fine. Back less so, but I'll live. I'll just pop another couple pills after breakfast, and I'll be fine."

"Lemme see." I turn around, and she gasps. "That fucking bitch will pay for this." She doesn't realize that my back was already in bad shape thanks to the crap with the guys in the theater the other day.

"I already broke her wrist, so I figure we're even." I shrug out of my towel, removing clean underwear out of my drawer and pulling it on. "Besides, Trent will go apeshit on her ass when he returns and finds out how cozy she's been with the enemy."

"She's not the only one. What's with that?"

"I don't know, but I'm determined to find out."

"Why are they sitting over there today?" I question Chad from our usual table in the cafeteria, staring at Cam, Jackson, and Sawyer as they sit at the head of the long table across from us. The empty seats beside them are rapidly filling up.

The fawning girls with googly eyes I understand to a point. Wentworth too, because I tossed him aside and he's always been a sniveling idiot with little between his ears. And now that Sawyer is our new QB, the cheerleaders and jocks make sense. But the few deflections from the inner circle don't, and I can't fathom why everyone is so blatantly defying the rules for a bunch of newcomers.

"I heard they're bribing people," Jane says, licking Greek yogurt off the back of her spoon.

"With what?"

"They're promising to break the code, end the elite's rule over the school, and give everyone freedom to do and say as they please," Chad interjects.

"Is everyone that unhappy?"

I know people resent obeying the code that's been in place for centuries, and they hate bowing to the arrogance of the elite, but there's no denying things run smoother in school with strict rules.

Fights rarely break out, and disruptions in class are minimal, because they aren't tolerated.

Everyone loyally supports the football team and all extracurricular events, because if the elite tells you to be there, you go or face the consequences.

Parties are planned to perfection, and all the booze and drugs on offer have come from reliable sources and are the best quality.

I hate the traditions myself, and I'm tired of walking the hallways with the guys acting like I'm superior to everyone else, but even I've got to admit school is a more pleasant experience when everyone is sticking to the rules.

Chad shrugs. "Sometimes people prefer change."

"That's not what this is," Jane says, lowering her voice as she leans in close to both of us. "I overheard some girls talking in the bathroom. They're buying their allegiance with cool stuff."

My brows climb to my hairline and my voice oozes disbelief. "Everyone in this school is wealthy, and there isn't anything their money can't buy."

"They're offering early access to the latest xNet6 cell phone, and Jackson's planning a race day at his father's private track in New York where he's promising everyone they can take some official team cars for a spin."

I snort. "Wow. That's bribery at its finest. Have they no shame?"

"They're new money, Abigail," Chad says, a look of disgust washing over his face. "Of course, they've no shame. This is what they do. Throw their money and their status around. It's so uncouth."

I look at Chad with fresh eyes, a grin spreading over my face as an idea surfaces in my mind. "I like you, Chad. I see now why the guys trust you." He blushes, running a hand through his light-brown hair, and it's so cute. I lean into him, my eyes glimmering as the plan takes shape in my mind. "I need you to grab a group of five or six. Only those you'd trust with your life. Can you have that set up by this weekend?" I'll need a few days to set this in motion.

"Absolutely." A wide grin plays across his full lips. "What do you have in mind?"

I shoot a scathing look at the table across the way, my eyes meeting Cam's, because even though he has the skank pawing at him from his lap again, his gaze is firmly locked on mine. "The new elite may use bribes to buy their way to the top but the old elite resort to blackmail to get what they want, and we won't stop now." My gaze bounces between Jane and Chad. "We'll uncover dirt on every defector and use that to bring them back on our side."

Because I'm fucked if I'll let everything turn to hell in a handbasket and have the guys say I told you so when they return.

Camden Marshall isn't going to get the better of me.

He's about to find out what happens when you dare cross a Manning.

CHAPTER TWELVE

Our last ballet rehearsal is in the bag, and I'm making my way out of the theater into the dark night, alone—because my last sighting of Oscar showed him hurrying out of the theater with his cell pressed to his ear—when someone grabs me from behind, shoving something black over my head, masking my vision completely.

I open my mouth to scream, but a large hand clamps over my lips, muffling my sounds through the covering. A meaty arm snakes around my waist, and I'm drawn back against a hard torso. Blood thrums in my ears and adrenaline courses through my veins as my heart accelerates wildly behind my ribcage. Someone binds my legs and hands together before I can invoke any self-defense moves, and panic bubbles up my throat. I'm roughly thrown over a shoulder, a hand plastered across the backs of my thighs, keeping me in place.

I try to calm down. To use my other senses to take in my surroundings, but with panic weighing on my chest and white noise screaming in my ears, I'm finding it difficult to concentrate. I focus on my breathing, drawing deep breaths in and out to stay calm.

A car door slams open and shut. Whispered words are just out of reach of my eardrums, and then I'm flung into a confined space, my knees shoved up to my chest as a loud bang startles me. More doors open and shut, and when the quiet hum of an engine purrs to life, I know I'm locked in a trunk. My body is jostled as the car moves off, and I lift my arms and stretch out my legs, as far as I can with the painful bindings cutting into my wrists and my ankles, testing how wide the space is.

Not wide at all is the answer, adding to my frustration and fear.

How the hell did this happen, and where on Earth did Oscar disappear to? Did they ambush him too? And who are these people?

The list of my father's enemies is long and far-reaching, and there are plenty of people who'd kidnap me for ransom too. Although, if they knew my father, they'd realize the futility of such a plan. My father would probably pay them to *not* bring me back. At least not until I'm due to walk up that aisle.

But, if I had to bet, my money's on the new elite. This smacks of something they'd attempt to terrorize me, to further drive their point home, and I'm damn well not going to play into their hands.

I don't know how long we travel, but it's long enough for the intense heat of the trunk to become cloying, sticking matted strands of my hair to my forehead under the heavy cloth bag covering my face. My lacy tank top clings to my damp back, and my skin's on fire under my thick hoodie. My wrists and ankles sting because whichever bastard tied them tied them too tight.

I will annihilate these fuckers.

When I'm done with them, they'll wish they were dead.

I cling to my anger the entire trip, refusing to consider any other scenario other than this is the work of Camden, Sawyer, and Jackson.

My body slams against the rear of the trunk as the car makes a sharp turn, and I cry out as pain zips up and down my back. I grit my teeth and try to ignore the throbbing in my spine as the car slows down. My chest heaves as panic rears its head again, and I resort to deep breathing to remain collected.

A clicking sound, followed by booted feet, confirms someone has opened the trunk. Firm hands grip my upper arms, and I'm pulled out. My legs protest, cramping up, and I slouch against a warm body.

"Fuck. Her wrists are bleeding," a familiar voice says, and rage is like a charging bull plowing through me.

"Barely," Cam replies to Sawyer before adding, "Do you have the feed ready?"

"Yes," he snaps, and I detect some tension between them.

They yank the covering off my head, and someone brushes my knotty, sweaty hair back off my forehead.

"Fuck, she's a mess," Jackson says.

"What did you expect when you threw me in the trunk?" I snap as I blink my eyes open.

"Hand me those cutters," Cam says, ignoring me as he takes them from Jackson and clips the plastic ties digging into the torn, bloody skin on my wrists. The relief is instantaneous but short-lived.

Cam unzips my hoodie, yanking it down my stiff arms and tossing it to Sawyer. He eyes my lacy silk tank with a calculated stare before yanking it down by the hem, exposing more of my cleavage.

My face burns with outrage, my mouth open with a slew of cusses lining up on my tongue, when he dips his hands into the cups of my bra, rolling my nipples between his thumbs and forefingers. I swat at his hands, but Jackson reacts fast, yanking them behind my back, pressing into the tender flesh of my wrists, causing me to cry out.

"I would've done that," Jackson says, and Cam levels him with a dark look over my shoulder.

"Get your fucking hands off me," I holler. "Or I'll scream."

"Go for it, sweetheart," he says, eyeballing me as his fingers continue to pluck at my nipples. I hate how they immediately stand to attention for him, but my body hasn't understood he's the enemy yet. "We're in an empty parking lot," he adds, urging me to examine my surroundings. "There's no one to hear you."

"What do you want? And what did you do to my bodyguard and my driver?"

"We created a diversion at your house to distract them. And we laid a spike strip out on the road to delay Jeremy on his way back," Sawyer says, not looking up from the laptop he's furiously typing away on.

"And let's just say Oscar is taking a little nap and leave it at that," Jackson confirms with a grin.

"If you've hurt him, I'll kill you," I cry out, terrified at what they might've done to him. Oscar was only working late tonight because I had a long rehearsal. Ordinarily, he'd be at home with his family, and I hate he's gotten mixed up in this.

It hasn't escaped my notice they know both of their names, and it's clear they've done due diligence. They are two steps ahead of me at every turn, and I've got to rectify that.

"This won't work," Cam says, removing his hands. "Give me the bag."

Jackson lets go of my wrists, and I shove at Cam's chest, forgetting my feet are still tied. I crash to the stone floor on my butt, biting down hard on my lower lip as a fresh wave of pain rattles my tailbone. Tears prick my eyes, but I refuse to set them free. "Fuck." I suck in a sharp breath as Cam crouches down on the ground, breaking the ties binding my feet.

"That was your fault." He hauls me up by my elbows, and I glare at him. "Hold her," he tells Jackson, taking the black Gucci bag from him.

"Hey! That's mine!" I protest as Jackson slides his arm around my waist from behind.

"Gold star for the rich bitch," Cam snaps, unzipping the bag and examining the contents.

"You're fucking assholes. All of you," I hiss as I watch him remove items from my closet. It appears Sawyer stole more than just panties.

"This should work," Cam says, grinning as he stands upright, dangling a black push-up bra from the end of his finger.

I gulp over the lump wedged in my throat. "I'm not putting that on." I pierce him with a venomous look.

"No one asked you to," he retorts, grinning.

"Arms up, beautiful," Jackson says into my ear, and I jab my elbow back, hitting him in the ribs.

"Fuck," he winces, letting go of me to rub a hand over his rib cage.

Cam yanks me to him by the elbow. "Didn't your father teach you that ladies don't hit?"

"I'm no lady," I grit out, trying to wrestle out of his hold.

"I'm getting that." Cam turns his head toward Sawyer. "Is that ready because she needs an incentive to cooperate. I'm already out of patience."

"It's ready."

Cam flings my bra at Jackson and drags me over to where Sawyer has the laptop perched on top of the hood of the Land Rover. "Watch," Cam demands, gripping my chin painfully and forcing my eyes to the screen.

Sawyer presses the play button, and all the blood drains from my face as the recording starts.

Jane is in her bedroom, buck-ass naked on top of her bed, with her legs open wide, pleasuring herself. I feel sick to the pit of my stomach, and I can't mask my horrified expression. She has her cell propped up against two fluffy cushions at the end of the bed, and I've no doubt my brother was watching or she was recording it to send to him. She calls out Drew's name as she pumps two fingers inside herself, her back arching off the bed, little whimpers leaking from her mouth as she works herself into a frenzy. I squeeze my eyes shut, not wanting to violate my friend any more than they have violated her. This is such a massive invasion of her privacy, and I'm equally incensed and disgusted. "Turn it off," I snap, but they ignore me, and I'm forced to listen as she climaxes.

"I've jerked off to that at least five times," Jackson says, right at my ear. "And I love how she's incorporated it into her daily nighttime routine. She's definitely missing your brother and so sexually frustrated I might have to do her myself."

"You leave her the fuck alone!" I yell. "This has nothing to do with Jane." My voice cracks. "Please. I'll do whatever you want. Just leave Jane out of this."

"Open your eyes," Cam instructs, and I snap my eyes open as Sawyer mercifully shuts the video off. "Do we have your attention now?"

"You already had my attention. Wasn't knowing my non-virgin status enough?"

"That didn't seem to motivate you sufficiently, so we improvised." Cam shakes his head. "We took this path because you wouldn't do what we told you. This is all on you." That truth sits in my gut like sour milk.

"As long as you cooperate," Cam continues, "that video won't see the light of day. Cross us, and we won't just share it with our classmates. We'll put it out all over the web, and she'll be infamous overnight for all the wrong reasons."

"How do I know you won't double-cross me?"

Cam smirks, and I want to smash his face with a mallet so he looks as ugly on the outside as he is on the inside. "You're just going to have to trust us."

"There's no honor between thieves," I hiss.

"You'd know," he instantly retorts, putting his face up in mine. *What the fuck does that mean?*

The look of pure hatred on his face has me stepping back instinctively.

"You have our word that the tape won't be released provided you do what we tell you," Sawyer says, sending a cautionary look in Cam's direction.

"Which is what?"

"Strip for starters." Jackson's gaze homes in on my tits. "I've been dying to see your tits up close and personal."

"You can't be serious?" I blurt, panic welling in my throat, beseeching Sawyer with my eyes because he seems to be the only one with some modicum of decency and self-control.

"You need to play the part of a seductress and that outfit, those tits," Cam says, waving his hands in front of my chest, "won't cut it."

A stabbing pain pricks my heart, but I harden it, knowing I'll do whatever it is they want me to do because the game has changed, and I'll do anything to protect Jane. It isn't her fault they've brought her into this. That *is* all on me and it's my job to ensure that video never gets aired. It would destroy my best friend and most likely convince Drew to commit murder. Not that I'm opposed to ending any of these assholes, but I'd rather keep my brother out of jail.

"Fine." I lift my tank top up, throwing it in Cam's face. Jackson chuckles. "Give me the bra." I hold out my hand, keeping my gaze focused straight ahead.

"No." Cam drops my top on the ground, snatching the push-up bra from Jackson's fingers. "You don't set the rules here."

I don't set the rules anywhere, but articulating that won't help, so I clamp my lips shut.

Cam moves toward me like a hunter ensnaring his prey. With his free hand, he snaps my flimsy lace bra open in one skillful move, dragging the straps down my arms until it falls away, leaving me topless.

My cheeks burn as I feel their heated eyes on me, but I continue staring ahead, looking straight through that bastard, not giving them the satisfaction of knowing how humiliated I am.

Cool fingers brush across one nipple, and my stomach twists.

"Don't touch her," Cam says, swatting Jackson's hand away.

"Aw, c'mon, man. You got to fuck her. At least let me suck her tits."

"Like I said, I'll be the only one touching her. You can't control yourself."

"That's bullshit, and you know it. You can't hide the fact your cock is hard too. I can fucking see the bulge in your jeans."

Cool air swirls around my exposed chest, and the longer this goes on, the more I seethe.

"Just put the damn bra on her," Sawyer says, frustration evident in his tone. "We have things to do unless your hormones have eradicated your brain function entirely."

"Don't take that fucking tone with me," Cam growls at his friend. He tilts my chin up. "Eyes on me."

I clench my jaw so hard I'm worried it might snap. His eyes drill into mine as he tweaks my nipples again. Sawyer sighs, but before he can say anything, Cam speaks indirectly to him. "We have little to work with, so some staging is in order."

My fists ball up at my sides, and I want to inflict pain on him so badly.

Keeping his eyes trained on mine, he lowers his head, sucking first one nipple and then the other into his hot mouth. "I remember how much you liked it when I did that," he says, swirling his tongue across my nipples one at a time

Loud groans echo in the empty parking lot, and my head snaps sideways. Jackson has his cock in hand, and he's frantically pumping himself as he stares at his friend sucking my tits.

"You guys are fucking pervs."

"You should be proud, beautiful," Jackson grunts, licking his lips as he strokes himself harder and faster. "Few girls can make me come without touching." A primal roar erupts from his mouth as he sprays cum all over the asphalt, his eyes rolling back in his head as he milks his release to completion.

A muscle pops in Sawyer's jaw, but that's the only sign he's mad.

"You like that, baby?" Cam says, finally lifting his head from my tits. "You want his cock inside you?" He grips my chin painfully. "Or are you still dreaming about mine?"

"The only place you feature is in my nightmares."

"Touché, sweetheart." He slides the push-up bra up one arm and then the other, hooking it over my shoulders, eliciting a rake of tiny shivers as his fingers brush against my sensitive skin, before clipping it in place. Then he reaches into each cup, molding my breasts until they look satisfactory, and my humiliation is complete. "Throw me that red top and the heels," he tosses over his shoulder.

Sawyer hands them to him. "Hurry the fuck up."

Cam ignores him, slowly pulling the red tank top down over my head, fitting it in place. Then he drops to his knees, removes my ballet flats one at a time, and slips my black Prada heels on. His touch is soft and his gaze focused as he fits my feet into both shoes. No one says anything as he gently cleans my wrists, applies Band-Aids, and then slips two gold cuff-bands on.

He dabs at my face with a tissue, mopping up any damp patches, and then he removes my makeup bag from my purse, adding blush to my cheeks and slicking gloss across my lips. The two other guys watch in some kind of morbid fascination. He runs his fingers through my hair next, fluffing it up, and a pleasurable warmth ghosts over my skull.

I hate he has magical fingers.

Fingers that turn me on with barely a touch.

But I hate myself more in this moment.

Because as soon as he removes his hands from me, I feel like crying.

How can I hate him and still want him?

How is it I'm jealous of Rochelle because she gets to sit on his lap every day?

He's an abusive prick, and I don't want to be attracted to him, but the chemistry is undeniable.

"Where did you learn to do that?" Sawyer asks, intrigue underscoring his words.

Cam smirks. "I used to spy on my older brother's girlfriend when she was getting ready in his room."

"With your cock in hand, I'm guessing," Jackson predictably says. Cam just smirks wider, neither confirming nor denying the accusation.

Cam brushes his thumbs across my cheeks, raising tiny goose bumps all over my body, and my nipples instantly salute him.

"Fuck it." Jackson groans again. "Her nipples are jutting through her top."

Cam's gaze lowers, and a smug smile spreads across his mouth. "That's the plan."

"I'm hard again."

"You've got a fucking problem," Sawyer says. "And you're not jerking off again. It's time to go."

"Go where?" I ask, fighting to compose myself, but it's hard because Cam has moved even closer to me, and his body heat is doing weird things to my insides.

"It's showtime, baby." His gaze drifts to my lips. My heart thuds in my chest, and heat floods my core as my eyes lower to his mouth. Cam jerks back quickly, as if he's only just realizing how close he's standing to me and how hard he's staring at my lips. When he raises his eyes to meet mine, the cold, harsh glare is back on his face. "Get in the car, and do everything we say or your friend will pay the price."

I climb into the back seat and he gets in beside me while Sawyer slips behind the wheel, and Jackson rides shotgun. Sawyer floors it out of there, leaving a trail of dust behind us.

"Is someone going to explain what's going on?"

Cam slams a hand down on my thigh, and I jump at the unexpected contact. "We're going to your father's place of business, and you will get us in."

CHAPTER THIRTEEN

I want to know what they're up to, but there's no point asking the question.

"What, no inane questions?" Cam asks, raising a brow.

"Why bother asking a question I know I'll get no reply to."

"Maybe you're not as dumb as you look after all."

"Screw you, asshole." I stare out the window, not wanting to look at any of them.

"Out of all the things I've said and done, that bothers you the most, doesn't it?" Cam ponders. "You don't like your intelligence being questioned."

"Does anyone?" I snap, glowering at him.

"In your world, it shouldn't matter. Aren't females groomed to look pretty, open their legs, and shut their mouths?"

"Just because that's expected of me doesn't mean I like it."

He stares at me for a long time, and I don't pull my eyes away, challenging him with a defiant expression. "Why?" he asks after several silent beats.

"Now, who's the dumb one."

His jaw tightens, and his eyes darken to almost black.

"We're here." Sawyer swings the car into a rest area around the corner from Manning Motors corporate HQ.

"This is how it will go down," Cam says, all hint of anger replaced with a serious expression. "You will seduce the guard on duty, distracting him so you can remove his security card and pass it to us."

"How the fuck am I expected to do that?"

"I recall you had some seductive skills, so just work a little of that magic on him." Cam scrubs a hand over his unshaven jaw. "And if you need a little extra motivation, imagine how embarrassed poor Jane would be if the world saw her jerking off while her elite boyfriend watched on his cell."

"I *don't* need extra motivation. You've made sure of that." I narrow my eyes at him. "What do you plan on doing about the security footage? If my father finds out I was here, he'll want to know why."

"We have that covered," Sawyer confirms. "You don't need to worry about discovery."

"Fine." I huff out a sigh. "Let's just get this over and done with."

"That's not all," Sawyer says, turning around in his seat. "We need about twenty minutes, so distract him while we're gone too."

I throw my hands into the air. "You've got to be kidding me. How the hell can I distract him for that long?"

"You're a beautiful girl," Jackson says. "I'm sure you'll think of something."

"I'm not fucking one of my father's employees!" I screech.

"No one said that," Cam coolly replies. "I'm sure you'll think of some other way to distract him."

"Dance for him," Jackson supplies. "Or give him a massage. There are plenty of ways to dangle the goodies without letting him sample."

"Jeez, thanks for those stellar suggestions."

He winks. "Anytime, beautiful."

Ugh.

"We need to go before the shift change. You good?" Sawyer asks, eyeballing me.

"I'm good," I lie, frantically trawling my brain for something I can use.

We pull up in front of the building, just out of sight of the glass entrance doors, hidden from the camera scoping out the empty parking lot. "Take this," Sawyer says, handing me a small black device. "Press that button when it's safe to enter, and we'll take it from there. When you feel it vibrating in your pocket, you have three minutes to distract him while we make our exit."

I'm mumbling under my breath as I climb out. Cam grabs hold of my arm at the last second, pulling me back. "Don't pull any shit, Abigail. Remember the consequences."

I yank my arm out of his touch. "I don't need you to constantly remind me. I got the message loud and clear, so just shut up about it." I plant my hands on my hips. "I'll play my part. Don't take too long."

He gives me a terse nod and I slam the door shut, tossing my hair upside down and tugging my top down as low as it'll go, ensuring the girls are on full display. Butterflies scatter in my chest as I plant a smile on my face and stroll toward the front door with my head held high, my back straight, and my tits pushed out.

The guard on duty looks up as my heels tap off the marble-tiled floor. He looks to be in his mid-twenties with broad shoulders, a firm build, sandy-blond hair, and navy eyes which flicker with interest as he rakes his gaze over me.

I swallow my disgust, keeping the smile fixed on my face as I lean over the counter, making sure he cops an eyeful of my cleavage. My eyes flit to the name badge pinned to the breast pocket of his uniform shirt. "Hey, Jed. Do you know who I am?" I flutter my eyelashes and drag my lower lip between my teeth.

"Sure. Ms. Manning." He clears his throat, reluctantly pulling his gaze away from my tits. "What can I do for you?"

"I know it's late," I say, rounding the counter and perching my butt on the edge of the desk. I lean down into his face, ensuring he gets an up close and personal view. "I hope that's not a problem," I rasp in a husky tone, pushing my tits into his chest as I bring my mouth to his ear. "But I was passing, and it reminded me I need a favor." His eyes are firmly glued to my cleavage, and I carefully reach down, slowly unclipping his security badge from the belt of his pants.

"A favor?" he chokes out, his eyes radiating excitement.

I hop up, rounding the counter again, slipping the card on the floor before leaning down to look at him. His disappointed face tilts up to meet mine, and I think this might be easier than expected. "I have this assignment for school," I say, twirling a lock of my hair, "and I was hoping I could interview you about your role here at Manning Motors?"

The disappointed look expands on his face, and I wonder what kind of favor he thought I was suggesting. "It will only take about twenty minutes of your time, and I'd be ever so grateful." I flash my cleavage at him again. "I'll put in a good word with my father."

He perks up at that. "Sure. I'd be happy to help."

"You're so sweet, Jed. And I really appreciate this." I move to his side, slowly leaning down and kissing his cheek. "Could you escort me to one of the side rooms so I can grab some supplies?"

"I can't really leave the desk, Miss."

I toss my hair over my shoulder, placing my hand on his beefy arm. "We'll be gone three minutes, tops." I smile, glancing over my shoulder. "This place is like a graveyard. No one will know." I squeeze his arm, deliberately licking my lips, and he bolts up out of his chair.

"Follow me." He shoots me a disarming smile, and he's kinda hot for an older dude.

I slip one hand into the pocket of my jeans, pressing the little button on the device Sawyer gave me as Jed escorts me into the closest meeting room.

I waste as much time as possible, opening and closing cupboards, waving my butt in the air as I bend down, ensuring I'm giving Jed an ample show. After four minutes have passed, I figure the coast is clear, and I walk back out to the lobby with a pen, pad, and a bottle of water. Jed carries a chair, placing it close beside his, and I check the time on the large clock suspended from the ceiling in the lobby as I kick start my fake interview.

Jed loves the sound of his own voice, and a few carefully chosen questions has him blabbering away about his role. I scribble notes as he talks, keeping an eye on the clock, ignoring the distaste in my mouth every time he leers at my tits. He's growing braver, moving in closer, pressing his thigh against mine, and brushing his arm against the side of my chest accidentally on purpose, but I say nothing, sending him flirtatious looks while I silently urge the guys to hurry the fuck up.

I'm running out of questions, and growing more anxious, as the minutes tick by, and I almost collapse in relief when the device vibrates in my pocket. "I'd like to go back to one of your earlier responses," I say, pretending to flick back through my notes. "You've said the night shifts play havoc with your health and your sleep, and as part of my proposal, I'd like to suggest some measures the company can deploy to help combat symptoms." I rise, standing behind him, placing my hands on his shoulders. "Close your eyes," I prompt.

"What are you doing?"

"I'm giving you a shoulder massage to help loosen up your muscles. You need to tilt your head back and close your eyes. Let me relieve that tension spreading from your shoulders down your back." I brush my fingers across his cheek, and he obeys with no further hesitation. "That's right, Jed. Just like that. Now keep your eyes closed until I tell you to open them."

Swallowing bile, I knead his brawny shoulders, digging my thumbs in deep as I rotate them in circular motions. Sawyer's head creeps around the side of the corner, and I urge him to hurry with my eyes as Jed emits a loud moan that sours my stomach. The three guys tiptoe across the lobby in their bare feet, carrying their shoes in their hands, as I dig my fingers in deeper, trying to ignore the growing bulge in Jed's pants as I continue massaging him. The guys have only just slipped out the door when Jed springs into action. Reaching around, he grabs me by the waist, yanks me onto his lap, and crashes his mouth down on mine.

"Jed! What the hell!" I rip my mouth from his, trying to get up, but his arms wrap firmly around me, trapping me in place as he buries his head in my chest, nuzzling my tits with his nose. "Get the fuck away from me!" I snarl.

"I know this was just a ruse," he says, looking up at me through hooded eyes. "If you wanted to fuck me, baby, you only had to ask. I knew you were checking me out last month when you were here."

I'd had to drop some papers off for Father a few weeks ago, but I don't even remember seeing Jed, let alone checking him out. This guy is so full of himself it's not funny.

He thrusts his obvious erection into my hips as he licks a line across my chest. I'm getting ready to shut this shitshow down when the front door swings open, and Cam charges across the lobby.

Jed's eyes widen in alarm, and he automatically loosens his hold on me. I scramble off his lap, and Cam pulls me protectively into his side. He glares at Jed, his eyes narrowing on the boner straining the front of his pants. "Did you put your hands on my woman?"

"What? No!" Jed immediately backtracks, standing and raising his palms in a conciliatory gesture. "She was just interviewing me. That's all."

"Baby." Cam circles his arms around me, reeling me into his warm chest. "Did he touch you?"

"Yes, but he'll pay for it once I tell Daddy."

"You little bitch," Jed barks. "You were coming on to me the whole time!"

"I did no such thing," I huff. "Why the fuck would I come on to you when I've got the hottest fiancé?" I'm sure Jed is aware I'm engaged, like most employees in my father's company, but I doubt he knows who Trent is or what he looks like, because he doesn't mix in those circles, so this seems like a good angle to take.

I snake my arms behind Cam's neck, eye-fucking him as I bite down on my lower lip, trusting he'll play along. His eyes flare darkly, and his hands move lower, cupping my ass. Electricity crackles in the space between us, and I almost forget we're pretending.

"She's mine," Cam hisses, leveling a vicious look at Jed. "And no one touches what's mine without paying the price."

"Oh, honey." I pat his chest. "Forget it. It's not worth it. He'll be fired by morning."

"As if your little punk ass could take me anyway," Jed sneers, poking the beast.

"Are you a complete idiot?" I intone, shucking out of Cam's hold and gesturing at him. "He'd crush you and you know it."

"I'm into MMA," Jed says, wiggling his fingers at Cam. "Take your best shot, asshole."

Cam removes his jacket, offloading it to me. "It'd be my pleasure."

I step aside, knowing it's pointless to intervene.

The guys circle each other, and then Jed lunges at Cam with a clenched fist. Cam deflects the throw, spinning around and shoving his foot into Jed's back, sending him crashing to the ground. Jed groans but pushes up on his elbows. Before he can get to his feet, Cam has him positioned flat on his back, straddling him as he pummels his face and upper torso with punch after punch.

Into MMA or not, Jed is no match for all the pent-up aggression Cam's unleashing.

Blood flies. Bone cracks. Cries ring out.

And that's when I step in.

"Enough," I say, hovering over Cam. "Unless you want to be charged with murder."

He stops hitting Jed, resting back on his heels as he wipes his sweaty brow with the back of his hand, breathing heavily. I extend my hand, helping him up, and we walk out of there without speaking and without looking back.

"What the actual fuck was that?" Sawyer roars the instant we slide into the back seat. Jackson is in the driver's seat this time, and Sawyer has his laptop open, perched on his knees.

"He put his hands on her without permission."

As if that's anything new.

"*You* put your hands on her without permission!" Sawyer yells. Tires screech as Jackson hightails it away from the building.

"She likes *my* hands on her," he replies with a conceited shrug, inspecting his cut knuckles.

I snort. "You're fucking unreal. In what realm did I enjoy you manhandling me?"

"Don't bullshit a bullshitter, sweetheart," he drawls, his lips curving up at the corners. "We both know you get off on that shit."

I'm speechless for once in my life. Because I can't believe the arrogance of this guy. And I also hate he's right.

"I don't understand you, Cam." Sawyer shakes his head. "This… This is not what we agreed to." He claws a hand through his hair, and it's the first time I've seen Sawyer rattled. "He saw your fucking face! He can identify you."

"You're getting your panties in a bunch for nothing. The cameras are still out, so they caught nothing. Chill the fuck out." Cam slouches in the seat, crossing his ankles.

Sawyer harrumphs. "You just beat the guy bloody, and you think he won't tell someone?"

"He won't," I cut in. "He's too embarrassed to admit a high school kid got the better of him."

"You can't know that for sure."

"I'm a good judge of character, but if it makes you feel better, I'll phone my father when I get home. Explain I was interviewing one of his guards for a school assignment, he assaulted me, and my friend came to my rescue. I'll tell him I paired with Chad on the assignment and it was him who was with me. He'll can his ass on the spot because it's not okay for *commoners* to touch an elite."

Truth.

He'll let his asshole best friend assault me, let Trent grope me, but if any normal man even dares lift a finger to me, God help them.

Sawyer and Camden stare incredulously at me, and Jackson is grinning through the mirror.

"What?"

"Not just a pretty face," Jackson murmurs as Sawyer drills a look into me, and if I didn't know better, I'd think there was a hint of admiration in his gaze.

"That'll work," Cam says. "Do it."

He looks out the window, and I flip him the bird. He could at least say thanks. The jackass. Jackson chuckles, noting my expression through the mirror, and I stick my tongue out at him as I lean my head back and close my eyes.

A short while later, I feel Cam's gaze burning a hole in the side of my head, so I open my eyes and face him. "If you've something to say, say it."

"What did you mean by commoner?"

"Nothing."

He continues staring at me, and I stare back, giving nothing away in my expression.

Jackson chuckles again. "I like you," he admits. "I like you a lot."

"I think your dick already confirmed that," Sawyer mutters, furiously typing on his keypad.

Cam sends daggers at Jackson's back, but he doesn't speak.

It's not the first hint of discourse in this group, and I'm intrigued to learn more. Sawyer has some beef with the guys, and Camden does not like Jackson flirting with me. And I haven't forgotten Cam's cryptic comment about an older brother earlier either. I tuck all these useful nuggets of information away and stare out the window, hiding the smug smile ghosting over my lips.

Keeping your enemies close pays dividends after all.

CHAPTER FOURTEEN

I'm still mulling over the intel I gleaned last night as I make my way to Jane's house bright and early the following morning. I don't know why the guys were snooping in my dad's business, but whatever plans they have could benefit me in the long run—if they intend to take him down. So, keeping on their good side is imperative even if I must bow at their feet and eat crow in front of the entire school.

Jane is still in the shower when I arrive, but her mom lets me up to her bedroom to wait for her. This time, I locate the secret camera in the TV socket, and I flip the guys off with a smug grin as I extract the device, pocketing it to give to Xavier over the weekend.

I've just finished canvassing the rest of the room, making sure it's clean, when Jane appears clouded in a layer of steam. "Oh, my freaking God!" she yells, slapping a hand over her chest. "You just scared the shit out of me!!"

"Sorry, babe. Your mom let me up."

"You're early," she says, shedding the towel and getting dressed.

"I didn't sleep well, so I thought I might as well get up and go to school early."

"Are you nervous about the show tonight?"

"Definitely." It's only a partial truth though. My mind refused to shut down after last night's kidnapping and breaking and entering expedition. Sleep evaded me on and off throughout the night, as more and more questions floated through my overactive mind. I'm surviving on copious cups of black coffee, adrenaline, and pain pills to blot out the soreness in my back. It'll be a miracle if I pull off a flawless performance tonight. But *Swan Lake* is the least of my worries right now.

I've been debating whether to tell Jane about the recording, and I'm oscillating between decisions. My instinct is to shield her from the truth because I know it will upset and embarrass her. The other side of my brain says it's wrong to keep it hidden from her because it was an invasion of her privacy and she has a right to know the recording exists. If things turn pear-shaped and it gets released, she should at least be prepared. And it's that thought that spurs me into doing the right thing. "Come sit with me," I say, patting the space on the bed beside me. "I have something I need to tell you."

At lunch, I'm in the middle of a hushed conversation with Chad when Cam hollers my name across the cafeteria.

Remembering the leverage they have, I grit my teeth, lift my head, and stare at him impassively. He clicks his fingers, gesturing me with a "come hither" expression.

Jane and I share a look. She's still visibly upset, but I'm not sorry I told her. She deserved to know, and it's validated my behavior. Drew was livid when he discovered what they've done, but at least he understands why I'm playing by their rules now. Charlie does too, and it surprised me how enraged he became when I explained what they made me do last night. Trent, predictably, didn't see it as a big deal, but he'll still publicly support Drew on this matter.

I wouldn't like to be in the new elite's shoes when Drew returns because he's out for blood.

"I hate this," Jane whispers, shooting daggers at the new elite's table. "I hate that they're using me to get to you." Guilt slithers through my veins because she's not aware they have other ammunition.

"It's not your fault," I say in a low voice. "If it wasn't your video, they would've found some other way." I shoot her a reassuring smile before sucking in a subtle breath and standing. I'm conscious of several eyeballs glued to my back as I walk toward the table the new elite have now commandeered as their own.

The whore is situated on his lap. *Again.* Her uninjured hand rubs up and down his chest as she nuzzles into his neck.

I've been slyly watching them every lunchtime, and while he appears content to let her use his lap as her own personal chair, he never touches her, and he deflects every attempt she makes to kiss him.

I haven't spent years observing human behavior to ignore the signs.

He's doing this to piss me off. He has no real interest in her. I'm sure.

Not that it makes it any easier to bear witness to, but it's showtime, so I plant my game face on and ignore her wandering hand.

"Yes?" I arch a brow.

"Fix me a tray."

"What?"

"Are you dumb *and* tit-less?" Rochelle taunts, snaking her arms around his neck and pressing her face against his left cheek.

"The only dumb bitch around here is you," I retaliate. "Not that long ago, you were professing love for my fiancé. If you think Trent will let this betrayal slide, you're even dumber than I thought."

Just to annoy her, I lean in to Cam's free ear and whisper, "She clearly enjoys my sloppy seconds."

His eyes narrow to slits as he pushes me back. "Get my fucking lunch, and make it snappy."

I guess whatever camaraderie I felt last night was just an illusion because he's an even bigger asshole today. I want to gouge his eyes out with my fingernails, and my look must convey that sentiment because Jackson chuckles, his eyes sparking with mischief as his gaze bounces between us.

"The king has spoken," he says, standing. "Better not keep him waiting." He holds out his arm for me, and Cam's jaw instantly tightens.

I wonder if they've butted heads over a girl before, because Jackson sure seems to enjoy riling him up about me. I'm not one to pass up an opportunity to piss Cam off, so I loop my arm through Jackson's, smiling up at him like he hung the moon, as he leads me to the lavish self-serve buffet.

"What does His Majesty like to eat?" I inquire, inspecting the rows of exquisitely prepared culinary delights. Our cafeteria would rival a Michelin-starred restaurant on any day.

"You can't go wrong with meat," he replies, and I immediately head to the vegetarian section.

Jackson smirks. "You just can't help stirring shit."

"What?" I toss him a faux innocent face. "If he had particular dietary requirements, he should've been more specific." I place a sea kale entrée, artichoke mille-feuille dinner, and mixed exotic fruit dessert on his tray while Jackson's mouth waters as he slides a steak on his own tray. I glance at the clock, taking my time as I drop ice cubes into a glass and add a bottle of water to Cam's tray.

"Ready?" I cock my head at Jackson.

"Hells yeah. I'm not missing this."

I smile sweetly as I approach Cam, carefully placing the tray down in front of him. "Your lunch, sir." I curtsy, because I've always had a flair for the dramatic.

"What the fuck is this?" Cam holds up a large kale leaf, scowling at it like it's done him some personal injustice.

"Sea kale," I supply.

"I'm not eating that." He shoves the tray away.

"It's high in fiber, proteins, and vitamins, and it's a natural anti-inflammatory. Figure you could use it after your *workout* last night."

"If I wanted dietary advice, I'd hire a fucking nutritionist. Get me a steak. Now."

I glance over my shoulder, smothering my satisfied grin. "Oh dear. It's too late. The buffet is closed."

His nostrils flare, and I turn to leave as Rochelle whispers in his ear.

"Get the fuck back here," he barks.

I want to flip him off so badly, but Jane's troubled face comes into view, and I know I can't risk it. The entire cafeteria is watching this play out, no one even pretending they're not fixated on the drama unfolding before their eyes.

"I warned you. Cross me and there are consequences." He repositions a smug Rochelle on his lap. "Kneel." He points at the side of his chair. "Right there. With your head bowed, and you won't speak or move a muscle until I tell you to."

"Camden." Sawyer's tone holds a silent warning which Cam ignores.

"On your knees, bitch," the whore says, practically bouncing on his lap.

"Seriously? This is how you repay me for last night?"

"What the fuck is she talking about?" Rochelle asks, the superior expression wiped from her mouth.

"You seem to be under a misconception," Cam says in a voice that is ice cold. "We're not friends. Or allies. You serve a purpose." He shrugs casually, but his shoulders are rigidly tense, and he's not fooling me. "Don't cooperate. See if I care. I won't be the one paying the price."

My fists ball up at my side and tears prick the back of my eyes.

This is going too far.

If I do this, I'll lose all respect.

I already feel the weight of the shocked stares from the inner circle. Even knowing my guys will decimate the new elite when they return is cold comfort.

Cam pulls out his cell, his finger hovering over the pad. "Kneel."

His piercing eyes drill into mine, and I'm shocked at the depth of loathing I see there.

Why does he hate me so much?

I've done nothing to earn this level of hatred. "Now." He moves his finger closer to the send button, and I sink to my knees. Shocked gasps and hushed whispers surround me on all sides as I bow my head, my cheeks hot with anger and humiliation.

Rochelle cackles, and I swear, there and then, that I will finish her like I should've done months ago. But I was trying to give her the benefit of the doubt. No more though. She enjoys sticking the knife in, and I won't feel an ounce of guilt when I ruin her life.

"Good girl," Cam says, petting my head like I'm a dog. Tears sting my eyes again, and I hate how vulnerable I feel.

"While you're down there," Jackson jokes, earning a round of laughter from the table, and I grind my teeth so hard I fear I'll end up with lockjaw.

Footsteps approach. "Get up, Abby," Jane demands, placing her hand on my shoulder. "You've no right to do this," she snaps at the guys.

"C'mon, Abigail." Chad extends his hand to help me up, but I shake my head.

"Just go." I plead with my eyes. "This is how it has to be right now." I send a silent message, and a muscle pops in his jaw as he acquiesces.

"No." Jane crouches down to me. "You don't have to do this. We'll find a way around it."

"Trust me," I mouth. "I know what I'm doing."

Her tormented gaze fixes on mine, and she stares intensely at me before nodding. Standing, she glares at Cam and Rochelle. "You will all pay for this."

"I'm terrified," Cam deadpans, picking at the food on his plate.

Lowering my head, I'm grateful I don't have to watch them laughing at my humiliation. Jane and Chad refuse to leave, standing behind me, and their quiet support is the only thing that gets me through this. I'm forced to listen to the inconsequential chatter around the table as they eat lunch, and the longer I'm on my knees, the more I seethe. The more I plot their downfall.

Jackson stands up on his chair at one point, whistling until he's claimed the attention of the cafeteria, inviting everyone to a party at his place tonight.

Sawyer doesn't utter a word during the whole ordeal, and he finishes his lunch superfast, leaving without saying goodbye. I only know he's gone because his chair protests loudly when he slams it back, and his footsteps are loud as he stalks away.

Gradually, the cafeteria clears out. "You make a great slave," Cam condescends, patting my head again. "Class is about to start. Get up."

Rochelle snickers as I rise, and Jane hisses at her. Pain slices across my chest, like a million tiny knives stabbing me all at once, but it only strengthens my resolve and my determination to act with dignity. "Laugh now because you won't be laughing for long," I threaten, sending daggers at her.

I'm trembling with rage, my fists clenched so tight the skin blanches white and my jaw hard and unyielding. I'll destroy her because I'm sure she's the one who suggested he do this. Her face pales, and she looks to Cam for assurance, but he locks his eyes on mine like always. My lips tug up at the corners. "Don't look to him. He won't and can't help you. You've dug your own grave, and I doubt anyone will mourn your loss."

With Jane and Chad by my side, I stalk out of the cafeteria with my head held high, refusing to give them any more victories today.

CHAPTER FIFTEEN

y father is a no-show at the ballet, and I'm genuinely shocked. He's never missed one of my performances, and I can only surmise that whatever is going on at Parkhurst is serious enough to merit staying longer than intended.

But I forget all about him as the show continues, letting everything from today go as I immerse myself in the music and the flow of my body as I dance my heart out. I barely even register the audience. My mind has gone to that magical place, and I'm Odette, pirouetting and spinning, dancing with elegance and poise, as I command the stage.

I'm full of pent-up emotion, and I let it fuel me, channeling a whole host of feelings as I glide effortlessly across the stage. I feel everything intensely. Odette's joy and suffering, her passion and grief, her hope and despair. As Liam—playing the part of the prince—shields me from the evil sorcerer, I wonder who will protect me from the guy who's manipulated and bewitched me.

When I return to the dressing room after our second curtain call, I'm exhausted but feeling lighter too. A smile plays across my lips as I blow an imaginary kiss toward the heavens, silently thanking my beautiful mom for introducing me to dance.

It has been my savior on so many levels, and I needed it tonight.

The smile drops off my mouth when I discover the large bouquet of roses waiting for me with an accompanying apology note from my father. But I know they're just for show. He doesn't really care he let me down. He only cares about public perception.

But I'm not my father's daughter. I couldn't give two shits what the public thinks of me, and I only pretend I do to keep up the charade long enough to plot my escape. However, my patience is at an all-time low today, so I take great pleasure in tossing the note and the flowers into the trash in front of my fellow dancers.

I drove myself here tonight, and I dismissed Oscar after the performance ended. He came with his wife and their two daughters, and I posed for pictures with them backstage.

He wanted to wait to escort me home, as he was technically on duty, and he's nervous after being ambushed the other night. He thinks it was a random guy who knocked him unconscious for a few hours, and I didn't correct him. Despite his vocal protests, I insisted he leave with his family. When that didn't work, I resorted to my usual blackmail, and he left the theater with a face like thunder.

Being followed by bodyguards all the time is exhausting, and today, more than any other day, I need to be alone.

Jane and her family came too, and she tried to convince me to sleep over at her place, but I just want to go home, get into my pajamas, eat my body weight in Belgian chocolate ice cream, and watch *The Godfather* movies for the hundredth time in bed.

I'm looking forward to all the violence and murder, and I'll be imagining Camden Marshall's face in place of every victim I see on the screen.

I say goodbye to the other dancers, making my way out to the parking lot alone. I click my key fob, and the lights flash on my Impress FX17, highlighting the figure cloaked in dark clothes loitering at the side of my car. My heart rate instantly spikes, and I reach into my purse for the pepper spray I always keep there when the stranger steps under the light.

A growl builds at the base of my throat as I close the distance between us. "I've had enough of you for one day," I bark, putting my face up in his, barely containing my rage. "Get lost, Cam."

"I thought you were made of stronger stuff than that," he coolly replies.

I deliberately don't reply, glaring at him, imagining all the different ways I could torture him.

He pulls the hood down off his head, stepping into me. His chest brushes against mine, and his eyes glimmer with challenge, flooding my body with a mix of raw desire and naked anger. Trent's words about hate sex pop into my mind, and while I'm loath to agree with anything my douchebag fiancé has to say, at this moment, I'd love nothing better than to slap, punch, and kick Camden Marshall's perfect face until he bleeds and then take his cock for the ride of a lifetime.

I step away from him the instant that thought lands in my mind, horrified that he infuriates and arouses me at the same time.

He closes the gap between us immediately, running the tip of his finger across my exposed collarbone, eliciting a rake of fiery tingles that makes my toes curl. "The more you fight me, the more I enjoy this," he whispers, pressing his mouth to my ear. "So, keep fighting me, sweetheart. Nothing turns me on more."

"Fuck you, Cam." I shove him away, stalking to my car and climbing inside. The passenger door opens, and he slides inside. "What the hell do you think you're doing?"

"Coming with you. Unless you already know the way to Lauder's place?" He examines the interiors like he's considering purchasing one.

"No, and no. Get out."

"Make me." He slants me a sexy, lopsided grin, and it only infuriates me more.

Fishing my pepper spray out of my purse, I uncap the lid and aim it at his face. But he reacts fast, and before I know it, he has me pinned to my seat with his fingers curled around my hand, trying to pry the canister out of my grip while I attempt to press down on it.

We wrestle for several minutes—me trying to get it to explode in his face and him trying to get hold of it. Our bodies touch repeatedly, and heat pours off him in hypnotic waves, threatening my concentration. I only drop the spray when he digs his fingers into my still sore wrists, and I yelp in pain. Opening the window, he throws the cannister outside. I let a string of expletives loose as he straddles me with his powerful thighs, encasing my body on both sides. I fight him. Trying to push him back, but he's an unmovable, solid block of muscle, and I emit a frustrated scream.

"I can do this all night, so feel free to keep fighting me."

I buck against him, raising my free hand to slap him, but he grabs both my hands over my head as he presses his body down on top of me. My chest rises and falls as heat and lust slam into me, and my nipples turn to bullets under my flimsy bra.

He turns rigidly still, easing himself back until he's sitting on my lap, his hungry eyes latched onto my chest. I suck in a sharp breath when I feel his hard-on pressing against my core, and I squeeze my eyes shut, wishing I could do the same with my thighs.

I hate him.

I hate him.

I hate him.

He's hurt me.

Humiliated me.

Groped me.

I do not *want to jump his bones.*

I keep repeating it over and over in my head, willing him to get off me, yet I can't articulate that request either. I am seriously screwed in the head when it comes to this guy, and nothing good can come from that.

A little whimper escapes my lips when his hot mouth brushes the sensitive skin just under my ear. I hold my breath as he trails his lips up and down my neck, inhaling deeply, while his grip on my wrists loosens and he rocks his hips against mine. Another whimper flies out of my mouth, and I curse my weak hormones.

I want to shove this asshole away, and deny him what he wants, but I also want to pull him closer and let him do wicked things to my body because I'm aching for him which is all kinds of fucked up. My pussy is throbbing with need, pulsing and jerking, as he thrusts slowly against me.

"How is it I crave the thing I hate most?" he whispers, his mouth moving to my jaw. "How do you do that? Make me want you when I despise you?"

"If you discover the answer, please enlighten me," I rasp, keeping my eyes shut.

"Open your eyes, Abigail." My name rolls seductively off his tongue, doing funny things to my insides. He peppers my jawline with kisses, and I'm on the verge of spontaneous combustion. My eyes blink open, and I stare into his beautiful face. He's so close I have no other choice. Conflict rages in his eyes, and I relate to the feeling. "I think you've been put on this Earth purely to torment me," he whispers, letting my wrists go so he can wind his hands into my hair. "I need you to hate me."

"Oh, trust me, I'm already there."

"Not nearly enough," he whispers, kissing the corner of my mouth.

"What do you want from me, Cam?" I whisper back.

He kisses the other corner of my mouth, and my dress is stuck to my skin, my body overheating with liquid lust, my core pulsing with an intense need.

"*Everything*, Abigail. I'm going to take everything."

Before I can respond, he crashes his mouth to mine, gripping my head in his large palms so he can direct our kiss.

Although calling it a kiss is a bit like calling a Ferrari an average car.

This kiss is the Rolls Royce of kisses.

It's a claiming.

A branding.

An invasion.

A promise.

An attack.

A challenge.

A punishment.

A reward.

And a hundred other things.

He devours my lips with a frantic need, plunging his tongue into my mouth, and grinding his hips against mine. Every nerve ending and cell in my body is hypersensitive, and I'm drowning in Camden Marshall, both hating and loving it at the same time.

My fingers trail across the nape of his neck, fondling the downy hairs there. Then I dig my nails into his scalp, dragging them up and down the shorn sides, and he growls into my mouth, clasping my head tighter, as his punishing lips bruise mine.

My head is swimming, and I'm drowning in his rough kisses, greedy touch, and the feel of his hot body grinding against mine. The devil on my shoulder taunts me to take, take, take, while the angel in my ear implores me to push him away.

Inside, I'm screaming.

Tormented and aroused.

Confused and clear at the same time.

I'm overheating, my body building to a crescendo as we claw at one another, thrusting our bodies together through our clothes, desperate to get closer and yet keep our separation. I scream into his mouth as my climax hits, throwing back my head and jerking violently as the craziest, most explosive orgasm rips through me with violent intensity. He grunts into my ear, his breathing labored, and my scalp stings as he yanks hard on the strands of my hair while rocking against me with his eyes closed.

I can't be one hundred percent sure, but I think he just came too.

My breathing returns to normal, my chest settles down, and a heavy cloud descends on top of me with the realization of what we've just done.

I don't trust that this isn't another part of whatever sick game he's playing, and I've just succumbed.

Again.

After the way he treated me today, making out with him is the absolute last thing I should be doing.

I'm sickened, and I couldn't hate myself any more than I do in this moment. "Get off me."

He climbs into the passenger seat without argument, and I pinch the bridge of my nose, fighting an inner battle as I cast a surreptitious look his direction. He looks equally pissed off by this weird chemistry we share, and I'm glad it's not only me.

Tension is thick in the air, and I want to slam my hands against the steering wheel and scream until my lungs bleed. But I won't give him the satisfaction, so I force myself to calm down.

"Drive," he bites out.

"I'm not going to your party." I need to get as far away from him as possible.

"I've one word for you." He angles his head, eyeballing me with his usual hateful mask in place. "Jane."

That ensures I'll do his bidding, and I'm sick to my stomach as I start the engine and maneuver the car out of the parking lot. He taps coordinates into the car's GPS system, and neither of us speaks for ages.

"That meant nothing," he eventually says.

"Less than nothing," I agree, flooring it when I reach the outskirts of town and hit the open road.

I watch him, on the sly, from the corner of my eye, inspecting every square inch of the car, running his fingers across the shiny dash with reluctant admiration in his eyes. "You like it?" I ask when the unbearable silence becomes almost claustrophobic.

"I fucking hate it," he spits, and I crank out a laugh.

"Well, that figures." His unspoken question lingers in the air. "I helped design it. My father wanted to design a car that would appeal to young, rich, society girls, and he roped me into working with the design team a couple summers ago." I'd never admit it to my father, but I really enjoyed that project. He's amassed an amazingly creative team who is a joy to work with. They didn't treat me as the owner's daughter. Or look down on me for being a spoiled, rich teenager.

They valued my opinions.

Challenged my ideas.

Expanded my creative brain.

I cast a quick glance at him. "So, it stands to reason you'd hate it."

Except I know he was coveting it too.

I think he has the same love-hate relationship with my car he has with me.

Silence engulfs us again, and I briefly consider putting some music on, but I prefer the awkward quiet as it reminds me he's my enemy. Something I seem to forget every time he touches me.

"Why do you do it?" he asks a few beats later.

"Do what?"

"All the elite bullshit."

"Why do you?" I throw back.

"I have reasons. Good ones," he replies with his face turned away so I can't see his reaction. Except I can make out his reflection in the window, and I detect the hatred blistering in his eyes, oozing like molten lava.

"As do I," I say.

His phone vibrates, and he glances at it quickly, a perplexed look appearing on his face. The cell continues to vibrate while he stares at it. At the last second, he answers the call. "Hey." He averts his eyes, looking out the window again. "I know. I'm sorry I wasn't there." His tone has lowered, and the reflection in the window shows his features have softened, and he looks kinda sad. "I promise I'll show up next time." He glances briefly at me before looking away again. "I can't really talk now." He's quiet for a few beats. "Yeah, I miss you too," he quietly says before ending the call.

I'm dying to know who put that whimsical look on his face, but I know better than to ask.

"Take a left here," he snaps a couple minutes later, and I turn into an open driveway lined with tall trees on either side. When we round the bend, an impressive modern building comes into view. The entire house is lit up like it's the Fourth of July, and with the flashing lights, thumping music I can hear through the windows of the car, and people stumbling across the lawn with beer bottles in hand, it looks like the quintessential party house.

The property stretches across two levels, and it's constructed of cherry wood and glass with an angled roof and a glass and silver balcony wrapping around the entire upper level. Cars are parked haphazardly on the gravel-lined space in front of the house, and I pull into the side, a little farther back. I want to ensure I'm not hemmed in so I can make my escape whenever I need to.

We exit the car together, walking silently into the house side by side. Rhythmic beats and multicolored strobe lights stream through the open door as we step into a wide foyer with winding glass stairs on either side. Strips of industrial-type lighting extend the length of the ceiling overhead, and the oak hardwood floors under foot are distressed, giving it an edgy, modern feel.

I follow Cam into a massive kitchen comprising glossy white cupboards and stainless-steel appliances and watch as he makes a beeline for the refrigerator. "Beer?" he offers, extending a chilled bottle to me.

I shake my head. "I'm good." There's no way I'm consuming any alcohol in the devil's lair. I need to stay sharp. Now that I'm here, I've decided I might as well use the opportunity to do a little snooping. "Where are Lauder's parents?" I inquire as he nudges the door shut with his hip, popping the cap on his beer.

"In New York."

"He lives here alone?"

He lifts the bottle to his mouth, wrapping his gorgeous lips around the rim and drinking greedily. The way his throat works as he swallows is ridiculously sexy, and I turn my head, avoiding getting caught drooling, looking out the window at the impressive outdoor space.

Separate basketball and tennis courts are off to either side, sandwiching a utilitarian garden with copious seating areas. A magnificent pool resides between the garden and the house, rimmed by an extensive patio area, cluttered with loungers occupied by fornicating couples.

The place is thronged with kids I recognize from school. Boys and girls holler and shriek while taking flying jumps into the massive swimming pool, spraying water everywhere. A frown furrows my brow as I rake my gaze over the assembled crew. At least some of the inner circle are here.

Traitorous pricks.

The guys won't be pleased to hear it.

"The three of us live here," Cam acknowledges, in between guzzling his beer. "And if you're thinking of doing any snooping, you can forget it. We locked our bedrooms."

"Whatever gave you that idea?" I tease, smirking, because a little thing like a lock won't keep me out.

"I'm beginning to understand how your mind works, and it's a waste of time. Besides, I didn't bring you here to aid your agenda."

"Why *did* you bring me here?"

He gestures for me to follow him, and I trail alongside him as we exit a different door than the one we came in. We enter a large living space that is operating as a dance floor. A DJ spins tunes from a makeshift booth at the top of the room, and heaving bodies jostle and grind as beats pulse across the space.

I spot more familiar faces.

Faces who should not be here.

A few of them scurry off, groveling as they throw apologies over their shoulder while they race out of the place. However, what's more worrisome is how most don't appear to care that I've spotted them. Cam's earlier humiliation has eradicated whatever respect I've heretofore commanded, adding to the reasons why I need to hold on to my hatred.

Cam pushes his way through the room, out into a long hallway. Moans and cries filter out from closed doors as we pass, and my mind, unhelpfully, conjures up images of Cam grinding on top of me back in my car.

He's the enemy. Never forget.

He takes the stairs two at a time, and I keep pace behind him. Stopping at the first door we come to, at the top of the stairs, he raps three times.

Jackson swings the door open, grinning as he peruses the length of my body in my conservative black and gold dress with matching heels. I was expecting my father to appear at the show, so I'd brought appropriate Daddy-approved clothing to change into, but I'm hardly party ready. "If you're aiming for the sexy secretary look," he says, standing aside to let us enter. "You've nailed it."

I poke my tongue out at him as he slams the door shut, grabbing my arm and pushing me up against it. "Next time you do that, I'll devour your tongue and your lips until your head spins."

"Promises, promises," I purr, sliding out from under his arm.

"Damn," he mumbles from behind. "Your ass looks hot in that dress."

I roll my eyes. "Let me guess," I toss over my shoulder. "You're hard."

Throwing back his head, he laughs. "How did you guess?"

"If you two are done flirting," Cam snaps. "We have business to attend to."

"Touchy, isn't he?" Jackson quips, and now it's my turn to laugh.

"Oh, you've no idea." Ignoring Cam and Jackson, I claim a seat at the table beside Sawyer.

The room is a home study of sorts complete with a fitted shelving unit, desk, and storage unit. This six-seater table occupies center stage in the room, in front of the large floor-to-ceiling window which offers prime viewing of the debauchery going on outside.

Several girls are now topless in the pool, making for an attentive male audience, many of them with their hands down the front of their shorts, stroking their cocks. In the other, more shaded, corner of the pool, couples are having sex, uncaring they have an audience.

"Jealous, beautiful?" Jackson asks, noticing the focus of my attention.

"Hardly," I scoff, leaning forward in my seat. "What is it you want now because I'm assuming you didn't bring me here to party."

"We didn't." Sawyer angles his laptop, so it's facing me. It's open on a Manning Motors log-in screen. "We need you to help us figure out your father's password."

CHAPTER SIXTEEN

"And why is it you think I'd know? I'm female, which means my father shares nothing in relation to the business with me."

"But you know important dates like birthdays and anniversaries and other personal data," Sawyer supplies. "That's usually what people use for passwords."

I collapse in a fit of laughter because the thought is so absurd. The guys stare at me as if I've taken a trip to Crazy Town. "Did we say something funny?" Cam questions.

"Yes," I say, wiping tears of laughter from my eyes. "You seem to have mistaken my father for a normal person. For a human. You expect him to act like every other businessman with a family does when that is not who he is."

Cam and Sawyer share a look. "Who is he then?"

"He's a ruthless monster who cares about nothing except wealth, power, and status. He's more likely to use something random and impersonal as his password."

"What about his fuck buddy?" Cam asks. "What's her name or date of birth?"

"They're as interchangeable as the weather, and he rarely has just the one. I doubt he even knows their names."

"And you know this how?" Jackson rocks back in his chair with his hands behind his head.

"Because subtlety isn't exactly his thing. He transformed the basement in our house into a sex den, and he spends most nights he's home down there with his friends and a slew of prostitutes and strippers."

"Fuck. Can we trade fathers?" Jackson jokes.

"I'd trade in a heartbeat; although, if the rumors are true, your father isn't exactly a saint either."

"He isn't, but there's no way my mom would let him build a sex room in our house even if they share an open marriage."

"Can we focus?" Sawyer slides a page across to me. "Write every birthday, anniversary, memorable date, and anything you think it could be."

"This is a waste of time. It won't work."

"Humor me."

I shrug, starting to write stuff down even though it's pointless.

Xavier regularly attempts to hack into my father's home and office computers, but he can't get through the firewall, and we've tried every computation of password we can think of without success. My father's computers are as well protected as the safe in his study—rock solid and impenetrable.

"What else could it be?" Cam asks, pacing the room. He hasn't sat down once, and I almost see the cogs turning in his head. He's agitated. Whether it's because of what just happened between us or this password issue is unknown.

"I. Don't. Know." I fold my arms across my chest.

Placing his palms down on the table, either side of me, he leans in. "Or maybe you do and you're just not saying." •

"What is it you're after, anyway?"

A malicious grin spreads across his mouth as he pushes his face in mine. "Answers and proof."

"Well, that narrows it down," I drawl sarcastically.

"Are we done here? I've weed to smoke and pussy to pound," Jackson says, jumping up with his cell in hand. "Maybe Abby can have a think about it overnight."

"Take the weekend to think about it," Sawyer says, closing his laptop and folding up the sheet of paper as my cell pings in my purse.

I remove it, smothering a groan as Trent's name flashes on the screen. An idea comes to me, and I answer the call before I change my mind. "Hey, baby," I purr. "I miss you so badly."

Initial silence greets me down the line. "Abby, is that you?" Trent asks, confusion clear in his tone.

And I get it.

I'm more likely to hurl insults than offer words of endearment.

"I'm at Lauder's party," I continue, ignoring his question. "It's lame ass."

Jackson grins, hauling me against his body in a fast move I hadn't anticipated. "I can rectify that, baby," he taunts in a seductive voice, loud enough for Trent to hear. "You only have to ask, and I'll show you a night to remember." He squeezes my ass, and I push him away, flipping him the bird while Trent shouts into the phone.

"Baby, he's being an ass on purpose. Relax, I only have eyes for you." I stare at Cam as I lie to my fiancé. "No one else even comes close to measuring up. No one else sets my body on fire like you do." It's a wonder I don't choke on the treacherous words. But they have the desired effect, and I watch Cam storm out of the room with a smug smile on my face.

Jackson shakes his head, whispering, "You never learn," before he follows Cam back to the party.

"I'm leaving," I tell Trent. "I'll call you back." I hang up before he can protest.

"I'll escort you outside," Sawyer says as I slip my cell back in my purse.

"You mean make sure I go home." I watch him lock the laptop in the top drawer of the desk. "It's not like I was planning on breaking into your office or planting a hidden camera in your bedroom," I add in a harsher tone.

"If you're expecting me to apologize," he says, placing his hand on my lower back and ushering me outside while he locks the door, "you'll be waiting forever. I don't do sorry."

"Wow. I pity the woman who ends up with you."

He shrugs, wordlessly guiding me down the stairs and out through the front door of the house.

"Give me your cell," I say, stopping just outside the entrance, with my palm out. He arches a brow, and I roll my eyes. "I'm adding my number, and then I'll message myself, so I have yours. That way, I can text you if I think of anything over the weekend." He places the cell in my palm, and I take my sweet ass time adding my deets before sending a quick text to myself. My cell pings in my purse, and I smile as I hand it back. "All done."

"Goodnight, Abigail." He spins on his heel, pausing in the doorway. "And a word to the wise." His eyes penetrate mine like laser beams. "Don't push him. Just do as he says, and you'll have an easier time."

What is he up to? Why would he care whether or not I have an easy time of it? "Noted." I tilt my chin up and walk away, heading toward my car. He watches me climb inside before disappearing from sight. I sit behind the wheel, not starting the engine, calling Trent back immediately.

"What the actual fuck is going on?!" he roars. "Wentworth sent me a recording from lunch. Why the fuck would you do something like that?"

"You know why!" I hiss. "If I don't comply, he'll release the video of Jane."

"So let him!" he snaps. "She's not your responsibility."

"She's my best friend, and I won't feed her to the sharks! If I have to kneel at his feet every day until I bring them down, I'll do it to protect her."

"I'm going to fucking kill that fucking bastard with my bare hands for disrespecting you like that."

Funny thing is, Trent's done equally disrespectful things to me, but it's okay if he's the one humiliating me.

"Rochelle put him up to it," I snap. "So, add her to your kill list. Although, by the time I'm through with her, she'll probably be begging you to end her suffering."

"What are you planning?"

"To teach that bitch a life lesson once and for all. And to reel the defectors back into our net. I'll have the inner circle on our side by the time you return, and you can dole out the punishment."

His dark chuckle raises goose bumps on my arms, and not the good kind. "This is why we're perfect for one another. Things will be different when I get home."

I'll believe it when I see it. "I need to go. I want to sneak back into the house and do some snooping."

"Fuck, babe, you're like my every wet dream rolled into one. I'm hard as a brick. FaceTime me when you get home. I need to see you naked."

In your dreams, douche. "I'll call you later," I lie, ending the convo. I kick my heels off in favor of my ballet flats, hook my bag crossways over my body, and get out of the car.

Creeping around the back of the house, I stick close to the walls and slip inside through an unlocked side door, emerging in the laundry room. The only way out is through the kitchen, and I open the door a smidgeon, surveying the lay of the land, grateful none of the new elite are in sight.

Keeping my chin up, I walk through the room like I belong there, and no one pays me a lick of attention. Avoiding the room where everyone is dancing, I take a back hallway I didn't see earlier because it seems to be quieter.

I'm halfway down the long hall when moans and groans accost my ears, and I halt, wondering if I should go back and risk going up the main stairs.

I flatten my back to the wall and inch closer to the noise. It's coming from the next room, and the door is slightly ajar, allowing the obvious sounds of fucking to trickle out into the hallway. If I was a betting woman, I'd put money on Jackson being in that room. But it's clear from the multitude of sounds that there's more than one couple inside. With blood thrumming in my ears, I take a risk and sneak a peek, instantly wishing I hadn't.

The room is awash with naked bodies engaged in all kinds of sexual acts. I'm no prude. I've heard Drew and Jane going at it plenty of times, seen couples fucking at parties before, heard tales of Trent's escapades, read my fair share of erotica, and even watched the occasional porno with my fiancé, but I've seen nothing like this before, in the flesh, and I'm in a weird state of shocked arousal.

I don't have a complete view from this angle, but I can see enough.

Threesomes.

Foursomes.

Guy on guy.

Girl on girl.

Everyone is too into it to even notice me gawking.

Then my eyes land on Jackson, and all the blood drains from my face.

He's butt naked, fucking an equally naked Rochelle from behind, fondling her massive tits and grunting as he thrusts into her hard.

With his free hand, he's fingering a girl who's lying flat on her back on the floor with her legs spread wide, knees folded outward. I recognize her as one of Rochelle's crew. She's one of the girls who was with her in the bathroom the day I broke her wrist.

But it's not Jackson who has me seething.

Cam is sitting on the couch with his shirt unbuttoned, showing off his ripped body and the impressive ink on his chest. His legs are spread apart, jeans pooled at his ankles, eyes closed, with one hand on the back of Rochelle's head as she sucks his dick.

He isn't making a sound, and the only muscle he's moving is the one between his thighs as he rams his cock into her mouth, holding her head firmly in place, forcing her to take all of him.

Stabbing pains perforate my heart, like a thousand pinpricks impaling me, and a messy lump of emotion clogs my throat as I watch her blow him while Jackson fucks her from behind.

I look away, gritting my teeth, swallowing back bile mixed with envy. I force myself to move, pushing one foot in front of the other, trying to erase the images of what I've just witnessed from my mind.

Hurt and anger comingle in my veins, and it's a lethal combination. My fists clench as I walk with more urgency, needing to create distance between me and that room. I sequester my jumbled emotions in a box, locking it away to analyze later while I focus on the task at hand. I'm even more determined now I'm bringing them all to their knees.

Screw Camden Marshall.

Damn him to hell and back.

I follow the hallway to the end, coming to a set of back stairs the staff must use. I climb quietly and quickly, materializing at the other end of the upper hallway.

It's quiet up here, but I'm still careful as I check each door. There are five on either side of the hallway. Most are guest bedrooms. One is the room we were just in. Three other doors are locked, and I don't need to be a genius to figure out these are the guys' personal bedrooms.

I remove my kit from my bag and expertly pick the lock, glancing left and right before I creep into the first room. Switching on my flashlight, I inspect the surroundings with my mouth hanging open. It looks like a garbage disposal threw up in here.

The bed is unmade, clothes are strewn everywhere, and empty pizza boxes compete with crumpled soda cans and discarded beer bottles for precious floor space. My nostrils twitch at the icky smell in the air, and I fight the urge to fling the windows open and air out the place.

This room is a pigsty, and I smirk as I instantly recognize Jackson's handiwork. No wonder he always looks like he just dragged himself out of bed and grabbed his wrinkled uniform from the floor.

I gingerly sidestep the crap on the carpeted floor, making my way to his desk.

Plaques and awards are haphazardly displayed on the overhead shelf, alongside pictures of him with celebrities, confirming Jackson is both a skilled driver and well connected. It's not surprising, given who his father is, but I thought he was more into underground racing based on the research Xavier discovered.

I pull out the drawers, inspecting the contents, but there's nothing of interest.

Next, I examine his bedside table, my stomach souring at the sight of his sex toys stash and the various empty condom wrappers. A large box of Durex is half empty, and flashes of the scene from downstairs flit across my retinas until I shut that shitshow down. Angrily slamming the drawer shut, I jump as my heart thumps, conscious I might have just given the game away. I wait a couple minutes, my blood pressure calming down when no one bursts into the room.

I shine my flashlight on the only items on top of his table: two framed photos.

In the first one, Jackson is in a padded jumpsuit, leaning against the side of a race car, grinning wickedly with his arms around an older man I recognize as his father. The second picture is him with a girl who looks like the spitting image of him. His sister, I presume. The one he mentioned was murdered. I snap a quick pic of it and then fight my way out of his room, carefully closing it behind me.

I know I've hit pay dirt when I slip into the next room, spotting Cam's black leather jacket hanging off the back of a chair. This room is much neater than I was expecting; although, after Jackson's mess of a room, that wouldn't be difficult.

A black, silk comforter and matching pillows adorn the large king-sized bed. Two glossy black tables on either side of the bed yield no major surprises. The requisite box of condoms is unopened, but I can't tell if that's a good sign or not.

I move over to the seated area, flipping through the stack of magazines and papers on the coffee table. A large wall-mounted TV occupies prime real estate in front of the wide black leather couch. A gaming station, controllers, and other gaming paraphernalia are neatly stacked on a unit underneath the TV. Posters line the surrounding walls, showing Cam is a fan of MMA and motorcycles.

I open and shut the drawers in his desk, rooting through papers on his shelves, shocked to find neatly written and labeled study notes. His laptop is protected by a password, which isn't of much use, but I snap a pic of the sticker underneath with device details in the hope Xavier might hack into it at some point.

A photo on the middle shelf claims my attention, and I take a pic as I examine it.

Cam, Jackson, and Sawyer are identifiable in the center of the pic. None of them are as tall or as built as they are now, and judging from the baby faces they're all sporting, it's at least a few years old, which raises alarm bells because Xavier's research indicated they've only known each other a couple of years, which clearly isn't the case.

I glance at the other three guys in the picture, wondering who they are. They are all dark with similar features, but none of them are familiar. One of the guys looks older, but the other two look younger.

A sketchpad on the desk claims my attention next, and my mouth hangs open as I flip through the pages. Most of the drawings are of a beautiful dark-haired older woman. Some are landscapes. Some are inanimate objects, like the remarkably detailed drawing of beer bottles in a bucket of ice on top of a table.

Some are of me.

My heart swells in my chest as my eyes skim over the drawing of me in his bed. I'm lying on my stomach with the covers draped at my waist. My back is bare, and my hair fans out all around me. My expression is peaceful, and my lips are arranged in a contented smile, even in sleep. I'd no idea he'd drawn me that night, and my heart pounds with unnamed emotion.

The sketch of me in the sea in my silk robe with water swirling around my legs, and my arms wrapped tight around my body, induces a level of intense pain I haven't felt since that night. You can't see my face, because it's drawn from behind, but the sense of hopelessness, of desperation and suffering seeps from the page, and a solitary tear trickles out of my eye.

My heart hurts as I remember how desolate I was that night. If Cam hadn't been there, if he hadn't coaxed me out of the water, I shudder to think what might've happened. My mind was in a dark place that night, and I'd lost all my strength.

Camden Marshall is the biggest thorn in my side, but I will never forget what he did for me that night.

I examine the last drawing of me, on stage in my leotard, and the pain in my chest eases. I run the tip of my finger over every line he's drawn, and I'm blown away by the attention to detail. He's captured me mid-dance, on pointed toes, with my arms curved upward, displaying every emotion on my face. I know he didn't have this pad with him the evening they gate-crashed my rehearsal, so he's drawn this from memory. I stare at it for another few minutes, marveling at how he sees me, and I know I've caught a glimpse into his soul.

He might outwardly hate me, but something inside him is drawn to me in the same way I'm drawn to him.

He *sees* me. He really sees me in a way few people do.

He's exceptionally talented, and he has a true gift for capturing the human form. I close the pad, putting it back in position as I perform one final scan over his desk. My eyes fall on a silver box tucked in against the wall, and a flash of red silk instantly claims my focus. I lift the lid, all softer emotions disappearing as I discover my stolen underwear. My blood boils, and just like that, I'm back to hating him.

I shove the panties into my purse, closing the lid on the box and replacing it where it was. I know the time will come when he discovers they're missing, and he pieces things together, but I don't care.

I've no idea what he planned to do with them, but I'm claiming this one small victory.

I like him finding out I've been in his room without his permission.

Let's see how he likes the invasion of privacy.

I'm only sorry I don't have a hidden camera of my own in my little spy kit, or I'd totally turn the tables on him. I make a mental note to ask Xavier if he can pick some up for me for future use.

Before I leave, I rummage around his closet, and I stumble across a bag on the floor shoved into the corner. I shine the flashlight on it as I lower the zip, my eyes widening as I take in the blood-stained jeans and a wad of cash tied with an elastic band. I don't want to touch it, and risk leaving my fingerprints, so I can't count how much is there, but it looks like at least a few thousand dollars.

The discovery does little to calm my nerves as a multitude of explanations swarms my mind. Whatever he's mixed up in, it's dangerous, and I decide it's time to cut and run.

I'm opening the door, just about to slip out of Cam's room, when footsteps approach, forcing me to duck my head back inside. I leave a teeny tiny gap open so I can determine who it is, praying it's not Cam and Rochelle taking the party to a more private setting.

With my heart thundering in my chest, I try to work out if I've enough time to hide in the closet, but it's too late. The footsteps stop outside the room across the way—the office we were in earlier. A long shadow falls across Cam's door, and I hold my breath.

"I've told him," Sawyer grits out. "What the hell else do you want me to do?!" I can't determine if he's with someone I can't see yet or talking on the phone.

"He knows," he says after a few silent beats, and I deduce he's talking on his cell because I'm only hearing one side of the conversation. "It's weird," he continues. "He's weird with her. About her." He sighs, and the wall rattles as he leans back against it. "He's obsessed, and *that's* driving his behavior not what we've told him. He's veering off plan, and the longer this goes on, the more of a loose cannon he becomes."

He pushes off the wall and I watch as he inserts the key in the office door. "Well, you fucking try then," he hisses down the line before disappearing into the room, slamming the door shut behind him.

I wait a couple of minutes, ensuring the coast is clear, before I sneak out into the hallway, slowly shutting Cam's door so I make no noise.

Deciding to forgo snooping in Sawyer's room, because it's too risky, and he's the least likely to leave anything lying around for me to find, I tiptoe quietly toward the stairs.

I'm on the third step when the office door swings open behind me and Sawyer steps out into the hallway. "I'll call you back," he says, and I silently curse under my breath.

Shit. Crap. Fuck.

"You want to tell me what the hell you're doing Abigail?"

CHAPTER SEVENTEEN

I wet my dry lips, planting a nonplussed look on my face as I turn to face him. "I was halfway down the driveway when I needed to pee, so I turned around and came back inside to use the bathroom."

He narrows his eyes at me. "Do I look like an idiot?"

Does he really want me to answer that? "What?" I flutter my eyelashes and bite down on my lip, flashing him an innocent smile. "You don't believe me?"

He bores a hole in my skull staring at me with his usual intensity plus an added layer of suspicion piled on top. I stare back at him, keeping a pleasant, non-guilty look on my face. "Let's talk." He points at the third locked bedroom. "In there."

I say nothing as I follow him into his room, stifling my grin as I drink in my surroundings when he flips on the light.

It's exactly how I thought it would be.

Clinical and devoid of any personality.

A dark navy comforter looks freshly laundered on his massive bed. Two wooden tables with lamps rest on either side of the bed. There's a large closet, a desk with overhead shelves like in the two other rooms, and a leather recliner chair resides in front of a mammoth TV.

But that's it.

There are no adornments and no personal belongings.

No items out in plain sight on his desk.

No framed photos or posters on the walls.

No trophies or bloody clothing.

It gives zero clue to the enigma that is Sawyer Hunt.

"Is something amusing?" He quirks a brow, watching me survey his room.

"Your room is exactly how I expected it to be."

"And how is that?"

"Perfectly presented yet giving nothing away." I hold his gaze. "A lot like its owner."

"And how would you describe Lauder and Marshall's bedrooms?"

I flutter my eyelashes, smiling. "I'd have to see them first to offer my opinion."

One corner of his mouth lifts as he sits down on the end of the bed, patting the space beside him. "Come sit."

He removes his silk tie, folding it neatly and placing it on the bed, before rolling the sleeves of his blue button-down shirt up to the elbows as I sit right beside him, placing my bulging purse on the other side of me. His eyes land on my bag, and I'm expecting him to snatch it up to examine the contents, but he doesn't.

Placing his hands on top of his black slacks, he leans slightly forward, angling his body so he's looking me directly in the eye. It's his preferred method of communication, as if he's always primed to interrogate, and I can imagine him working for the CIA or the FBI someday.

"You're not exactly dressed for a party," I blurt, conscious our thighs are brushing together.

"Likewise," he instantly replies, his eyes dropping low on my body for a split second.

"I didn't know I was coming here, or I would've dressed appropriately, but you live here. Yet you still dressed like that."

"I had a meeting before this, and I haven't had time or the inclination to change."

"Will you work in your father's business after you leave school?" I inquire, wondering if that's why he's dressed like he's just spent a day in the office.

"After I graduate from Stanford, yes."

"Is that something you choose to do, or it's expected?"

"It's both. I would never commit to something I didn't want to do."

"You're lucky you have a choice."

There's a pregnant pause, and he stares at me. "There are *always* choices. Even if it doesn't seem like that."

"Why does that sound like some kind of hidden message?" I ask, instinctively leaning closer to him. I might've been wrong in my assessment before. Sawyer was the least interesting to me previously, coming across as dull and boring, but I'm sensing that's because he holds his cards close to his chest. He's a lot like Charlie in that regard. And they share a pragmatic sense of obligation too.

He moves his face closer to mine, and his hazel eyes are more green than brown today with little flecks of golden elevating them from ordinary to extraordinary. At this proximity, I can also make out the light smattering of freckles across his nose and cheeks, and I'm betting he was adorably cute as a little boy. His spicy cologne swirls around me, and I relax, which is dangerous because he's no less of a predator than the other two jerks.

"Because maybe it is." He tucks a stray lock of hair behind my ear while burrowing his gaze into mine.

Butterflies scatter in my chest as his piercing gaze does funny things to me. When we're this close, his intensity is less intimidating and more intimate somehow. "Is this some new angle? Because Camden's humiliation tactics aren't enough?"

He shakes his head. "I'm being truthful, and Cam is doing what he thinks he must, but that's not who he really is."

I snort. "Yeah. Sure."

"His reactions to you are deeply entrenched, but he's conflicted."

"Conflicted how?"

He trails the tip of his finger around my jawline, and I suck in a sharp breath as his electrifying touch heightens all my senses. "He's conditioned to hate you," he admits in a softer tone, his eyes fixating on my mouth. I'm not sure if that admission is deliberate or unplanned, and I've no clue if it's genuine, but I don't want to lose this connection or whatever the hell is happening between us right now. Not if it'll give me the answers I need.

Slowly, I raise my hand, running my fingers lightly through the silky strands of his dark brown hair. "Why?" I whisper. "Why does he hate me so much?"

Sawyer rubs his thumb across my lower lip, and I'm scarcely breathing at this point. Indecision flickers in his eyes but I know not to push it. So, I wait, trailing my fingers through his hair as he continues to rub his thumb across my lip while staring at my mouth. "Have you ever considered that maybe we're on the same side?"

My heart thuds behind my rib cage, fear constricting my oxygen supply as I contemplate whether they've discovered my secret. "What do you mean?"

"Maybe we—"

"What the fuck?" Cam roars, and I jump as the door to the bedroom slams viciously against the wall.

He's standing there like an unholy vision, oozing danger and aggression from every pore, and his commanding presence devours all the oxygen in the room. His jeans are hugging his slim hips, his shirt still undone, showcasing his beautiful body, and it's impossible not to stare.

The potency of our attraction is undeniable at this moment, and our eyes lock together as if drawn by some magnetic force.

Sawyer slowly removes his thumb from my mouth, purposely adjusting himself in his pants as he stands, cocking a brow and smirking at his friend. "You're interrupting," he coolly says, his eyes darting to mine, breaking the standoff with Cam.

Cam stalks into the room, nostrils flaring and eyes burning with rage. "What is she doing in your bedroom? I thought she fucking left!"

He speaks as if I'm not in the room, eyeballing his friend and blatantly ignoring me, and it's just another form of intimidation.

Well, fuck this shit.

I've had enough for one day.

I snatch up my purse and stand. "I came back, asshole." I prod my finger into his arm. "You might've noticed if you hadn't been otherwise preoccupied," I snarl.

Visions of Rochelle blowing him resurrect in painful clarity in my mind, and I glare at him, pouring every ounce of hate in my heart into my expression.

A cruel smile tugs up the corners of his mouth as understanding dawns, and I want to hurt him. To rake my nails across his flesh until I draw blood. Rip out his ball sack and feed it to sharks. Bite, slap, and punch him until he's a messy, broken pulp at my feet.

The craving to inflict pain is unlike anything I've felt before, and that's saying a lot because I *am* engaged to Trent and I regularly want to beat on his ass.

But violence isn't an option, so I do the next best thing.

Stretching up, I fling my arms around Sawyer's neck, catching him completely off guard as I plant one on him. It's a hard, brutal kiss. One laced with every venomous emotion festering inside me. If he minds, he doesn't act like it, kissing me back without hesitation.

When I pull back, I run my hand along his chest, smiling at him as if my world starts and ends with him. "Thank you. For the talk and…" I let it hang in the air, delighted he doesn't call my bluff, wondering if maybe we *are* on the same side.

I shoot a scathing look at Cam, deliberately shoulder-checking him as I walk out of Sawyer's bedroom, thrilled at the angry, frustrated expression contorting his beautiful face. I know he'll punish me for it, but, for now, I'm claiming it as a win.

"Girl, you're playing with fire. Are you sure you know what you're doing?" Jane asks the following morning as we stroll along the beach after breakfast.

"Yes. No. I don't know." I sigh, picking up a stone and skimming it across the surface of the water. A gentle breeze whips my hair around my shoulders as we resume walking.

"What if they tell Trent? He'll go apeshit on your ass." She pins me with a worried expression. "And then he'll wage an even bigger war on the new guys. Not that I'm opposed to that. I hate those assholes for what they did to me. What they're continuing to do to *you*, but I don't want you to suffer any more than you have."

"If they say anything to Trent, I'll lie my way out. He knows they're sniffing around me, so it won't take much to convince him they're winding him up. The only witness with Jackson was Oscar, and he'd never rat me out. I made out with Cam in my car in an empty parking lot, and I kissed Sawyer in his room. Even if Cam confirmed it, Trent would expect that and not find it believable."

"I still can't believe you've kissed all three."

"It's not like I planned it. And I hate them." I fling another stone out to sea. "I really do." Except maybe Sawyer. I glimpsed something last night, and I don't think he's as bad as the others.

"But you're attracted to them too."

I think about that for a few moments while we walk, smiling at an elderly couple out walking their dog as they pass by with their arms linked.

I'm not really into Sawyer or Jackson. Sure, they're hot guys, and it could be fun, but it's nothing deep. Neither of them ignites an inferno in my body, throws my mind into complete chaos, or sends my heart into a wild tailspin like Cam does.

I hate that I'm so attracted to him.

That the chemistry between us is palpable.

That I can't stop thinking about him.

And I'm worried what it says about me because he's bullied me, groped me, and humiliated me in public.

Yet I still crave his touch.

Long to feel his body moving against, and inside, mine again.

I loathe how badly I want him.

And how much last night sickened and upset me.

I've never once thought about Rochelle touching Trent, but I spent most of last night curled into my pillow with a piercing pain stabbing my chest as images of her with Cam tormented me for hours. I hate that she touched him intimately, and I tortured myself imagining what else happened after I left.

Did he trade places with Jackson and fuck her too?

Or fuck the other girl?

Fuck both of them?

I feel nauseous at the thought, and what kind of sick bitch does that make me?

Perhaps there is more of my father in me than I like to believe because it's the kind of fucked-up shit he'd get off on.

"You look troubled," Jane says, looping her arm through mine and squeezing.

"Do you think I'm screwed up like my father?"

"What?" She slams to a halt, forcing me to face her. "No! You are nothing like that monster."

"Then why do I want Camden Marshall so badly? How can I hate him for everything he's done and still want his hands all over me?"

I shake my head, hating this confusion. I wish I could tell her I lost my virginity to him, but I'm scared of giving her that knowledge. I know if I asked her to keep it from my brother she would, but it wouldn't be fair of me to ask her to do that, and I worry it'd come back to bite her.

When it comes out, and it *will*—hopefully, when I'm a million miles away from here—I don't want her to know anything. When my father grills her, I want her to look him in the eye and say she didn't know and for it to be the truth, so he takes nothing out on her.

So, as much as I want to confide in my best friend, I say nothing.

"You can't help who you fall for. Just like you can't force yourself to feel things for Trent."

I loop my arm in hers again, pulling her forward. "If only it were that simple."

CHAPTER EIGHTEEN

"**I** come bearing gifts," I say, plonking into the chair beside Xavier, handing him a coffee and doughnut.

"Thanks. I'm starving. Been at this for hours."

I kiss his cheek. "Thank you. I appreciate it."

"We still need stuff for two of the envelopes."

"That's why I'm here," I say, sipping on my coffee. "Put me to work."

"I have your workstation set up and ready to go." He points to the screen directly in front of me. "But tell me about this other information you want me to investigate."

I show him the pics I took in the guys' bedrooms last night asking if he can identify the other boys from the photo and find out exactly what happened to Jackson's sister. "There's one other thing too." I drain my coffee, tossing the empty paper cup in the trashcan. "Camden let something slip. He mentioned he had an older brother, but you said he was an only child."

He nods. "It's well documented. He *is* an only child."

"That makes no sense. Why would he say he had an older brother if he didn't?"

Xavier looks contemplative. "Maybe he had a cousin or a best friend who lived with them and he considered him a brother?"

"Or maybe there was another child, and he died?" I suggest, because that's where my mind wandered. "And why does the world think the guys only met two years ago at the academy when this picture shows they've known each other for longer?"

He scrubs a hand over the scruff on his chin. "It's puzzling, but we'll get to the bottom of it. Leave it with me." He purses his lips and frowns. "I'll add it to the long list of things I have to do for you."

I nudge him in the ribs. "I pay you extremely well."

"You do."

"And I'm your favorite client."

"You'll be my only client at this rate," he murmurs, tapping away on his keyboard. "Senior year is kicking my butt already, and I won't have much downtime coming up to exams."

Xavier isn't from around here, and he only moved to Boston when he graduated high school three years ago. He attends Rydeville University on a full scholarship, thanks to his nerdy tech brain. "You should consider yourself privileged."

"With you, I already do." I smack a kiss off his cheek again. "And I know you secretly love me," I tease.

"If I was into chicks, you'd be it for me." He winks, and we both laugh.

He shows me where he's set everything up, and I scroll through files until I find a few clues and follow the trail, compiling evidence and printing it off before sealing it in the envelopes, carefully writing the names on the outside.

Xavier has been busy finishing his presentation, and he hands me a USB key when I'm ready to leave. "Just plug it into your laptop and insert the password I'll send to your cell. Then you'll be good to go. Any issues, call me."

I hug him. "Thanks for this, and I will."

I move to ease out of his arms, but he keeps hold of me, peering at me with a troubled expression on his face. The silver ring in his eyebrow glints as it catches the light. "You'd tell me if you were in danger, right?"

I offer him an amused smile. "I'm in danger every day, Xavier. You know who my father is. What his associates are capable of. What lies in store for me if I go through with the wedding to Trent." I cup one side of his face. "It's why I made the deal with you. It's why you're trying to find something I can blackmail my father with so he'll leave me alone once I leave Rydeville."

"You could leave *now*. I can make it happen. With my skills, and my contacts, I can hide you. I can keep you safe."

"I want to believe that so badly, but my mother tried to escape, and she paid for it with her life. I owe it to her to learn from her mistakes. The only way I can make this happen is to hold something over him. Something that would ruin him. Even then, he might still hunt me down, but it's insurance, and it should at least buy me some time." I kiss his forehead. "I love you for caring so much, but I can't leave until we have something to blackmail him with."

"I'm worried we're running out of time."

I exhale loudly, shucking out of his arms. "I know. I constantly feel like there's a ticking time bomb strapped to my back."

"And I don't like this new elite. I have a bad feeling they'll make a shitty situation even shittier."

I clasp his face in my palms. "Which is why we'll find something to use against them." I drop my hands, pulling out my cell. "I almost forgot to tell you. I planted the chip on Sawyer's cell last night. I'm texting you his number now."

"Fucking A!" He fist pumps the air. "I'll load the surveillance feed right now."

I prop my butt on the edge of the long desk. "What exactly will it give us?"

"Access to all his texts and messages, and we can listen to live calls. I should also be able to trace all activity on his cell, so whatever he's browsing, apps he's using, etcetera."

The biggest grin spreads over my mouth. "Let's hope we get something fast. The situation at school is getting out of hand."

"This should help rectify that," he says, gesturing at the five envelopes in my hand.

"It will. But that's only one part of the problem. I need to get those guys off my back before they release that recording." Xavier is aware they are using Jane to manipulate me although I still haven't told him about my non-virginity status and the fact Cam is also using that to force my hand.

"I'm working on hacking into their systems, but it's proving challenging because all their shit is encrypted and hidden behind badass firewalls thanks to Techxet's latest malware software, but I'll keep at it. I promise."

I press a kiss to the top of his head. "I have faith in you and your mad skills." I waggle my fingers at him. "I'll call you later to tell you how it went."

"You got this, babe," he says, blowing me a kiss before burying his head in his computer.

"What is this?" Chad asks, staring at the envelope with his name on it.

"If everyone could take a seat," I suggest, waving my hands toward the couches.

Oscar helped me set up this makeshift office in one of the old living rooms we no longer use. We pushed the stuffy couches to one corner to make way for the desks and chairs I ordered. A large screen is screwed to the wall over the ornate fireplace, and every workstation has a MacBook Pro, a printer, stationery supplies, bottles of water, and snacks. Investigative work is hungry work, especially with the amount of testosterone in the air.

"Don't open those yet," I tell the four boys and two girls. I'd asked Chad to find a small, trustworthy group loyal to the elite, and he delivered.

Which is why I hate giving him that envelope, but I'm taking no chances. Too much is at stake.

When they are all seated, I sit on the arm of one couch, facing them. "Thank you so much for coming here today and for agreeing to help even though you don't know what's involved. I value and appreciate your loyalty and support."

I clear my throat, eyeballing each person. "What I'm asking of you is illegal, but I can assure you no one will find out it involved you unless anyone in this room squeals." I peer into Chad's eyes, beseeching him to understand. "What's in those envelopes is insurance. It will mutually benefit all of us. Ensure that what happens in this room stays in this room."

I place my hands on my knees. "Certain members of the inner circle, and others at school, seem to have forgotten their place in the order of things. Forgotten the importance of abiding by the rules and traditions that have governed Rydeville High for years. The new elite is causing waves, and we must stop them. I'm dealing with them myself, but you'll help me regain control and restore authority and order to school."

"How?" the pretty girl with the cute strawberry-blonde pixie haircut asks.

"It's Emily, right?" I say, recognizing her from my AP world history class. All I know of her is that she's quiet, super smart, and keeps to herself.

I already like her.

She nods.

"Every person has secrets," I say, standing and slowly pacing. "Secrets are weaknesses, and we're going to exploit those weaknesses to gain the upper hand."

"We're spying on people?" Adam Vitte asks, his eyes popping with interest.

"Yes. I will give each of you a list of names, and your job is to hack into their private and school systems and dig up dirt. Internet research is also remarkably useful. Especially if the secrets are more of a family nature. We need to find one thing to threaten each person with."

"And are these empty threats, or you plan to follow through?" Chad inquires, looking noticeably worried, and I understand why.

"I will follow through if I'm ignored or challenged, but I have a plan. I will make an example of a couple of people, and that, combined with the evidence we uncover, should be enough to scare the others into toeing the line."

"This sounds vindictive," the girl with the fiery-red hair says. "And I'm not very comfortable with that."

"This isn't revenge. It's survival, and you're involved now. There's no backing down."

Tense silence filters through the air, and it's time to nail their allegiance. "Open your envelopes. Take your time perusing the contents," I add, walking to the coffee station at the top of the room and brewing a fresh pot.

Chad jumps up, his face puce, stalking toward me with transparent fear etched upon his face. "Can I talk to you outside?" I set my coffee cup down and follow him out into the hallway. "How the hell did you get hold of this?" he asks, shaking the crumpled papers between his clenched fist.

"I hacked into your computer and downloaded the photos from

your hard drive. It really wasn't difficult at all. You need to be more careful if you want no one else finding out."

"That file was password protected!"

"We have software which decrypts most passwords. Only systems with high-end tech are secure."

His chest heaves, pain glimmering in his eyes, and guilt presses down on me. "Chad." I move in closer to him, staring him straight in the eye. "I'll tell no one. I know you won't betray me, so that information will never see the light of day. I promise."

"So why do it then?" he croaks, now visibly shaking.

"Because I'm putting myself on the line, and I need insurance. It's not personal. You know this is the way things work."

"Please don't tell Trent, Drew, or Charlie. They respect me and—"

I take his shaking hands in mine. "Drew and Charlie would still respect you if they found out you're gay, but Trent's a homophobic asshole who would ruin you. I know that as well as you do. I won't tell any of them. Contrary to what most people think of me, I don't enjoy hurting others. I swear you have nothing to fear if you don't cross me."

He bobs his head, and air whooshes out of his mouth. "Okay."

"Chad." I grip both sides of his head, forcing him to eyeball me. "I swear it will go no further. You can trust me." I scan his face. "Can I trust you?"

"With your life, Abigail."

Sincerity drips from his words and oozes from his expression, and I believe him. I nod, smiling. "So, we're good?"

"Yeah, we're good." He smiles too, and his shoulders visibly relax. "C'mon then. We've got work to do."

It shocked the others at how easily I uncovered the skeletons in their closets, but if anyone was wavering before, they're not now.

I play the presentation Xavier compiled with step-by-step

instructions on how to conduct online investigations, explaining basic hacking techniques and how the software he installed works, and everyone is focused and attentive as they watch.

Holding people to proverbial ransom works every time.

It also never ceases to make me feel like a worthless piece of shit, because resorting to manipulation and blackmail is my father's go-to strategy, and I hate I'm forced to use those tactics too.

But there's a bigger picture here, and my life is on the line, so I do what I must.

We work late, making great progress, and when I call it a night at ten p.m., we have almost a third of the envelopes prepped.

I move everyone out to the pool house, which is a lot more modern, and a lot more comfortable, than the main house.

I convinced Daddy Dearest to upgrade it last year after failing to persuade him to modernize the mausoleum we live in. He refuses to change anything in the house, spouting the usual traditional bullshit. I know from looking at old photo albums that the current design has been around for centuries, and it shows.

I'd live out here if father permitted it, but he's denied my request every time I've asked.

I take in the sumptuous surroundings as I fix drinks for everyone with a surge of pride swelling my chest. I hired Alex Kennedy's interior design company to handle the remodeling, and I got a real kick out of meeting her in the flesh, explaining how Mom had been a big fan of her Kennedy Apparel brand when she was alive. Every time I come in here, a genuine smile crosses my face as I think of how much Mom would love what Alex did with the place. It has her signature style stamped all over it.

I distribute drinks, and we shoot the shit, while watching a movie and eating pizza, and I can't remember the last time I felt so at ease.

I silently question why I've kept these people at arm's length for so long. As part of the inner circle, even Father wouldn't openly criticize me for hanging out with them; although he'd draw the line at any close friendships, because in his mind their families are inferior to the main elite even with their wealth and social standing.

We repeat the process the next day and a couple of evenings that week after school, and by Thursday night, we have everything ready.

Now, it's showtime.

CHAPTER NINETEEN

All week, I've been getting Cam's lunch even though I want to stab him in the eye with his fork every day when he smirks as I slide a tray in front of him like he's fucking royalty.

And every day, without fail, that bitch Rochelle is a permanent fixture on his lap. I can't wait to wipe that smug, superior grin off her face. We're taking this weekend to run over the plans one final time, and we'll execute first thing Monday morning. Until then, I'm acting like a loyal slave even if it's chipping away at my soul, bit by bit.

Sawyer is aloof, as usual, and Jackson is being his normal flirty self. Apart from that, the guys are lying low, and I'm keeping my head down too, pretending like I don't notice how most everyone has defected to support our enemy and how much they enjoy taunting me as they grow braver in the absence of the guys.

I'll enjoy watching them come crawling back on their hands and knees.

The triad is waiting for me at my locker when school ends Friday, surrounded by adoring groupies fawning over their every word. It's pathetic how these girls throw themselves at them with zero shame, self-control, or self-respect.

I shove my way through the crowd, ignoring the guys, as Jane and I get books out of our lockers. Without a glance in their direction, I link arms with my bestie and attempt to walk off, but someone fists a hand in the back of my jacket, reeling me back. My book bag slips off my shoulder onto the floor, and I sway unsteadily on my heels before an arm wraps around my waist, and I'm hauled against a hard chest. "Careful, beautiful. Don't want you falling and messing up that pretty face."

I shove Jackson's arm off and spin around. "Aw, you think I'm pretty?" I flutter my eyelashes and deliberately pout. "I think you're pretty too," I add with a sly smile, deliberately pausing for a beat. "Pretty fucking gross."

"Now, we both know that's a downright lie." He steps all up in my private space. "You didn't think it was gross when my tongue was licking the inside of your mouth or when I had your ass cheeks cupped in the palms of my hands," he murmurs, nipping at my earlobe.

I spy Rochelle scowling out of the corner of my eye, and I can't resist winding her up. Placing my palms on his chest, I stretch up so I can whisper in his ear. "I was referring to the fact you stuck your disease-ridden dick in that whore's saggy cunt." I ease back, shaking my head as a shiver works its way through me. "Ugh. I thought you had more class than that."

He grabs me to him, grinning like a maniac. "If I didn't know better, I'd say you're jealous. But that couldn't be right, because you're engaged to the love of your life." He quirks a brow, grinning knowingly, and I push him away, knowing it's time to end this convo before it turns nasty. I take my bag from Jane as she shoots me a worried look, propping a hand on my hip, and leveling the guys with a "get a move on it" look.

"Leave us," Cam instructs the fangirls, and they scatter like dust in the wind but not before sending me scathing glares. Rochelle doesn't budge, looping her arm through Cam's and sticking her tongue out at me like she's reverted to six years old. Cam turns to her with an icy look. "Are you deaf?" he growls in that mean, gruff tone of his which never fails to heat my blood and stir my desire.

I'm still fucked in the head when it comes to him.

She flinches, the smug grin slowly disappearing from her face. "Surely, you don't mean me?"

He growls at her. "You're getting on my last fucking nerve." He throws her arm away.

"Get lost, Rochelle," Jackson supplies, clicking his fingers dismissively. "You're not wanted."

"And she is?" she fumes, jabbing her finger in the air at me.

Cam grips her chin. "Who said you could question us?"

Jackson moves behind her, and she's trapped between both assholes but not in a good way. "The only time you should open that mouth is to suck cock," Jackson says. "Otherwise, keep your mouth closed and your opinions to yourself."

I resist the urge to tell her I told you so, and I don't gloat either. I take a leaf out of Sawyer's book and adopt a disinterested look. "I've got plans, so whatever you need to say, say it now or I'm gone," I supply, eyeballing Cam.

He releases Rochelle's face, walking away without a second glance. "You're coming with us." He takes my elbow and steers me forward.

"I'm coming too," Jane pipes up, shooting hostile vibes at all three boys.

"No!" I glance over my shoulder at her. "Take the car and go home. I'll text Oscar and call you later."

"Abby. Please."

"Run along now, cutie," Jackson says, squeezing her waist. "I'm sure you have plans too." He waggles his brows, and a naughty glint appears in his eye. "Like hot, naked, phone sex with your fiancé."

All the color drains from my face as I shoot daggers in Jackson's direction. Jane's face turns fire-engine red, and Jackson chuckles.

"You're an asshole," I snap.

"So you've said." He winks, placing his hand on Jane's lower back as he moves her forward.

"I'll be fine," I reassure her when we reach the door. "Just go." I kiss her cheek, giving her a gentle nudge toward the car waiting at the bottom of the steps.

Cam moves to take my elbow again, but I sidestep him. "Unless you want my bodyguard all over your ass, I suggest you stop manhandling me." I plant my hands on my hips, challenging him with my expression. "Where are you taking me, anyway?"

"It's a surprise," Jackson singsongs, swatting my butt as he eyeballs Oscar with a grin. My bodyguard is now out of the car, a perplexed look puckering his brow.

I sigh. "Give me a minute to fix this."

"I'll pull the car around," Sawyer says, skipping down the steps.

I walk toward Oscar with a sunny smile planted firmly on my face. "I've got a group assignment to finish with the guys. I'll get one of them to drop me home after."

"Is everything okay, Ms. Abigail?" he asks, glowering at Cam and Jackson over my shoulder.

"Everything is fine. Stop worrying. Just make sure Jane gets home safe."

He rubs a hand across the back of his neck. "Your father will kill me if he discovers you're hanging out with the new elite."

"He's not here, and he won't find out. This is one of those times when I need you to turn a blind eye, Oscar." Indecision washes over his face. "Trust me. Please. I've got this, and Drew is fully aware."

"Call me if anything happens. And watch your back. I don't trust those punks."

That makes two of us, buddy.

I press a kiss to his cheek. "They won't hurt me," I lie. "Stop worrying."

Sawyer pulls his Land Rover to a halt at the curb, and I wave at Oscar as I get in. Cam rides shotgun while Jackson gets in the back with me, sitting way too close for comfort. But it's part of his M.O. and I don't move because that would give him the upper hand and I'm already weak in their eyes.

"You're friendly with the help," he teases. "You banging him?"

I pin him with a disgusted look. "You're unbelievable. He's older than my father!" I ram my elbow in his side. "And I don't use sex as a bartering tool. Unlike some."

"Yet you're keeping him in line," Cam says, turning around in his seat. "If you're not using your body, how are you manipulating him?"

I fold my arms over my chest and smirk at him. "That's for me to know and you to find out."

"Our little virgin is keeping more secrets," he taunts.

"Stop calling me that when you know it's not true."

"I'm curious," he says, smoothing a hand over his skull tattoo. "Have you fucked anyone since me?"

"Wouldn't you like to know," I drawl.

"That's why I asked." He cocks a brow, waiting for me to answer.

"Aw, you're worried you didn't measure up."

An arrogant smirk appears on his face. "We both know I fucking rocked your world." He licks his lips, and I hate how my eyes greedily follow the motion. "I'm just wondering if the rumors are true."

"Okay, I'll bite," I say, leaning forward. "What rumors?"

"That you're fucking Trent's ole man behind his back," Jackson replies.

"I'd die before I touch that sleazebag," I hiss, shuddering as my stomach simultaneously twists into painful knots. A muscle ticks in Cam's jaw as he penetrates me with his piercing brown eyes, and Sawyer glances at me through the mirror with a slight frown. Rage is a slow burn in my veins as I consider the shit people are spreading about me. "Let me guess," I say through gritted teeth. "That bitch started the rumor."

Jackson chuckles. "She sure hates you."

"Believe me, the feeling is mutual."

Any last-minute guilt evaporates. Rochelle deserves everything coming to her, and I can't wait to see her face on Monday as her world falls apart.

Sawyer pulls up in front of a diner downtown, killing the engine and getting out. He opens my door, offering me his hand, and Jackson sniggers. I take hold of his warm hand, letting him help me out. "Thank you."

He smiles, and it reaches his eyes. Wonders will never cease.

We take a booth in the back of the diner, and Cam slides into one side after me while Sawyer and Jackson sit across from us. After the waitress has taken our order, we get down to business.

"I still can't crack your dad's password," Sawyer says, keeping his voice low. "You've got to give me more to work with."

"I've sent you hundreds of suggestions. I don't see what else I can do." Xavier has a massive file of passwords we've already tried, and I'm sending some each day to Sawyer to keep them off my back.

No one speaks as the waitress sets our drinks down, doing little to disguise her blatant ogling of the guys.

And I get it.

They're hot as fuck and hard not to drool over.

Even I'm struggling to keep my emotions in check, but at least try to be subtle about it, girl!

"It might help if I knew what you were looking for," I say, taking a sip of my sparkling water.

"We want to search his computer, *and* we need access to his home office," Sawyer says, being vague on purpose.

I shake my head. "I can't help you with that. He has cameras all over his study, and he locks everything away in his safe." I know because I've already searched the place from top to bottom, and he leaves nothing incriminating lying around.

"You know how to alter the camera feeds so you can cover our tracks," Sawyer says, and my spidey senses are on full alert.

How does he know that, or is he just assuming?

"Even if I got you in there, you won't find anything. He isn't stupid enough to leave important stuff lying around."

Cam sighs heavily, his leg tapping anxiously off the ground. "We need something to go on because this is taking too long."

"Again, if you told me what you're looking for, I might offer more helpful suggestions," I snap.

Cam slams his clenched fist down on the table. "This is getting tiresome, and none of us are buying the helpless little girl act."

"I'm not acting." I stare deep into his eyes. "You seem to have vastly misjudged my father. You have no idea what you are up against. *None.*" I let my gaze drift between them. "Whatever you're after, whatever you're planning, you need to up your game because your current strategy won't cut it."

"Those cabinets store all the microfilm by year, categorized by local and national news," the helpful librarian explains, showing me row upon row of filing cabinets that occupy the back portion of the red-bricked building, which houses our town's only library. "Select which film you want, and bring it to one of those machines. The instruction sheet taped to the side explains how to load the film and navigate through the images."

"Okay, thanks. I think I can figure it out."

"I'm Mary. Come find me if you run into difficulty, Abigail."

"I will. Thank you again for your time."

She leaves me alone in this empty section of the library, and I walk through the rows until I come to the nineteen eighties, deciding to start there. I skim my fingers over the boxes of files until I come to a box marked nineteen eighty-seven, and I take it with me, sitting down at a machine and loading the film per the instructions.

It takes an hour to locate the article from the *Gazette* that accompanied the photo Xavier found online—the one that showed my parents with Trent's and Charlie's fathers, Atticus Anderson, and Emma and Wesley Marshall.

The article talks about Rydeville High's annual sports day and family barbecue, including mention of the founding fathers and their successors, but it contains nothing useful, and my hope deflates. I spend another hour randomly scanning through various microfilm until I switch the machine off and sit back to think.

I didn't realize there would be so much information to wade through. I could easily spend years of my life in front of this machine with nothing to show for it. I chew on the corner of my pen as I cogitate ideas.

I need a more structured research plan.

One that is likely to yield results in the shortest timeframe. Removing my notepad and pen from my bag, I start a list.

Old Elite – Parents:
Michael Hearst
Olivia Hearst -Manning (deceased)

Christian Montgomery
Sylvia Montgomery (nee Fleming)

Charles Barron II
Elizabeth Barron (nee Dasher)

Atticus Anderson
Emma Anderson (nee Marshall – deceased)

New Elite - parents:
Wesley Marshall
Ruth Marshall (nee Winston)

Ethan Hunt
Ava Hunt (nee Synnott)

Travis Lauder
Laurena Lauder (nee Vergara)

The new elite have some beef with my father—that much is clear—and considering how interconnected they all are, it makes sense to delve into our parents' backgrounds.

My gut is telling me the answers I seek lie there, and I've learned to listen to that intelligent inner voice, so I focus on the four founding families and the Marshalls because they are all tied to Rydeville. I'm not sure what part the Hunts and Lauders play, but I'll leave them till last for the moment.

But where exactly to start?

I ruminate for a little longer, and then I focus on births, marriages, and deaths as a logical starting point and work from there.

I know my father was born in nineteen seventy-two and my

mother the year after, so it makes sense to focus on those two years as they were all in school together, so they must have been born within that timeframe.

Mary comes to my aid again, pulling out two huge dusty old leather books and hauling them to her office for me to go through. She seems to have bought my lie this is research for a history assignment and doesn't bat an eye when I open up my iPad to type notes.

It takes hours to scroll through the ledgers, but by closing time, I've a list of birth dates, parents and grandparents' names, and while it could be a complete dead end, at least it feels like a start.

Unfortunately, the library isn't open on Sundays, so I'll have to wait until next weekend to come back and scroll through the marriage and death records. They were all scanned from nineteen ninety, so it should be easier and quicker to search by microfilm.

I drop my bag in the back seat of my car, opening my two cells for the first time in hours. I'd muted both to avoid distractions, so I'm only seeing the multitude of missed calls and texts from Xavier now. I sit in my car in the empty parking lot outside the library and return his call.

"About damn time, woman! I've been calling you nonstop."

"Where's the fire?"

"I've intercepted a message from Hunt to Marshall. Something's going down tonight, and I think we should check it out."

"*We?*" I ask in an incredulous voice because Xavier has made it clear, time and time again, that he's most comfortable behind a screen not doing field work, as he likes to call it.

"Yes. *We.* They're going to the Grid, and I'm not letting you go there alone."

"What's the Grid?"

"It's an underground fight club in Marbay, notorious for illegal fighting. Rich assholes with deep pockets bet heavy, and as it's unsanctioned, it gets vicious. The crowd is crazy, and it's not unheard of for fighting to break out among the audience. Hell will freeze before I'd let you get within a mile of that place alone."

"Okay, you've made your point. What time am I picking you up at?"

"These things start late, so drop by about ten thirty."

"It's a date."

CHAPTER TWENTY

"I'm not getting on that thing," Xavier grumbles, crossing his arms over his chest and glaring at my beloved motorcycle. "They are fucking deathtraps."

"You wouldn't say that if you'd ever ridden on one," I reply, handing him a helmet. "Because the feel of the wind swirling around you, and the exhilaration as your body moves as one with the bike, is unlike anything you've ever experienced. Honestly, it's the biggest thrill."

He still doesn't look convinced, and I chuckle. "What's so funny?"

"You." I wave my hands in front of his persona. "You look like this wild, reckless punk with your blue hair, ink, and piercings, but really, you're a big, squishy softie."

He flips me the bird. "Less of the squishy, please." He pokes a finger in his lean stomach. "These abs are solid, babe."

"I'll take your word for it." I grin. "Now, are you going to continue to act like a baby or grow a pair?"

"I'll get on your fucking deathtrap. No need to insult me." He mock pouts.

"Just get on the bike, and quit your bitching and moaning." I roll my eyes as I tuck my hair into a ponytail and pull my helmet on.

Xavier has his arms wrapped so tight around my waist it's a miracle I'm still breathing, but at least he isn't screaming or demanding to get off.

When we arrive at the main street in Marbay, he directs me toward the shoreline, and then we take a succession of narrow back roads, venturing farther away from the residential parts of town. We pass vast, empty fields, devoid of all signs of life, until we come to a crossroads, and he points at me to take a winding, bumpy road on the left, surrounded on both sides by leafy woodland.

Our bodies are repeatedly jostled as I carefully maneuver the bike over rough terrain before coming to a stop when Xavier tugs on my elbow. "Park it behind that tree," he instructs, sliding off and handing me his helmet.

I meet up with him after I've stashed the bike and helmets away from prying eyes, shoving my hands in the pockets of my ripped, skintight black jeans after yanking the hood of my zipped black hoodie up over my head. "What?" I ask, feeling his eyes examining me.

"I don't think I've ever seen you looking grungy." He grins. "You look hot."

I snort. "That wasn't the intention. I want to blend in. The last thing I need is for the guys to find me here."

"You'll fit in, and we'll hang back and observe from the shadows. Whatever happens, don't leave my side. If you need to piss, go in the woods now."

I pin him with a sharp look. "If you think I'd ever pee in public, you don't know me at all. I'm good, but if I wasn't, I'd just hold it."

He chuckles. "Such a badass."

Now it's my turn to flip him the bird.

We walk swiftly but quietly, and my apprehension grows when we emerge from the forested path into a wide-open space cluttered with expensive cars, SUVs, and a few monster trucks.

Music blares from the large warehouse in the near distance, the corrugated-iron roof shaking slightly as the beats literally rock the place. I quirk a brow at Xavier wondering if we're attending a fight or a rave. "Keep your head down, and let me do the talking," he says as we approach the door.

I do as he says, ignoring the beady eyes of the two bulky guys manning the entrance. Both have muscles stacked upon muscles, shaved heads, armfuls of ink, and handguns visibly strapped to their hips. "Hood down," one orders in a guttural voice, and I remove my hood, tilting my chin up with more confidence than I feel as I eyeball him.

"That face is far too pretty to hide," he leers, his eyes raking up and down my body. "And it's rare we see women at these events." Ignoring the urge to retaliate with my words, I school my lips into a neutral line, letting him take his fill.

Xavier hands two tickets to the other guy, and he scans them on a handheld device before snapping red bands around both our wrists and stepping aside to let us enter. I release the breath I was holding, yanking my hood back up again.

"Let your hair down," Xavier whispers "and keep the hood back further on your head so you don't draw attention for all the wrong reasons." I remove my hair tie, letting my wavy tresses fall around my face before loosely covering my head with the hood. Xavier nods his approval, taking my hand and drawing me into the room.

The large open space is packed to the rafters, and intense heat slaps me in the face. Two overhead balconies house lines of rich pricks in expensive suits, standing pompously with drinks in hand, surveying the crowd below. Down here, everyone is standing, heads bobbing to the rock anthems bouncing off the walls, while sipping beers, huddled around a large elevated ring in the center of the room.

The light dims on the crowd, and spotlights illuminate the ring, as Xavier tightens his grip on my hand, maneuvering us to the far side of the room and into an empty space just under the stairs. We can see this side of the crowd and the ring from here, but it's not exactly a prime spot, so we're not surrounded, which hopefully means we can stay relatively hidden.

A loud roar ripples through the room as a man in gray pants and a white button-down shirt, rolled at the elbows, appears in the ring. He shouts into the mic, his loud voice booming around the cavernous space as he rallies the crowd for the first fight.

I scan the masses, looking for any sign of the guys, but I can't find them in the darkly lit overcrowded space. "We'll never find them in here," I holler into Xavier's ear.

He slips something into my hand. "I'll scout the room. You stay here. Keep your head down. Don't budge from this spot. If anyone gives you trouble, press the button, and I'll come straight back."

I nod, and he slinks away as the first two fighters land in the ring.

I watch the sick display with a kind of warped curiosity the entire time Xavier is gone. No one even notices me. They're all too engrossed in the fight.

The barbaric crowd shouts encouragement, hurls insults, and pumps their fists in the air as the bloody fight continues round after round. The two guys are beating the crap out of one another. Fists are flying. Blood is spraying everywhere. And even when they both take tumbles, at different times, they are back on their feet straightaway, eager for more.

Xavier returns as the fight ends with one contender lying unconscious on the ground. The noise from the crowd is deafening when they announce the victor. "Well?" I ask, handing him the device.

He shakes his head. "I didn't spot any of them, but I think I've figured out why," he says, slipping the device into his jeans pocket as the next two fighters advance on the ring.

Time seems to slow down as I watch the men enter the ring, and my pulse kicks up, my eyes drinking in the sight of Cam's naked chest as he stands rigidly still at one side of the ropes, weighing up his opponent with eyes that are equally controlled and reckless.

His contender is no slouch. He's not as tall as Cam, but his shoulders are broader and he's stockier. His shaved head, cold eyes, and hard face scream brutality and adrenaline courses through my veins as unprecedented fear washes over me. "Holy fuck. That guy looks savage. He'll annihilate Cam."

"You sound worried." Xavier cocks a brow, expecting an answer, but I don't give him one.

My feelings for Camden Marshall are a clusterfuck of epic proportions. One I haven't worked out myself yet.

"I overheard a couple of guys talking. Seems Cam is a bit of a legend in the underground New York fighting scene, and there's fierce excitement he's here tonight. Over three hundred K has already been bet on this fight, and I'm guessing there'll be a last-minute rush."

"You can't be serious?"

"As a heart attack," he quips. "I've heard of fights where over a million has been laid down. It's only pocket change for the rich assholes upstairs."

I hold my breath as I watch Cam standing in the center of the ring not moving a muscle. The other guy is bouncing from foot to foot, cricking his neck from side to side and bumping his gloved hands together every few seconds as he snarls in Cam's direction.

Cam is like a statue. Rock solid. Unflinching. Face like stone. Only his dark, disturbed eyes give away the fact he's fully alert and taking it all in.

When the bell chimes, and the fight starts, his opponent charges at Cam, and I watch him dance around the ring, avoiding impact, while making no move to hit the guy.

There's an elegance to the way Cam moves his powerful, ripped body. A fierce determination etched across his face as his lips tug up in amusement. His contender emits a loud roar as the crowd boos, demanding action.

Things ramp up fast. My breath stutters as Cam slams his fist into the guy's face, and he stumbles back, falling against the ropes with blood spurting from his nose. Cam advances on him with ninja speed, landing blow after blow to his face and body, his features contorted into a mass of anger and aggression.

Each strike is calculated.

His body ripples with danger and power, and God help me, but I'm so turned on right now I feel like charging into the ring and climbing his body like a spider monkey.

"Damn," Xavier murmurs in my ear. "Please tell me you're as turned on as I am."

"Guilty as charged," I rasp, never taking my eyes off Cam. He's magnetic, and the same energy pulls me to him even with the distance separating us.

The stocky guy recovers, swinging blindly with his fists, glancing the side of Cam's jaw, forcing him back. Then it's on, and they go at one another with everything they've got.

The crowd is going wild. Beats continue to thump from loudspeakers, and the energy in the air is electrifying. I don't agree with this shit at all, but I'm starting to understand the attraction, the addictive draw.

The guys continue beating one another, and it's a wonder Cam's opponent can see with the blood leaking into his eyes from a nasty gash on his forehead.

Cam's lip is cut, trickling blood, and his left eye is swollen, but he still looks like he could go another hundred rounds. His next punch flattens his opponent to the ground, and then Cam is on top of him, straddling him as he pummels his face and his chest with punches. He doesn't stop, hitting him over and over, even when it's obvious the guy isn't getting up again and the victory is his.

It's a terrifying display of naked aggression that has all the tiny hairs lifting on the back of my neck.

Eventually, someone pulls Cam off him, holding his arm up in the air, confirming his victory.

It's only then I spot Jackson and Sawyer, entering the ring and pulling a sweaty, bloodied, and bruised Cam out of there.

"That dude has serious issues," Xavier says, pulling my hood up more firmly. "And I think we've seen enough. Let's get the fuck out of here."

I don't argue, letting him create a path through the crowd, dragging me by the hand, as I think things through.

I now understand where the bloody jeans and the bundle of cash in Cam's closet came from. Although tonight's display was scary, in a sexy, weirdly arousing manner, it's a relief to know he's not a murderer. Not that I ever truly believed that, but the thought had crossed my mind.

Cam hasn't shown me anything of his true self since he arrived in town. He's completely guarded, giving nothing away, and it's bugged me. He's content to play the sneering, guarded bully, and it's a role he plays to perfection. But I've suspected it's a front, because that's not the guy I met at the beach all those months ago. And, tonight, I saw another side of him. A side that's completely at odds with the sweet guy who claimed my virginity.

Tonight, I witnessed his pain. His deep-seated anger. The self-torment that is ripping him apart on the inside. While I don't know what's driving it, it explains a lot.

I should be even more frightened of him.

But I'm not.

All it does is ramp my intrigue up another notch.

"Fuck. That dude is one crazy bastard. Hot as fuck," Xavier says when we're outside, navigating our way through the rows of vehicles. "But scary crazy." He stops, planting his hands on my shoulders. "I don't want him anywhere near you. He's messed up in the head."

I'm not surprised Xavier has observed the same thing. He studies people as I do. "I know," I agree. "But aren't we all to some extent?"

He peers into my eyes. "Shit. You're into him, aren't you?"

I nod because there's no point trying to deny it. I've been playing that game with myself since he showed up in town and it's time to admit the truth to myself. "I don't want to be, but he does something to me." I bite down on my lip. "He…he makes me feel alive. Makes me feel so many things and it excites me as much as it scares me."

"Girl." He shakes his head, grinning as he takes my hand, and we walk again. "You're even more screwed up than me."

"I wasn't aware it was a competition," I joke. "And I thought you always knew I was a mess."

"A beautiful, smart, kick-ass mess," he corrects, smiling.

"I got so lucky the day I met you," I say, yanking him to a stop.

He throws back his head, laughing. "Are you kidding? You wanted to remove my liver and eat it with some fava beans and a nice Chianti."

"Nerd," I tease, laughing at his movie reference as we resume walking. "It might've been true at first, but that was before I got to know you. Besides Jane, you're my only best friend, and I hope you know you mean more to me than what I pay you to do."

"And what might that be?" a hard voice asks directly into my ear as I'm ripped away from Xavier.

CHAPTER TWENTY-ONE

"Let me go!" I wriggle against the arm wrapped around my waist from behind.

"Stop fighting, and I might," Cam growls.

"Get your fucking hands off her," Xavier shouts, and I look up to see him being restrained by Sawyer.

"Over here," Jackson hollers from the place where my bike is stowed.

"I can walk unaided," I snap as Cam marches us forward with his arm still glued to my stomach.

"This way's much more fun," he rasps in my ear, pressing his groin into my ass. My body sparks to life at the feel of his erection prodding into me, and I quit arguing. His belly rumbles with a silent laugh. "Yeah, thought as much." I flip him the bird and gnash my teeth. "Careful, baby," he murmurs, "You don't want to piss me off after a fight."

When we reach Jackson, Cam tightens his hold on me, using his free hand to tug my hood down and push my hair aside, and nuzzles his nose into my neck. A tiny whimper escapes my mouth before I can stop it. Jackson shoots me a smug look while Xavier looks like he wants to rip Cam's head from his shoulders. Which is dangerous, because after what we've just witnessed, there's no way Xavier could ever take him on and expect to win.

"I said take your hands off her, asshole." Xavier bravely pushes on, trying to shuck out of Sawyer's grasp but he towers over him, and he's at least twice his width too.

"No." Cam's tone brokers no argument, and then he leans down, running the tip of his tongue up and down my neck before sucking on that sensitive spot between my neck and my collarbone.

My legs turn to Jell-O, and I slump in his arms, hating my reaction but powerless to stop this train wreck from happening. His hard-on is digging into my ass, and my body is short-circuiting at the thoughts of him taking me there.

"I enjoy putting my hands on her," he adds, slipping one hand under my hoodie and tank top, palming the skin on my tummy. His touch is like a branding iron on my flesh, and I bite down on my lip, hard, to stem the moans lying idle on my tongue.

"Aw, hell, beautiful," Jackson says, cupping the bulge at his crotch. "Now look what you've done."

"Abby, what the fuck is going on here?" Xavier asks, his confused gaze bouncing between us.

"Who is he to you?" Cam grits out, his words laced with venom as his hand moves farther up my stomach.

"He's my friend," I pant, too turned on to feel any embarrassment at my obvious state of arousal.

"Friends with benefits?" Jackson, predictably, asks.

Xavier and I both laugh at that, and Sawyer rolls his eyes. "You two fuckwits are too obsessed with her to recognize the truth when it's staring you in the face."

Jackson's brows knit together, and he stares at Xavier, the lines on his forehead smoothing out as he inspects him. He grins. "Might've known *you'd* sniff out the homo, dude," he says, and Sawyer flips him the bird, letting Xavier go at the same time.

"Wait a sec." I yank Cam's hand out from under my clothing and step away from him, gawking at Sawyer. "You're gay?"

Why did I not pick up on that?

Sawyer glares at Jackson for letting the cat out of the bag. "If I'd known I never would've kissed you. Sorry."

"What?" Xavier shrieks the same time Sawyer says, "I'm bi."

"Well then, I take it back," I reply, looking at Cam through hooded eyes. "I'm not sorry I kissed you." I lick my lips. "It was a hot kiss."

"Have you gone stark raving mad?" Xavier asks, flapping his hands about. "You can't go around kissing guys. Especially him!"

"Guess now isn't a good time to mention we made out," Jackson unhelpfully supplies, blowing smoke circles into the air. "Or she gave Cam her virginity."

Deadly silence greets that statement, and I could happily throttle Jackson until he turns blue. "What?" He looks between us, confused. "You heard her. He's her *bestie*." He scoffs. "He already knows."

Xavier walks up to me, hurt and anger flashing in his eyes. "Is it true?"

I gulp over my panic, nodding. "I'm sorry."

"Why didn't you tell me?"

"You know why." I reach for him, but he steps away, and a heavy weight presses down on my chest. "Please, Xavier. You know more about me than anyone. Jane included. But I couldn't tell anyone this. No one else knows."

"*They* do!" he snaps.

"I didn't know who he was when I slept with him! Or that he's an asshole who kissed and told." I send daggers in Cam's direction.

"I wasn't the one who revealed that," Cam says. "That's all on you."

"This is all making a lot more sense," Xavier adds, his anger redirecting. "They're blackmailing you with this too." He puts his face right up in Cam's with no trace of fear. "If I find out you've been forcing yourself on her, I will make it my life's mission to see you pay."

"No, Xavier." I pull him back before Cam punches him. "It's not like that. Well, mostly not like that," I add, remembering the times he groped me without permission. But I'm only fooling myself. If he'd asked, I would've let him because he has this toxic hold over me I can't explain.

"What the fuck does that mean?" Xavier places his hands on my hips, pulling me in close to his side.

"It means it's none of your Goddamned business," Cam snarls. "And take your hands off her before I make you."

"Excuse me?" I shuck out of Xavier's hold, glaring at Cam. "You get no say in who touches me."

"Want to spout that bullshit again?" he says in a low, deep voice that sends shivers fleeing all over my body. He steps into me, and I step back, but he closes the gap again, and we play this little game where he moves and I move until my back slams into a tree and I'm caged in by his powerful arms. "I'm waiting."

"You can keep waiting because I'm not in the habit of repeating myself. Especially not to bullying assholes who think they can push me around and force me into submission."

"Oh, baby. We both know I wouldn't have to force you into anything." He presses the length of his body against mine, and I silently pray for strength I know I don't possess.

"Get off me," I say, but it sounds weak, and Jackson sniggers.

"Make me. Because I can do this all night, sweetheart." He nips at my ear, dragging it between his teeth, and the pleasure-pain sensation radiates throughout my body, eradicating all logical thought. "Remember what I said? Fighting me only turns me on," he whispers against my face, his warm breath sending me into a daze as he thrusts his cock into my pelvis. "And I'm always horny as fuck after I fight."

"I hate you," I whisper, my hands sliding around his bare sweat-slickened torso.

"I hate you too," he whispers back, roughly grabbing my neck and yanking my mouth to his.

He assaults my mouth with kiss after bruising kiss, sucking my essence from a dark hidden place inside me. I claw at his back, dragging my nails down his flesh, and I know I'm drawing blood. His tongue enters my mouth, licking me all over, and I can hardly breathe with the way he's devouring me. My nipples are so hard they could cut glass, and I'm sure he can feel the taut buds pressing against his chest even through my hoodie.

Grabbing my wrists, he hoists them over my head, grinding his cock into my pussy, and I cry out into his mouth. When he tugs on my hair, stretching my neck back, I wince from the sharp sting radiating across my scalp, lifting one leg and wrapping it around his waist, rubbing against him in a desperate attempt to ease the almost unbearable friction climbing inside me. I'm this close to begging him to fill me up when a throat clearing breaks through the sex fog in my head, and I remember we're not alone.

Holy shit.

I blink my eyes open, turning my head sideways, forcing Cam's lips away. "Get. Off. Me," I grit out in a more determined tone, shoving at his chest.

"That was so fucking hot and disturbingly arousing," Jackson says before adding, "I jacked off again." Cam pushes off me with a gloating grin. "You going for a world record, beautiful?" Jackson asks, in between drawing on his blunt. "Because that's twice I've come without you touching me. Dat's true talent."

"Shut up, Lauder. Just, shut up," Sawyer says, pinching the bridge of his nose. "And you!" He glares at Cam. "Make up your damn mind because you're driving me insane."

Cam gets all up in his face. "Don't fucking push me." He shoves at Sawyer, but his broad shoulders barely move. "And don't forget who's calling the shots."

I've wondered whether Cam or Sawyer was in charge, and that answers at least one of my questions. I don't know why Cam is purposely letting everyone think Sawyer is in control, when I know now that's not the case.

"Meet us back at our place," Cam says, taking hold of my elbow. "And don't blow us off because then we'll just pay another little visit to Chez Manning."

I yank my arm away. "Fine."

"I want you there too." He points at Xavier.

"And I want to blow Hozier but that's just a pipe dream."

A sly grin lifts the corners of Cam's mouth. "I'd hate for Abigail to pay the price for your non-cooperation. I've missed seeing her kneeling at my feet."

My lip curls up in disgust, and I brush past him to my bike, lifting our helmets and handing one to Xavier. "I need to get out of here before I end up in court on a murder charge," I hiss, securing my hair in a messy bun before putting my helmet on. I get onto the bike and rev the engine, impatiently waving Xavier forward.

"Oh, fuck," Jackson says, dropping to his knees. "Kill me now." He blows a kiss in my direction. "That's so fucking hot." I'm wondering if all the weed he smokes has wiped a few brain cells or he just has sex on the brain twenty-four-seven.

An amused grin appears on Sawyer's mouth, but Cam looks like he wants to choke me with his bare hands.

What the fuck's his problem now?

Probably blue balls. I smirk as the thought lands in my mind.

Xavier climbs on the bike, wrapping himself around me like a koala, and I rev the engine again, press my foot to the pedal, and floor it out of there, bits of mud and leafy debris spraying up in my wake.

We arrive at the house before the guys. They've locked the gate, so I park the bike, and we both sit down on the ground with our knees raised, waiting for them to show up.

We discuss strategies for the impending conversation, debating the pros and cons back and forth, until we agree on an approach.

"What's going on between you and those guys?" he asks. "And no bullshitting or hiding the truth this time."

"I couldn't tell you the virginity stuff, and I held back on some other shit because I was afraid you'd storm Rydeville High and confront the guys."

"It hurts that you didn't confide in me," he admits. "I thought we were friends."

I turn into him, pleading with my eyes. "We *are* friends. Please don't let this come between us. I'll tell you everything now, but you must promise not to physically retaliate. The best way to get back at them is the way we've planned."

I tell him how it all went down, from that first encounter with Cam in Alabama when he was merely a handsome stranger, and he listens attentively as the story pours from my heart.

It feels good to get this off my chest.

Then I explain the shit that's happened since school started. Some of it he knows, but most of it I've kept from him because I knew what his reaction would be. He climbs to his feet, pacing, with his jaw pulled tight and murder glimmering in his eyes when I finish. "I fucking knew it!" His fists clench at his side. "Those fucking assholes."

I stand. "It doesn't matter."

"The hell it doesn't! They can't do that shit to you!"

I shrug. "They've done it, but things will change."

"How?" He grips my shoulders. "If the news gets out about your virginity, your father will literally kill you, and I know you won't throw Jane to the wolves."

"That's why we'll find something to blackmail them with! I know there's something, and we'll unearth it and bury those fuckers."

"Are you sure that's what you want? Things seem…intense between you and Marshall, and it doesn't look like you've much self-control around him."

"Maybe I'm seducing him," I throw out.

"Are you?"

"No." I sigh, rubbing the back of my neck. "I told you I was all messed up."

"I didn't realize it was this bad."

The quiet purr of an engine pricks my ears, and I look over his shoulders at the approaching vehicle. "They're here. And remember." I narrow my eyes. "You promised. We do this my way."

His only reply is to hop back on the bike as the gates automatically open, and we follow Sawyer's Land Rover up their driveway.

The instant we disembark, Xavier charges at Cam, and I roll my eyes, muttering cusses under my breath.

So much for promises and restraint.

He rams his fist into Cam's face as I stand there with my mouth hanging open. "That's for assaulting her and humiliating her in school. And if you fucking touch her without her permission again, I will end you." He pushes his chest into Cam's. "That's a promise."

Cam surprises me by turning around and walking into the house without uttering a word or punching him back.

We follow Sawyer through the door into the wide lobby and enter the large living space that functioned as party central the last time I was here.

A massive cream leather couch is the focal point in the room with all the other furniture centered around it. Cam slumps in one of the leather recliners with his leg tossed casually over the arm. His feet and upper body are bare, and the top button of his jeans is undone. His lip is bloody, his cheek and eye swollen, and the faint hint of bruises already appears on his jawline and across his rib cage, but he's still the sexiest guy I've ever seen, and my libido reawakens with gusto.

Stupid damn hormones.

Sawyer drops onto the couch, gesturing for us to sit beside him. Jackson wanders into the room from the direction of the kitchen, gulping down water and offering bottles around. He sits cross-legged on the floor in front of the couch, winking at me. Ignoring his deviant, flirtatious ass, I take sips of water as I wait for the interrogation to begin.

"Who are you, and how do you know Abigail?" Sawyer asks Xavier, not beating around the bush.

We've already discussed this, and I see no harm in being mostly truthful. If we lie about the obvious stuff, they'll catch us on it because Sawyer has tech skills too. And I want none of this coming back to bite Xavier.

"Name's Xavier Daniels. I'm in my senior year at Rydeville University, studying computer science. And I met Abby when I hacked into her computer and attempted to extort money from her."

Cam sits up straighter. "That true?"

"Yes." I nod.

Sawyer frowns. "How did you two become friends then?"

Xavier grins. "Because she turned up at the meet with my cash and a loaded gun. When she pressed the muzzle into my temple, I nearly shit myself, but then she made me an offer I couldn't refuse."

"What kind of offer?" Cam rests his arms on his knees, invested in the conversation.

Xavier looks at me, silently communicating with his eyes, ensuring I'm still okay to do this. It's risky. I know that. But I think the potential wins outweigh the risk, so I'm willing to go there. I nod, letting him know it's okay.

Xavier eyes the three guys. "She asked me to help uncover dirt on her father we could use to blackmail him with."

CHAPTER TWENTY-TWO

You could hear a pin drop in the room, and the expressions on the guys' faces are comical. Sawyer looks deep in thought. Cam looks suspicious. And Jackson looks strangely smug.

"Why do you want to blackmail your father?" Cam asks, his expression sober.

"Why do you think?" I half-laugh.

"I don't know. That's why I asked."

I sigh, moving my head from side to side, attempting to loosen my stiff muscles. The guys watch me like hawks, and I wipe my clammy palms over the front of my jeans. "I hate him," I say. "He's a horrible human being and a lousy husband and father. He used to beat my mother, and he didn't care to conceal it. After she died, he did nothing to help us. We were seven years old, and we'd lost the only real parent we'd ever known. He left us to grieve alone, working long hours and whoring around in his sex dungeon, while an army of paid help raised us." I swallow over the painful lump in my throat, as all four guys listen attentively.

"He gets off on bullying people, especially women," I continue. "He sees all women as weak, and he loves controlling me, telling me what to wear, what to do, who I can hang out with, insisting I'm driven everywhere, and that bodyguards breathe down my neck. I have no freedom. No control over my life. The only reason he plans on keeping me around is so he can marry me off to Trent and forge a strong working relationship with that asshole Christian Montgomery."

"And?" Cam prompts.

"And I'm not a pawn to be used in whatever nefarious game he's concocting!" I hiss. "And I can barely abide Trent. The thought of being married to him makes me physically ill."

"But I thought you loved him and missed him badly."

His arrogant smirk pisses me off, but I might as well get everything out on the table. "I might've said that to piss you off." I shrug. "Big deal." His smug grin expands until it's sucking up all the oxygen in the room. "Oh, please. Don't sit there acting all smug. You've been parading that slut on your lap for the past two weeks. We all know you did that for my benefit."

He shoots me a lopsided grin. "Trust me, I was benefiting."

My hands ball into fists at my side, and I chew on the inside of my mouth. "Trust me, *I know.*" My stomach sours. "I saw her blowing you while your stoner friend was fucking her. I hope both your dicks turn rotten and fall off."

Jackson bursts out laughing, dropping back onto the ground and clutching his stomach as if he's in pain.

"He's totally stoned," Xavier says, "and I really need some of that shit." He slides onto the floor, nudging Jackson to sit up.

"Can we attempt to keep this conversation focused," Sawyer asks, sighing in exasperation. "Why are you telling us this?"

I pull my knees up to my chin. "One, you asked. Two, you mentioned we might be on the same side before, and you're right. I thought it was time we stopped pussyfooting around one another and laid our cards on the table." He nods, encouraging me to go on. "You hate my father. So do I. You want something to hold over him. So do I. You're trying to access his files, and we've spent the last five months attempting it. Neither group is making enough leeway, but maybe if we combine forces, we can succeed."

"How do we know this isn't a trap?" Cam asks, worry lines furrowing his brow.

"You don't. Guess you'll just have to trust me." I love throwing his words back at him.

He scowls, instantly making the connection. "That's not exactly reassuring."

"Listen, dipshit," Xavier intervenes. "Abigail has way more at stake here than you do. You have shit on her, and she's much more to lose. That should be all you need. She didn't have to tell you any of this stuff, but she did."

"How do we know you don't have shit on us?"

My eyes narrow to slits. "Because if we did, I'd have already used it."

"How did you know I was fighting tonight?" Cam asks, staring me down.

I'm sorely tempted to say it's a coincidence, but that won't wash. I know I must fess up. "Because I implanted a tracking device on Sawyer's cell last night, and Xavier intercepted your messages."

The look Cam levels in Sawyer's direction is nothing short of pure evil.

But Sawyer *actually smiles.*

The biggest fucking smile I've ever seen on his face, and his entire body rumbles with laughter, his deep chuckles echoing around the room.

"Wow," he says, when he's composed himself. "No one's ever gotten one over on me." His eyes shimmer with wicked intent. "I'm so impressed I could kiss you."

Cam growls. "I dare you to try it."

Jackson and Xavier are sharing a blunt between them, watching us with very different expressions.

"You're too easy to wind up when it comes to her, and that's a big fucking problem," Sawyer admits, all trace of humor fading.

"Why do you keep saying that?" I ask, my gaze jumping between them.

"Because it's true," Jackson butts in. "You two have smoking-hot chemistry. I say you just fuck each other until you get it out of your system."

"Helpful as ever," I say with a hefty dose of sarcasm.

"Come with me," Cam says, extending his hand.

"What?" I splutter.

He rolls his eyes, and he even makes that look sexy. *Ugh.* I rub a tense spot between my brows.

Now, I sound like Bella Swan mooning over Edward Cullen. He wanted to suck her blood, and I think Camden Marshall would bleed my veins dry and suck my soul clear out of my body if I let him, so it's a rather apt comparison.

"I want to talk to you. That's all." I eye him warily, unsure if it's wise to be alone with him when I have zero impulse control around him. "And I need to clean up. I won't touch you. I promise."

"Go with him," Sawyer says. "You're safe." He drills a warning look at Cam.

I stand, but I don't take his hand, trailing him out of the room, up the stairs, and into his bedroom. It's locked again, and I wonder if it's just habit or they're suspicious for a reason.

We walk inside and he enters the en suite bathroom without uttering a word. I follow him inside, taking the first aid kit from his hands. "Sit on top of the toilet seat," I instruct, and surprisingly, he complies.

I wash and dry my hands before removing supplies from the box.

I press sterile gauze against the bottle of iodine and then gently dab his lip. It's stopped bleeding, but it's dry and encrusted, and I'm sure it stings, not that you'd know from his stoic reaction. "I'm guessing you're used to this," I say, cleaning his lip thoroughly.

He stares at me but doesn't acknowledge my statement. "Okayyy." I toss the bloody gauze in the bin, removing another piece and dabbing that with iodine too. Then I clean the area around his eye and his swollen cheekbone before inspecting his bruised jawline with tender fingers.

"How long have you been fighting?" I ask as my fingers gently probe the bruised flesh along his ribcage.

"A while," he says, hissing, and I pull my hand back.

"Sorry."

He takes my hand, rubbing circles on the back of my wrist with his thumb. "You did nothing wrong, so don't apologize."

"Why do you fight?" I press on, trying to ignore the soft warmth creeping up my arm from his touch.

"Why does anyone do anything they enjoy?" He shrugs.

"You enjoy beating the crap out of others?" I caress his damaged face with my free hand. "Feeling pain?"

His eyes bore into mine, and silence descends for a few beats before he slowly nods. "You told me the night we met you wanted to feel something real. To feel in control. To feel alive." I nod, remembering. "Sometimes I need to feel all that too."

"And fighting does that for you?"

"Yeah." He brings my wrist to his mouth, kissing my sensitive skin.

My eyes close for a second, but I force them open. "Did you know who I was that night?"

Tense silence filters through the air. "No," he eventually admits, looking me directly in the eye. "I only found out who you were a few months later."

Maybe I'm a fool, but I believe him. "Why do you hate my father?"

He drops my hand and a cold, harsh glaze drapes across his dark eyes. A muscle pops in his jaw. "That's a conversation we need to have with the others." He stands, walking into his bedroom like he's carrying the weight of the world on his shoulders. "I need to understand why you think you have to blackmail your own father."

"Why does it matter?"

He drops onto his bed, resting his back against the headboard and I climb up beside him. "Humor me."

I lean back and close my eyes. "My entire life, I've been playing at being me, and I'm sick of it. The thoughts of performing an expected role for the rest of my life depresses me so badly."

"Is that why you were in the sea that night? You wanted to end your life?"

I open my eyes and turn my head to face him. "Yes, although it wasn't premeditated. It was more of a spontaneous reaction even if it had been brewing for a few days."

"Why then? And why were you in Alabama?"

"My aunt had just passed. She had cancer," I explain with tears pricking my eyes. "She's the only one who ever truly understood. She rebelled against this life and got away. She forged a different path, pursued her passions, but she never fully left it behind, because it's not the kind of life you ever fully escape from."

It's why I'm so focused on blackmailing my father because it's the only way I'll genuinely be free.

"She was my last link to my mother. The only relative besides Drew who loved me with no agenda. Her loss devastated me." I keep to myself the things she divulged on her deathbed.

He's quiet for a few beats, and I look up at the ceiling, wondering where all this is leading. "And what is it you want out of life?" he asks.

"I'm not altogether sure except I want to be free to make my own choices." I look over at him again. "I don't want to be a trophy wife. To stand on the sidelines looking pretty while my husband fucks other women behind my back. I don't want to endure his cruel words and violent hands while pretending everything is peachy. And I definitely don't want to pop out kids to a timeline agreed in a business contract." I shake my head. "I would rather die than live that life."

"So just leave. I'm sure you have a *trust fund*." He spits out the words, his disgust evident, and I don't understand.

"I do, but why is that an issue?"

"I didn't say it was."

"You didn't have to." I sit up a little straighter, scrutinizing his face.

"Don't look at me like that," he snaps.

"Like what?"

"Like you pity me."

My mouth opens and closes a few times before I find the right words. "Why would I pity you? I'm just trying to understand why you're pissed. Your father is loaded, and I'm sure you have a trust fund too, or does he want you to make your own way in life? And I've got to say, if he does, I respect the hell out of him."

He snorts, his eyes blazing as he glowers at me. "You would say that! Because you don't know what it's like to live poor."

"And you do?" My brow puckers as I stare at him. I have no clue what the hell he's talking about.

His chest inflates and deflates, and he grinds down on his teeth, his jaw pulsing. Without warning, he jumps up. "I don't want to talk about this anymore."

Moody fucker.

"Okay." I slide off the bed. "What do you want to talk about?"

"I don't need to talk anymore. I've heard enough." His stomach rumbles loudly, and I frown.

"When did you last eat?"

"What?" A perplexed look appears on his face at my left of field question.

"When did you last eat something substantial?" I know how much food Drew packs away, and Cam's just exerted a ton of energy so he's probably starving.

He shrugs. "A few hours ago. I'll grab something after I shower."

"I'll make you something while you shower."

"Why would you do that?" he asks, suspicion underscoring his tone as he unbuttons his jeans all the way.

"Worried I'll poison you?" I taunt, planting my hands on my hips.

"The thought had crossed my mind."

I smirk. "If I wanted to kill you, I'd prolong it. Enjoy torturing you and ensuring you suffered. I'm offering to make you something, because the sooner we get done here, the sooner I can go home." It's an effort to keep my eyes trained on his face when he kicks his jeans away, standing in front of me in skintight boxers that do nothing to conceal the giant boner he's sporting.

"Anxious to escape me, huh?" He lowers his voice as he walks toward me, and my pulse spikes.

"Of course. It's not like I enjoy your company."

He grabs the nape of my neck and pulls me to him. His cock jerks against me, and I slam my lips shut to avoid an embarrassing leakage. "Maybe Jackson's right," he whispers, sending tingles skating over my skin. "Maybe we need to fuck this weird chemistry out of our system."

I duck under his arm before I do something I regret.

Like agree.

"Never happening again."

"Guess I'll just be imagining your tight pussy hugging my cock as I stroke one out in the shower," he casually says, and my mouth turns dry as he slides his boxers down his legs and grips his hard length in his hand. "Or visualizing you on your knees, feasting on my dick," he adds with a gleeful smile when he notices my discomfort.

I gather myself, thrusting my shoulders back and lifting my head. "You do that, because it's the closest you'll ever come to sex with me again."

I can't get the image of Cam's impressive cock out of my head, and it's a wonder I've managed to serve up edible food. The others all professed hunger when they heard I was cooking for Cam, and I ended up making steaks and salads for all four guys.

"This is so fucking good," Jackson muffles, his mouth half full. "Now I'm even more convinced you should become Marshall's new fuck buddy. You can stay over and cook for us all the time."

I swat the back of his head. "Not happening. Why don't you ask his current fuck buddy to cook for you—although, I doubt Rochelle has many culinary skills."

"Speaking of culinary skills," Sawyer cuts in fast, "where did you learn to cook like this? Don't you have hired help?"

"We do. Mrs. Jenkins runs the kitchen, and she taught me how to cook. When my mom was alive, we used to make cupcakes and cookies and other baked goods, and I loved spending that time with her. When she was gone, and Dad and Drew were away at Parkhurst, I loved spending time with Mrs. Jenkins. It felt less lonely." I shrug, my cheeks heating as I instantly regret my little outburst.

"Remind me to thank her," Jackson says, shooting me a soft smile that's genuine. "Because she taught you well."

"It's only steak and salad," I murmur, growing uncomfortable with the praise. I get up and clean the kitchen while the boys eat in silence. I'm surprised when Cam clears the plates, rinsing and stacking them neatly in the dishwasher, but I don't remark on it.

We stay in the kitchen, and Sawyer and Cam make coffee while Jackson heads to the bathroom. "You okay?" Xavier whispers, clasping my hand under the table.

"Yeah," I whisper back. "Although I'd be better if we can just finish and leave. They're getting under my skin."

"It's been interesting," he admits, bobbing his head.

"What are you two whispering about?" Cam asks, eyeing our interlinked fingers through narrowed eyes. A flash of irritation, and something darker, glints in his eyes, but it's gone before I can decipher it.

"Nothing important," I say, accepting a mug from him. Our fingers touch in the exchange, and it's like I've plugged my hand into an electrical socket. If we'll be working as a conjoined team, I honestly don't know how long I can resist temptation.

When everyone is seated, I ask my question again. "Why do you hate my father, and what is it you're trying to find?"

The three guys trade looks, and some silent communication passes between them. Xavier and I share a knowing look, wondering how much of the truth they'll impart. There could be many reasons they have it in for my father, but I'm guessing it's something to do with his business dealings.

I couldn't have been more wrong.

"It goes without saying," Sawyer says, "that whatever we discuss is confidential, and it remains between all of us."

"Of course," I agree. "And we expect you to keep our confidence too. We've all got stuff to lose."

Sawyer nods at Cam.

Cam leans his elbows on the table, his eyes burning with anger. "Your father killed my...aunt, and I want to make him pay."

CHAPTER TWENTY-THREE

I'm momentarily dumbfounded, but I quickly find my voice. "Are you talking about Emma Anderson?" I frown, my gaze jumping between them. "Didn't she take her own life?"

"Your father staged it to look like a suicide."

"How do you know that?" It's not like I'm disputing he's monstrous enough to do something like that, but it seems like a stretch even for him.

"The aunt you mentioned upstairs," Cam says. "That was Genevieve?" I nod. "Your aunt knew my dad from their Rydeville High days, and she asked to meet him shortly before she died. She told him your mother believed Michael killed Emma."

He swallows hard, his Adam's apple bobbing in his throat. "Apparently, your mom had evidence to back it up, but she died before she could use it."

"What evidence?" My heart is thumping wildly behind my rib cage, and I'm wondering if this is the reason my father killed my mother. The other possibility is Aunt Genevieve lost control of her mind in the run up to her death. But, no, I don't really believe that. She seemed lucid. If this was any other man, and any other place, I'd be highly suspicious of my aunt's deathbed claims. Telling me my father killed my mother and telling Cam's father he killed his sister seems a little too coincidental.

But my gut tells me it's true.

And that we might finally be getting somewhere.

"She found the prescription for the medication used to end my...her life. Your father's physician wrote it not Emma Anderson's family doctor, the same man who had treated her all his life. And she had proof Hearst had paid for it."

He clenches his knuckles so tight the skin is blanched white, and a muscle ticks repeatedly in his jaw. He's sitting stiffly in the chair, as if every bone and sinew in his body is wired tight.

"And where is that proof now?"

"Your father has it," Sawyer quietly confirms.

"He killed my mother for it," I deduce, slouching in my chair, all the wind knocked out of my sails. I thought he killed her because she was planning to escape. Or maybe it was for that reason too.

"You knew?" Cam asks.

"When Drew and I got older, we suspected he'd done something because we both remember crying under the covers, terrified, when we were little, listening to Mom's cries as he beat her. He used to fly into a rage at the slightest thing, and it was always Mom's fault." An errant sob slips from my mouth, and I squeeze my eyes shut to blink the memories away. "But it was only when Aunt Genevieve told me she believed my father had staged the car accident I started to accept it."

"And what about your brother?" Jackson asks. "What's his take on all this?"

I gulp back the lump in my throat. "Drew hates him too, but...he wants to take over the family business, and he knows he needs to keep him on his side, so..." I can't articulate it, so I stop speaking.

"He's happy to pretend like it never happened," Cam snarls, his warm brown eyes almost black as he glares at me.

I don't want to bitch about my brother when he's not here to defend himself. We've fought enough about it over the years, and I'm not going there with a group of guys I distrust, so I ignore Cam's assumption. I clutch Xavier's hand under the table. "Xavier and I have tried to prove it, but all the evidence points to it being an accident."

"Because your father bribed the local authorities," Cam says. "They're all in his pocket, and you can't trust any of the paperwork you've uncovered. It's all fabricated. Just like the reports of my aunt's suicide." He almost chokes on the words, and I reach out with my free hand to take his without hesitation.

His eyes divert to his knee, where my hand rests atop his, and his chest heaves. When he lifts his head, the look of pure hatred on his face confuses me. I withdraw my hand quickly, but I refuse to back down from his heated stare. "Do you blame me for my father's actions? Is that why you hate me so much?"

"I despise everything about you. I don't need your father's reprehensible acts to convince me of that."

A piercing pain slices across my chest, but he's not getting the last word. "You think you know me, but you don't. You know nothing about me!"

He jumps up, his chair crashing to the tile floor. "I know you've wanted for nothing in your life!" he shouts. "Growing up in that creeptastic mansion, being waited on hand and foot, swimming in cash. You and your brother ignoring everything your father has done. Everything *you've* done! Attending fancy dinners, going to ballet and plays, pretending like you're not all monsters masquerading as pretentious pricks!" Spittle flies from his mouth, and his entire body is primed to attack.

"Fuck. You." I stand. "I'm not staying here to be spoken to like that." Especially not after I spilled my guts earlier, and now he's throwing it back in my face.

"Do what you do best, sweetheart." Cam invades my private space, putting his face all up in mine. Right now, I've no clue who he is. I thought we'd made some progress tonight, but I was wrong. "Pretend like shit isn't happening."

Xavier hops up, ready to explode in Cam's face, but I hold on to his arm, cautioning him to stay back. Sawyer stands, pulling me behind him, protecting me from Cam's vicious stare, which pleasantly surprises me. "You need to calm down and remember the bigger picture."

"Fuck this shit. I can't do this," he says before storming out of the kitchen.

"This isn't really about you," Sawyer says, turning to face me. "You're just an easy target."

"Bullshit." I shake my head. "You told me he's conditioned to hate me. And that's exactly what that was!"

"It's hard to shake misconceptions you've believed your whole life," Sawyer says.

"So, you're saying the Marshalls hate me and my brother because we grew up rich and pretended like our father didn't kill his aunt?" My tone elevates a couple of notches. "Do you hear how ridiculous that sounds? And fucking hypocritical because his family is as loaded as mine." I'm fuming now, and I need to leave. "We're going, Xavier."

"This isn't how I wanted the night to end." Sawyer sighs. "Can we agree we have common ground and meet again to discuss how to combine our efforts?"

"On one condition." I fold my arms and dare him to challenge me with a cold look.

"What condition?"

"That you don't interfere on Monday at school. You let things happen as they should."

"What's happening on Monday?" Jackson asks, ending his silent spell.

"Things are returning to their rightful order."

Sawyer's brows climb to his forehead. "We won't intervene provided it doesn't involve us."

"It doesn't."

When I take them down, it'll be a much more sophisticated plan.

"Then it's agreed. Do what you must."

Jackson grins. "I look forward to the show."

I send him a tight smile. "Make the most of your time with your fuck buddy, because she won't be around much longer."

He shrugs. "I'm done with her, anyway. Rochelle gives great head, but she's a whiny bitch. There's plenty more pussy to go around."

"Spoken like a true manwhore," I say, shaking my head as I walk toward the exit.

Sawyer escorts Xavier and me to the front door, and I make one final condition. "Tell the asshole he's getting his own lunch from now on."

"Is everyone clear?" I ask one final time before we enter the school premises and put our plan into motion.

"Crystal," Chad says. "We've got this, and we won't let you down."

I turn to our little motley crew. "Thank you. I couldn't have done this without you, and I won't forget it." I smile a genuine smile. "Now, let's restore control."

We split up, finishing our rounds with plenty of time to spare so we're able to watch as it goes down.

Gradually, the school halls fill up as students arrive, everyone sharing puzzled looks as they spot the envelopes taped to lockers.

Cries and gasps ring out as they open the envelopes, and pride surges through me.

It's incredible the number of secrets we uncovered, and no one was immune.

Not the guy whose father is fucking the local priest or the girl with the questionable heritage whose parents paid a generous bonus to their Latina maid before she skipped town seventeen years ago and certainly not the family hiding the fact their bank account contains a lot less zeroes than they're claiming.

"You've got some fucking nerve," Wentworth says, shoving his envelope in my face, his ears burning red. "And if you think this little stunt will win everyone back on your side, you're even more pathetic."

I straighten up, and Chad moves in closer to my side. "If you don't think I'm serious, the joke's on you. No skin off my nose if you want to risk it." Wentworth has little between his ears, and I'm banking on him calling my bluff. I'll enjoy making an example of him almost as much as I'll enjoy destroying Rochelle.

"Everyone knows you're Cam's little bitch. He'll go ape on your ass when he discovers this shit."

"I wouldn't count on it. But go for it. Please."

He looks like he wants to hit me, but even he's not that stupid. He storms off, cursing at me over his shoulder, and I look forward to never seeing his ugly face again.

I climb onto the chair outside the nurse's office, cupping my hands around my mouth. "Listen up," I holler, my voice carrying down the hallway. All chatter dies off, and a hush descends over the place. "Your little vacation is over now. Order is restored, effective immediately. You know the rules. Abide by them or pay the consequences. And if you think I'm bluffing, I'm not. If you test me, I will distribute the contents of that envelope far and wide. Obey and you have nothing to fear from me or the other elite when they return." I skim my gaze over my audience, spotting tears, red faces full of rage, and abject horror. "Now, get to class before you're late."

Chad helps me down as familiar laughter tickles my eardrums.

"Nice speech, beautiful," Jackson says with a wink.

"Can I still count on your cooperation?" I ask Sawyer.

"Absolutely. We're all on board."

I know that was directed at Cam, and I need reassurance. I eyeball him, trying not to flinch at the mottled bruises on his face and the swollen purply-blue mess around his eye. "And is His Highness aware I'm not his punching bag any longer?"

"He said we're on board, didn't he?" Cam grits out. "I give you my word."

I snort. "As if that means anything."

"I'm not getting into this with you again." He stalks off without waiting for his friends.

"Oh dear. Was it something I said?"

"Naughty, Abigail. Very naughty. And you know he'll make you pay," Jackson says, and while I know he meant it as a threat, all I'm thinking about are the many delicious ways that asshole can make me suffer, already starting a mental countdown in my head.

The morning classes go by smoothly, but not everyone is toeing the line, as predicted, so I execute the next stage of my plan once everyone is seated in the cafeteria at lunchtime. Most everyone that had defected from the inner circle has returned to our section, and I welcome them warmly, noticing how they visibly relax. Little do they know I'm leaving their punishment up to the boys when they return. There's no way we can have them thinking they can deny the rules without some consequence.

"Ready?" Chad asks, his finger hovering over the button on his iPad.

"Do it."

Cells ping in quick succession around the room, and I smile as everyone opens up the group message we've just sent.

"You fucking whore!" Rochelle exclaims, jumping up and running toward me, closely followed by Jackson, Sawyer, and Cam. Chad and a few of the guys stop her before she reaches me, keeping her back. "You filthy slut!" she screams, attempting to shuck out of their hold, baying for my blood.

"Stop stealing my lines, Rochelle, or should I call you *Chastity*." I snigger. "Oh, the irony." I walk around her as the sounds of *Chastity* performing for her clients echo around the room. "I knew you were a whore, but I didn't realize you were prostituting yourself out for money. I thought you spread those legs for free."

I shake my head, tut-tutting. "I felt a responsibility, as an upstanding member of this community, to notify your *employer* you were underage." Her nostrils flare, and it only spurs me on. "So, unfortunately, you've been fired." I shoot her a faux apologetic look. "But I had to ask myself what would compel a high school senior to get naked and perform sex acts on camera for random perverts to drool over in the first place? It couldn't be because she needed the money. Not when her father is a senior stockbroker for one of the biggest stockbroking firms in Massachusetts."

I walk around her, aware of my captive audience—well, the half who aren't still glued to the show on their cells—and I definitely have a flair for the dramatic.

The large screen descends from the ceiling, and I hold my hand out for the remote. Chad places it in my palm, and I smile at Rochelle, not in the least bit sorry.

Jackson grins, more than enjoying the show, and I blow him a kiss.

"Imagine my surprise," I continue, projecting my voice around the room, "when I discovered you're about to be kicked out of school for unpaid fees." I circle her like a hunter stalking her prey as I turn the TV on, pausing it for now. Tears roll down her face when she sees her father on the screen, and a tiny flicker of remorse erupts in my chest, but I soldier on, remembering all the things she's done to me.

I'm not doing this to her.

She's done it to herself.

If she hadn't started a war with me, I wouldn't have come out all guns blazing.

"I understood then why you were taking your clothes off on camera and meeting clients for paid sex behind your employer's back." I eyeball Cam as I speak my next words. "No wonder the guys in school were complaining about how loose you are. Let's hope they all wrapped it before they tapped it, or a visit to the doctor will be in order."

"You won't get away with this." She sobs.

"Oh, I think you'll find I will." I lean in close. "And your ex-boss really isn't happy with you. Didn't you know meeting clients for sex was a breach of your contract, not to mention against the law," I glance at the Tag Heuer watch on my wrist. "The cops will pay him a visit right about now." The sleaze deserves it, and it feels like I've done something good getting his operation shut down.

"Just after they've finished handing your no-good father over to the feds." I press play on the CNN newsfeed, watching her entire body crumple as the reporter confirms they have arrested her father on multiple charges of fraud and embezzlement.

It seems he was doing some shady deals on the side, and when they went sour, he borrowed funds from the company he worked for, only digging himself into a bigger hole when he continued to lose big.

Not only has he bankrupted his own family, but he's obliterated hundreds of pension and investment funds, causing hardship and suffering to multiple families. "I hope they lock him in jail and throw away the key. He deserves to die there because he's destroyed hundreds of families due to sheer greed."

She stares at me through glassy eyes. "What, no more insults?" I stand in front of her, and she's broken. "It didn't have to be this way, but you left me no choice."

Some of her fire returns, and she spits in my face. I slap her, just once, but it's enough to make my point.

Taking a tissue from Chad, I carefully wipe her saliva from my face. "Chad will escort you outside where a car is waiting to take you to your house," I calmly say. "It's being repossessed as we speak, but the bank has assured me you can keep your clothes and some basic belongings. I believe you're moving to your maternal grandparents' farm in Ohio." I wiggle my fingers in her face. "Bye, now. I'd say we'll miss you, but that would just be a lie."

I turn my back on her, muting the screen before fixing my sights on Wentworth.

I wait until Chad and the others have removed Rochelle, and then I send the next group message. Cells ping around the room for a second time, and Jackson chuckles, obviously enjoying the drama.

I load the video on the large screen, and the sounds of sex echo around the room. "Harder, Wentworth," the middle-aged woman pants as he holds her facedown over a table while pounding into her from behind.

"You like this, don't you, you dirty bitch," he shouts, thrusting into her harder as sweat drips down his face. "What would your son think if he knew you let me fuck you like the filthy, cheating slut you are?"

"You motherfucking bastard!" Elijah Lantiss jumps over the table, grabbing Wentworth by the neck, and they both tumble to the ground in a tangle of limbs and swinging fists. Wood splinters as the chair he was sitting on breaks apart. I spot the vice principal hurrying my way with a face like thunder, and I stop the recording, pressing the button to retract the screen.

The school authorities know their place, and they turn a deliberate blind eye to most of our shit, but they usually call our fathers if we cross a line. I was expecting intervention, and Drew has already smoothed things over with father. I'm not sure what lies he's told, but all I care about is my father will back me up when the principal makes the call.

The VP backs down when he sees I've turned off the video, shooting me a cautionary warning before exiting the room, leaving the boys beating one another on the floor.

More outraged shouts ring out as the recording sent to everyone's cell phones progresses through the images of Wentworth fucking several of his friends' mothers. It turns into a bloodbath as more boys join the melee. I move closer with the new elite keeping close to my side. "Enough," I command in an authoritative voice when the beatings turn one-sided.

I want him conscious for my finale.

Cam and Jackson pluck guys off Wentworth, tossing them aside and warning them to stay back.

Wentworth groans, spitting blood and a couple of loose teeth out onto the floor. "You stupid cunt," he hisses, sitting up on the floor and glaring at me. Blood spurts from his nose and trickles from multiple cuts on his lips. Both eyes are already closing, and his shirt is torn and bloodstained.

"I warned you, but you were always an arrogant idiot." He attempts to climb to his feet. "Surely, you didn't target your friends' mothers, record yourself fucking them, and expect to get away with it?"

He sways on his feet, clutching onto the back of a chair to keep himself upright. "Hacking into someone's computer is illegal, and I'll go after you for it."

I move one step closer, raking my gaze over him in a derogatory manner. "You need to learn to keep your stupid mouth shut because all it does is dig you in a deeper hole." I cross my arms and smile at him. "I have sent a copy of that recording to your parents along with a copy to every one of those women's husbands. I wouldn't be surprised if there's an angry mob waiting for you outside."

The smile drops off my face, and I lean in to his ear, not wanting to divulge this to the masses, but only because I'm protecting his sister. "I found the file with the recordings of your sister. You're a sick bastard, and you're going down for what you did to her."

His face pales behind all the blood. "What did you do?" he stutters.

"I sent those to your parents too, along with a copy to the police chief."

A loud roar rips from his mouth, and he wraps his hands around my throat before I can stop him. He squeezes hard, his bloodshot eyes bulging out of his head, as he tries to strangle me. He's yanked off me almost straightaway, and I stagger back, drawing deep breaths as I watch Cam punch Wentworth repeatedly until he slumps unconscious to the ground.

"You okay?" Sawyer places a hand on my lower back as Chad reappears in the cafeteria. Cam stares at my neck, and I detect a fleeting flash of guilt in his eyes before it disappears.

"What happened?" Chad asks, his eyes darting from me to Wentworth's bloody, beaten body on the ground.

"He tried to strangle her," Sawyer says, and Chad's eyes pop wide.

"I'm fine." I hold up a palm. "Cam pulled him away before he could do any damage."

A commotion at the door claims our attention, and we watch as a team of police pushes their way through the crowd, making a beeline for us.

I smooth a hand down over my uniform, holding my shoulders upright, projecting confidence, as Cam moves to the other side of me and the five of us line up to face the authorities.

CHAPTER TWENTY-FOUR

Things return to normal at school after the showdown, and we have restored order. The new elite continue to sit at their existing table, but they are alone as everyone else has returned to the old arrangements. Classes are no longer disrupted, and the principal even overlooked the confrontation in the cafeteria, backing up our version of events with the police and declining to call my father.

Rochelle has left town with her family, and Wentworth is behind bars awaiting trial.

Life is—temporarily—good.

"You did well, little sis," Drew says on the phone Friday night while I'm preparing to sneak out to meet the guys. "I'm proud of you."

I roll my eyes even though he can't see me. "That's not something you should be proud of me for."

"Sure, it is. You removed an illegal sex operation from business, stopped Rochelle's father before he bankrupted more people, and put a rapist in jail. That's what I'm proud of. Not the fact you regained control in school; although I'm grateful as we've enough on our plate without having to deal with that upon our return."

"What do you mean?" I ask, shimmying my leather pants up my legs.

"It's not something I can discuss."

I snort. "Right. Shady Parkhurst shit. Got it."

"How's Jane?" he asks, deliberately changing the subject.

"She's good. Happy now I got the recording off the new elite and they're no longer threatening to expose her." It surprised me when Cam handed it over Monday night, but Sawyer assured me it was a show of good faith and that it didn't bode well to start a working relationship by using threats and coercion.

"Thank fuck, but I will still beat their asses for it. And I don't like you pretending to form an alliance with them. It's risky if they discover you're double-crossing them."

"They won't," I say, trying to dampen down my guilt.

Drew thinks I've made an agreement with the elite whereby they are exempt from following the rules once they don't interfere with our control. He thinks I'm putting on a front in school to keep them in line until they return and squash them. If he knew it's all part of the plan, he'd be so disappointed in me.

Drew chose his side a long time ago, and while I hate we're on opposing teams, I can't lose sight of my long-term goals.

Thoughts of leaving here, leaving Drew behind, always bring tears to my eyes, but we want different things from life, and I can't find any way to reconcile our issues. I only hope that, in time, once Drew has assumed full control of Manning Motors and our father no longer has the same power, we can rectify things and rebuild our relationship.

And he has Jane.

It's not like I'm leaving him all alone. I trust my friend to take care of my brother after I flee.

"I've got to go." I hear voices in the background. "I love you, and tell Jane I love her too. I can't wait to see you both next week."

"I love you too," I croak over the messy ball of emotion wedged in my throat.

I'm the last one to arrive at the guys' place, and Cam snaps, "You're late," when I stroll into the sitting room.

"And you're still acting like you've got a giant stick up your ass," I retort.

"Issues?" Sawyer asks.

"I had to create a diversion so my bodyguard wouldn't see me sneaking out," I admit, dropping my helmet and leather jacket on the arm of the couch.

Louis is grating on my nerves these nights. He barely spends any time standing guard in the hallway outside my room, preferring to smuggle his latest fuck buddy onto the grounds for sexy time. The problem is, he's been bringing her to one of the unused outdoor buildings on the edge of the garden, and it's way too close to where I enter the forest from the tunnel. I stumbled upon them earlier in the week and almost got caught, so, tonight I sent a virus to the camera system, timed to impact just before I planned to leave, knowing he'd be called to assist and I could leave without fear of discovery.

"Hey." Xavier pulls me into a hug, kissing the top of my head. "Don't mind Grumpy McGrumpy. I only just got here."

"Looking sexy as fuck, beautiful," Jackson says, removing a blunt from his pocket as he trails his gaze over my tight black lacy tank top, skintight black leather pants, and black wedge boots.

Sawyer snatches the blunt off him. "I need you alert with all brain cells functioning. And stop hitting on her to wind Marshall up. I'm sick of refereeing."

I smirk, perching on the arm of the couch. "Aw, are you two still fighting over me?"

"Don't flatter yourself," Cam drawls, flopping into the recliner chair. "You're just another pussy. Nothing special. And it's not the first time Lauder and I have hit on the same woman."

"Try telling that to someone who believes it, dickwad," Xavier says, sitting down beside me and sending daggers in Cam's direction.

"And this is exactly what I'm talking about." Sawyer sighs, throwing his arms out in exasperation. "We'll make no progress with everyone throwing shade, so just quit it and focus."

"Have you had any luck finding an expert who can advise us how best to open the safe?" Cam asks Xavier, immediately getting down to business.

"I've contacted one guy, but I'm still checking his credentials."

"We're running out of time," Cam replies. "They're back next week."

"They won't be back until late Friday," I confirm. "So that gives us a full week."

"Why don't we just have a stab at the safe ourselves?" Jackson suggests.

"Because Xavier and I have already tried it. Attempting to work out the code, even using high-tech software, still gives us a list of combinations that's too long to test. And it's composed of certain materials which mean it's virtually impenetrable. Besides trying to cut into it would be messy, make too much noise, and the security team would catch us. Or my father would know someone compromised the safe."

"We need the element of surprise with the evidence," Sawyer agrees. "Hearst can't know we've been in his safe and copied the contents."

"This seems like a dead-end idea." Jackson taps his leg impatiently off the hardwood floor. "I don't see how we'll ever get into that safe."

"Career criminals have tools that will enable us to crack the code on the safe but it's not like we can just find their number listed in the

Yellow Pages," Xavier replies. "And I need to vet any guys I find online because Hearst, Montgomery, and Barron are in cahoots with a lot of these people. The last thing we want is to make arrangements with one of their contacts, compromise our plans, and lose the element of surprise."

"Which is why I think we'll struggle to pull this off in the next week," Cam says. "We need more time to plan. Rushing risks mistakes."

"Look." I place my elbows on my knees and cup my chin in my hands. "It will be easier to pull this off while my father and the elite are away, but if we have to do it after they return, so be it. I'll think of some way of getting them out of the house so you guys can work without risk of discovery."

"And we'll still have the security detail to handle anyway," Xavier adds.

"I can manage that. I have Oscar under my thumb, and I'll use him to create some diversion which will pull the others away. We'll manipulate the camera feed, overlaying a blank image of the hallway to mask our comings and goings."

And if all else fails, I can get them out using the tunnel infrastructure, but I'm not mentioning that as it's only a last resort. I still don't trust these guys as far as I'd throw them.

I spend the next day at the library, digging through more of the records. This time, I pull up every news article I can find on Emma Anderson's suicide. I asked Cam why my father would kill his aunt, and he gave me one of his usual shouty non-answers, but I sense he knows more than he's letting on.

God, would it kill the jerk to throw me a bone?

I remember Mrs. Anderson with fondness even though I was only about four or five the last time I saw her. Before she had a falling out with my mother, they were best friends and we spent a lot of time with her and the Anderson boys.

I had a little crush on Maverick Anderson, but he barely knew I existed. He was four years older than me, and he enjoyed tormenting me and making me cry.

I remember this one time he chased me around the pool when we were over at their house and I fell on the stone patio and cut my knee. Mrs. Anderson sent him to his room and took me into the kitchen to clean me up while Mom watched the rest of the hooligans jumping in and out of the pool. She gave me vanilla ice cream with strawberries and strawberry syrup, and I remember thinking it was the most delicious thing I'd ever eaten. Mom was strict with treats, only allowing us to have candy on Saturdays, and Mrs. Anderson made me promise to keep it a secret.

I never told.

Not even Drew, and we told each other everything back then. But he was best buddies with Kaiden Anderson, and I was afraid he'd blab to him. I didn't want it getting back to his mom because I didn't want to displease her.

That ended up being one of the last times we all hung out together. Then the moms stopped talking, and a few years later, Emma was found dead after overdosing on pills. Her youngest two sons were only one and two respectively at the time of her death, and I remember the baby crying incessantly at the funeral and how the entire congregation was in floods of tears.

Mom was inconsolable.

Then six months later, she was dead too.

I read every article I can lay my hands on, and they all say the same.

She committed suicide.

No foul play suspected.

Case closed.

Atticus Anderson fell apart after that if the reports are reliable. He lost his business and his home and moved the family out of Rydeville.

I wonder if they moved to be with Cam and his family? If the older brother Cam mentioned by accident is one of his cousins? I suppose it'd make sense. If Atticus Anderson had lost everything, wouldn't he'd turn to his family for help?

I want to bring it up with Cam, but he's so closed off and he's not likely to volunteer any information. Plus, if he finds out I've been digging into old records, he'll probably be pissed and shut me down. So, I've got to time it right. To look for an opportunity to bring it casually into the conversation and see if I can uncover more.

After the library, I drop by Jane's for a while, eating dinner with her family, before I return home. I spend an hour dancing in my home studio, working up a sweat as I glide around the polished floor to a mix of tunes on my cell. I do some of my best thinking when I'm dancing, and while ballet is my favorite, I love contemporary too.

Cam's question about what I want to do with my life has been playing on repeat in my mind all week. I've been so focused on plotting my escape, and making it happen, that I've given little thought to what I'll do when I'm free to make my own choices.

I want to dance. Maybe on Broadway or the West End in London.

And I want to travel. To explore different continents and cultures. To expand my horizons.

Or maybe teach, because I'm academically minded and I'm one of those weird kids who enjoy school. That could be because it got me out of the house and away from my father every day, but I like to think it's more than that.

I definitely want to attend college. And I've already researched Juilliard. Getting to go there would be a dream come true.

But all it can be is a dream. For now.

Because I can't get my hopes up.

Not until I know I'm free to make my own life decisions.
And everything is still hanging in the balance.

Jane and I spend Sunday at the beach topping up our tans. Although it's late September, this weekend has been unseasonably warm, and it'll probably be the last opportunity we get to do this for a while. We swim, chat, listen to music, and share the picnic Mrs. Jenkins prepared for us, only leaving when the beach is almost empty, and our tummies are rumbling for more food. I pull my thigh-skimming strapless gold beach dress up over my black and gold bikini and slip my feet into my Gucci flip flops before we make our way through the thick sand.

We're walking toward the grassy path when I spy a forlorn figure, hunched over a sketchpad drawing, sitting on top of one dune.

Cam has his head half down, and a look of fierce concentration is etched upon his face. His hand flies across the page, his wrist skillfully angling, his fingers smudging the drawing. His entire body appears relaxed in a way I rarely see, and I instantly know sketching is for him what dancing is to me.

Memories of the sketches I looked at in his room surge to the forefront of my memory, and a little niggle tickles the back of my mind. Jane notices my attention has wavered, and she angles her head in the same direction. "Isn't that…"

Cam's head whips up as if some invisible force has called to him. His Adam's apple bobs in his throat as he drinks me in. He's got a ball cap on backward, and he's bare chested, only wearing khaki shorts and sneakers on his feet, with his sketchpad balanced on his bent knees.

We stare at one another as Jane and I walk by, but he doesn't move to acknowledge me, and I do the same. Electricity swirls around me, igniting the air between us, heightening my senses. All the tiny hairs lift on the back of my neck, and butterflies are running amok in my chest. Honestly, this freaky attraction between us is getting out of hand.

"Holy hawt chemistry," Jane jokes once we've moved out of earshot, fanning her hands in front of her face. "You can stay with him if you like. I'm cool to make my way home."

"I'm not ditching you." I loop my arm through hers. "Especially not for a Grade-A jerk like Camden Marshall."

"How's that denial thing working for you these days?" she quips.

"I'm hanging on by a thread," I admit.

"You sure you don't want to take advantage before Trent returns and breathes down your neck again?"

"Ugh." I chew on the inside of my mouth. "Please don't remind me. These past few weeks without him and Father have been bliss. And Trent will be hopping mad when he returns because I've refused to send him any naughty pics and I hang up every time he initiates phone sex."

"All the more reason you should climb the hottie like a tree while you can."

I slam to a halt. "Who are you, and what have you done with my best friend?"

She smiles softly. "I just want you to grab happiness where you can. I hate that you're forced to be with someone you don't love."

"Forget love. I don't even *like* Trent," I remind her.

"Exactly why you should get with Cam while you can."

"But I don't like him either." I send her a knowing look. "And you shouldn't too, not after what they did to you."

"I hate the thought they've seen me like that, but there's nothing I can do about it." She shrugs. "It's survival of the fittest, and it's not like our guys haven't pulled shit over the years."

"True, but it's never been at our expense."

"If you're trying to switch the subject, it won't work." I flip her the bird, and she smirks. "You don't have to like him to make out with him, and it's obvious you two are hot for one another, which," she adds, threading her arm in mine and pulling me forward toward the parking lot, "is something you must work on. If Trent sees the way you two stare at one another in the cafeteria when you think no one's looking, there'll be hell to pay."

"I didn't realize I was so obvious."

"Sparks fly when you two are in the same vicinity, and I'm sure I'm not the only one who's noticed."

"Great," I groan, sighing. "One more thing for me to worry about."

We drop Jane off first and set out for the ancient monstrosity I call home. "What time did Oscar leave?" I ask Louis, frowning when I see I still don't have a reply to the text message I sent him twenty minutes ago.

Louis shrugs. "I don't know. About two hours ago?"

I roll my eyes. Honestly, I don't know how he's still on my father's payroll. He's less than useless. All he could tell me when I got back to the car—startled to find him waiting with Jeremy when I was expecting Oscar—was he went home to deal with some family emergency. I didn't hesitate to message Oscar immediately, concerned, wondering if there is anything I can do to help.

I put my cell away when we turn into our driveway, leaning my face against the window as I vow to cherish my last week of freedom before everyone returns.

But when we round the bend, and I spot the row of cars parked out front, my stomach dips, and disappointment slams into my gut.

They're home early.

Shit.

That fucks up things with the guys. I guess that means we move to Plan B.

Using my bag to shield me, I tap out a quick text on my burner cell to Xavier to let him know my father is back early, asking him to relay the message to the new elite. Then I quickly stow it in the concealed inner pocket of my bag, plant a fake happy smile on my face, and get out of the car to greet the controlling bastard.

CHAPTER TWENTY-FIVE

"What the hell are you wearing?" my father barks from his position in the lobby. He's propped against the marble table as if he was waiting for me.

Hello to you too.

"Beachwear." *Dumbass.* "I was at the beach all day with Jane."

"You look like a common whore."

His nostrils flare, and he's a little red in the face.

Is it bad I hope it's because of ill health? Like terminal heart disease or stage four lung cancer?

My hands ball into fists at my side. "This is what everyone wears to the beach."

"You're not everyone!" he snaps, pushing off the table and stalking toward me with a muscle ticking in his jaw. His eyes glimmer with cold menace, and it's a look I've seen countless times before. Panic bubbles up my throat. "You know the rules. You look and act respectable, in public, at all times. The beach is no exception."

I want to tell him to go fuck himself, but he's riled up about something, and I don't want to give him further ammunition to lash out at me. So, I bite my tongue and say what he needs to hear. "I'm sorry, Father. It won't happen again."

He grabs my arm and drags me down the corridor toward his study. His nails dig into my arm, hurting me, but I know better than to mention it, so I absorb the pain, trying to keep myself calm as adrenaline floods my system and alarm bells blare in my ears. When he shoves me into his study and I find Drew, Trent, Charlie, Mr. Barron, and that sleazebucket Christian Montgomery waiting, my panic accelerates to new heights.

This cannot be good.

"What's going on?" I inquire, my eyes searching Drew out. He subtly shakes his head, letting me know he's as much in the dark as I am.

I jump as the door slams shut, startling me.

"That's what I'd like to know," my father growls, grabbing a piece of paper off his desk and walking toward me. His eyes are manic, the veins in his neck bulging, and he looks primed to detonate.

Fear crawls under my skin, and pressure settles on my chest. I back up until I hit the wall, throwing panicked eyes at Drew over my father's shoulder. Drew and Charlie stand rigidly still, their brows creased with worry while Trent watches with curiosity etched all over his face. Mr. Barron, Charlie's dad, shuffles awkwardly on his feet, rubbing the back of his head in an obvious tell. Trent's father smirks, almost gloating over what's about to go down.

"Whatever it is you think I've done you're mistaken," I blurt, hating how shaky my voice sounds. I'm guessing they've found out something about the shit that's been going on while they've been away and they're unhappy with how I handled it.

Or maybe they were in cahoots with Rochelle's father or Wentworth's father and I should have checked with them before I took them down. "And I'll fix it. I swear."

"I'd like to know how the fuck you intend to reinstate your hymen!!" my father roars, and all the blood drains from my face. Drew straightens, sending me a perplexed look while Charlie stares at the floor, hiding his face from view. For once, Trent looks confused.

No. Please, God, no. He can't have found out.

He shoves the paper in my face. "Someone sent this to Christian," he confirms as I try to focus on reading the words on the page, but my vision is blurry as panic races through my body at an unprecedented rate. My legs buckle, threatening to go out from under me, and I grip onto the wall to steady myself.

"Read. It," my father demands. "Out. Loud. Or I'll take you outside and put a bullet through your skull right this second."

Forcing back bile, I wet my dry lips and read the words typed in large, bold font.

ABIGAIL MANNING IS A LYING LITTLE SLUT. SHE'S ALREADY SPREAD HER LEGS AND THE JOKE IS ON YOU AND YOUR SON.

That's all it says. It's like one of those blackmail letters you see on crime shows except this letter isn't demanding any ransom. It's just sealing my fate.

"It's not true," I blurt, in a complete state of panic, not thinking it through. "When would it have happened? I'm surrounded by the guys or my bodyguards all the time. And Jeremy drives me most everywhere. Whoever sent this is messing with you. It's probably a student at school, and this is their sick way of trying to get back at me for this week."

My heart is racing so fast I'm worried I'm on the verge of a coronary. My palms are slick, and my brow is dotted with little beads of sweat.

My father grips my chin painfully. "If you're lying to me, you'll be sorry."

"I'm not lying," I lie, silently praying for divine intervention. Begging him to believe me and drop it even though I know it goes against my father's M.O.

He releases my chin and steps back, scrutinizing my face carefully. I try to hold his gaze with confidence I don't feel, but it's challenging when my whole body is trembling and I'm this close to puking.

The instant a smug grin tips up the corners of his mouth, I know I'm screwed. "There's an easy way of determining this," he says in a lethal tone, yanking me to him and dragging me across the room. He slams me across his desk, holding my face down with one meaty palm while he yanks my flimsy beach dress up with the other. "Trent, son, get over here."

My heart is pounding frantically, and my breathing is labored. I can even smell my fear. He presses his palm tighter on my face, smooshing my cheek into his desk, but I barely feel any pain because my body's gone into shock as he rips my bikini bottoms off in front of the room. Cool air swirls around my naked buttocks, and I wish the ground would open up and swallow me.

"Father, I—" Drew's anguished eyes meet mine as he attempts to intervene. Charlie jerks his head toward his father, but I can't see his expression.

"You dare to interrupt me, Andrew?!" My father roars at my twin. "This is business. Exactly the thing we've trained you to deal with. If you can't handle it, you know where the door is. But don't expect me to support you if you walk out."

"Daddy, please," I sob, not above begging if it'll save me from this new humiliation. Christian Montgomery licks his lips as his eyes flit from my face to my bare ass. Nausea swims up my throat at the sight of the growing bulge in his pants.

My father's large palm swats my ass, and I cry out as stinging pain sears my flesh. "Shut your mouth, and spread your legs, Abigail, and I'll make this quick."

"Michael, is it necessary to do this here? You could conduct an examination in private," Mr. Barron says, and I could kiss him for attempting to reason with my father even though I know it's futile. Both he and his son are averting their eyes, only making me respect them more.

"Stay out of this, Charles. I don't tell you how to deal with your children, so butt out of my affairs."

"Trent, son, you're the only one who can do this," my father says, working hard to keep a level tone. I can tell he's seething. "Shove your fingers inside her, boy!" he barks, lifting me up by my waist so my ass is at a higher angle. Then he roughly forces my legs apart, and a loud sob rips out of my mouth, birthed straight from my wounded soul. "Feel if her hymen is still intact," he commands.

I've never let Trent touch me down there because the thought of him touching me intimately sends tremors of fear rushing through me. I never imagined his first time fingering me would be like this.

Tears roll freely out of my eyes as he plunges his finger inside me, pushing it up as far as it will go and feeling around, making my humiliation complete. The jagged edge of his nail tears me inside, but I bite down on my lip, determined not to make another sound. Silent tears continue to pour from my eyes, and something inherent shatters inside me. The pain in my chest is so intense it feels like I can't breathe.

Drew keeps his eyes locked on mine, an apology written on his face. Both Barrons continue to stare at the floor, but it makes little difference. They are still in the room to bear witness to my humiliation.

"What's the verdict?" my father asks.

"I...I don't know," Trent says. "She's very tight."

"Bend down and look inside her," my father commands, and my heart cracks wide-open. I can't keep my cries locked inside any longer, and I openly sob. Drew silently pleads with me to hold it together, but I can't. This is the worst affront to my privacy. An invasion I'll never get over. I can't believe Drew is allowing this. That his half-assed attempt at intervention was all he tried before accepting this as inevitable. If someone turned the tables, I'd have yelled bloody murder before I'd let him humiliate my twin.

"What am I looking for?" Trent asks as if he's never seen a vagina before.

"If her hymen is intact, there should be a thin layer of skin covering her opening with a small hole in it." Either my father Googled this before I came home or this isn't his first rodeo. I'm inclined to believe it's the latter.

"I see nothing like that," Trent says, using his fingers to open the front of my vagina, probing my folds to ensure he's doing a thorough job.

I want to die. To curl into a ball and cease to exist.

I should have just come clean instead of lying.

At least I might have been spared this humiliation.

A loud knock on the door sends my heart rate elevating to heart attack territory as thoughts of what he has planned next swirl through my fractured mind.

"Come in," my father calls out as if he doesn't have his almost-eighteen-year-old daughter spread-eagled across his desk with her ass and pussy on display.

"Ah, Doctor Cummings," he says, finally lifting his hand from my head. "Thank you for attending on such short notice. And on a Sunday too. I appreciate it."

Drew finally moves, pulling my dress down over my naked ass and helping me up. I slap his hands away, crossing my arms around my trembling body. I avoid looking at Trent, not wanting to see the smug expression on his face. Tears continue to cascade down my cheeks, and I'm powerless to stop them. A sharp ache lances across my chest, and a choked lump clogs my throat as the worst pain attacks me from all angles.

"I'm always at your disposal, Mr. Hearst," the doctor says in a monotone voice. "Is this her?"

"Yes." My father pulls me over by the arm. "I need your professional opinion on whether or not her hymen is intact."

That fucking bastard.

I glare at him.

He'd already summoned the doctor, so this was for pure show. A way to prove to Trent's father he's taking the accusation seriously. A way to punish me for my crime. Another means to try to break me.

"I'll need a private room with a bed," the doctor says.

"I'll have Louis take you to her bedroom. You can examine her there." I half-expect my father to march everyone with us, but he lets me leave with the doctor alone. "Don't let her out of your sight," he tells Louis, and the asshole nods with a gloating smile.

I glance over my shoulder at Drew, begging him to do something, but he hangs his head, and I know I'm on my own with this. Charlie finally lifts his head and looks at me. The tears in his eyes almost undo me, but I'm desperately trying to lock everything up inside until I can let it loose when I'm alone.

The doctor is cold and unfriendly as he instructs me to lie on my back on the bed, bend my knees up, and spread my legs wide. Louis wets his lips as he watches from the doorway. The asshole could easily keep watch from outside, but he's enjoying seeing me suffer. I could ask the doctor to send him away, but I have a feeling the request would fall on deaf ears, and I won't give Louis the satisfaction of knowing this is getting to me.

I squeeze my eyes shut when the doctor inserts his gloved finger inside me, and my ruination has come full circle. He flashes a small flashlight into my vagina, and more tears leak out of the corners of my eyes.

When he's done, he hovers over me with steely eyes. "You need to come back downstairs with me."

"I need to use the bathroom first," I say, and he nods.

"Make it quick." His tone is scathing.

I pull panties out of my laundry basket in the bathroom and pull them on before swiping angrily at the hot tears coursing down my cheeks. I blot my eyes and dab at my damp skin, fixing my hair and brushing my teeth, before I leave and rejoin a smirking Louis and the coldhearted doctor.

"What is your professional opinion?" my father asks the instant we step foot back in his study.

"She's not a virgin," the doctor coolly states, signing my death warrant.

"Thank you, Doctor Cummings, that will be all."

Louis escorts the doctor out, and the second the door is closed, Trent flies across the room, grabbing me by the throat. "You fucking, lying, cheating whore!" he spits, his eyes burning with rage and indignation.

"Get your filthy hands off her," Drew says, grabbing Trent's elbow and trying to pull him back.

"I'll fucking kill you, you slut!" He tightens his grip on my throat, restricting my oxygen supply. His neck muscles strain, and pure liquid venom spills from his eyes as he continues to squeeze me.

My eyelids flutter as black waves wash over my retinas. "Do it," I rasp while Drew and Charlie attempt to pry Trent's hands from my throat, but his hold is firm, and he's not giving up easily. Mr. Barron is shaking his head sadly, and Christian Montgomery looks like he wants to join his son in throttling me. He's no longer ogling me with desire, so that's at least one positive to come from this epic clusterfuck.

"Trent, I need you to let Abigail go," my father says. "I'll deal with this."

"She's my fucking fiancée," he growls.

"She's my daughter." My father squares up to him. "Let her go."

"Son, let her go," Mr. Montgomery says, and Trent drops me instantly. I crumple to the floor, gasping for air, rubbing my sore neck as tears spring from my eyes. Before I've had time to catch my breath, my father hauls me up, slamming me roughly into a chair he's placed in the center of the room. He ties my wrists and ankles to the arms and legs of the chair, and I wonder what new humiliation he has in store for me.

An icy-cold river sweeps through me, replacing all the blood in my veins, and a protective layer closes around my heart, sealing everything warm and humane behind it. My tears dry up, my previous anguished emotions replaced with an angry numbness I cling to.

My father stands in front of me, barely concealing his fury. "I'll ask you some questions, and I want answers. Refuse me, and I'll beat you to within an inch of your life."

I school my lips into a neutral expression and stare impassively at him. If he thinks I'm giving him anything, he's deranged.

I try one last-ditch attempt at changing my fate even if there's little hope of success. "Father, I swear to you I'm a virgin. I could've broken my hymen dancing or horseback riding. It's well known there are several ways it can happen. Ask the doctor. He can't say with one hundred percent certainty I'm not a virgin."

My father looks contemplative for a moment, and I can almost see the wheels turning in his brain. I'm giving him an out should he choose to take it and run with it.

But Trent's father isn't buying it. "Stop." Christian's nostrils flare as he steps up to me. "Just stop lying. If you dare to disrespect me and my son, the least you can do is own up to your sins."

I snort. "The way you own up to yours?"

He slaps me so hard my head jerks back painfully, and it feels like it's disconnected from my neck. "I want the truth," he demands, shooting my father a look which says the game is up and there's no point in me trying to stick to my claim of innocence. Even if I was pure, they wouldn't believe me.

A fresh wave of anger washes over my father's face as he leans into me. "Who have you had sex with?"

Even though it appears the new elite have reneged on our deal and fed me to the sharks, withholding Cam's name will infuriate my father, and that's all I care about now. If he thinks humiliating me, and beating me, will give him answers, he's sorely mistaken.

"I'm not telling you," I hiss, earning myself another slap in the face.

"I want his name." Placing his palms on either side of me, on the arms of the chair, he leans in, putting his menacing face up in mine.

"Fuck. You." My voice is detached as the words leave my mouth.

My head whips back as he punches me twice in the face. Tendrils of pain emanate from my nose, shooting angry shards all over my face.

"How many men have you let into your treacherous cunt?"

I smirk, licking the trickle of blood that leaks onto my lip from my swollen nose.

He punches me in the stomach, and I gasp, grappling for air as slicing pain ricochets through my upper torso.

"When did this happen?" He continues berating me.

"I'll never tell." I pant, still trying to recalibrate my breathing, earning a punch to the ribs this time. Agonizing pain rattles around my rib cage, and I cry out.

Grabbing hold of my chin, he roars, "Who was it?" His eyes are bulging and his nostrils flaring, and the scary, dark expression on his face promises a world of pain.

I ache everywhere, but there's a certain sense of release with the pain. I'm doing this on my terms now. He can beat me until I stop breathing if he likes. I'll never divulge the details.

"Who was it?" He punches me in the face again. "Answer me, you stupid cunt!"

I spit on him, and he goes crazy. Raining punches on me as he straddles the chair.

Voices bounce off the walls, in the background, but I can't make out who it is or what's being said.

We fall to the ground, the chair smashing into pieces underneath me, the full weight of his heavy body pressing down on me. His large hands close around my already bruised throat, and the last thing I hear before I black out is Drew pleading with my father to stop.

CHAPTER TWENTY-SIX

Every bone in my body aches when I finally come to, opening my eyes to the dark confines of my bedroom.

Drew is asleep in a chair at the side of my bed, his clothes wrinkled and a frown marring his beautiful face even in slumber. I reach one arm out from under the covers, my fingers crawling along the top of my bedside table, searching for my cell, when a throbbing pain radiates from my back, over my shoulder, and up my arm, and a whimper escapes my mouth.

Drew jerks awake, eyes wild and immediately on alert. "You're awake," he mumbles in a sleep-heavy tone. "How are you feeling?"

"How do you think?" I hiss, a fresh wave of pain blanketing me as the events of last night resurface in my mind.

Remorse washes over his face. "Abby," he whispers, tears pricking his eyes. "I'm so sorry."

My fingers continue searching for my cell, and he gently places it in my hand. I cradle the cell to my chest, attempting to scoot up the bed, but the pain circling around my torso is excruciating, and I cry out as tears slide from my eyes. Drew moves toward me, and I cower back, not wanting him anywhere near me. Sadness clings to his moist eyes. "I won't hurt you," he whispers. "Let me help you."

"I needed your help last night, and you did nothing." I sniffle, ignoring the pain to pull myself upright.

He hangs his head in shame. "I failed you, and I'll never forgive myself for as long as I live."

"I would never have let him do that to you." I sob, wincing again as another wave of pain moves through me.

Drew empties two pills from a box on my table, handing them to me with a glass of water. "I got the doctor to come back. He strapped up your bruised ribs and prescribed these strong painkillers. He says you most likely have a concussion and you need bedrest to heal."

"How could you let him touch me when I was unconscious?" I hiss, feeling like I've been assaulted all over again.

Drew's face drops. "Your entire body is broken and cut up, and you blacked out. I was fucking terrified, and I had to do something!" He smooths a hand over the five o'clock shadow on his chin. "I had no one else to call, and I was panicking. I stayed in the room the whole time he was here."

"Jeez, that makes me feel so much better." I level him with a sharp look. "You were in Father's study the whole time too, and that didn't stop me from being violated!"

He sinks to his knees, tears rolling down his face. "We didn't know, Abby! They yanked us out of training and told us we had to return early, but none of us knew why. We were completely blindsided when it went down. I went into shock. Didn't know how to stop it."

"You barely even tried," I whisper, clutching my cell almost painfully. "You let Trent do that to me," I sob, tears cascading down my face. "You let father humiliate me. You didn't even come up here when the doctor was examining me, and that asshole Louis had a front-row seat."

"He what?" Drew growls, and I narrow my eyes at him.

"Save your indignation, Drew. You're too fucking late!"

Sniffling, I glance at my cell, noting the time. "Can you call Jane and ask her to come here?"

"What are you doing?" he asks, as I shove the covers back, gingerly sliding my legs out of the bed. There isn't a single part of my body that doesn't feel some level of pain.

"Getting ready for school."

"You're not going to school." He looks incredulous. "You need to rest."

I glare at him. "I'm not staying here on my own with Father. I'm going to school."

"I'll stay home with you," he offers.

"What makes you think I want to stay here with you either? You're as bad as him."

His face crumples, but I don't feel an inch of remorse.

He stood by and did nothing.

I will never forgive him.

Never.

"I'll get Jane to stay with you then. Please, Abby. You have a concussion. It's serious."

"What happened to me was serious, but that'll just get brushed under the carpet, won't it?"

He clenches his jaw. "I don't know what'll happen. Father went over to Montgomery's last night to try to salvage your marriage. Trent stormed out of here, ready to explode." He drags a hand through his hair. "Everything's all up in the air."

"If the deal falls apart and I'm released from my obligation to marry that jerk, at least something good will have come from it." I stand, instantly assaulted with a barrage of pain, and I slam my hand down on the table to stop my legs from going out under me.

Drew slides a gentle hand behind my back, helping steady me.

"You can barely even walk. Please, A. Please get back in bed."

"No." I grit my teeth, forcing my feet to move. "I'll be fine once the medication kicks in, and I need to pee and shower."

I force Drew to leave my en suite bathroom after he helps me inside and turns on the shower. I stare at my reflection in the mirror with growing horror.

My nose is busted up, my lip torn where I must've bitten down on it, and multicolored bruising covers my cheeks and one side of my jaw. Gritting my teeth to bite back the pain, I manage to get my nightdress off, staring in disbelief at the myriad of bruises swathing my body. A thick white bandage is wrapped around my middle from my chest to my waist, damaged skin peeking out from both ends. Small cuts and grazes line my arms and lower legs. I'm guessing broken debris from the chair must have embedded in my skin as I was lying on the floor with my father beating me to a pulp.

Anger trundles through me, and I vow to get revenge as I move slowly toward the shower, every step knocking the wind out of me as pain skitters over every inch of me.

My father will pay for this.

So will Trent.

And Drew is as good as dead to me after his non-action.

I pant heavily as I step under the warm water, biting back my cries as the water stings my battered body.

I absorb the pain.

Clinging to it.

Letting it sink deep into my marrow.

I want to remember this feeling.

The pain.

The humiliation.

The rage and the disappointment.

I want it to fuel my vengeance. To use it to destroy the new elite because this betrayal goes more than skin deep. It's soul deep.

They are the only ones who knew. The only ones who could have done this to me.

I just don't understand why. *Or why now?*

It makes little sense.

Not unless they've figured out a way to get into my father's safe without me.

But maybe it was never about that to start with.

Maybe everything they've said and done has all been a ruse.

There's only one surefire way to find out. I need to get to school and confront them.

"I know you're pissed at Drew. I am too," Jane says as she helps me out of the house and into the car. "But I agree this is crazy. You're in agony, Abby. You need to stay in bed."

"Stop fighting me, and just help me do this," I snap with zero patience.

Her red-rimmed eyes are welling up again. When she arrived to help me get dressed, she burst out crying at the state of me. Drew had already told her what happened, and she's furious with him for not protecting me. I expected anger when she found out about my non-virgin status, but she has said nothing. Yet. I expect she's granted me a reprieve because of my current fragile state, and I know she'll want to talk about it at some point.

"I'd like some privacy, please, Jeremy," I ask once we're seated, unable to stomach Louis's smug, leering face on the ride to school. I still haven't heard from Oscar, and I'm worried my father has done something to him. At least, I was spared the ordeal of having to face the sperm donor this morning. According to Drew, he never returned last night, so he obviously stayed the night at the Montgomerys'.

Jane and I don't speak for ages. I stare blankly out the window, barely seeing the mansions and fields flash by, consumed with plans for revenge.

My heavily made-up features mostly disguise my injured face—there isn't much I can do about my swollen nose—and I've buttoned my shirt up to my neck so the indentation marks from Trent's fingers aren't visible. I'm wearing knee-high socks which cover the scrapes on my legs.

On the outside, I look near perfect.

On the inside, I'm broken into a million jagged pieces.

"Abby," Jane whispers when we're a few miles out from school.

"Yes." I turn to face her.

"I'm so sorry this happened to you." Tears slide down her cheeks. "I always knew your father was a monster, but I can't believe he did this." She clasps my hands in hers. "Parents are supposed to cherish and protect you. Not hurt and violate you."

She's openly sobbing again, and I brush her tears away with the pads of my thumbs. "I stopped believing in that a long time ago, and I've always known what he was capable of. I'm lucky I'm still alive." But I don't know for how much longer.

"Don't say that!" she cries out.

"It's the truth, Jane. If he loses his deal with Christian Montgomery, he may well kill me. He needs Montgomery's company's skillset to launch Manning Motor's auto-drive car program. Christian's research team is the foremost experts on robotics, and they've both invested heavily in the project to date."

"Which is why Christian won't pull out," Jane says, attempting to reassure me.

"The difference is, Christian owns the intellectual property," I say, relaying what Drew's previously told me in confidence. "That only becomes shared after my marriage to Trent. If the marriage doesn't go ahead, Christian will have no difficulty finding a new car manufacturer to partner with. My father stands to lose his shirt on this project, not to mention market share, when news gets out. If Christian partners with a competitor brand, Manning Motors will no longer hold the title as the world's largest, most successful car manufacturer, and my father will kill me with his bare hands."

"Shit."

"Yeah. You could say that."

"We're here, Ms. Abigail," Jeremy says through the sound system. My door swings open a minute later, and Jeremy helps me out of the car. Thankfully, the pain pills have kicked in, and while I'm still sore all over, I can at least move one foot in front of the other at a reasonable pace.

Drew and Charlie are waiting at the bottom of the steps for us. Crowds swarm them, greeting them like long-lost warriors returning from battle.

It all seems so stupid now.

All the rules and the battle to regain control.

My view of the world has tilted on its axis again, and I'm struggling to find my new equilibrium.

Drew moves to my side, purposely ignoring the evil eye his girlfriend is sending in his direction.

I'm sure this wasn't the homecoming they had planned.

He attempts to circle his arm around my shoulder, but I stop him with a vicious look. "The time to protect me was last night. You're too late."

"Abby, please."

The forlorn expression on his face does nothing to alter my resolve, because the new me is harder of heart. "Just leave me alone, Drew. As far as I'm concerned, I don't have a brother."

I walk ahead, leaving him behind with Jane. Footsteps thump

behind me, and Charlie's spicy cologne swirls through the air. I don't acknowledge him, but he forces my hand when we step foot into the hallway, racing around me and stopping right in front of my face. "Can we talk?"

"I've nothing to say to you either." Truth is, I don't blame Charlie as much as I blame Drew. He's not my brother. Although I consider him a close friend, and as my friend, he should've tried something. His father attempted to intervene, but they all allowed it to happen, and I'm so sick of everyone being afraid to stand up to my father. I appreciate that he didn't look. That he helped restrain Trent and helped Drew pull my father off me at the end, but it doesn't change the fact he didn't stop it.

And the other truth is it's hard to look him in the face knowing he knows what happened in that room last night.

I'm embarrassed and ashamed.

"That's fair and I deserve it. We all deserve it." Tears stab his eyes. "He had no right to do that to you. And the Montgomerys are every bit as bad as your father." A lump forms in my throat when he lifts his hand, carefully cupping my face. "You're too beautiful, too inherently good, and far too strong and brave to let them tear you down. Dad and I wanted to intervene, Abby, but we couldn't." His eyes plead for understanding I don't possess. "And we only stayed in case he took it too far. Then we would've stepped in, consequences be damned."

"What consequences?"

"There's so much you don't know, Abby. Things I wish I could tell you, but it'd be dangerous for all of us. Just know how bad I feel for failing you last night. It was unforgivable, but I swear to you, here and now, that I will never fail you again." A determined look materializes on his face. "Starting with making them pay."

"What do you mean?"

"I mean I'm done with all this bullshit elite rules and regulations. I've never agreed with the whole arranged marriage thing, and I sure as shit don't agree with your father's callous parenting style. He doesn't get to do that to you and get away with it. We'll fucking make him pay. I don't know how yet, but it'll happen."

For the first time in hours, a small smile plays on my lips.

This is what I needed to hear from Drew.

To know he's finally taken my side.

But all my brother has offered is weak excuses and meaningless apologies.

"I can count on you?" I drill him with a serious look.

"Completely." He slowly reels me into a tender hug. "I'm here for you, Abby. You're not doing this alone."

CHAPTER TWENTY-SEVEN

Charlie's support has bolstered my confidence, and he couldn't know how badly I needed him on my side. I've barely paid attention in class all morning, as I run over everything in my mind.

I still can't fathom what angle the new elite are playing. Jackson acted his usual flirtatious self in math class, and it genuinely seemed like he didn't have a clue. He didn't eye me warily or check me out any more than usual, and wouldn't he if he knew they'd dropped a bomb? I had already asked Xavier to message them to explain my father was home early before everything went down, so, if they'd sent the letter, they would know why he came back early, and wouldn't they check for signs of a confrontation?

Unless Cam did this alone.

He hates me enough to do it.

But I circle back to the same question: *Why?*

And that's when another unpleasant thought enters my mind.

What if it wasn't them?

Xavier recently became acquainted with that knowledge too. In theory, he could have sent the letter although I don't want to believe that. But my mind is seriously fucked, and I don't know what to believe or who I can trust.

And then there's a third possibility. That it's someone I don't know. I've seen how easy it is to unearth secrets and invade people's online privacy.

Could one of my father's enemies have discovered my secret? Has someone been watching us? Overheard us talking? Or am I overthinking this, and the simple truth is the new elite played me for a fool?

I rub at my throbbing temples, urging my mind to quiet down, at least until it's lunchtime and I've gauged their reaction.

I know how I want to play this.

Drew and Trent will not be happy.

Father will swing for me again if he finds out.

But I'm done playing their stupid games.

Father pushed me, and now he'll find out just how I push back. I've zero fucks to give anymore.

The bathroom is empty when I step inside minutes after the lunchtime bell has chimed. I lock the door, remove the makeup wipes from my bag, and erase all traces of the thick foundation masking my injuries. I open the top few buttons of my shirt, stuffing my tie in my bag, and I secure my long hair in a sleek ponytail, ensuring my bruises are on full display.

I look like I lost a fight with a semitruck.

But that's the point.

Drawing brave breaths, I take one final look in the mirror, silently championing myself as I exit the bathroom and head toward the cafeteria.

The hallways are empty. The only sound the tap-tapping of my shoes. Noise wafts from the busy cafeteria out into the hall as I stand with my hand gripping the door handle, blood thrumming in my ears and butterflies skating around my chest.

My mouth is dry as I push the doors open and step foot inside the packed room.

No one notices at first.

I keep my head held high, my shoes squeaking across the floor, as I make my way to the new elite's table. A few shocked gasps ring out as people gradually take notice. Brief flashes erupt around me as people take photos on their cells. And a deathly hush descends on the room when I slam to a halt at the new elite's table, dropping my book bag onto a chair with a loud thud.

The guys stop talking and eating, looking up at me. Sawyer blinks repeatedly, a look of horror appearing on his face. Jackson's lopsided grin instantly slides off his face, and his head whips in the elite's direction. Cam's hands ball into tight fists on top of the table as his eyes skim over my bruised flesh. Fire burns in his eyes, and he holds himself rigidly still, his face a scary mask of pent-up aggression. "What the fuck happened?" Cam asks.

"You tell me." My eyes seethe as I examine their faces for clues, but all I'm seeing is genuine shock and anger.

"I don't understand." Sawyer's brows knit together. "Why would we know?"

I don't have time to waste on bullshit. Placing my palms on the table, I lean down. "Did you send Trent's father a letter telling him I was no longer a virgin?"

Sawyer's shocked eyes meet mine. "No! Hell no." He lowers his voice. "Why would we do that when we're working together?"

"Your father did this to you?" Cam asks in a low, menacing tone.

"My father and Trent," I say in a louder voice, uncaring who hears.

"Motherfucking bastards," Jackson says in a clipped voice.

A shadow looms on either side of me, and I straighten up, my face grimacing as pain twists my back into painful knots.

"What are you doing, Abby?" Drew asks, reaching for my arm.

"Asking the enemy if this was their doing," I confirm, acknowledging

Charlie with a nod. I deliberately did this in public for several reasons, this being one.

"And was it?" Drew asks, frowning when I shuck his hand away. Out of the corner of my eye, I spy Trent glowering in this direction. He has a petite blonde perched on his lap, which is a first. Not that I care.

I'm done with Trent.

If my father patches things up with his father, I've decided I'm just going to take my money and my fake ID and disappear. I'll worry about how to protect myself when he comes after me at a later stage.

"No." Sawyer stands. "We had nothing to do with this."

Cam swings his body over the table, sending plates crashing noisily to the ground. He grabs Drew around the neck, his eyes wild as he stares at my brother. "You let them do this to her?"

"You don't understand." My brother pants. "I couldn't stop it."

Cam shoves him away, and Drew falls on his butt on the ground. "You're right. I don't." Cam casts a venomous glance over his shoulder at Trent. "Because if he did that to my sister, he'd be under six feet of rubble by now."

Drew climbs to his feet, looking strangely at Cam. Then his eyes narrow, his nostrils flare, and he swings his fist at Cam, growling, as he punches him in the face. "That's for spying on my fiancée."

Cam deflects his second hit, grabbing Drew's wrist and holding him back. "You don't get to do this. Not after you let Abby down." He glances over his shoulder at Trent. "And you're still cozying up to that asshole."

"Trent will pay for hurting Abby," Charlie says. "That's a promise."

"Were you there?" Sawyer asks, looking slightly confused.

Charlie tersely nods his head.

"How the fuck did this happen," Cam growls, throwing the

weight of his anger in Charlie's direction, and now, *I'm* confused.

"Oh, shit," Drew exclaims, looking behind me. I turn around, watching Trent saunter toward us, towing the little blonde with him, wearing false bravado to disguise the rage bubbling under the surface. As if he has any right to it.

I'm the one who was humiliated and violated.

He doesn't get to throw his anger in my face.

Drew and Charlie stand by either side of me as Jackson comes around the table to stand beside Cam and Sawyer, just behind me.

Trent's gaze slowly rotates among us. "Barron, Manning," he says, jerking his head in acknowledgment at the guys. "Whore," he seethes, pinning murderous eyes on me.

"Small dick," I reply, happy to finally be playing this game. It takes a lot of self-control not to lunge at him and claw my talons down his face. Looking at Trent has always been difficult, but now, I'm sick to my stomach at the sight of him, remembering how he caved to my father's commands without hesitation.

He barks out a laugh. "Funny. I think most of the chicks in this room can attest to the opposite."

The bimbo at his side giggles, and I roll my eyes. "And you have the nerve to call me a whore."

"If you hadn't been such a frigid bitch, I wouldn't have had to look elsewhere," he sneers, and the plaything under his arm giggles again.

"I thought I was a whore. Now I'm frigid?" I arch a brow. "Make up your mind." His nostrils flare, and I move a step closer. "I'll help you out," I say, ensuring my voice is loud enough for those close by to hear. "I have standards hence why I wanted your STD-ridden cock nowhere near me. Hell, I can barely even tolerate looking at you." I narrow my eyes and glare at him. "And now I can add sex offender to the list of adjectives I use to describe you. I'll remember to include that when I'm making my police report."

He laughs, and I raise my hand, ready to slap him when Charlie wraps his fingers around my wrist, pulling me back. "He's not worth it."

"Forgotten what team you're playing for, Charlie boy, or you think you finally have a chance at getting into her panties?" Trent pushes all up in Charlie's face. "Trust me, she's far too much work." A wicked glint appears in his eye. "And after I had my fingers in her cunt last night, I can confirm her pussy's nothing special. She was so tight I'm wondering if she *did* accidentally break her hymen riding a bike or something."

The blonde giggles again, and I've officially run out of patience. "Chad!" I holler, gesturing him forward. He's by my side in a nanosecond. "Please take out the trash."

"My pleasure, Abigail." He turns to the blonde. "Don't make this any harder than it has to be."

She laughs, clinging to Trent's side, but he's too much invested in this conversation to waste time with distractions. He shoves her away without even looking at her. Her whiny voice bores through my sore skull as Chad leads her away.

"As I was saying," Trent interjects before anyone else can put in a word. "My guess is she's still a virgin. Not that anyone will believe that now." He sends a smug grin my way. "Sucks to be you."

I smile sweetly at him. "Sucks to be *you*, and I hate to burst that self-inflated bubble, but I didn't break my hymen riding a bike. I did it the traditional way." I lick my lips. "I had sex with a guy who rocked my world all night long, and it was a million times better than it would've been with you." I rake derisory eyes over him. "I chose a guy who knew how to take care of my needs." I prod him in the chest. "Not a selfish fucking prick who jerks off and runs, with no regard for his lover."

"You didn't," he seethes through gritted teeth.

I flash him the biggest grin. "Oh, I did. *Over and over and over again.*" I drag the words out, really going to town. "And the next day, when my body ached deliciously, I replayed it in my mind, and I laughed at the thought of getting one over on you." My grin expands even wider. "I've been laughing at you for months, Trent, because this entire time you've been trying to force your way into my bed, thinking you would be my first, when another guy already beat you to it." I cup my hands around my mouth. "Loser!" I whisper-shout, and he lunges at me, but I'm ready for him this time.

Adrenaline temporarily papers over the pain in my body, supercharging my arm as I swing it around, landing a punch square on his nose. He's caught off guard, stumbling back against a chair, falling clumsily to the ground, and I'm on him in a flash, unconcerned about retaliation as I jump on him, landing punches to his face and his chest, pulling his hair and dragging my nails across his face.

Strong arms lift me up off him, and I thrash about, kicking my legs out, hoping I might catch him in the balls. "Get her out of here," Drew says, handing me off to Charlie. "I'll deal with Trent."

Charlie cradles me against his chest as all the fight leaves me in a rush. I rest my head on his shoulder, locking eyes with Cam as Charlie carries me out of the room. I expect to see a smug expression on his face after the compliments I just showered him with. But a conflicted look paints his face instead, and a plethora of different emotions stare back at me. His mask is down, and he wants me to understand he's showing me something real. He doesn't take his eyes off me for a second, and unspoken words pass between us, and I know, without a shadow of doubt, that Camden Marshall did not write that letter.

I'd stake my life on it.

But if the new elite aren't behind this, who is? And what do they have to gain by revealing my secret?

CHAPTER TWENTY-EIGHT

By mid-afternoon, I'm flailing. I used up whatever additional reserves of strength I had during the confrontation in the cafeteria. Combined with the fact I neglected to bring my pain pills with me, and my body aches like a bitch, I'm fading fast.

The teacher's voice drones on, and I rest my head on the table, trying to blank out his voice and the darts of pain rattling through my skull. The longer he goes on, the worse I feel. Heat radiates from my bruised ribs, burning me up under my uniform. Sweat sticks my shirt to my back, and damp tendrils of hair curl around my brow. Nausea swims up my throat, my stomach churns violently, and I fear I'm going to be sick.

I jump up, swaying dangerously as I grab my book bag and stagger from the room, ignoring the teacher's questions. The door crashes against the wall as I body slam my way out into the empty hallway, clutching a hand over my mouth while my body heaves.

I can't even cry out when I'm unexpectedly drawn into a warm body, and a sturdy pair of arms slide under my thighs. "I've got you," Cam says, running with me in his arms toward the nearest bathroom.

He's only just deposited me in a stall when I throw up the contents of my meager lunch into the toilet. My body continues to heave, rejecting whatever I have in my stomach, until there's nothing left to expel. My ribs throb, my head feels like it's splitting wide-open, and I'm on fire, burning up as if my body is engulfed in flames.

I slump against the back of the stall as Cam speaks into his cell in hushed tones, his worried eyes roaming over my face. I try to remove my jacket, but my arms won't cooperate, flopping at my sides every time I try.

Cam ends his call, pocketing his cell, and crouches down in front of me. "Where does it hurt?" he asks, scrutinizing my eyes.

"Everywhere," I rasp, squeezing my eyes shut as blinding pain rips through my skull. "Too hot," I murmur, feebly attempting to remove my jacket again.

"Can I?" he asks, in the softest tone, and I force my eyes open. I can barely summon the energy to nod, but my eyes convey my permission.

With gentle hands, he strips me out of my jacket and shirt, leaving me in a camisole and my bra, before scooping me up into his arms again. The jostling movement of his body lulls me into a sleepy state, and I slump against his shoulder, my arms loosely hanging around his neck. "Sleep, baby," he murmurs. "I'll take care of you."

And for the second time in less than twenty-four hours, I black out.

When I wake, I'm in a strange bed, covered in black silk sheets that feel incredibly soft under my aching body. "Abigail," an unfamiliar voice says, and I jolt awake, jerking away from the stranger perched on the side of my bed.

"Hey, it's okay," Cam says, appearing on my other side. "He's here to help you."

"Who are you?" I ask, whimpering as my sore limbs protest when I sit up. I'm still in my camisole and bra, and someone—Cam most likely—removed my skirt, socks, and shoes, leaving me in my white silk panties.

"He's my cousin," Cam blurts, leveling the good-looking dark-haired guy with a strange expression.

"I'm in Harvard training to be a doctor," the cousin says. "Cam asked me to come by and check you out."

"I'm fine. Just sore and need to sleep," I mumble.

"That's not what the doctor who examined you last night said," he calmly refutes, his brown eyes challenging me to argue.

"You've spoken to that asshole?" I ask, and he chuckles.

"Not exactly."

"I hacked into the doctor's system and pulled the report," Sawyer confirms, and I jump at the sound of his deep voice.

I look around the dimly lit room, finding him straddling a chair. My eyes do a quick recon of the space, and I'm surprised. "I'm in your bedroom?" I ask Cam, and he blinks at me.

"Where else would you be?" he says, looking at me like I'm crazy for even asking.

"In one of the guest rooms?"

"You're staying here, and that's final," he growls.

I'm too tired and sore to argue with him, so I say nothing, accepting it even if I don't understand it. Guess he hasn't realized the panty stash is missing yet, and he doesn't know I broke into his room and did some snooping.

Jackson's trademark chuckle wafts around the room. "Is everyone here?" I inquire, squinting to make out his form in the dark room.

Jackson swivels around in the gaming chair at the end of the room, game controller in hand. "We were worried about you, beautiful. We all wanted to make sure you were okay."

"Why am I in your house?" I ask, as the door opens and a familiar face walks in.

"We felt it was the safest place," Charlie says, leaning over me and planting a kiss on my forehead. I don't miss the scowl Cam throws his direction or the way my heart rejoices at his obvious possessiveness.

"And you're okay with this?" My voice drips in disbelief.

"It's not safe for you to go home. Your father is on the warpath. Apparently, talks broke down last night, and he's like a caged lion, according to Drew. He's at the house trying to calm him."

"And where does my father think I am?"

Charlie sits on the edge of the bed, tucking my hair behind my ears. "He believes you're staying at my house." He places his finger against my lips when I open my mouth to speak. "Don't worry. I squared it with my parents. If your father asks, you are recuperating at our place. I told my father you were with trusted friends, and he won't pry."

I arch a brow. "Trusted friends?" My eyes flit to Cam, and his scowl deepens.

"It's a stretch, I know, but I've spoken with the guys, and they assure me they mean you no harm. They'll take care of you." Charlie stares at Cam, and Cam sends him back an equally suspicious look.

"Better than you assholes did," Cam challenges.

Charlie stands, his body wired tight. "Do not fucking push me, Marshall. You're skating on thin ice as it is. We know how you've treated her in our absence." He looks two seconds away from ripping Cam's head off his shoulders. "This is a temporary truce." He steps up to him. "And if you harm one hair on her head, I will beat the ever-loving crap out of you."

Cam smirks. "I'd love to see you try."

"Step down, Barron," Drew says entering the room, holding Jane's hand. "We've agreed. Don't go fucking things up."

I lock eyes with my brother, puzzled. "So, what, you're all friends now?"

"Lines have been drawn, A." Drew presses a kiss atop my head as he takes the spot Charlie vacated. The room is becoming claustrophobic with so many bodies in the space. "And the new elite have agreed to help. You need protection, and they can offer you that. You can't come home. Father is unhinged in a way I've never seen before. It's not safe, and I'm terrified of what he might do, especially if Montgomery ends their arrangement."

He glances briefly at Charlie over his shoulder, and they share a worried look. "Trent won't want anything to do with you after today," he continues. "Goading him like that wasn't smart."

"Don't start, Drew," Jane snaps. "Trent's had that coming for a long time." She folds her arms across her chest. "Good riddance. He's a fucking psycho, and you shouldn't want him anywhere near Abby."

"I would never roll over after what he did to me," I hiss. "He's lucky I'm injured; otherwise, his dick wouldn't still be attached to his body." Even thinking of that bastard sends me into a rage.

"You're lucky we don't stick Cam on you," Jackson says, walking toward the bed, having abandoned his game. "How could you stand by and watch while that happened?"

"Does everyone know?" I whisper, embarrassment crawling over my skin.

Initial silence greets me, and I have my answer. I drop my head into a pillow, unable to face everyone knowing they're privy to all the facts.

"Hey." Jane lies down beside me, curling her body into mine. "Look at me." I blink back tears as I peer into my bestie's concerned eyes. "You have nothing to be ashamed about. You're the only innocent in all this." She cuts a sharp look at Charlie and Drew, making her meaning clear.

A throat clearing breaks through the tension in the air. "Okay, I think it's time you all leave. I need to attend to Abigail, and I can't do that with you here," Cam's cousin says with authority.

"I'm staying," Drew proclaims.

"No, you're not." Jane beats me to the punch line. She kisses me on the cheek before jumping off the bed. "Abby doesn't need an audience."

The others leave the room, one by one, but Cam makes no move to exit.

"Out," Drew says, eyeing him warily and jabbing his finger toward the door.

"Cam's staying," I supply. I don't want to be left alone with a stranger even if he seems nice, and Cam's the only one I don't feel embarrassed around.

Go figure.

"Why does he get to stay, and I don't?!" Drew asks in a snippy tone.

"Because he didn't stand by while they humiliated me and do nothing!" I shout.

"I said I was sorry."

"Sorry doesn't magically make everything right, Drew. You're my brother. My *twin*. The only real family I have. You're supposed to always have my back. And you. Did. Nothing."

His chest heaves, and he looks like he might cry. Yet, it changes nothing.

Anger still simmers in my veins. I avert my eyes, unable to look at him anymore, and my gaze instantly finds Cam's. He stares at me, and it's like I'm properly seeing him for the first time. His eyes betray sympathy and respect and so many other things I can't figure out.

A low growl emits from the back of Drew's throat, and I see the instant the pieces align in his brain. "It was him, wasn't it?" He glares at Cam. "I don't fucking believe it!"

"What's he talking about?" the cousin asks.

"Nothing," Cam and I answer in unison, sharing a conspiratorial look.

"It wasn't Cam," I say, hating that I'm lying to my brother's face, but the truth is, I don't trust him any longer. Don't trust any of them. "He only arrived here a few weeks ago, and I told you this happened months back."

Drew stares at me for so long, unmoving, his eyes unflinching, he might as well have turned to stone. Finally, he snaps out of it. "If I find out you're lying to me—"

"I'm not," I lie, cutting across him. "And you need to go. I ache everywhere, and I need pain meds."

"I'll be back later. Call anytime, day or night, if you need me." I don't reply to that, because, right now, Drew's the last person I'd rely on. "I love you," he says from the doorway, his tone and his facial expression betraying his fear.

He knows he's messed up.

That he might have lost me for good.

He's waiting for my usual response, and the fear on his face grows with every passing silent moment.

"I love you too," I eventually answer, almost choking on the lump in my throat. I might be disappointed and pissed at him, but I'll always love my brother. For so long, it was just him and me, and while I won't ever forget how he failed me when I needed him the most, it doesn't diminish my love.

Drew pulls the door closed behind him, leaving me alone with Cam and his cousin. "Can you at least sit down," I say, looking up at Cam. "You're making me nervous looming over me with that perpetual scowl on your face."

His cousin attempts to smother his laughter with a cough, but he's fooling no one. Cam grabs the chair at his desk and pulls it over beside the bed. "Happy?"

"Delirious," I deadpan, jerking as cool gloved fingers unexpectedly touch the inside of my arm.

"Sorry. I didn't mean to startle you," his cousin says. "I just want to put a line in and get a drip going as it's the fastest way to administer morphine."

"How'd you get your hands on that?" I ask.

He taps the side of his nose, smiling. "There isn't much you can't acquire with the right contacts and cash." True. I've seen that my whole life. "Have you had any issues with IVs before?" he asks, and I shake my head. "Good. I'll make this quick and painless. And I'm Maverick, by the way, although everyone calls me Rick."

"Maverick Anderson?" I ask, watching as he swabs my arm and applies a tourniquet.

His eyes flash to Cam's for a second. "Yes. You remember me?"

I nod, wincing at the small pinch where the needle impacts my skin. "You used to pull my hair and try to dunk me under the water in the pool."

Cam snorts, rolling his eyes at his cousin, and I automatically seek the framed photo I noticed when I was snooping in Cam's room before, but it's missing. Looking at Maverick now, I'm almost certain he was one of the guys in the picture. "How are your three brothers?" I ask, wondering if he'll take the bait.

"They're good," Rick cryptically replies while he removes the needle, fitting a tube into the catheter that leads to the bag elevated on a stand beside my bed. "I'll tell them you said hi," he adds, applying tape to my arm to secure it in place. He flicks the tube, watching to ensure the medication is flowing through.

"You do that," I murmur, sinking deeper into the bed. Cool liquid seeps into my veins, and a contented sigh escapes my lips.

"That won't take long to work, and you shouldn't feel as much pain. It's important to eat regularly and get plenty of sleep," Maverick adds. "I'll alternate the bag to administer fluids, but still drink lots of water."

"Thank you, and you're forgiven." He stops what he's doing, looking at me with a lopsided grin. "For tormenting me as a kid," I confirm.

"You know I only did that because I secretly had a little crush on you." He waggles his brows, and his brown eyes glint mischievously.

"I might've had a little crush on you too," I murmur, smiling.

He leans in closer, slanting a look at Cam as he says. "You're even hotter now you're all grown up. I think I feel another crush coming on."

Cam loudly clears his throat, muttering *asshole* under his breath, and I laugh, instantly whimpering as pain slices across my rib cage. "Fuck. Don't make me laugh. It hurts too much."

"You need me to look at your ribs?" Maverick asks, all trace of flirtatiousness gone.

"The asshole doc strapped them up, so I think I'm good for now."

"And are you hurting anywhere else?" he quietly asks.

This is so embarrassing, but I need to heal, because the longer I'm out of action, the more at risk I am. "I'm a little sore down below," I whisper. "His nail cut me…"

Cam stands, pacing the room with his knuckle stuffed in his mouth.

"Time is the best healer for that," Maverick says, watching Cam closely. "But warm baths will help too. And no sex for a while."

I splutter. "Yeah, I need no convincing. Having sex with your cousin got me into this mess in the first place." Shock splays across Maverick's face, and Cam stops pacing. "Oops. Was I not supposed to mention that?" Cam's entire body is rigidly stiff, and a muscle ticks in his jaw. I stifle a yawn as my eyelids grow heavy. "I thought guys bragged about stuff like that."

"Well, Cam didn't kiss and tell," Maverick says in a clipped voice, packing up his bag. "Which is a little weird," he adds, as I drift into unconsciousness. "Because it's not how he usually rolls."

That's the last thing I hear before I plunge into peaceful, dark depths.

CHAPTER TWENTY-NINE

A gentle rustling disturbs my sleep sometime later, and I sense someone in the room. "Cam?" I whimper, trying to force my eyes to open, but they won't cooperate. Eerie silence surrounds me, and all the tiny hairs lift on the back of my neck. I attempt to move my head, to force myself to wake up, but dark tendrils reach out for me, pulling me back under.

"Abby." A soft voice pricks my ears as a gentle touch brushes across my cheek. "Wake up, Abby. You need to eat."

I blink my eyes open, staring into warm amber-flecked brown eyes. "I brought you a tray," Cam says, and I sit upright, yawning as I fix the covers across my lap. Cam places the tray down, and it's laden with food. Two different eggs, bacon, toast, waffles, and a massive bowl of chopped fresh fruit with a pot of Greek yogurt. "I didn't know what you like, so I made a variety," he says, flopping into the chair by my bed.

"You did all this?" My brows lift in surprise. He nods, looking a little sheepish, which is an odd look on him. He's dressed casually today, and he looks hotter than ever in his gray sweats and fitted white T-shirt. "Thank you." I tuck my hair behind my ears before tasting the scrambled eggs. They're perfectly cooked. Light and fluffy, just how I like them. "This is so good." I shovel another forkful into my mouth. "You want some?" I ask, in between eating. "I'll never finish all this."

"I already ate, and it's okay to leave what you don't want."

Silence engulfs us as I eat, and it's weird to be in this setting with Cam without either of us baiting the other. "Where is everyone?" I inquire, picking at the bowl of fruit.

"Lauder and Hunt have gone to school. We figured it'd look suspicious if all of us were absent. They'll spread the news I've gone to visit my father in New York for a couple days, so I can stay here with you."

"You don't have to do that," I protest, sipping my orange juice. "I'm sure I can manage fine."

He eyes me quietly for a few beats. "Do you always push people away when they're trying to help?"

I shrug. "Since my mom died, I've learned to rely on myself. Apart from Drew and Jane, and more recently Xavier, there's been no one who cared." I'm not seeking sympathy. Just stating facts.

"About Xavier." He leans forward, and a woodsy, citrusy smell tickles my nostrils.

My skin prickles, and I'm instantly on guard. "What about him?" My tone is intentionally harsh as I set the tray aside.

"Have you considered he might've been the one to betray you?"

"No," I lie. "And I haven't exactly ruled you out." I'm not being truthful, because I pretty much *have* ruled him out, but his insinuation it's Xavier pisses me off, even if I've had niggling doubts myself.

"I didn't do this. *We* didn't do this." He drills earnest eyes at me. "I know I threatened it, but I would never have followed through."

I believe him because I see the truth written across his face. "Why threaten me at all then?"

"Because I needed something to manipulate you with, and that was the obvious answer."

"Because you wanted my help to nail my father?" He nods, but I still get the sense I don't have the full picture. "Why not just ask me for it?"

"Because we didn't realize you hated him. That you had your own reasons for wanting to take him down."

I mull it over in my head, and that stacks up, but I can't shake the feeling I'm missing something vital. Something that is staring me in the face, but I can't see it. "It was all for nothing anyway, because I doubt I'll be able to help any longer. I'll probably have to leave town before my father murders me for messing up his plans."

"We won't let that happen, and you can stay here for as long as you need to."

"Why are you doing this?"

He drops his head, looking at the floor, and I wait him out for a few minutes. "Because it's the right thing to do. Because we misjudged you. Because you're not the enemy?" I don't know if he's making statements or questioning himself.

"You've been a complete asshole to me. Why should I believe a word that comes out of your mouth now?"

"You shouldn't," he says, surprising me. "And I expect no less of you, but we'll prove it to you. That's my promise." I lie flat on my back, staring at the ceiling, wondering when my life became such a spectacular clusterfuck. "Starting with finding out who did this to you," he adds.

I turn on my side, sliding my hand underneath my face. "I don't think Xavier did this."

"But?" He quirks a brow.

"But I've learned not to completely trust anyone in my circle." I sigh, and my heart throbs at the thought he could be behind this.

"Don't feel bad," he says, as if he can read my mind. "It's smart to think like that, and until we question him, you can't know it wasn't him."

"What do you mean *we?*" I push up into a sitting position, ignoring the pain the movement produces, and narrow my eyes at him. "I'll be the one talking to Xavier. He's *my* contact. My friend."

"Don't get your panties in a bunch," he says, rolling his eyes. "We knew you'd want to be there, so that's why he's coming here tonight. We can grill him together."

"No." I shake my head. "I'll speak to him alone. He'll just clam up if you guys are interrogating him."

"Christ, you're so fucking stubborn." His eyes flash darkly.

"You're one to talk," I retort.

He stands, shaking his head and mumbling something under his breath. "Fine. You talk to him first, but if you don't get answers, we're taking over."

"Agreed. Now that wasn't so bad, was it?" I smile sweetly at him, laughing when he flips me off.

"I'll run you a bath, if you're finished eating."

"I am," I say, glancing at the tray of barely touched food. "Sorry, but I don't have much of an appetite."

"It's fine." He runs his hand through his hair. "Stay put, and don't move." With that parting instruction, he stomps off into the en suite bathroom.

Grabbing my bag from the floor by the bed, I rummage through the contents, extracting my cell and removing one of my contraceptive pills. I swallow it with the remainder of my orange juice as I swipe through my messages and missed calls, cursing when I spot all the abusive texts from Trent.

"What is it?" Cam asks, lounging against the bathroom doorway.

"Trent being his usual psycho self." I flip the covers back and swing my legs over the side of the bed, moaning as pain batters me from different angles.

"Take these." Cam empties two pills from a bottle by my bed. "Rick had to return to Harvard, and he didn't trust Lauder enough to leave spare bags of morphine, so he got this prescription filled for you instead. He said to take two every four to six hours."

I take the pills, ignoring how my heart flutters and my skin tingles when our fingers touch. Cam hands me a bottle of water, never taking his eyes off me as I swallow. His eyes drift momentarily to my bare legs, and I'd almost forgotten my state of undress. His hot gaze wanders the length of my legs, and need pulses, thick and heavy, between my thighs. "Why didn't he trust Jackson?" I blurt, needing to deflect the growing charge in the air.

Cam slants me one of his special trademark smirks. "Haven't you noticed his propensity for getting stoned? Jackson likes to amble through life in a blissed-out state of numbness. None of us trusted him not to sneak in and try to siphon some of your morphine while you were sleeping."

His words spark a memory, and I wonder if it was Jackson I heard rummaging around in my room in the early hours of the morning. I don't say a word to Cam, tucking it away in a mental box to ask Jackson later.

"What nightmares is he hiding from?" I ask as I attempt to stand. My ribs protest, and I cry out in pain. Cam scoops me up carefully as if I weigh nothing, and the feel of his skin against my legs elevates my desire to new levels.

I'm so fucking screwed with this guy. Especially if he acts nice to me.

"The pain of his sister's death," Cam quietly confirms as he enters the bathroom and sets my feet on the ground. Steam fills the room, along with the fragrant scent of jasmine from whatever he put in the water. "You need help to undress?" he asks, and I shake my head.

"I've got this," I lie, wondering how much darker my soul is after all the lies I've told recently.

He turns around, facing the door and leaning against the wall. "I won't look, but I'm not leaving yet, in case you need me."

Tears sting my eyes at his obvious concern, and if I thought my head was messed up over this guy before, it's not a patch on the chaos in my mind right now. I think I preferred it when he was being cruel and deliberately hurting me, because I knew where I stood. Now, everything's in a tailspin, and I hate feeling so mixed up.

I tug my tank up over my head and toss it to the floor before angling my head around, wondering how I'll remove the bandage to bathe. I stretch a hand around my back, to where it's pinned in place, but I can't reach. "I need help with my bandage."

He turns around and walks toward me, keeping his eyes fixed on my face. Sweeping my messy hair to one side, he works the bandage off from behind, his hands brushing my outstretched arms as he unwinds the gauze from my torso. Heat floods my body and creeps up my neck as memories swarm my mind.

I remember his hands roaming my curves, his lips gliding against my sensitive skin, and the feel of his cock as he thrust inside me, and my legs buckle underneath me.

"Woah. You okay?" he asks in a deep, gruff tone, his arm sliding around my waist. I was so lost in thought I didn't even realize he'd fully removed the bandage.

"I'm fine," I croak, resisting the urge to lean back into him. "Could you unclasp my bra?" I quietly ask.

His fingers brush against my skin as he deftly unhooks my bra, letting the straps slip off my shoulders. I let it fall to the ground and kick it away so it doesn't get wet. Placing one hand on the edge of the tub, I attempt to pull my panties down, but my ribs throb when I bend over, and the effort is too much.

"I won't look," he says, moving around in front of me before I've asked for his help. He looks off to the side as he hooks his thumbs in either side of my panties and draws them down my legs until I'm standing butt naked in front of him. It's not like it's the first time he's seen me naked, but I'm covered in bruises and cuts, and I don't want him to see me like this.

He stands, continuing to avert his gaze, and tears spring forth again.

Fuck.

I'm stuck in an emotional maelstrom, my heart ping-ponging all over the place.

"It's okay," he says, seeing my confusion. "I've got you." In one fell swoop, he lifts me up, gently placing me in the water. My limbs instantly relax, my body immediately soothed under the warmth of the bath.

His arms are soaked when he pulls them out, grabbing a small towel and stalking from the room without saying a word. He returns a few seconds later with a hair tie, kneeling beside the tub and running his fingers through my hair. The sensation is orgasmic, and I close my eyes, leaning against the edge of the tub as he fixes my hair into a messy bun on top of my head.

"You want me to stay in here?" he asks, his voice dangerously low, and I open my eyes.

His gaze roams over my torso, and my heart beats wildly. Despite the noticeable bulge in his sweats, he's concentrating on the sweeping bruises spread across my ribs and stomach. Anger burns red-hot in his eyes.

"You should go," I whisper, because the longer he stays, the more

I risk begging him to strip and get in here with me.

Without warning, he lowers his head, pressing the softest of kisses to my lips.

And it's everything.

Everything he hasn't said.

Everything I'm feeling.

And I realize how deep I'm buried.

His lips leave mine, and he cups my face, peering deep into my eyes, his expression determined and sincere. "They won't get away with this, Abby. I'll ensure those bastards pay for what they did to you."

I wake a few hours later, yawning as I stretch out in the bed. After the warm bath, I had zero issue falling asleep again. I look over at Cam, fast asleep in the chair. He's leaning on his side with his hands under his head, and he looks so young and so peaceful in slumber. A craving to crawl into his arms hits me full force though I'm not surprised anymore.

My visceral reaction to him has been almost instantaneous.

Even when he was being a nasty prick to me, I still wouldn't have passed up an opportunity to jump his bones.

His sketchpad lies discarded on his lap, and I can't help myself. In careful movements, I crawl over and retrieve it, propping my back up against the headrest as I leaf through it, skipping the ones I already saw, looking at his more recent drawings. My finger brushes across the image of Jackson and Sawyer, a smile playing on my lips.

He caught them in an unguarded moment, and neither of them is sporting the usual masks they wear. Their heads are close together, their bodies relaxed, as if deep in conversation. Sawyer's hand grips a bottle of beer, while Jackson's fingers curl around a joint. Jackson's mouth is curved into a wide smile.

Not the type he's infamous for at school.

But a real honest to goodness genuine smile that lights up his whole face, highlighting how truly beautiful he is with his scruffy blond hair, high cheekbones, and full lips. Sawyer has lost the impassive face he wears like battle armor, and his grin—although not as wide as Jackson's—is carefree and unburdened. He doesn't look as serious as he usually does, and his suave, dark looks radiate from the page.

Fuck, Cam is such a talented artist. I've never seen any drawings that bring people to life in the same way.

My heart is in my mouth as I take in every detail of the last two additions.

Both drawings are of me, and I get an inordinate thrill knowing he's still sketching me. It means I'm on his mind as much as he's on mine, and if I needed any further proof he feels the same pull as I do, this is it.

The first picture is the day at the beach. I'm lying on my towel, propped up by my elbows, my head thrown back, laughing. My hair cascades down my back, and he's captured every nuance of my body and facial expression. It's exquisite, and from the attention to detail, it's obvious he was watching us for a while that day. A thrill works its way through me at the thought, but I caution myself not to get carried away.

He's done some shitty things to me. And I still don't trust him.

Doesn't mean I'd kick him out of bed though.

Sighing at how weak I am to be ruled by my hormones, I turn the page, looking at his current drawing. I'm asleep in his bed, my hair fanning out around me on the pillow, one hand tucked under my chin. It's not finished, and he was clearly sketching it now, but I can already tell it will be epic. The way he's shadowed and contoured my face shows the depth of his skill, and I wonder if anyone knows he can draw like this.

"Didn't anyone teach you it's rude to snoop?" he says in a sleep-heavy tone, startling the heck out of me.

A little shriek of surprise flies from my lips. "Did anyone teach you?" I throw back at him.

"You weren't supposed to find that." He holds out his hand for the sketchpad, and I reluctantly hand it over.

"You are so talented, Cam. Wow. I…I'm blown away. They are seriously good."

Color stains his cheeks, and my mouth hangs open. Holy smokes. *Did the badass Grade-A jerk just blush at my compliment?*

"They're private. I don't show them to people for a reason." His tone is gruff, but he doesn't bark at me like he usually does when he's pissed, so I consider that progress.

"Why have you been drawing me?"

He shrugs nonchalantly. "I was bored, and you were there." He looks at me as if he's looking through me. "Don't read into it."

I'm sure it's a lie, but his easy dismissal hurts all the same.

I can't cope with any more shit right now, and I no longer want to look at his annoyingly perfect face. "I hear you loud and clear." I give him a tight smile. "You know, I'm feeling a lot better now. I don't need you to babysit me all the time, so you can leave." It takes effort to be polite.

"I'm going nowhere."

"I wasn't asking." I glare at him. "Get out. I want to be alone."

"This is *my* room." He arches a brow, daring me to argue.

I fling the covers off and crawl out the other side of the bed. "Fine. I'll find somewhere else to sleep. I'm sure Jackson won't mind me sharing his bed."

Cam jumps up, growling. "Get back in the fucking bed. I'll leave."

I turn my back on him, so he doesn't see my smug grin.

Yeah, he can try to fight this.

Pretend he doesn't give a shit, but time and time again, he proves he does.

My sour mood evaporates as quickly as it appeared, and I slip back under the covers with a satisfied smile.

The door closes quietly behind him, and I stare up at the ceiling, wishing I knew why I was so attracted to the moody bastard and wondering why he blows hot and cold on me all the time, when he suddenly reappears in the doorway.

"I like to draw people because human nature fascinates me," he explains. "I sketch the people in my life because I want to immortalize them on my page. I want to capture certain memories so I can look back and always remember them the way I want to remember them. Other times, I draw strangers. Those who intrigue me. Those who stand out by their individuality or their quirkiness. And I'm especially drawn to those who are an enigma. Those people whose inner beauty radiates from their every pore like a beacon. That's why I do it." He pushes off the doorway, his eyes like laser beams as they pierce me. "Perhaps now you can figure out why you're my latest muse."

CHAPTER THIRTY

"I will murder the bastards in cold blood," Xavier says, hugging me gently as if I'll break. "And I might murder these assholes too for not calling me the instant they knew what'd happened." He glares at Jackson, Cam, and Sawyer who are eyeing him up like the murderous intent is mutual.

"Come through to the living room." I take his hand. "The guys will give us privacy to talk." I drill a warning look at the three amigos, making sure they don't renege on their promise. They refused to allow Xavier up to the bedroom, so we compromised on the living room. That way they are close by if they need to rush in and protect me.

Their words. Not mine.

I'm still hoping above all hope that Xavier is innocent. I don't want to believe he's guilty of this, but that sliver of doubt is in my mind because of how we met. And the fact he only recently discovered the truth.

The timing is either coincidental or deliberate.

I'm about to find out.

I purposely take Cam's preferred recliner, so Xavier is forced to sit on the couch by himself.

"I'd have come sooner if I'd known," Xavier explains, leaning his forearms on his thighs. "I'm so sorry this happened to you, sweetheart. They're fucking animals." His Adam's apple bobs in his throat, and he runs a hand through his newly dyed purple locks. "How badly are you hurting?"

"I'm bruised and sore all over, and I have a mild concussion, but it could be worse." He opens his mouth to disagree, but I shut him down. "My father threatened to put a bullet in my skull at one point."

"Fuck." He shakes his head. "He really is a heartless son of a bitch."

"Did you do it?" I blurt. Tact has never been my forte. "Did you send the note to Christian Montgomery?"

"What?" He half-laughs, inspecting my face to see if I'm serious.

"I don't want to believe you'd do something like that, but someone sent that letter, and the list of suspects is pretty small."

Anger twists his face as he jumps to his feet. "How could you think that for even one second!?" he shouts, jabbing his finger in the air. "Of course, I didn't send it! I'd never do anything that'd hurt you." He paces, tugging hard on the ends of his hair. "They put you up to this, didn't they?!"

I climb awkwardly to my feet, walking over to him. "Xavier, look at me." Hurt radiates from his face, and I feel like the biggest bitch. "I'm just trying to figure this out. They were the likely suspects, but it wasn't them, so I had to ask you next. I know you're mad, and you've every right to be, but I need to work out what's going on, and that means I need you to look me in the eye and say that to my face."

He cups my face, forcing himself to calm down. "I didn't betray you. I swear it." He presses his forehead to mine. "I'd hurt myself first before I'd ever hurt you."

I circle my arms around his waist, relieved tears welling in my eyes. "I believe you." His body visibly relaxes, and I hate I've upset him. "I'm sorry. Please don't hate me."

"Even if I wanted to, it's impossible to hate you. You're far too easy to love."

I rest my head on his chest, pulling him in closer. "The new elite didn't appear to have any problem," I mumble into his shirt.

"That's water under the bridge, beautiful," Jackson says, sauntering into the room wearing nothing but a pair of black sweatpants. With more tenderness than I expect from him, he removes me from Xavier's arms before enveloping me in his embrace. "And we don't hate you now." He looks over my shoulder, his eyes glinting mischievously. "I'd say some of us even *love* you."

"Stop stirring shit," Sawyer says, entering the room with a thunderous-looking Cam.

"He just can't help himself." I sigh, attempting to move out of Jackson's hold. My cheek is pressed against his warm, naked chest, and I'm uncomfortable. Jackson trails his hand carefully down my back before flattening his palm against my ass in what is a blatant attempt to goad Cam. "Jackson." My tone brokers no argument. "Get your hand off my butt."

He pats my ass a couple times before releasing me, grinning at Cam. Cam does not return the sentiment, flipping his friend the bird instead.

"You're all even bigger assholes than I thought," Xavier says, still quietly seething. "I know you planted the seeds of doubt, and you can all fuck right off."

"We had to be sure," Cam says, standing in front of the fireplace with his hands shoved into the pocket of his jeans. "Which is why Sawyer and Jackson broke into your warehouse earlier today."

"You did what?" Xavier splutters, his face turning an unhealthy shade of red.

"Relax, man." Sawyer slaps him on the back. "Our search turned up no evidence, so you're in the clear."

"That's crossing a line." Xavier gestures between himself and Sawyer. "From one hacker to another, you suck. Big-time. And don't think I'll forget this. If anything is missing or messed up with my shit, I'm coming after you."

"Chill the fuck out," Cam says. "Your stuff is fine."

"You're on my shit list," Xavier points to Jackson. "You too, pretty boy."

"What da fuck did you do to your hair?" Jackson asks, seemingly only noticing it now. He rubs a hand across his chest, and my eyes follow the movement as if they've a mind of their own.

Xavier cocks his head to the side. "You don't like it?"

"Whatever floats your boat, man," Jackson says, blowing smoke clouds into the air.

"When the hell was anyone going to tell me about this?" I huff, pissed Cam made me ask Xavier to his face when they already knew the truth. Fucking shitheads.

"Calm down, princess," Cam says. "Everything's on a need-to-know basis." He leans in close to my ear. "And you didn't need to know." Smoke billows from my ears, and I'm about to rip him a new one when he whispers, "FYI. You look hot as fuck in those yoga pants." He discreetly bumps my hip with his pelvis, brushing his growing hard-on against me. "And Angry Abigail turns me on like you wouldn't believe." He waggles his brows suggestively before stepping aside, leaving me confused and horny.

"You're still an asshole," I grumble.

"I wear the label with pride."

He salutes me, and I long to kiss the smug grin off his mouth. Instead, I invoke my tried and tested distraction strategy—focus on something non-sexy. Something guaranteed to take the sexual tension down a notch or ten. "Okay, we need to get real about this. If none of you ratted me out, who did?"

Everyone instantly sobers up. "It has to be one of your father's enemies," Xavier says. "Although how we'll narrow the list down is beyond me. Your father has more enemies than Hitler."

"Does it really matter who's behind it, anyway? The damage is already done," Sawyer says.

"It matters if they're planning something else."

"You have other skeletons hiding in the closet, beautiful?" Jackson asks.

"As if I'd tell you," I harrumph, working hard to avoid staring at his impressive chest. "But I agree with Sawyer, to a point. Trying to find the culprit will be almost impossible, and we can't lose sight of our goal. Now, more than ever, I want to nail my father's back to the wall."

"Then we stick to the plan," Jackson says, shrugging as if it's no biggie. His tight abs lift with the movement, and my eyes are like ab-seeking missiles as they greedily drink in the sight.

Cam snarls, and every head turns to him. "Put a fucking shirt on before Abigail develops eye strain," he snaps at Jackson. "And if you dare laugh, I will beat you the fuck down and enjoy every second of it," he adds, flexing his knuckles.

"Wow. Someone needs to get laid." Jackson makes an obscene gesture with his hand and finger as he backs out of the room. "Hurry and get better, beautiful," he adds, and Cam takes a step toward him. "Just a suggestion." Jackson blows me a kiss before he leaves.

The conversation ends shortly after that with Xavier confirming he's moved to negotiating terms with the safecracker expert.

Cam orders pizza, and we all watch an action movie in the living room. I lie on the couch with my head in Xavier's lap, much to Cam's obvious disgust, and I fall asleep with a self-satisfied smile on my face.

The next couple days follow the same pattern, and by Thursday night, I'm chomping at the bit to get out of the house and do something. I wander off in search of the guys, finding them in a huddle with Drew and Charlie in the living room. "What's going on?" I eye them with a certain amount of suspicion.

"Nothing," Drew says, plastering a fake smile on his face.

Things are still strained between us even though he drops by every day and sends multiple texts, checking up on me. "I call bullshit. What's going on?"

"Nothing for you to worry your pretty little head about," Cam says, rolling up a large piece of paper they were poring over.

"Could you be any more insulting or any more cliché?" I snort. "Who the fuck am I kidding. This is *you* we're talking about." I roll my eyes to the ceiling. "You're as stereotypical as they come."

"Keep going, babe," Cam says, his endearment earning him a caustic look from my brother in the process. "You know what I said about Angry Abigail? Well, Sassy Abigail has the same effect."

My eyes lower of their own accord, and Cam doesn't attempt to disguise the boner nudging the crotch of his jeans. Drew stands, pointing between me and Cam. "This shit isn't happening. Our agreement does not extend to you screwing my sister."

I slap Drew across the back of the head. "Don't be so vile." I smile sweetly. "I'm free as a bird now, which means I get to *screw* whoever I like. You don't have a say."

"I'm down with screwing," Jackson says, circling his arms around my waist from behind. Brushing my hair aside, he plants a kiss on my bare shoulder, and shivers skate over my body. "I'm all about free loving."

"He's not doing babysitting duty," Drew snaps, rubbing a spot between his brows. "Hunt, you stay. You seem to be the only one capable of keeping your hands off my sister."

"True," Sawyer says, and I spot the wicked glint in his eye before he says. "She's the one who has issues keeping her lips off mine."

Drew's jaw snaps in frustration. "That better be a Goddamned joke."

"Jeez, bro." I shake my head. "I think I need to have a word with my bestie, because you need to get laid, stat. You're tense."

"Why the hell does every serious conversation we have end up in a discussion about sex?" Xavier cuts in. "I'm into fucking as much as the next guy, but time and place, people, and we need to make a move." He rubs his hands. "Chop-chop."

"Lauder's staying," Cam says to Drew. "And he *will* keep his hands to himself." Cam drills him with a look, and Jackson holds up his palms.

"Fuck, you're all so uptight. It's a joke. I'll be on my best behavior. Scout's honor."

"You still haven't told me where you're going or what you're doing?" I shout as they move toward the door.

"We're going out," Cam says.

"For burgers," Drew adds.

"And we might catch a movie after," Xavier supplies.

"She doesn't leave your sight," Sawyer says, sending Jackson the evil eye.

"Sorry," Charlie says, kissing my head. "We'll tell you everything when we get back."

I shove my middle finger up. "I hate you all!" I shout after them, stomping my foot in annoyance.

"Holy shit," Jackson exclaims, chuckling. "You stomp your foot and have the nerve to tell Cam he's cliché?" He tuts. "I didn't have you down as a stomper."

"Sometimes, situations call for it," I holler, heading into the kitchen.

"Stop waving your ass at me," he says, while I'm bent over with my head buried in the refrigerator rummaging for ice cream. He walks to my side, his eyes glued to my butt. "Unless you want me to rip those pants down and fuck you from behind." He rolls his hips suggestively.

"You're not allowed to flirt with me. Remember?" I take out the chocolate ice cream and pop the lid, licking my lips.

"And I don't follow the rules. Remember?" He smirks, moving in so close his chest brushes against mine. "They really shouldn't have left me here with you. Who knows what I'm liable to do?"

I nudge him aside, removing two spoons from the drawer. "Nice try, Casanova, but that won't work." I grab his arm. "We'll eat ice cream while you tell me what's going down."

"We could get naked and eat it off one another," Jackson suggests when we're in Cam's bedroom, sitting cross-legged on the bed in front of one another, dipping our spoons into the tub.

"Have you ever done that?" I ask, genuinely curious.

"Kind of," he cryptically says.

"How do you *kind of* eat ice cream off a chick's body?"

His eyes darken. "I licked ice cream out of this chick's pussy one time. It was hot." He chuckles. "Well, it was hot for me. It was probably cold for her." He frowns, thinking about it. "Nah, she was definitely into it. Sweetest thing I ever tasted."

I throw a pillow at him. "I'm sorry I asked."

"I'd offer you an opportunity to experience it, but I value breathing."

"Quit stalling, stud. What's going down?"

"The guys are torturing the safecracker dude to see if he's trustworthy," he casually throws out, and I spit chocolate ice cream all over Cam's black silk sheets.

"What the ever-loving fuck?" I ask, spitting more bits of ice cream over Cam's bed.

"Oh, my God. You should see your face. It looks like someone shit all over it." His chest rumbles with laughter as he grabs the box of tissues from the bedside table and hands them to me.

"Who came up with that harebrained idea?" I huff, wiping my mouth clean. "Wait. Let me guess. It was Neanderthal Fighter Boy."

"Actually, it was Charlie Barron's idea."

"No way. Charlie's not like that."

Jackson sends me an incredulous look. "You know what they do at Parkhurst, right?"

I shake my head. "I only have my imagination because the guys say jack shit about what goes on there."

Jackson leans in closer, his eyes twinkling. "We've heard rumors it's a front for an elite sect-like organization. They have to do all these mad, dangerous initiations to pass through the ranks. Including killing people."

I want to deny it, because it sounds like something Hollywood would make up for a movie, but I'm not some naïve cookie cutter little rich girl. I know how ruthless my father and his associates are, so it's not that hard to believe.

"That's… I have no words." My emotions are veering all over the place. I can imagine Trent feeling right at home someplace like that, but not my brother and Charlie.

"Yeah. It's some fucked-up shit all right." He takes a blunt out of his pocket.

"Do you ever not smoke weed?"

He thinks about that for a second. "When I'm asleep?"

I swat him with the pillow again before shoving him onto the floor while I change the sheets on Cam's bed. Then we lie back, side by side, propped against pillows, as we shoot the shit and pass the blunt back and forth. When we're stoned, Jackson decides it'd be funny to watch a porno, and we roll about the place laughing at how staged and cheesy the whole thing is.

I don't remember falling asleep. Only waking up, in the early hours of the morning, as the bed violently shakes. "Ow!" Jackson moans, his voice heavy with sleep. "What the fuck d'you do that for?"

"What the fuck are you doing sleeping with her?"

"Christ. Hunt's right. You're a real fucking psycho when it comes to Abby."

I rub my tired eyes, blinking repeatedly to ensure I'm seeing things straight. Cam has Jackson in a headlock, and he looks like he wants to rip him limb from limb.

"You're overreacting, Cam," I venture, sliding off the bed. "We're both still dressed, and we were on top of the bed. We just fell asleep."

At that precise moment, a loud moan echoes throughout the room. On the TV screen, a woman is being fucked by two hot cops with big "sticks" in an alleyway. "Yes, Officer. I've been a very bad girl. Punish me," she purrs, moaning as he slaps her ass with his cock.

"What the actual fuck?" Cam says, staring wide-eyed at the TV.

I burst out laughing because it's so comical. I'd say Jackson would laugh too, if he wasn't turning a scary shade of blue. "Let him go, Cam, before he chokes to death." I turn on the light in time to see Jackson drop to his knees, gasping for air.

"You're lucky I love you like a brother, man," he pants.

"I could say the same." He pulls him to his feet, "You good?"

Jackson slaps him on the back. "I'm good, psycho." He winks at me before fixing his gaze on Cam. "And for the love of all things holy, lock that shit down."

CHAPTER THIRTY-ONE

"That shit's not to happen again," Cam growls, pulling his shirt over his head, balling it up, and throwing it in the laundry basket's direction.

"Fuck off trying to tell me what to do." I plant my hands on my hips and glare at him.

He steps up to me, leaning his face in close. "We both know you're mine, so quit trying to piss me off."

My mouth drops open, and my heart swoons at his words before my head interjects, reminding me he's a cruel, arrogant a-hole. Cam smirks, walking off into the bathroom, and I hear the shower turn on straightaway.

After a few minutes, the sound of the shower being switched off snaps me out of the argument doing circles in my head, and I stomp into the bathroom. Cam has a towel wrapped around his hips, and beads of water trickle over his wet skin as he stands at the sink with one hand under the faucet, wincing as water cascades over his split knuckles.

"Let me see." I push my way in, trying not to drool over his semi-naked body, pretending my panties aren't damp, as I take his hand, lifting it up for closer inspection. "And the other one." I take both his hands, examining the bloody torn skin. "I presume you played the role of chief asshole tonight?" I bring both his hands under the water, gently cleaning them.

"Actually, that accolade belongs to your brother." He winces a little. "And I thought *I* had anger management issues."

Jackson's earlier words resurface, and I wonder how well I know my brother and Charlie. Trent is such an arrogant fuckface he doesn't shield who he is from anybody.

But have my brother and his other friend been hiding who they are? What really goes on at Parkhurst, and how afraid should I be?

"What's the verdict on the guy?" I inquire, patting his hands dry with a towel.

"Suspect. Guy shit his pants which doesn't invoke a lot of confidence."

"So, we're back to square one?" Disappointment washes over me as I apply antiseptic cream to his damaged skin.

"We're mulling over options." He tilts my chin up with one finger. "We'll figure this out. I promise."

I'm still wide-awake an hour later, listening to Cam toss and turn in the chair as my mind refuses to shut down. I bolt upright, flinging the covers back on the empty side of the bed. "This is ridiculous. We're up for school in a couple hours, and neither of us is getting any sleep. Just get in the bed already."

He must be exhausted because he's slept in that chair the last three nights. Which is ridiculous with the number of spare beds in the house. But he refuses to leave me in the room alone, and I've got to admit I feel safer with him in here.

I expect him to argue, but he complies without uttering a word. My pulse thrashes wildly in my neck as he slides under the covers, turning on his side to face me. We stare at one another, neither of us making any attempt to go to sleep.

My heart thumps so loud I'm sure he must hear it. My eyes drink him in, and he's so beautiful up close. Almost too beautiful to be real. His eyes are like giant pools of liquid chocolate, and I'm diving right in.

Electricity swirls around us, and every part of my body tingles in anticipation. His eyes lower to my mouth, and my tongue darts out, wetting my lips. I gulp over the tension in the air, silently begging him to make a move.

The longer we stare at one another, the more heated my body becomes until I'm inwardly screaming, my body achy and needy, my lips crying out for his.

In the end, we both move as one, falling into each other as if some invisible force is drawing us together at the same time. His arms wind around my waist, and our lips collide in a searing-hot kiss that curls my toes. He draws me in flush to his body, keeping his palm flat on my lower back as he angles his head, deepening the kiss. Our tongues tangle, and I'm devouring him like he's the luscious chocolate ice cream I was eating earlier.

Tasting him again brings all my memories flooding back, and I can't deny what I feel for him anymore.

It doesn't matter how obnoxious he is to me, because he burrowed his way under my skin that first night, and I can't dig him out.

I'm desperate and needy, clinging to him and thrusting my hips against his, feeling his erection pushing against me through his sweats and my sleep shorts. He moans into my mouth, and I'm panting and writhing, my skin itching with unbridled desire.

When he pulls away, we're both struggling to breathe. My thin tank is stuck to my back, and my leg is thrust between his. He grasps both sides of my face, kissing me softly in a way that undoes me worse than the frenzied kissing. "Sleep, baby." He pulls my head to his chest, and I press my ear over his heart, allowing the strong rhythm to quickly lull me into sleep.

Cam wakes me the following morning, fully dressed, with his hair still damp from the shower. He pecks my lips. "Time to get up, princess. Unless you've changed your mind about school?"

"I haven't," I say, yawning.

"I'll make breakfast while you shower. Don't be long."

I wear a lopsided grin the entire time I'm in the shower, but I physically wipe it from my face before I step foot in the kitchen.

The guys are quiet as we eat breakfast together, but it's not awkward.

We are making our way out of the house when Cam pulls me back inside at the doorway, wrapping his arms around me before leaning down for a long kiss.

My lips are swollen when we finally break apart. "What was that for?"

"Two reasons," Cam says, taking my hand as he activates the alarm system. "I'm reminding you you're mine, and no one is touching you but me."

He pulls the door shut, and I roll my eyes even though my heart is somersaulting in my chest. "And two?"

"If anyone gives you shit today, I want to hear about it immediately. I'm the first person you come to. Understood?" He opens the door to the back seat, grips my hips, and gently lifts me up before going around the other side and sliding in beside me. "Answer me," he demands. "And put your seat belt on."

I shove my middle finger up as I simultaneously smile at him and buckle my belt. He sends me one of his death glares that have never felt menacing to me. "I got it. You don't need to go all caveman on me. I'll call you if anything happens."

"Good girl." I'm opening my mouth to let a few expletives loose when he leans across and kisses me hard, instantly muting me.

Jackson chuckles. "If you're going to kiss her every time she sasses you, you'll be doing nothing else."

"I have zero issues with that." Cam sends him a smug smile, and Jackson laughs louder.

"If you guys are doing this, you'll need to hide it at school," Sawyer says, looking at us through the mirror as he maneuvers the car out of the driveway and onto the road.

Cam's good humor evaporates as he leans forward, putting his hands on the back of the driver's seat. "Do I look like a fucking idiot? We both understand the need for discretion." He sits back, threading his fingers in mine. "We've got this."

We say nothing else during the journey, but the silence is amicable and relaxed.

Charlie is waiting in the parking lot for us when we arrive at school, and he opens my door, helping me out. "Where's Drew?"

"With Trent."

"What the fuck?"

"Relax, Abby. It's all part of the plan." Charlie looks over my head. "Didn't you fill her in?"

"There wasn't time," Cam coolly replies.

"You had time to kiss me!" I snap, shoving at his chest. "You could've made time to tell me."

Charlie arches a brow but says nothing, taking my hand and walking toward the entrance. "Drew needs to stay tight with your father and Trent so we know what's going down. As far as Trent is concerned, I'm siding with you and Drew is siding with him."

"Great," I grumble. "Now he'll be all smug and superior thinking he's turned my twin against me."

"Who gives a shit what the douche thinks," Cam says, coming up alongside us. "And if you value your life, you'll remove your hand from hers," he adds, giving Charlie the evil eye before turning his attention to me. "What part of no one else touches you didn't you understand?"

"What part of fuck off trying to tell me what to do didn't *you* understand?"

"People are staring," Sawyer says, subtly pushing his way in between us. "And Charlie should continue to hold her hand. It'll deflect attention."

Cam looks like he wants to pummel Sawyer into the ground, but he says nothing, stalking ahead of us with frustration leaking from his pores.

"You sure you know what you're getting into, Abby?" Charlie asks, just as we reach the steps.

"Nope," I honestly admit. "But I've paid my ticket, and I'm on this crazy train now, so I might as well see where it takes me."

Morning classes crawl by, not helped by the murmured whisperings and finger-pointing that follows me everywhere. I have one class with Trent and Drew, and the gossipmongers have a field day as we all purposely ignore one another. My cell pings with an apologetic text from Drew which I don't respond to.

I know he's doing this for me.

But I don't know if it's just to try to get back in my good graces or if he's genuinely doing what needs to be done in the interests of keeping me safe.

Drew has a long way to go to prove his loyalty to me.

That's the only thing I know for sure.

Lunch is fun. Not.

The division between the old elite has completely upset the balance of power.

Charlie and I sit at the new elite's table, joined by some members of the inner circle, but most have sided with Trent and Drew, which doesn't surprise me. Chad sits with me, and I squeeze his hand, barely flinching from the kick Cam gives me under the table. "I really appreciate your support," I say. "I know it can't have been easy."

Chad has been one of Trent's most loyal minions over the years.

"He made it easy," he says, throwing a filthy look in Trent's direction. "The minute he laid his hands on you without permission is the minute he lost my loyalty."

No one outside the new and old elite knows exactly what went down last Sunday night, but I said enough in the cafeteria on Monday for them to get the gist.

Not that it's garnered much sympathy for me or diluted female interest in my ex-fiancé.

In case there's any doubt, I returned his ghastly engagement ring in an envelope Charlie gave him after first class. Drew had retrieved it from my bedroom when he was packing up my stuff. Word spread fast, and now girls are foaming at the mouth at the prospect of backfilling my shoes. It almost makes me lose faith in the female race.

Jane looks miserable sitting at Drew's side, picking at her salad, and I hate she's caught in the crossfire. This is the first time she's really feeling what it's like to be a part of this life.

To have your choices taken away from you.

To be forced to do something you don't want to.

I never wanted her to experience that, but it's inevitable.

I'm walking to the bathroom after lunch when someone yanks on my hand, pulling me sideways into an empty classroom. A palm clamps over my mouth as I prepare to scream, and Cam's warm breath fans across my ear. "It's me."

"What the hell?!" I spin around in his arms, shoving at his chest. "Are you trying to give me a coronary?"

"Sorry," he murmurs, not sounding in the least bit genuine as he rubs his nose along my neck. "I just needed to see you."

"Why?" I'm instantly on alert. "Has something happened?" My eyes search his for the truth.

"I just needed to do this," he says before smashing his lips against mine. He ravishes my mouth as he locks the door and pulls down the blinds. Then he spins us around, pressing me up against the wall, and I melt against him. He rocks his hips against me, and I'm whimpering into his mouth as we devour one another with our lips and tongues. He kisses me like he never believed he'd get to do it again, and I barely have time to draw air into my lungs, but I'm not complaining.

Kissing him is something I'll never tire of.

His lips move from my mouth to my ear, and he nibbles on my earlobe as he grabs one leg, pulling it around his waist. Stars explode behind my eyes, and I grab the bottom of his shirt, tugging it out of his pants so I can slide my hands underneath.

His skin is warm under my fingers as I inch my way up his back, and he flinches at my touch, trailing his lips down along my neck, loosening my shirt so he can press kisses along my collarbone. I'm bucking against him as the throbbing between my legs grows more insistent.

My breath hitches in my throat when he slides his hand under my skirt, his fingers dancing slowly up my thigh. I cry out when his hand brushes against my damp panties. "Are you still sore?" he whispers in my ear.

"No. I'm good." I pant.

He lifts his head, his seductive eyes swallowing me whole, and his lips are glistening from our hot kisses. "I want to make you come." I bob my head enthusiastically, and his lips tug up at the corners. His mouth descends on mine again the same time he slides my panties aside, pushing one finger inside me. "Fuck, baby. You're so wet."

"More. Faster," I demand, shamelessly riding his finger. He inserts a second digit and moves them up and down inside me, while his thumb draws circles on my sensitized clit. I drag my lip between my teeth, stifling my moans, as I thrust against his hand, panting into his mouth, my chest heaving.

Pressure builds in my core, spiraling and spiraling, and when he curls his fingers inside me, hitting my G-spot while his thumb presses down on my clit, I explode in a colorful burst of sensation, my limbs sagging as the most amazing waves of pleasure wash over me in fast succession. He continues pumping his fingers until I collapse against him, sated and deliriously happy.

Slowly, he draws his fingers out of my body, bringing them to his mouth where he licks my essence in exaggerated swipes of his tongue.

It's one of the hottest things I've ever seen, and my mouth is dry, my panties the complete opposite. It's dirty as fuck, and it makes me want to climb his body like a monkey. "I could get addicted to this taste," he purrs, his voice dripping with lust.

I slide my hand down the gap between our bodies, cupping his hard-on. "I want a taste of my own," I say, crouching down, but he stops me, pulling me back up and wrapping his arms around my waist.

"I'll take a rain check." He kisses me so sweetly I feel like crying. "We're already late." He smacks my butt as I slip out of the room first, and his devious laughter follows me all the way to class.

I offer to cook dinner for the guys once we're back at the house after school, but they insist I rest up, ordering from my favorite Thai place, and who am I to argue with three bossy gorgeous guys?

Charlie shows up later while Cam and I are lounging in the living room, arguing over what to watch on TV. Jackson has gone for a run, and Sawyer is at football practice.

"You're early," Cam says, not even lifting his head up to look at Charlie.

"I wanted to talk to Abby before the others arrive."

"We're having a meeting?" I ask, pinning Cam with accusatory eyes. He hasn't mentioned a word about anyone coming over.

"Yes. We need to discuss next steps." Charlie sits beside me on the couch, his face softening as he turns to me. "Trent came over to my house, demanding to see you."

Tension cords my stomach into knots. "What did he want?"

"I don't know. He wouldn't say, but he was throwing his weight around, shouting at Dad, making threats if we didn't get you."

"Does he suspect I'm not living there?"

"I don't think so, but we need to be more careful. From now on, I think I should bring you to and from school." He glances at Cam, challenging him to disagree.

Cam leans forward in his chair, a resigned, unhappy expression on his face. "I hate to agree with anything that comes out of your mouth, but I won't jeopardize Abby's safety." He looks to me. "That means you've got to stay indoors too. It's too risky otherwise."

"I can't stay cooped up in here all the time. I'll go stir-crazy."

"It won't be forever," Charlie says, instantly agreeing. "Just until we figure this out."

"My father won't let me stay at your place indefinitely. Especially if he discovers I've taken sides with the new elite."

"He won't do anything to rock the boat while he's isolated. He's still at loggerheads with Christian over their deal, and he knows my father is disgusted with him for the way he treated you. He's on his own for now, so he'll let it go."

"For now." My worried gaze bounces between the two guys.

"It buys us some time," Cam says, opening his arms. "Come here."

I go willingly, curling myself into his lap, where I stay while we chat and aimlessly watch TV until the door chimes, signaling the others have arrived. I crawl out of his lap, happy when a scowl appears on his face. "I don't fully trust my brother," I admit.

"I'm with Abby," Charlie says. "Drew's been acting off lately."

My brows knit together as I stare at him, wondering what kind of behavior he's noticed and what it means exactly.

CHAPTER THIRTY-TWO

"I don't understand why I can't go," I fume after the meeting has ended, stomping my way around Cam's bedroom. "It's not safe for me around here, so a trip to New York makes perfect sense."

"We don't trust the guy, Abby, and they could be walking into a trap. He's agreed to teach them how to use the safecracking technology, and we've paid him a small fortune to rent the hardware, but that doesn't mean he hasn't sold us out to a higher bidder. This weekend trip is fraught with risks, and none of us want you exposed. Our main priority is keeping you safe, and that means you stay here with me this weekend."

I pull spare bed linen from the closet as he walks up behind me, pressing the length of his body against mine. I hate how badly I want to melt into his arms, but I'm frustrated enough to resist. "Look at the positives," he whispers, nuzzling against my neck. "We have the place to ourselves all weekend."

I spin around, glaring at him. "If you think that'll appease me, think again." I narrow my eyes, making sure he gets the message. "I hate being babied, and it's completely unfair. You should've stuck up for me."

"This *is* me sticking up for you. It's not my fault you're acting unreasonable."

My nostrils flare as I shove the pillows and blankets at him. "Try this for unreasonable. You're sleeping on the floor."

I feel a teeny bit vindictive the following morning when I wake from a comfortable sleep to find Cam curled at an awkward angle in the chair with the covers halfway off his body. But then I remember all the shit he's pulled on me, and all sympathy evaporates.

I'm in the kitchen, finishing my eggs and bacon, when Cam saunters in, rubbing the back of his neck. "Have the others already left?"

"Yes." I gesture toward the note on the counter. "They were gone by the time I came down."

"Something smells good." He props his back against the counter, sniffing the air.

I pop the last bit of bacon into my mouth, grinning. "It was." I pat my full tummy, gloating.

"Any for me?" he inquires, looking around, and my grin grows wider.

"I'm not your slave." I point at the refrigerator. "Knock yourself out, champ."

His eyes darken, but he says nothing as he forages yogurt, fruit, and oats, slamming the cartons down on the counter.

It takes colossal effort not to ogle his naked chest as he fixes his breakfast. The ink on his body fascinates me, and I wonder if the designs have any special meaning. My eyes home in on the sharp V-indents on both of his hips, and I automatically lick my lips.

Now I've seen how religious he is about his daily two-hour workouts in the state-of-the-art home gym in the basement, it's no wonder his body is so well defined.

Boy, does he take his fitness seriously.

"See something you like, babe?" he asks in a smug tone, and I stick my tongue out at him.

"I was just daydreaming into space." I shrug, getting up with my plate. "Don't go reading into it." I just love throwing his own words back at him.

I place the empty plate and dirty silverware into the sink to rinse them, shrieking as his hands dig into my hips and he pulls me back against him. His morning wood digs into my ass, making me instantly hot and bothered. "I think you get off on pissing me off," he growls into my ear.

"You do too," I retort, placing my hands on the counter.

"Everything about you gets me off. I've been on a permanent boner since I arrived in Rydeville, thanks to you." He thrusts his erection into me, simulating sex, and my legs buckle.

"What about Rochelle?" I snap, the image of her blowing him suddenly popping into my mind. "Did she give you a permanent boner too, or you just fucked her for shits and giggles?" I shove my elbow back into his gut, pushing him away.

"I should lie and really piss you off," he says, sounding a little winded, "because that was unnecessary, but I guess I deserve it, and it's not like I haven't pulled shit on you."

I squeal as I'm unexpectedly lifted. Cam places me on the counter, nudging my legs apart and situating himself between them. He grips my hips, staring earnestly into my face. "The only permanent thing Rochelle gave me was a headache, and I didn't fuck her."

I snort. "Don't lie. I saw your little orgy." Bile travels up my throat and I avert my eyes.

He grips my face, forcing it back to his. "I had a momentary lapse in judgment, and I let her blow me that one time. It was your fault anyway, for winding me up about Trent." His eyes darken. "But I never let her touch my cock again. I never even kissed her. It was all an act to piss you off."

"You let her paw at you and say nasty shit to me every day at lunch." I narrow my eyes, and he grips my chin harder.

"There's so much you don't understand, Abby. Things I want to tell you but can't. Not yet." His Adam's apple bobs in his throat. "I've no basis for asking you to trust me, and you're smart, so I know you don't, but I'm asking for a chance."

"What kind of chance?"

"A chance to prove that the guy you met on the beach in Alabama is the real me."

"Why?"

"Why what?"

"Why do you want a chance? You don't even like me."

He smirks. "Oh, I like you, and I think you already know that." He thrusts his hips into me, drilling his point home.

"Just because you're hot for me doesn't mean you like me. Sex and like is the same as sex and love in that regard."

He brushes his thumb across my cheek, sending a flurry of tingles across my skin. "I'll prove it to you." His eyes bore into mine and he seems genuine. "And I regret the shit I pulled. You're not who I expected you to be."

"What does that even mean?"

He sighs, dragging a hand through his tousled hair. "It will all make sense soon. I promise."

He leans in, kissing me, and I run my nails gently through the shorn sides of his scalp. "Does this have special significance?" I ask, running the tip of my finger along the cross inked on his skull.

"It's a reminder."

I arch a brow, peering deep into his beautiful eyes. "A reminder of what?"

"That we're all persecuted in some way."

We spend the day hanging out in the garden. I whip his ass at tennis—much to his disgust—and after lunch, we cool off in the pool. The day is overcast, but the temp is still warm enough to swim. "You're a good swimmer," I observe as we swim lengths of the pool side by side.

"I spent a lot of time in the water as a kid."

"It must've been lonely growing up an only child." I'm fishing on purpose, holding my breath as I wait to see if he takes the bait.

He swims to the side, placing his arms on the ledge with his back to me. "I got by, and I had Rick and the guys." He turns around, stretching his arms out behind him, his abs and biceps bulging in the process, and I know my mouth's hanging open.

He is hot as fuck, and there's no way I can't stare when all that naked skin is tempting me. "Come here." Lust glints in his eyes as I swim toward him. He brushes his thumb across my mouth. "You had a little drool there."

He smirks, and I shove his chest. "You're an ass."

"I think we've already determined that." He lowers his hands into the water, pulling me into him at the waist. "And yet, here you are."

"I'm an idiot with you," I truthfully admit, sliding my hands up his wet chest.

"And why is that?" he asks, toying with the strings on the side of my bikini bottoms.

"Because my hormones overrule my brain every time."

"If it helps, I haven't been able to get you out of my head since we met."

I tilt my head to the side as his hand slips into the back of my bottoms. "Why?"

"Because you intrigue me. You never do or say what I expect, and you don't take no for an answer." He nips my earlobe. "Your strength and your fighting spirit are the sexiest things about you. I loved it every time you fought me."

"You helped me with that," I say, sliding my hand down between our bodies to stroke his hard length through his swim shorts.

"I did?"

"That night." I gulp, remembering how far my mind had ventured. "I had all but given up on life." My eyes lock onto his as he palms my bare ass cheeks, sweeping his thumbs across my naked flesh.

"I know," he whispers, trailing hot kisses up and down my jaw. "You wanted to feel something real. To feel you were in control even if it was only an illusion."

"You remember." I slip my hands under the band of his shorts, and he sucks in a sharp breath.

"I remember every single thing about that night." He presses a kiss to the corner of my mouth. "I remember how lost you looked. How dead your eyes were until you were writhing underneath me and you came to life."

He kisses the other side of my mouth. "I remember how incredible it felt to be inside you."

He licks a trail up my neck, and I moan as intense needs pulses between the apex of my thighs. "How wet and tight you were." I thrust my pelvis against him, swiping my thumb along the precum leaking from the crown of his cock. He bites my lower lip, sucking it between his teeth as he devours me with his eyes. "How responsive your body was to mine, and I replay every second of our encounter every morning while I'm jerking off in the shower to thoughts of you."

His hand moves around to my pussy, and he slides two fingers inside me.

"Oh, God." I grip his cock, pumping it in my hand as my head drops to his shoulder. "That feels so good," I whisper, as he curves his fingers inside me, and I ride his hand with abandon. "But it's not enough." I lift my head up. "I want you inside me again." I kiss his mouth hard. "Fuck me, Cam. Fuck me like you did that night at the beach."

He doesn't ask if I'm sure this time, ripping my bikini top away and lowering his mouth to my puckered nipples. I'm stroking him as he's finger-fucking me while devouring my tits, and our joint mutual groans are carried away on the wind. "These are perfect," he murmurs, licking, nipping, and sucking at my breasts before cupping them in both hands. I cry out at the loss of his fingers inside me. "And if you ever felt differently, I'm sorry. It was all part of the play."

"Let's not talk about that now," I deadpan, glaring at him as I remember how he taunted me for having small boobs. "Unless you want me to change my mind."

I squeal as he lifts me up, placing my butt on the cold ledge. He yanks my bikini bottoms down, sending them floating alongside my top. "It's too late, princess." His grin is feral as he parts my thighs, bringing his mouth to my pussy and feasting.

I grip his hair, tugging on the dark strands, as he eats me out, his hot tongue thrusting inside me while his fingers toy with my clit. When he places my legs over his shoulders, I arch my back, spreading my legs as wide as I can to give him greater access. He pumps his fingers inside me, curling them up as his tongue swirls around my clit, and I explode, bucking my hips and screaming out his name as my climax hits.

I've barely time to recover when he pulls me back into the pool. His shorts join the floating clothes party, and he pulls me against his throbbing cock. "You're on the pill, right?" he asks, and I nod.

"I'm strict about taking it, and I haven't been with anyone since you."

"Neither have I," he admits, startling me. "And I'm clean; otherwise, I wouldn't do this." Grabbing my legs roughly around his waist, he slams into me in one fast thrust, and I cry out as he fills me up. "Hold on tight, baby, because this won't be gentle."

I grab hold of his shoulders, tightening my legs around his waist, as he slams in and out of me. Throwing my head back, I moan as pressure builds inside me again. "Kiss me," he pants, and I instantly oblige, lowering my mouth to his. Our tongues wrangle as our bodies collide, and it's not long before we're both screaming as we chase orgasms at the same time.

I collapse against him, my limbs like liquefied Jell-O. He rubs his nose into my wet hair, smoothing a hand up and down my back. "You okay?"

"Peachy," I murmur in a sleepy voice, and I can almost feel the smile spreading across his mouth.

We take a shower together, intending to clean up, but we end up indulging in round two before falling in a tangle of limbs into bed, engaging in rounds three and four.

I wake sometime later, my body aching deliciously in places I never knew I could ache. Outside the window, night has fallen, and the crescent moon in the sky reminds me of the night I met Cam. "You hungry?" he asks, his seductive voice sending goose bumps all over my body. I look over at him, sitting in his usual chair, with a smile on my face.

"Starving," I admit, looking at him through hooded eyes. "But not for food." I pull back the covers, patting the empty space beside me. "Come back to bed."

He smiles, a wide genuine smile that reaches his eyes, and it's like being hit by a thousand volts of electricity. "What?" he asks, frowning as he inspects my face while putting his sketchpad aside.

"You should smile more often," I softly admit, as he crawls in beside me. "Or maybe not." I pout, thinking of how many more admirers he'd gain if he smiled around school. "Only with me." I push him down and straddle his hips. "Promise I get all your smiles, and I'll let you have your wicked way with me."

"What makes you think you have any choice in the matter?" He pulls me down on top of him, kissing me passionately. "You're mine, Abby." He runs his hand over the curve of my ass, tracing a path up my spine before clasping my neck. "Mine to do with as I please." He tightens his hold on my neck, so it's not quite painful, but it gets his message across. "Mine to kiss." He presses his hot mouth against my lips. "Mine to tongue." He slides his tongue into my mouth, licking me all over. "Mine to fuck." Grabbing my hips, he positions me over his cock and slides me down his hard length.

I ride him, bouncing up and down on his cock, my tits jiggling with the movement. "But I'll give you my smiles too," he adds, running his hands up my body and rolling my nipples between his fingers. "When you've earned them." His wicked grin masks his intent as he flips me over, shoving my head into the pillow and thrusting my ass up in the air. Then he's slamming into me, over and over, and all logical thought flees my mind.

It's only much later I think about the fact he never said he was mine.

CHAPTER THIRTY-THREE

Over the course of the next month, Jackson, Sawyer, Charlie, and Drew return to New York every weekend to complete their training while Cam and I fuck our way around every room in the house.

It's like a switch has been flicked inside my body, and I'm insatiable for him.

We're cohabiting now, in every sense of the word, and nothing has ever felt more natural or more right. Going to sleep and waking up beside a guy is something I never imagined I'd love, because the only guy in the frame was Trent, and I'd rather cut off a tit than share a bed with that douche.

I've settled into a comfortable routine in the house, and I'm enjoying living with the guys. But, as much as I'm growing closer to them, I'm still in the dark over much of their plans, and they still keep me at arm's length.

Especially Cam.

He tells me it's his way of protecting me, but I call bullshit on that.

Every time I broach the subject of his childhood, he clams up. All he's told me is that he met Jackson and Sawyer when he was ten. A fact that isn't widely known. Or the fact his childhood was difficult.

But he won't elaborate beyond that, and with the little background there is on him online, I'm at a complete loss who Camden Marshall really is.

Is he the observant stranger who made tender love to me that night on the beach? A guy I still see flashes of. *Or is he the cold bully who roughly fucks me with hatred sometimes still evident in his eyes?*

I don't have the answers to these questions, and it concerns me, because every day that passes, I fall a little bit more.

Our most heated arguments are regarding his real agenda. He keeps insisting proving his aunt was murdered is what brought them here in the first place, but I'm not buying it, and he knows it.

My gut tells me there's more to it than that, and Xavier agrees. It's a constant source of tension between Cam and me, and it does little to ease the kernel of distrust that exists between us.

My mood swings alternate like crazy. When he's sneaking kisses at school, cuddling me on the couch, watching guard over me at ballet class, mess wrestling with Jackson when he calls him pussy-whipped, or burying himself balls deep inside me at night, peering into my eyes as he explores my body with unrivaled passion, I know I'm falling in love with him, and I trust him with my heart. With my life.

But when he's cagey with his answers, sneaking off to make calls in the middle of the night and refusing to divulge details of his past and the real reason he came to Rydeville, I feel like a lovesick fool, and I don't trust him with anything. Especially my heart.

Being cooped up during my free time doesn't help either even if I agree it's for the best. I miss Jane terribly, but apart from the odd visit, I haven't seen her. Both Drew and Jane are circumspect with their visits in case Father has someone following them.

Xavier is my saving grace. He drops by whenever he has free time, and he's even visited Mary at the library, picking up on my painstaking research. So far, with no results to show, but at least I feel like something is getting done.

Trent is regularly sending me abusive texts, and he parades around school with a different girl attached to his mouth, daily, as if it will upset me, but I couldn't care less. However, he's made no retaliatory move, and that worries me.

My father's lack of action troubles me too.

Drew says things are coming to a head between him and Christian and that it's only a matter of time before the deal is officially off the table, so I don't understand why he hasn't come for me.

Charlie's parents continue to lie on my behalf, and I'm grateful, but even that makes me suspicious. No one does anything out of the goodness of their heart. Not unless there is something in it for them.

"Lauder will stay with you," Cam says, strapping a gun to the belt around his waist. "But no pornos this time."

Drew cocks an eyebrow. "Do I even want to know?" I'm continuing to keep him in the dark about my relationship with Cam; although I'm sure he has his suspicions.

We're like dogs in heat, and although we try our best to disguise it, I'm certain he's picked up some clues.

"Probably not." Sawyer clips and unclips his gun before ensuring the safety is on and slipping it into his gun belt.

"I hate being left out of the action." I'm aware I'm pouting, but I don't care. I'm sick of being sidelined like some precious cargo in need of protection.

I'd sneak out and follow them only it'd get Jackson in trouble, and I'm afraid it'd distract the others, and they might make a fatal mistake. There's a lot on the line tonight, and at least they allowed me to participate in the planning.

It was my suggestion to bring my bodyguard Oscar on our side. He's been with his family for a couple weeks as someone knocked his youngest daughter off her bike and she was in the hospital for a while, but he's back to work now, and he's been peppering Drew with questions about me. I sent him one text message from my burner cell, confirming I was fine and that I was staying at Charlie's. He didn't buy it, and he told Drew as much. Drew used the opportunity to ask for his help in creating a distraction tonight. Oscar purposely asked not to be informed of the plans, agreeing to help purely for me.

Drew sweet-talked Trent into arranging one last-ditch attempt at a resolution. They are having dinner with both fathers at the gentleman's club downtown, and Charlie is on surveillance duty outside, to ensure they don't leave, while Cam, Sawyer, and Xavier break into my father's safe.

Because things are tense with the Montgomerys, Father is bringing most of his security detail, leaving only Oscar, Louis, and two other guards at the house. Louis will be busy entertaining his latest lady friend, so Oscar only needs to preoccupy the other two.

He's given us one hour tops, which is tight but doable.

"No one would properly concentrate if you were there. They'd be too busy worrying about you." Drew's attempt to appease me is feeble.

"I could help. One hour is tight. I know how to fix the camera feed. I could implant the fake footage and then reinstate the live system when we're ready to go. I can add value."

"Xavier has it covered." Drew places a patronizing kiss on my cheek, and I shove him away. He's still on my shit list, and he knows it.

"You may need Xavier to crack the safe," I say, continuing to push my point. "You've all said yourselves it's a skilled art and you've only had a crash course. If Sawyer can't crack the code, Xavier will have to step in. Who'll take care of the camera stuff then?"

"I'll implant the fake feed in seconds, and if I don't get back to reactivate the system, I'll hack in remotely and do it." Xavier cups my face, shooting me an apologetic look. "I know you hate this. And we all know how capable you are. But your father is a madman who has already expressed murderous intent toward you. You can't be anywhere near that house. Near this. If he finds out we hacked his safe, it's better he can't connect you to it."

"C'mon, babe." Jackson links his arm through mine. "Let them risk their lives. We'll stay here and eat ice cream." His eyes glimmer mischievously. "Naked." He waggles his brows.

"He's joking," I say, elbowing him in the ribs before Cam smashes his fist in his face and gives our relationship away. "Well, about the naked part. Not about the ice cream. I'm going to eat my bodyweight in chocolate fudge brownie because that's what I do when I'm pissed off, and I'm majorly pissed off now."

"We'd never have guessed," Cam deadpans, and I flip him the bird.

"Withhold sex tonight," Jackson whispers in my ear. "And maybe next time, he'll fight for you to go."

I harrumph as Drew approaches. "This will all be over soon, and then you can come back home," he says, like returning home is something I desire.

Living here has been a breath of fresh air, and I'm in no hurry to leave.

"I don't want you to go back home," Cam murmurs, pulling me in close to his side after Drew's left.

"Then you should be on my side more."

He lets me go, sighing. "Is it too much to ask for a little maturity?"

I instantly see red. "Fuck you. I'm plenty mature. I'd like to see you cope with being sidelined."

He scrubs a hand over his prickly jaw. "It's dangerous, babe. We're not bringing guns for the hell of it. If the bodyguards return and find us, they won't hesitate to open fire."

"I know my way around a gun." I poke him in the chest. "And that's another way I could help, but, no, we've got to lock the princess in her ivory tower until she dies of boredom."

Jackson chuckles. "Of course, you know your way around a gun."

"My father had me at the shooting range as soon as it was permitted."

"Oh, yeah?" Cam sends me a cocky smile. "Care to make a little wager?"

That pricks my interest, even if I know he's doing this to distract me. "What did you have in mind, caveman?"

"A shooting contest out back. You and me. Best of five. Whoever gets closest to the target wins."

I can't stop the massive grin spreading across my face. "You're on." I stretch up and kiss him. "And you're going down."

"If I wasn't leaving, I'd demand a rematch," Cam pouts, and this time, he's not pretending. He's competitive as fuck, and he hates losing. Especially to a girl.

"And I'll still beat you next time."

"Damn, girl. That was hot. Ditch the caveman, and come share my bed," Jackson jokes, running his fingers through my hair.

"Unlucky for you, I'm addicted to the asshole. I couldn't ditch him even if I wanted to."

"Aw, you say the sweetest things." Cam's sarcastic drawl matches his dark mood as he shoves Jackson away, reeling me into his arms. "Behave while I'm gone."

"Yes, Dad."

He squeezes his eyes shut. "My patience reserve is in low supply tonight, and I really don't want to fight with you before I leave."

"I'm not fighting." I smile sweetly at him, pecking his lips. "I'm in winning form." I stick the knife in because, yeah, maybe I am a little immature at times.

"I'd love to know how you hit every mark dead center," Cam says, shaking his head in disbelief as he backs away.

"It was easy," I call after him. "I just imagined it was your face, and I hit the bull's-eye every time."

I spend an anxious couple of hours pacing the floor in Cam's bedroom, chewing my fingernails to the bone, as I glance at the clock every few minutes. When I hear the front door opening, I race out of the room and down the stairs like I'm on skates, almost slumping in relief when all four of them walk in unscathed. "Well?" I ask, propelling myself into Cam's arms.

"We did it."

"Fucking A, dudes." Jackson high-fives them.

"And did you find the evidence?"

Cam's face drops. "It doesn't appear to have been there."

"Damn." Air whooshes out of my mouth in disappointment.

"But Cam made a copy of all the paperwork in the safe, and there could be something in there once we go through it," Sawyer adds. Because Cam hadn't taken part in the safecracking training, he was on copy duty.

"Let's do it now. Where is it?"

"We stashed it someplace safe," Sawyer says, and I frown.

"Why?"

"If your father figures out his safe was broken into, this could be the first place he comes looking," Cam coolly replies. "So, we're keeping it offsite for the time being."

Alarm bells ring in my head. "Where?" I ask, planting a "don't mess with me" look on my face.

"It's better you don't know," he says, adopting a cold, indifferent mask.

"Excuse me?" I drill him with a cold look of my own.

"If your father comes asking questions, at least you won't be lying when you tell him you don't know." He scrubs a hand over the stubble on his chin. "Don't fight me on this, Abby." He pushes past me into the kitchen, and I race after him.

"Did Drew agree to this plan?" I demand, shooting daggers into the back of his head as he opens the refrigerator, grabbing a few beers.

"Drew wasn't there, and we felt it best to make some last-minute alterations."

"Bullshit. I don't believe you. This reeks of subterfuge."

He shrugs, and it infuriates me. "I told you to trust me, so do it."

A red haze coats my eyes, and my fists ball up at my sides.

"You look tense. Have a beer," he says, sliding one to me, knowing damn well this will only rile me up more.

Right now, I have no clue who the guy I'm sleeping with is, and goose bumps sprout up and down my arms. I take the beer, keeping my eyes locked on Cam's, as I throw it at the wall, watching as it shatters against the tile, the glass breaking into tiny pieces, beer spraying everywhere.

"Mature." Cam gives me a tight smile, and I flip him the bird as I stalk out of the room with Xavier hot on my heels.

"Wait up," Xavier says.

"What? Were you in on this plan too?"

He shakes his head, looking cautiously over his shoulder. "No. We split up. Charlie came to get me, and the two of them went off on their own. I'd no idea they planned that until we met up outside, and they said they'd dropped the documents off. Your brother will lose his shit when he hears. We were supposed to duplicate the records and give him a copy, but they didn't do that either."

"They're up to something." I tap a finger off my lip. "But what?"

"I don't know, but I'll find out."

"You're the only person I trust," I whisper. "You and Charlie."

"I'm with you on that front," he whispers back.

I press my mouth to his ear, looking over his shoulder, but the guys aren't listening; they are too busy arguing among themselves in the kitchen, their voices growing louder as they bicker. "When I'm gone upstairs, go back in there and say I'm in a foul mood and to leave me to cool off. Then drive to the lane at the side of the house and wait for me."

"What are you going to do?"

"I'm not sharing a bed with that liar any longer. I'll stay at Jane's for a while."

"Is that wise?" His brow furrows with concern.

"It feels safer than staying here."

He thinks about it for a few seconds. "Okay. Go. I'll wait outside for you."

I hurry to Cam's room and lock the door. Then I race around the room grabbing my clothes and toiletries and shoving them in the bag Drew brought for me from home. Thankfully, I hadn't unpacked half my shit, so it doesn't take me long to zip it up. I pull my hair into a ponytail and change into a hoodie, yoga pants, and sneakers. When I'm ready, I take one last lingering look around the room, and a pang of nostalgia slaps me in the face. I've had tons of happy times in this room with Cam, but now, I wonder if any of it was real.

Quietly, I open the French doors and slip out onto the balcony. I tiptoe along the length of the balcony until I've reached the side of the house, then I secure my bag over my shoulders, and shimmy down the pipe. When my feet hit the ground, I start running, and I don't look back.

CHAPTER THIRTY-FOUR

"He's left more messages," Jane says the following day, skimming through my cell phone.

"I don't care." I roll over on my side, wishing that was true. I stayed up half the night filling Jane in on everything that's gone down with Cam the last few weeks, including how I feel used.

"Are you sure he was just playing you?" she asks, tossing my cell on the bed. "He seems genuinely worried about where you are, and he wouldn't have shown up here first thing if he didn't care."

"This isn't about caring or not caring. It's about controlling all the moving pieces. He still needs me for something, and that's the only reason he's eager to find me. Thank God, I snuck in last night and your mom doesn't know I'm here; otherwise, she'd never have been able to lie convincingly to his face."

"And thank God for Xavier's mad tech skills. If he hadn't rerouted your cell signal, I'm sure Sawyer would've already traced you to here."

"Have you heard from Drew yet?" I ask, wondering if he's done lashing the guys for their double cross.

"He just texted me. He, Charlie, and Xavier are holed up in Charlie's place trying to figure out where the new elite may have stashed the paperwork. He said they're refusing to hand over anything."

"School on Monday should be fun," I droll. "We'll be drawing more new lines in the sand." I glance at the time. "We need to go if I'm to make my appointment on time. You're sure you're okay to drive me to the doctor's?"

"Of course." She snatches her keys up. "Let's go."

An hour later, I stumble out of the building in a daze as a new layer of horror settles on my chest. Tears pool in my eyes, and strangled sobs rip from the back of my throat as I scan over all of Cam's missed calls and texts.

He sounds so genuine, and the panic in his voice seems real, but I don't know what to think or who to trust.

I'm wandering toward the place where Jane parked, too trapped in my mind to pay attention to my surroundings, when a hand clamps over my mouth and a damp cloth is pressed against my lips. I'm dragged backward, my feet scraping the ground as panic bubbles up my throat. My assailant keeps one arm tight around my waist, and the other holds the cloth tight to my mouth so I can't breathe.

The last thing I register is a sweet-smelling concoction before I pass out.

When I wake, I've lost all concept of time. Darkness bathes the room, and it's clear I've lost hours. I sit up, rubbing my bleary eyes, cursing out loud when I take in the familiar surroundings of my bedroom.

Nothing is out of place since I left here five weeks ago. I stagger past the open window as nightfall encroaches on my private space, traipsing into my en suite bathroom to pee. When I return, I close the drapes and grab my bag, searching heedlessly for my cell because my fucking father has taken it. Thank fuck, I have a retinal scanner and passcode set up on that cell too.

A superior smile slips over my mouth as I open the secret panel in my bag, extracting my burner cell. The battery is low, and I don't have my charger, so I waste little time tapping out a text to Drew and to Jane, explaining what's happened. I open up the message Xavier sent two hours ago.

I've found out something you need to know about Camden Marshall. Meet me at the warehouse at nine. I need to show you this in person.

It's almost nine now, so I tap out a text telling him I'm on my way. I check my bedroom door, and it's locked. No big surprise there. But I don't need to exit that way to get outside. I dress warmly and then head into the secret tunnel.

I emerge into the woods, shivering as the haunting sounds of an owl hooting resonates all around me, lifting all the tiny hairs on my arm. I jog toward the shed, to collect my bike, with blood thrumming in my ears.

I unlock the door, screaming when I'm confronted by Louis pointing a gun at me. "Going somewhere?" he sneers, urging me back a few steps.

"Oh, my God. You startled me." I slap a hand over my chest, giggling. "What are you doing here?" I attempt to downplay it because Louis isn't the sharpest tool in the box.

"Attempting to flirt your way out of this won't work," he says. "I've a long memory," he adds, roughly grabbing my arm. "And you'll rue the day you blackmailed me." He drags me back through the woods. "Tell me how you're getting out of the house, and I'll plead with your father for leniency."

"Screw you."

"I would've been down for that," he snarls, yanking me harder.

"And I've been dreaming about that tight pink pussy of yours since the doctor gave me a free viewing, but even I'm not that stupid."

Mercifully, he stays mute the rest of the walk back to the house, and I don't put up a fight, because I don't trust him not to shoot me.

He opens the back door, prodding the gun into my back and forcing me inside the house.

"Look who I found trying to escape," he says, shoving me into my father's study. "And she had this on her." He pulls my burner cell from my pocket, holding it out.

My father gets up from behind his desk, puffing on a cigar as he walks toward me, taking the cell from Louis. He swipes at the screen. "What's the code?"

"Fuck. You." I'll take that code to my grave. He's not getting into that phone and finding any connection to Xavier.

He raises his hand to slap me when Mr. Barron speaks up. "Michael, don't. We can't have her face marked. It will look suspicious."

I glare at Charlie's father, wondering what his deal is or if this is some new angle he's playing.

Has my father been aware I haven't been at his house this whole time?

I don't believe it because there's no way he'd leave me with the new elite if he knew I was there. So, I don't get it. Behind my father's back, Charles Barron Senior, mouths at me to say nothing. I keep my lips closed, but only until I've had time to think this through.

"You're right," my father huffs. "You disappoint me, daughter." He grips my chin, and I see the effort it takes to be gentle. "But you have a way to redeem yourself now."

My eyes narrow to slits. "How?"

"All will be revealed tomorrow. In the meantime, you will stay in your room. Don't escape again, because you won't succeed." He looks at Louis. "Take her back upstairs, and make sure she stays put."

Louis attempts to take my elbow, but I shove mine in his ribs, enjoying the grimace that appears on his face. "I can walk upstairs without you manhandling me." I hold my chin up, staring impassively at my father. "I'll do whatever it is you want me to do without argument," I lie, "once you tell him to stay outside my room."

My father's sharp gaze swings to Louis. "I haven't touched her, boss," Louis rasps. "She's just trying to cause trouble."

I eyeball my father with confidence. "He stayed in the room the entire time the doctor examined me, and he just told me how much he enjoyed the show. He also told me he wanted to fuck me, so excuse me if I don't trust him to keep his hands to himself."

My father examines my face for a few minutes before picking up his phone and calling the head of security. "I want another man assigned to watch over my daughter at night," he barks into the phone. "Fine. Send Maurio to my study now." He slams the phone down.

He'd have zero issue if it was any of his rich, pervy friends sleazing over me, but Louis is an employee. A *commoner*. Lowest of the low in my father's eye, and I knew he'd balk at him leering at me.

In some ways, he's utterly predictable.

But it's all the ways he isn't that worries me.

"And you." He points at Louis. "You're lucky I'm not firing you. My daughter is off-limits. From now on, you're reassigned to my son."

"No problem, boss," he says through gritted teeth, and I smother my gleeful smile.

The smile is long gone from my face the following day though. He has locked me in my room with nothing but my e-reader, the TV, and my panicked mind for company. Xavier must think I stood him up, and Drew hasn't darkened my door even though he has to know what's going on.

He's now permanently on my shit list.

When the door opens in the early evening, I swing my legs off the bed and stand, my trepidation mounting as the strange woman and man enter the room. "Who are you?"

"I'm Ava, and this is George," the gorgeous redhead says, while the gaunt-looking man with the slicked-back blond hair wiggles his fingers at me. "We're here to do your hair and makeup."

"What's the occasion?" I ask, my nerves instantly spiking.

"Oh, we're sworn to secrecy," Ava says with a glowing smile as if it's some wonderful big surprise.

My mind churns relentlessly as they work me over, and my panic spirals to new heights with every passing second. When they're done gushing over how gorgeous I look, Ava disappears for a few minutes, reappearing with a strapless red dress, and a layer of stress lifts from my shoulders.

The dress is stunning with a frill over the bust, and it stops just above my knees, showcasing my slim legs encased in gorgeous black Jimmy Choo heels. "Your father said not to wear any jewelry and to come to his study when you're ready." Ava air kisses me on the cheek. "You are breathtaking. Have a wonderful night!" She claps her hands with glee before they exit my bedroom.

I glance at my reflection in the mirror, conceding they did a great job. My makeup looks natural even though it feels like it's caked on. My eyes are smoky, rimmed with a subtle layer of black eyeliner and lashings of thick, black mascara, and she painted my lips in a nude color with loads of gloss on top. Ava tried to persuade me to go for statement red lips, but that's too cliché. George has styled my hair in soft bouncy waves that cascade down my back.

I might enjoy feeling like a million dollars if I wasn't so anxious. I half-expected them to hand me a white wedding dress, and I sagged with relief when it wasn't that, but it's only taken the slightest edge off my nerves.

My father is up to something, and instinct tells me I won't like it one little bit.

I'm wound up tighter than a ball of yarn as I leave my bedroom with my purse in hand. Maurio walks alongside me without saying a word.

We have just entered the long corridor leading to my father's study when the distinct sound of gunfire outside halts both of us in our stride. Maurio speaks into his mouthpiece in hushed whispers, nodding his head as if the person on the other side can see him. "Stay here, Miss Abigail. I won't be long." His boots make a loud noise as he runs toward the rear of the house.

An arm jerks out from the nearest door, and I'm yanked into the bathroom before I've had time to scream. Cam covers my mouth from the front with his callused palm. "Don't scream. We don't have long."

I pull back away from him. "What the hell are you doing here?" I snap, eyeing him warily.

His eyes darken, in a familiar way, and he's on me so fast I don't have time to preempt his move, startled when his lips press against mine.

It feels like weeks, instead of days, since he last kissed me, and my body instantly forgets I distrust him, melting into his arms. When my brain finally reengages, I shove him away, hating how badly I've missed him and how much I wish things were different. "You don't get to do that anymore. Not unless you're here to tell me the truth."

"I've been trying to reach you since you ran away to tell you everything."

"My father kidnapped me, and he locked me in my room without my cell. I tried to escape, but his bodyguard caught me and brought me back."

"Fuck. I didn't know. I've been sick with worry." He rubs the back of his neck, and, for the first time ever, Camden Marshall looks *terrified*. "I shouldn't have pushed you away, and I want to make it right. You deserve to know the truth." He caresses my cheek. "I wanted to talk to you before this went down, but we're out of time now."

He reels me into his arms, holding me tight. I squeeze my eyes shut, desperately wanting to believe him, but I'm so confused.

"I didn't want you finding out like this, and it's my fault because I was scared." He tilts my chin up, pecking my lips briefly. "You'll hear some stuff that'll shock you, but please give me a chance to explain. Come home with me tonight, and you can ask me whatever you want. I'll tell you everything."

A noise outside startles both of us.

He releases his hold on me. "You better go back."

"Did you do that?" I ask as realization dawns.

He nods. "We needed a distraction so I could get you alone." His lips crash down on mine in a brutal claiming, and he wraps his arms around me, holding me close. "You look so beautiful," he says in a breathless tone, his gaze roaming over my every curve as he nudges me toward the door. At the last second, he takes my hand, stalling me. "You're my everything, Abby," he chokes out. "Don't forget. And no matter what you hear, know that what we share is real."

I don't have time to respond because Maurio shouts out my name, so I dart out of the bathroom, without uttering a word or even looking back at Cam, closing the door behind me. "I needed to pee," I say before he can ask, slipping my lip gloss from my purse and touching up my mouth. "Is everything okay?" I ask as we walk.

"False alarm," he says. "Some idiots set off fireworks at the back of the garden, but they ran off before we could apprehend them."

I bet that was Jackson's idea, and I purposely cough to disguise my laughter. Maurio is a man of few words, and we don't talk again while he escorts me to my father's study. He opens the door for me and then leaves.

"Charlie?" I query, arching a brow as I step toward my friend. I wasn't expecting to see him here, but I'm grateful for the friendly face. He looks incredible, dressed in a sharp, fitted black suit with a blinding white button-down shirt and a red silk tie. His hair is styled back off his handsome face, and his jaw is clean-shaven.

The only other people in the room are his parents, his younger sister, my father, and Jane and Drew. Jane pins me with sorrowful eyes, and it's clear she knows what's going down. Hurt lances me on all sides as I add her betrayal to the litany of others I've suffered, but I don't have time to deal with that now. I need to figure out what's going on.

Both fathers are drinking scotch while Mrs. Barron has a glass of champagne in her hand. She puts it down on the desk, rushing to my side with a box in her hand.

"Abigail, darling, you look so gorgeous." She beams at Charlie while I continue to shoot him "what the fuck" looks. "And these will work perfectly," she adds, removing a stunning diamond necklace and matching bracelet from the box. "Charles." She glances at her son. "Fasten the necklace on Abigail."

I feel like I'm having an out-of-body experience. Like I'm not really here, and I'm floating overhead watching everything go down. I lift my hair on autopilot, and Charlie fixes the necklace in place, his warm fingers brushing the nape of my neck.

Charlie's mom kisses me on the cheek. "I'm so excited for you both," she squeals before returning to her champagne. Charlie's dad nods at him.

"What the hell is going on?" I whisper, narrowing my eyes on Charlie.

"Do you trust me, Abby?"

"Well, there's a loaded question." I purse my lips, noticing my father scowling in my direction.

Charlie hauls me into him, placing his hand on my lower back as his mouth drops to my ear. "Just follow my lead, and go with it. I promise I've got your back." He presses a kiss to my temple, and I'm instantly on guard. "Smile as if you're pleased with what I'm saying," he whispers. "Quick, before your father intervenes."

I plant the biggest smile on my face, gazing at Charlie as he tenderly strokes my face, and my father retreats, the scowl on his face smoothing out.

What the ever-loving fuck is going on?

"I'll fill you in on everything after. I promise," he adds, leaning in to kiss my cheek. "Just play along for now."

"It's time," my father says, swiping the empty glasses from Mr. and Mrs. Barron. "Let's go."

Charlie offers me his arm, and I loop mine through his. His mother beams at us adoringly, and I realize she thinks we're a couple. I gulp over the burgeoning panic bubbling up my throat as we follow everyone out of the room and down to the ballroom.

When Mom was alive, she hosted lavish parties in this room on birthdays and anniversaries and at Christmas, but the room has seen little use since then.

I step inside the ballroom for the first time in ages, trying not to gawk. At some point, over the last few weeks, my father has had this room redecorated. He spared no expense.

Dazzling chandeliers glisten above glossy hardwoods floors. Ornate gold and red velvet drapes dress each window, complementing the elegant round tables covered in crisp white and gold linens, adorned with beautiful centerpieces of fragrant lilies.

The room is crowded with families from the elite and inner circles, along with business associates of my father.

Applause breaks out as my father leads our small group through the room, shaking hands and fake smiling as he passes well-wishers. I keep a bright smile plastered on my face as my body trembles in nervous anticipation. Charlie tightens his hold on me, reassuring me with his confident smile.

My father steps up onto the newly constructed stage at the back of the room, and we all follow suit. We stand in a line behind him as he takes to the podium, tapping the microphone to ensure it's working. The crowd quiets as they turn to face us.

"Thank you all for coming at such short notice. I'm delighted you could be here with us tonight for this very special occasion." He glances over his shoulder at Charlie and me, and my blood pressure skyrockets. "I know your invite said this was a party, but it's actually much more than that. I'd like to ask Charles Barron the Third and my daughter to step forward." He extends his arm, smiling adoringly at me as if he's the proudest father in the universe.

"Just run with it," Charlie reminds me, steering me forward.

The next few minutes happen as if in slow motion. The crowd gasps as Charlie drops to his knee in front of me, holding out a small black box. He pops the lid, and the large round diamond ring glints and sparkles in my face.

My mouth hangs open in shock. Now, I understand why Charlie didn't tell me the full story back in the study. He wanted my expression to look suitably surprised, and he knows me well enough by now to know there's no way he would have gotten me up on this stage, without screaming bloody murder, if I knew this was an engagement ambush.

"Abigail Aveline Hearst-Manning. You have been in my life for as long as I can remember, but you're more than just one of my best friends. You're someone I've admired and respected for a very long time. Someone who is already an integral part of my family. More recently, I've realized how deep my feelings extend."

He forces a tear to his eye, and I want to shout, "someone give that man an Oscar," but naturally, I keep that sentiment locked up inside.

"I think I've always been in love with you," he continues, "but I was too afraid to admit it even to myself."

I've got to hand it to Charlie. He's putting on the performance of a lifetime. As he peers at me with adoring love-struck eyes, even I almost believe it. But I know better. This is my father's Plan B; although I'm perplexed.

While an arranged marriage to Charlie continues the elite bloodline, it does jack shit for my father's business because Charlie's father is a banker. He owns one of the state's oldest and most reputable banking firms, but my father doesn't need money for his auto-drive car program. He needs technical know-how, and an alliance with the Barrons doesn't give him that. So, I'm confused why he believes this needs to happen.

What am I missing?

The sound of a commotion at the back of the room distracts me, but I can't look away when Charlie is mid-proposal, so I keep my eyes fixed on his. "I love you, Abby, and I want to spend the rest of my life making you happy. Would you do me the enormous honor of agreeing to be my wife?"

CHAPTER THIRTY-FIVE

Hushed whisperings filter through the crowd as someone shouts, "Get the fuck away from me!"

My head whips up, my eyes finding Cam's across the packed room. Sawyer, Jackson, and Maverick are restraining him, and he's livid. His eyes glimmer with confusion, anger, and hurt as he stares at me. Charlie tugs on my wrist, reclaiming my attention. His eyes warn me to stick with the plan, pleading with me to trust him, and I force all thoughts of Cam aside as I wet my dry lips and smile at the man on one knee in front of me.

"I would be honored to marry you," I dutifully reply, and the crowd breaks out into rapturous applause.

Charlie stands, flashing me another adoring smile as he slips the ring on my finger.

From the corner of my eye, I spy Trent glaring at both of us even as some brunette clings to his side.

"This needs to seem real," Charlie whispers as he draws me into his body. Clasping the nape of my neck, he pulls my mouth to his. He holds me firmly against his hard body, keeping one hand on my lower back and another at my neck, gently dipping me down as he kisses me passionately.

I'm grateful he doesn't push his tongue into my mouth, because that would take the charade a step too far, but he's not holding back on this kiss, and holy hell, can Charlie Barron kiss.

Must be all that practice with college girls, because I'm having trouble seeing when he pulls me back up and tears his lips from mine.

The crowd whoops and hollers, and my father is grinning like the cat that got the cream. Charlie's parents advance, enveloping us in hugs and loud congratulations, and I'm in a daze the whole time, wondering where Cam is and why the new elite are here. There is no way my father invited them so they must be gatecrashing.

"Congratulations, Abigail," my father says, pressing a chaste kiss to my cheek. "I hope you'll be very happy. Charles will make an excellent husband." In my ear, he whispers, "And if you do anything to mess *this* arrangement up, you'll be joining your mother in hell."

Charlie tucks me under his arm, as if he heard his horrid words, and I cling to him as my body trembles in very real fear.

Daddy Dearest doesn't realize I've already messed up his plans, and I've no idea what I'm going to do.

Drew and Jane are next up, and it takes colossal willpower not to hiss and spit at my brother. "You are on my permanent shit list," I tell him with a smile as I accept his congratulations.

"Everything I've done is to protect you," he says, returning my forced smile. "And you'll see that in time."

"I'm sorry," Jane whispers as she pulls me into a hug, both of us sporting huge fake grins. "I wanted to tell you, but Drew wouldn't let me near you."

"We'll talk later," I say before allowing Charlie to pull me away.

"On a scale of one to ten how mad are you?" he asks.

"Oh," I say, smiling up at him as if he hung the moon. "About a hundred."

"What is the meaning of this?" I hear my father say, and I glance over my shoulder at him. His face is slowly losing color as he glares at something or someone in the crowd.

"Shit." Charlie positions me in front of him, wrapping his arms around my waist as I watch a somewhat familiar tall man in a gray pinstripe suit advance through the crowd, followed by a lanky man, sporting glasses, who also looks a little familiar. Behind them are Cam, Jackson, Sawyer, and Maverick with two other dark-haired boys who look younger.

"What the hell is going on?" I ask, leaning back to look up at Charlie. "And why do those men look familiar?"

"The guy leading the charge is Atticus Anderson, and the man behind him is his brother-in-law, Wesley Marshall. I'm guessing we're about to find out the real reason the new elite showed up in town."

"Guards!" my father shouts through the microphone. "Clear the room. The party's over, folks. Thanks for coming, and be safe getting home." He gestures at Maurio and Louis who are both standing off to one side, wiggling his fingers in a come hither motion as Atticus Anderson steps up onto the podium, snatching the microphone from my father's hand.

"Don't be so hasty to leave," he says, his voice projecting around the room. "Some of you will remember me. I'm Atticus Anderson. A descendant of one of the original founding fathers, and I think you'll want to hear what I have to say."

Cam steps up onto the stage, leaning close to Atticus and whispering in his ear. Cam's jaw is tense as he speaks, his harsh eyes locked on mine the entire time.

The other guys step up behind them, and my father bristles as a line of armed men stand protectively to one side. I detect the bulge of guns strapped to their waists or shoved down the backs of their pants, and apprehension prickles my skin.

Maurio and Louis reach for their guns, but my father shakes his head.

Some men and women in the crowd have stopped, turning around to listen, but my father's men are ruthlessly pushing people out of the ballroom whether or not they like it. "Whatever you've planned will have to happen without an audience, Atticus," my father says, grabbing the mic back off him and handing it to Maurio.

Atticus shrugs, a satisfied smile gracing his lips. "They'll find out soon enough," he cryptically says. "And the main players are all here." He nods at Charlie's dad before fixing cold eyes on Christian Montgomery.

In all the confusion, I hadn't noticed him and Trent making their way onto the stage. Trent's date is nowhere to be seen, so I'm guessing he sent her home because this is elite business, and she's no right to be here.

The wide ballroom doors clang shut, and a row of my father's guards line up in front, blocking the exit.

"Fuck," Charlie whispers in my ear. "This won't end well."

Cam's eyes lower to where Charlie's hands hug my waist, and I'm tempted to escape his embrace, but I desperately need his strength, so I stay put even though it's upsetting my lover.

"We both know what you're going to say," Christian supplies, maneuvering into place beside my father. "And empty words mean nothing."

"Words aren't empty where there's proof," Wesley Marshall, Cam's father, says, speaking up for the first time.

"Bullshit," my father says. "You have nothing."

"We have the contents of your safe," Atticus says, "and what a revelation that was."

My father laughs, but it's humorless. "Nice try, but I'm not buying it. My safe is impenetrable."

"Only because that's what we wanted you to believe." Atticus eyeballs an on-edge Drew. "If you don't believe me, ask your son. He was involved."

A muscle clenches in Drew's jaw, and my breathing has turned erratic. My brother might be on my shit list, but I want nothing to happen to him. I turn pleading eyes on Cam, but he's still looking at me like he wants to strangle me.

My father stares at Drew, seeing the truth in the sweat beads dotting his brow and the wild look in his eyes.

All the blood drains from my father's face, and he isn't fast enough in disguising his panic.

Atticus notices, grinning. "I've waited a long time for this day, Michael." He steps right up to my father with no trace of fear. "You took everything from me, and now, I'll return the favor." Then he turns to Christian Montgomery. "And your day of reckoning will come too."

Atticus turns around, sending a sympathetic smile in Jackson's direction as he holds out his hand.

Wesley Marshall hands him a large brown envelope, and Atticus waves it in front of my father's ghostly white face. "Genevieve came to see me before she passed because your wife had confided in her shortly before she died. Did you know Olivia had proof you murdered my wife? Is that why you arranged for her to have that car accident? Or was it when you realized you killed the wrong woman? That the love of my life was still on this Earth and planning to run away with me?"

"What?" Maverick asks, stepping forward with a puzzled look on his face.

Atticus steps over to his son, planting a hand on his shoulder. "I'm sorry I haven't been fully truthful, son." He looks to where Cam has moved beside the two younger boys. One of them is visibly upset, fighting tears, and Cam has his arm over his shoulder. "I'm sorry that any of you boys have to hear this, but nothing good comes from hiding the truth. Everyone in this room is about to learn that lesson."

He walks to the upset boy. "I loved your mother, son, but she wasn't the love of my life. Emma always knew Olivia Manning was the only one for me, and if Olivia'd had a choice, she would've married me, but stupid elite bullshit, and that conniving asshole over there, stepped in our way."

My head is spinning, cluttered with questions, and I won't waste this opportunity to find answers. "Did my mother love you in return?" I ask, and Atticus turns to face me as my father snaps at me to shut my mouth. I ignore him, grateful Anderson's guards have their guns trained on him and that he can't stop this without it turning into a bloodbath. While I know he doesn't care about the majority of people in this room, he won't risk injury to Drew, as his only male heir, even if he now knows of his betrayal.

"Abigail, my dear." Atticus steps toward me with a funny smile on his face, and I spot Cam's shoulder's tensing. "Your mother loved me. We were childhood sweethearts, and we were destined to marry until your father set his sights on Manning Motors and your mother. He deliberately seduced Olivia and knocked her up to get her away from me. I was heartbroken, but life moves on, so I married Emma. She was Olivia's best friend, and I knew she'd always been secretly in love with me. It was a good marriage at the start, and things were good between us for those first few years."

He runs a hand through his hair, turning halfway to his boys with an apology in his eyes. "Until Olivia came to me for help. Michael was beating her, and he even stood by and watched while that monster raped her." He glares at Christian, and my stomach sours. "Olivia feared for her life and yours." His gaze bounces between me and Drew. "And I couldn't abandon her when she needed me."

Charlie tightens his hold on my waist, and I wrap my hand

around his forearm, clinging to him as I prepare myself for the bombs I know Atticus is planning to drop. "After we married other partners, we'd kept our distance from one another, but our feelings never changed. We began an affair—"

"That's why they stopped being friends," I cut in, all the pieces forming in my head. "Your wife found out about it, didn't she?"

He nods. "Yes. She begged me to stay away from Olivia and I did, for a while, but I could never deny her anything, and we started seeing each other again, but we were more discreet this time. Or so we thought." He glares at my father. "Do you want to take over this part of the story, or shall I go on?"

"I'm glad you've used that word because a story is all this bullshit is," my father seethes, clenching and unclenching his fists at his side.

"Come now, Michael." Atticus bravely slaps my father on the back. "At least have the balls to own up to your part. Genevieve gave me proof that confirms you murdered Emma. You paid for those pills in her name, and you forced them down her throat. Tell me, did you stay there and watch as her life force ebbed away?"

"You fucking murdering bastard!" Cam lunges for my father, but Louis steps in front of him, pressing the muzzle of his gun into Cam's chest.

I break free of Charlie's hold and run to Cam's side, trying to pull him back. Louis is an unpredictable hothead, and I wouldn't put it past him to shoot Cam deliberately to start a war.

"He's not worth it." I tug on Cam's arm. "Please, Cam. Walk away."

"He killed my mother!" he shouts, showing every emotion on his face.

"What?" I stutter, as Charlie steps forward and pulls me back.

"He really didn't tell you, did he?" Atticus says, looking between me and Cam. "Camden Marshall isn't his real name." Atticus looks at Wesley, and his tone softens. "Camden Marshall was Wesley's boy. He died when he was two." Wesley hangs his head, and his shoulders heave. "My brother-in-law is notoriously private, and he kept the news out of the media. When I needed help, Wesley stepped in and allowed us to use his son's identity to hide Kaiden so he could return to Rydeville and do what needed to be done."

"I fucking knew it!" Drew steps forward, jabbing his finger in Cam's direction. "I fucking knew I knew you. How could you not tell me? You were my best friend!"

"Until we were five," Cam—Kaiden—says, unperturbed.

"You could've at least told my sister!" he hisses, stalking forward and pushing his chest into Kaiden's, confirming he's known about me and him all along.

"Okay." Atticus separates them. "We're getting a little ahead here. Step back, son." Maverick pulls Kaiden back, and I stare at the guy I'm in love with, wondering if anything he's told me or shown me is true.

Atticus palms my face, reclaiming my attention.

"Don't touch her," Kaiden says, and we lock eyes for the first time since the truth was outed. I see so much written on his face, but I don't know what to believe.

I can't believe I've been sleeping with Kaiden Anderson, and I didn't know it.

I should've made the connection when I saw that picture in his room or when he slipped up and mentioned an older brother or when I met Maverick. Kaiden and Drew were joined at the hip when we were little, and while a lot of those memories are hazy now, Kaiden was a big part of my life at one time.

I can't believe he kept his real identity from me. Pain slices across my chest, and his betrayal cuts deep. I'm drowning, and Charlie is my only anchor right now. The only person in this room I trust. I look away from Kaiden, because I don't want him to see how heartbroken I am.

"Kaiden." Atticus sends a warning look in his son's direction, and he clams up, but he's not happy about being reprimanded in front of everyone. The vein bulging in his neck and the fierce look in his eyes contest to that.

"As I was saying, Abigail, your mother and I were together again, but your father found out, and that's when he took my wife from me as punishment. Olivia was distraught."

"I remember," I whisper. "She cried all the time." I was only seven, but I'll never forget her tears.

"She blamed herself, as I did." A muscle pops in his jaw. "But Emma was gone, and I couldn't bring her back, so my priorities shifted. I knew I had to get you all out of that house, away from that murdering bastard"—he snarls at my father—"and I needed to find a new home for my boys. One that didn't remind them daily of what they'd lost."

He rubs a hand over his chest. "We had everything planned. We were going to take all you kids and move overseas, but we needed to bury the bastard first. Putting him in jail for Emma's murder was the only way we'd be truly free, so Olivia got the evidence we needed, we bought a property in France, and booked open-ended flights."

He looks at me funny again, and this time, I read the expression. He's torn.

Like one part of him hates me and another part of him shows sympathy. "We would have succeeded if you hadn't given the game away."

"Me?" I look between Kaiden and his father. "What did I do? I knew nothing about you and my mother! This is the first time I'm hearing it."

"You overheard your mother on the phone with me, talking about the new house. You blurted it out to your father, and he pieced it together from there." An icy chill seeps into my bones. "You were the catalyst that ruined my life," he adds. "I lost everything. My business. My wealth. My home. My reputation. My wife. The woman I planned to grow old with. My sanity."

"She was only a kid, Dad," Kaiden says, interjecting. "It wasn't her fault."

"I see that now," he quietly says, as I watch Louis slowly stepping back off the stage, his eyes darting to the side door. *What the hell is he up to?*

"And you're helping to put things right," he cryptically says.

"What have you done, you little bitch?" my father shouts.

"Do not speak to Abby like that." Kaiden glares at my father.

"Fuck you, punk." My father eyes his tattoos with disgust, and suddenly, I can't wait until he hears my news.

He'll disown me for sure.

Either that or bury me ten feet under.

"I sent the note to Christian," Atticus says, and shock splays across Kaiden's face. Atticus smiles at my father. "I needed to distract you so you wouldn't notice what was going on right under your nose."

"I didn't know," Kaiden blurts, staring at me with pleading eyes, as if that atones for it.

The more I hear, the more I'm sure everything that happened with us was all part of the strategy. I glare at him, holding onto Charlie's arm tighter.

"We have copies of the documents you and Christian falsified to get me thrown off the board of my own company," Atticus continues, stepping right up to Christian and my father. "It's taken me years, but with Wes's help, I have enough to bury you, along with the evidence proving you orchestrated Emma's murder," he adds, pointedly staring at my father.

"It'll never hold up in court," my father says with false bravado.

"And we'll tie you up in legal wrangles for years," Christian adds, his voice dripping in arrogance. Trent stands beside his father, smirking.

"We're even better connected than we were years ago." My father shoves Atticus back. "So do your worst. It'll come to nothing. We'll still win." He steps forward, shoving Atticus back another step.

Keeping his arms around me, Charlie retreats toward the edge of the stage. "Things will turn nasty soon," he whispers in my ear. "When I tell you to run, I want you to run toward the back door, and get the hell out of here. Oscar is manning that exit point, and he'll see that you're taken to safety."

Atticus smiles. "I thought you'd say that, which is why I have insurance. You taught me that, Michael. I guess I should say thanks."

"Okay, I'll bite," my father says, not looking too bothered now he thinks he has his ass covered because he has so many cops, lawyers, and judges in his back pocket.

"We have a copy of Olivia's will. I didn't realize she'd changed it just before we were planning to escape. I know it wasn't the version produced at the official reading of the will, but I'm guessing few know a new will exists."

My father looks like he's about to keel over, and I'm silently cheering Atticus on even though I'm also cursing him, because he hasn't been nice to me.

"And I'm certain neither of your children know the terms."

"I might've known," Drew says, "if your asshole son furnished me with a copy of the paperwork like he promised."

"That was necessary, son," Atticus says, attempting to placate Drew.

"What does the will say?" I demand.

Atticus is gloating at my father as he turns to me. "In the event of your mother's death, all family shares in Manning Motors pass to her surviving children once they turn eighteen."

Drew and I lock eyes, each as surprised as the other.

"There was one caveat in the small print that the lawyer advising her overlooked. It's an old family will that was modified, and he mustn't have noticed. If your mother were alive, she'd hate she missed it, because it's the one clause that sealed her fate." He touches my cheek. "She'd be appalled if she knew you were being forced into an arranged marriage too."

He looks at Charlie, but there's no malice in his eyes. "If you marry," he continues, refocusing on me. "All your shares pass to your husband."

My eyes dart to my father's and I see the truth he's trying to hide. "You son of a bitch," I roar. "That's why you were trying to force me into marriage! All so you could hold on to your precious company!"

He must've been afraid the real will would become public knowledge, and he was covering all the bases. Clearly, this was part of the deal with the Montgomerys. He obviously agreed to something with Christian, which meant Trent would sell his shares back to him so he could keep control. And the same deal must apply now with my new engagement. I try to break free of Charlie's hold, but his grip is firm, and I wriggle and writhe to no avail.

The irony is, if my father had asked for my shares in exchange for my freedom, I would have readily agreed.

But not now.

Now I want to take everything from him.

I slide the engagement ring off my finger and throw it at my father's face. "You can keep that as I won't be needing it now."

"Careful," Charlie whispers in my ear. "The game's not up yet."

I will myself to calm down, because I know Charlie's right.

"You'll pay for this," my father says to Atticus in a low voice that promises evil deeds.

"You're not calling the shots here," Atticus shoots back.

"I fail to see how this revelation gives you any bargaining power," Christian says.

I glance over at Charlie's father, curious, because he hasn't said one word. He's watching everything going down with a sober face, standing protectively in front of Charlie's mom and sister, not missing a thing.

"That's the beauty of this plan."

I'm momentarily distracted by the sound of urgent whispering. Maverick is frantically spouting stuff in Kaiden's ear, gesturing wildly with his hands. It's how I happen to be watching the instant the look of horror overtakes Kaiden's face.

Atticus rubs his hands together. "There's another clause in the will." He glances at me. "Abigail's shares in Manning Motors will ultimately be mine the moment she marries my son."

Everything locks up inside me as I watch him remove something from his inside jacket pocket.

Nausea swims up my throat as realization dawns.

My head whips around to Kaiden, and tears are rolling unbidden down my face. There's a blank expression on his face, and I can't read him. Pain grips my heart in a vise grip, and I wonder if it's possible to physically rupture your heart, because that's what it feels like right now.

"I've had about enough of this," my father says. "Guards."

The unanimous clicking of guns echoes around the room as my father's guards descend from all corners with their weapons raised. Atticus's men surround the perimeter of the stage, pointing their guns at the approaching guards, and my breath hitches in my chest.

"Get ready," Charlie whispers in my ear.

"Call your men off," Atticus coolly replies. "Your daughter doesn't need this stress. Unless you want to be held accountable if anything happens to our grandchild."

CHAPTER THIRTY-SIX

"What the fuck have you done, you stupid cunt?!" my father roars.

"Your daughter has been in a relationship with my son behind your back. You know," he taps a finger off his chin. "I think they might be in love." He winks at me as he hands the printout to my father. "It's kind of poetic. A little like history repeating itself. Only this time, Kaiden will be the one to get the girl. The will says Abigail will forfeit her shares in the event of an unplanned pregnancy unless she marries the father."

My knees threaten to go out from under me, but Charlie keeps me upright. If what Atticus is saying is true, and I want to keep my shares away from my father, I have to marry Kaiden, only then I'll be handing the reins to *his* father. But if I don't marry him, then my father wins.

I'm damned if I do and damned if I don't.

Atticus looks wistfully at me. "You look so much like Olivia, and you're every bit as beautiful as her. My son is a lucky man."

Father takes one look at the page in his hand and crumples it in his fist. I'm sure it's a copy of the document I got at my doctor's appointment yesterday morning confirming I'm three weeks pregnant.

"You whore!" Trent shouts as Christian holds him back with a smug grin. "And sleeping with the enemy to get back at your father is pathetic. I'm glad I kicked you to the curb."

I shut Trent out, mentally swatting him away like an annoying fly instead of correcting his mistruths.

More tears leak out of my eyes as I stare at Kaiden in disbelief.

I didn't want it to be true.

I wanted to believe it was an accident, but at least now I know exactly how I got pregnant.

He deliberately sabotaged my birth control, and I was the stupid bitch who let him have sex with me whenever he felt like it.

I've been so naïve. Believing he felt something for me. I should've known better after all the shit he did to me. This has just been a different form of bullying and now an innocent child is caught in the mix.

I vow to extract retribution. I don't know how or when, but one day, I'll make Kaiden Anderson pay for all the ways he's betrayed and humiliated me.

Shock splashes across Sawyer's and Jackson's faces, and I'm glad to know at least they weren't in on the pregnancy part of the plan. Charlie's dad is holding Drew back, and he's shouting all kinds of threats at Kaiden from across the stage. Slowly, Charlie moves us again, a small step at a time.

"I'm prepared to make a deal," Atticus says. "I won't strip you of everything like you did me. I'll give you enough to enjoy a reasonable standard of living."

"If you think I'll broker a deal with the likes of you, you really don't know me at all," my father says. An evil grin spreads over his face as he quickly pulls a gun out of the back of his dress pants and shoots Atticus in the chest.

Bedlam ensues as everyone on the stage—except for the women—

extracts guns and starts shooting. Jane screams as bullets whizz over our heads.

"Abby!" Kaiden shouts, firing his gun indiscriminately while shoving his two younger brothers over the other side of the stage toward his father's bodyguards. He looks conflicted as he stares between them and me.

"Run now, Abby," Charlie says, blocking Kaiden from sight as he shields me with his body. He pushes me toward Drew while dialing nine-one-one on his cell.

"Don't let anything happen to Kaiden," I beg, clutching onto his arm. I hate him, and I'm planning to get revenge, but I'm determined my child won't suffer because of my mistakes. Kaiden is still my baby's father, and I don't want my son or daughter growing up without having both parents in his or her life. I know what that's like, and I wouldn't wish it on any child.

"Don't worry. He knows how to look after himself, but I'll watch out for him," Charlie assures me.

"I love you both," Drew says, shoving me and Jane toward the steps at the side of the stage. "Get to safety."

I want to argue. To grab a gun and join the fight.

But I can't.

Because this baby growing inside me is innocent, and it's my job to protect him or her. It doesn't matter how he was conceived or that he's already a pawn in the despicable game our fathers are waging, I already love him, and I'll do everything in my power to protect him.

"Stay safe," I shout at Drew and Charlie, taking Jane's hand. We fly down the steps, flattening our backs to the wall behind Charlie's mother and sister as we inch out of the room.

Everyone is too busy firing at the enemy to notice our escape. Some guards are trading fists now, having emptied their rounds. A few men lie on the ground. Some are unmoving. Others lie in pools of blood that are growing wider.

"Quick," Oscar says, racing forward to meet me as Benjamin, another guard, ushers the Barrons out to safety. "You need to get out of here."

"Abby!" Kaiden's frantic shout reverberates behind me as Oscar ushers us out into the corridor, pulling the door shut behind us.

"We need to split up." Oscar jerks his head at Benjamin as we run. "Take Mrs. Barron and her daughter and Jane and drive them to the Barron residence. I need to get Ms. Abigail as far away from here as possible."

I want to stay with Jane, but I trust Oscar. We hug quickly. "If anything happens to you or Drew, I'll die," Jane sobs, hugging me again. "Don't take any risks, Abby."

"I promise I won't. It's not just me anymore," I say, placing my hand on my tummy.

I know she's dying to talk to me about it, but this isn't the time. "Go. I'll call as soon as I can."

Benjamin takes the three of them out the front of the house while Oscar brings me out the back. "I have my car stashed in the woods," he says. "Are you able to run?"

I yank the Jimmy Choo sandals off my feet and throw them away. "I am now."

We take off running through the grass, and I hope the guards are too preoccupied to notice us. I push my limbs harder than I've ever pushed them to keep pace with Oscar. I'm breathing so heavily I don't hear the footsteps chasing behind us until the last minute. "Someone's running after us!" I pant.

"Go, Abby." Oscar flings his keys at me. "Keep running, and don't look back. No matter what you hear."

Tears stream down my face as I keep running and Oscar hangs back. Blood is pumping through my veins, and sweat coasts down my back as I run for my life. Sounds of a struggle emanate from behind me but I don't stop.

Not even when the gunshot rings out.

Adrenaline flows through me as sobs wrack my body, but I push on, empowered by this new life depending on me.

I enter the forest, barely feeling the pain as my bare feet race over debris on the forest floor. The pounding of footsteps chasing me spurs me on, and I run faster, swiping tears from my eyes as I pray like I've never prayed before.

Oscar's car appears in my line of vision just as someone jumps me from behind.

I go down hard, landing on my stomach, and I scream for help as a solid body pins me to the ground, smooshing my face into the muddy earth. I yelp in pain as a sharp sting pricks my upper arm. My eyelids grow heavy and my veins move sluggishly as whatever he injected me with works its way quickly into my bloodstream.

"Don't hurt my baby." I sob before darkness swoops in and claims me.

TO BE CONTINUED

The story continues in *Twisted Betrayal*, coming August 2019. Available to preorder now.

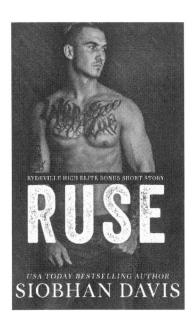

Subscribe to the author's mailing list to get this exclusive short story narrated by Camden Marshall. Copy and paste this link into your browser: https://claims.prolificworks.com/free/JXWYABMB

Faye Donovan has lost everything. After her parent's tragic death, she's whisked away from her home in Ireland when an unknown uncle surfaces as her new guardian.

Dropped smack-dab into the All-American dream, Faye should feel grateful. Except living with her wealthy uncle, his fashion-empire-owning wife, and their seven screwed-up sons is quickly turning into a nightmare—especially when certain inappropriate feelings arise.

Kyler Kennedy makes her head hurt and her heart race, but he's her cousin.

He's off limits.

And he's not exactly welcoming—Kyler is ignorant, moody, and downright cruel at times—but Faye sees behind the mask he wears, recognizing a kindred spirit.

Kyler has sworn off girls, yet Faye gets under his skin. The more he pushes her away, the more he's drawn to her, but acting on those feelings risks a crap-ton of prejudice, and any whiff of scandal could damage the precious Kennedy brand.

Concealing their feelings seems like the only choice.

But when everyone has something to hide, a secret is a very dangerous thing.

This box set includes the first three books in the highly addictive Kennedy Boys series from USA Today bestselling author, Siobhan Davis, and is over 950 pages of heart-stopping drama, intriguing twists and turns, and angsty romance. Complete trilogy that has a happy ending and no cliffhanger.

FREE TO READ IN KINDLE UNLIMITED

ABOUT THE AUTHOR

USA Today bestselling author **Siobhan Davis** writes emotionally intense young adult and new adult fiction with swoon-worthy romance, complex characters, and tons of unexpected plot twists and turns that will have you flipping the pages beyond bedtime! She is the author of the bestselling *True Calling, Saven,* and *Kennedy Boys* series.

Siobhan's family will tell you she's a little bit obsessive when it comes to reading and writing, and they aren't wrong. She can rarely be found without her trusty Kindle, a paperback book, or her laptop somewhere close at hand.

Prior to becoming a full-time writer, Siobhan forged a successful corporate career in human resource management.

She resides in the Garden County of Ireland with her husband and two sons.

You can connect with Siobhan in the following ways:
Author website: www.siobhandavis.com
Author Blog: My YA NA Book Obsession
Facebook: AuthorSiobhanDavis
Twitter: @siobhandavis
Google+: SiobhanDavisAuthor
Email: siobhan@siobhandavis.com

BOOKS BY SIOBHAN DAVIS

TRUE CALLING SERIES
Young Adult Science Fiction/Dystopian Romance

True Calling
Lovestruck
Beyond Reach
Light of a Thousand Stars
Destiny Rising
Short Story Collection
True Calling Series Collection

SAVEN SERIES
Young Adult Science Fiction/Paranormal Romance

Saven Deception
Logan
Saven Disclosure
Saven Denial
Saven Defiance
Axton
Saven Deliverance
Saven: The Complete Series

KENNEDY BOYS SERIES
Upper Young Adult/New Adult Contemporary Romance

Finding Kyler
Losing Kyler
Keeping Kyler
The Irish Getaway
Loving Kalvin
Saving Brad
Seducing Kaden
Forgiving Keven
Releasing Keanu^
Adoring Keaton*
Reforming Kent*

STANDALONES
New Adult Contemporary Romance

Inseparable
Incognito
When Forever Changes
Only Ever You
No Feelings Involved
Second Chances Box Set

Reverse Harem Contemporary Romance

Surviving Amber Springs

ALL OF ME DUET
Angsty New Adult Romance

Say I'm The One ^
Let Me Love You^

RYDEVILLE HIGH ELITE SERIES
Dark High School Romance

Cruel Intentions
Twisted Betrayal^
Sweet Retribution^

ALINTHIA SERIES
Upper YA/NA Paranormal Romance/Reverse Harem

The Lost Savior
The Secret Heir
The Warrior Princess
The Chosen One^
The Rightful Queen*

^Releasing 2019
* Coming 2020.

Visit www.siobhandavis.com for all future release dates. Please note release dates are subject to change based on reader demand and the author's schedule. Subscribing to the author's newsletter or following her on Facebook is the best way to stay updated with planned new releases.

Made in the USA
Las Vegas, NV
14 October 2021

32374209R00231